GEORGIE'S BIG GREEK WEDDING?

BY
EMILY FORBES

THE NURSE'S NOT-SO-SECRET SCANDAL

BY
WENDY S. MARCUS

ES

D0477122

005053000 3

Emily Forbes began her writing life as a partnership between two sisters who are both passionate bibliophiles. As a team, Emily had ten books published, and one of her proudest moments was when her tenth book was nominated for the 2010 Australian Romantic Book of the Year Award.

While Emily's love of writing remains as strong as ever, the demands of life with young families has recently made it difficult to work on stories together. But rather than give up her dream Emily now writes solo. The challenges may be different but the reward of having a book published is still as sweet as ever. Her inspiration comes from everywhere: stories she hears while travelling, at mothers' lunches, in the media and in her other career as a physiotherapist.

If you would like to get in touch with Emily you can e-mail her at emilyforbes@internode.on.net, and she can also be found blogging at the Harlequin Medical Romance blog: www.harlequin.com

Wendy S. Marcus lives in the beautiful Hudson Valley region of New York, with her husband, two of her three children, and a much loved Bichon Frisé named Buddy. A nurse by trade, Wendy has a master's degree in Healthcare Administration. After years of working in the medical profession Wendy has taken a radical turn to write hot contemporary romance with strong heroes, feisty heroines, and lots of laughs. When she's not writing, she enjoys spending time with her family and blogging/e-mailing/tweeting with her online friends. To learn more about Wendy visit her website: www.WendySMarcus.com

GEORGIE'S BIG GREEK WEDDING?

BY
EMILY FORBES

MILLS &
BOON

All the characters in this book have no existence outside the imagination of the author, and have no relation whatsoever to anyone bearing the same name or names. They are not even distantly inspired by any individual known or unknown to the author, and all the incidents are pure invention.

All Rights Reserved including the right of reproduction in whole or in part in any form. This edition is published by arrangement with Harlequin Enterprises II BV/S.à.r.l. The text of this publication or any part thereof may not be reproduced or transmitted in any form or by any means, electronic or mechanical, including photocopying, recording, storage in an information retrieval system, or otherwise, without the written permission of the publisher.

This book is sold subject to the condition that it shall not, by way of trade or otherwise, be lent, resold, hired out or otherwise circulated without the prior consent of the publisher in any form of binding or cover other than that in which it is published and without a similar condition including this condition being imposed on the subsequent purchaser.

® and TM are trademarks owned and used by the trademark owner and/or its licensee. Trademarks marked with ® are registered with the United Kingdom Patent Office and/or the Office for Harmonisation in the Internal Market and in other countries.

First published in Great Britain 2012
by Mills & Boon, an imprint of Harlequin (UK) Limited.
Harlequin (UK) Limited, Eton House, 18-24 Paradise Road,
Richmond, Surrey TW9 1SR

© Emily Forbes 2012

ISBN: 978 0 263 89164 5

Harlequin (UK) policy is to use papers that are natural, renewable and recyclable products and made from wood grown in sustainable forests. The logging and manufacturing process conform to the legal environmental regulations of the country of origin.

Printed and bound in Spain
by Blackprint CPI, Barcelona

Dear Reader

Georgie and Josh lived in my imagination for close to a year before I had a chance to begin their story. I thought it would be easy because I knew them so well by this time. I was wrong! (Please keep that to yourself as it's something my husband would love to hear me admit!)

This story was a battle of wills: mine versus my characters. Almost always my characters take on their own very distinct personalities, but I usually still feel that I am in control of their story. Not this time! Georgie and Josh refused to behave. But they're like my kids—I still love them even if they're misbehaving, and I do like it when they show a bit of spirit.

So eventually, with much angst on my part and much rebellion on their part, we found a way to compromise. They might have tested my patience, but I was very pleased ultimately to give them the happiness they deserved.

I hope you love Georgie and Josh as much as I did.

Best wishes

Emily

Recent titles by Emily Forbes:

BREAKING HER NO-DATES RULE
NAVY OFFICER TO FAMILY MAN
DR DROP-DEAD-GORGEOUS
THE PLAYBOY FIREFIGHTER'S PROPOSAL

**These books are also available in eBook format
from www.millsandboon.co.uk**

CHAPTER ONE

JOSH swung himself out of the ocean and onto the back of the pontoon. Slipping his dive fins from his feet and his mask from his face, he held them in one hand as he used his free hand to haul himself into a standing position. The air tank on his back was ungainly, making his balance awkward, but he was used to the sensation and after more than two hundred dives he knew better than to try to lean forward while changing position.

He dropped his fins, mask and snorkel into his dive bag and checked his watch, noting the dive time and depth. It had been a fairly standard dive, pleasant but certainly not the best. The visibility had been reasonable but aside from a few eels and one huge Maori wrasse he hadn't seen anything spectacular.

He was disappointed. He'd hoped the easy access to the world-renowned Great Barrier Reef dive sites off the coast of Cairns in northern Queensland would make up for the fact he'd had to transfer to this country town. He unclipped his buoyancy vest and slung it from his back. Okay, to be fair, Cairns was a large regional centre, not a typical Australian country town, but it definitely wasn't a big city. He'd spent the past two and a half years in Brisbane, a city of two million people, working his way up to a senior position, or so he'd thought, only to find himself banished to the sticks for six months.

But he'd survived smaller towns before, much smaller, all for the sake of experience, and he just hoped this move would pay dividends too. Besides, it wasn't like he'd had much of a choice. His six-month stint started tomorrow and he'd have to make the most of it.

He would take the opportunity to have one last holiday before he prepared to knuckle down and work hard to achieve the goals he'd set himself. He would be free to do as he pleased on his days off but once he returned to Brisbane he imagined days off would be few and far between.

Have fun, he told himself as he pulled his thin dive shirt over his head before running his hands through his hair to dry it off, but remember to think of the bigger picture and of what you stand to gain, that was the way to get through the next six months.

Georgie pushed herself out of the warm water and onto the ledge at the back of the pontoon that was moored permanently at Agincourt Reef. She removed her mask and snorkel as she dangled her legs in the ocean and watched the myriad holidaymakers splashing around, enjoying the beauty of the reef.

Her stomach rumbled as she basked in the afternoon sunshine, reminding her that she'd skipped lunch in favour of a longer snorkel. She pulled the flippers from her feet so she could stand and threw her borrowed diving equipment into the containers at the back of the pontoon. The deck was almost deserted now that most of the day-trippers had consumed their lunches and returned to the water, so she'd go and see what remained of the buffet.

She hung her life jacket on the rack and let her eyes roam over the handful of people gathered on the pontoon. Her gaze lingered on the starboard side where a group of scuba divers had just emerged from the water and were now laboriously removing their equipment. She searched the group for her brother Stephen and his girlfriend, Anna, who were visiting from Melbourne and had come out to the reef to go scuba diving, but she didn't see any familiar faces. They must still be in the water.

They'd tried to talk her into doing an introductory dive and initially she'd been keen, but she'd chickened out when they'd reached the pontoon and she'd seen the huge expanse of empty ocean. Who knew what was lurking under there? She decided she felt safer splashing about with all the other snorkellers. Being able to lift her head out of the water and see the pontoon and the catamarans that had ferried them to the reef gave her a sense of security out in the middle of the vast Pacific Ocean.

She continued to watch the group of divers, smiling at their attempts to shed their equipment. They'd looked so graceful under the water when she'd seen them from her snorkelling vantage point but out of it they looked ungainly. She was glad she'd changed her mind about the introductory dive—she wasn't sure she could be bothered with all the paraphernalia and the air tanks looked awfully heavy.

There was one man, however, who managed to make the tank look as though it weighed no more than a sleeping bag. Georgie watched as he unclipped his buoyancy vest and slung it and his air tank off his shoulders before he removed his thin dive shirt by pulling it over his head. His torso was bare and she was treated to a rather attractive view of a smooth, lightly tanned back and rippling muscles as he stretched his arms overhead. His dark blond hair was cut short and when he ran his hands through it the salt water made it stick up in all directions. He had the physique of a man who worked out. He had broad, square shoulders that tapered nicely into his waist and the muscles on his arms were well defined.

He threw his shirt over his shoulder as her eyes travelled down his back. She could see the two small dimples at the base of his spine just visible above the waistband of his shorts. His shorts hugged the curve of his buttocks and were patterned like the Australian flag. If all divers looked like him, perhaps she would take up the challenge.

'Help, somebody, please, help us.'

Georgie spun around, her meandering thoughts interrupted by a woman's cries. The sound came from her right, out in the ocean. She searched the water and it took her a second or two to locate the woman. She was about fifty metres off the back of the pontoon in one of the snorkelling areas marked out by floating buoys. The woman was waving one arm and hanging onto someone else with her other hand. From the corner of her eye Georgie saw a flash of movement as someone dived off the starboard corner of the pontoon. She turned her head. The guy in the Australian flag board shorts had disappeared. In the time it took her to process the cries for help and to find the source of the sound he had dived into the water and was now swimming strongly towards the distressed woman.

A couple of crew members had raced to the back of the pontoon, one unhooking a lifebuoy and the other carrying a first-aid kit. Seeing other people in action galvanised Georgie. She made her way across the pontoon, past stunned tourists, to offer her assistance as the crewman with the lifebuoy jumped overboard and struck out towards the woman, trailing in the other guy's wake.

Georgie followed him with her eyes. She could see that the diver in the Aussie flag shorts had almost reached the woman but it was getting difficult to see everything that was happening as the swell had picked up and the small waves breaking on the top of the reef were obscuring her vision. With two more over arm strokes, the guy in the board shorts had reached the woman and taken over control of the person she was supporting. He had hold of the person's chin and Georgie could see him making his way back to the pontoon with a strong sidestroke action, dragging the person with him. The woman was doing her best to follow but she was being rapidly left behind. The crewman with the lifebuoy swam up to her, slipped the lifebuoy over her head and under her arms and started towing her back to the pontoon.

The guy in the board shorts was already back at the pontoon with the rescued man in his grip. One of the crewmen knelt down at the edge of the pontoon and hooked his hands under the distressed man's armpits and hauled him onto the deck.

'He's complaining of chest pain,' the diver in the board shorts told the crewman as he helped to lift the man's legs out of the water, 'and I suspect he's aspirated some salt water.'

What sort of person used the term 'aspirated'? Georgie wondered. It was a medical term but perhaps it was common in diving as well? She watched the diver as he hoisted himself up onto the deck. His biceps and triceps bulged as he lifted his weight clear of the sea. Salt water streamed from his body as he stood. His chest was smooth and tanned and despite having just swum a fast fifty metres while towing a heavy body, he was breathing normally. He didn't appear to be even slightly out of breath.

There were now several people gathered around the back of the pontoon and Georgie was able to blend into the crowd. The guy seemed oblivious to her scrutiny so she let her gaze travel higher.

She was pleased to see that he had a face to match his body. He had an oval face with strong features that complemented his chiselled physique. He had full lips set above a firm jaw, which had a day's growth of beard and perfectly symmetrical, sandy brown eyebrows that framed his eyes. His nose was straight and narrow and his teeth, when he spoke, were even and white. He was rather cute.

'Let's clear the area and get him comfortable. We don't want to encourage extra blood flow to his heart. I don't want to stress it more than necessary.'

The cute guy, as Georgie now thought of him, continued to issue instructions as he directed the crew to reposition the man where he wanted him. Because of the board shorts he was wearing she'd initially wondered if he was an overseas tourist but he spoke with a definite Aussie twang. Foreign or not, the cute guy was sounding more and more like he had a medical background. Which reminded her of why she'd crossed the deck in the first place. It hadn't been to ogle a complete stranger, she'd meant to offer assistance. There were more important things to focus on than an attractive scuba diver.

She took a couple of steps away from the cute guy and towards the crew member who was standing nearby, holding the first-aid kit.

'Have you got a towel or something we can use to dry him off and keep him warm?' she asked.

He nodded and Georgie took the kit from him so he could go and find what she'd asked for. She squatted down and spoke to the cute guy. 'I'm a paramedic. Can I help?'

He nodded in acknowledgement but kept his head down and directed his words at the patient. 'I'm a doctor so between us we should be able to get you sorted.' For a moment Georgie thought he was going to ignore her but when he finished reassuring the patient he looked across at her. His eyes were an unusual shade of grey. Silvery grey, almost metallic in colour, they reminded her of the paint the Navy used on its ships. 'Can you have a look and see what's in the first-aid kit?' he asked.

She flipped the catches open as she listened to the conversation going on beside her.

'Can you describe your pain to me?'

'I feel like someone has punched me in the chest.' The man spoke with a British accent and he sounded out of breath, as though each word took great effort. He was going to have a holiday to remember, Georgie thought, assuming they managed to pull him through this crisis.

'Have you had chest pain before?' Cute guy had his fingers on the man's wrist pulse and his eyes on his dive watch, counting the seconds. His fingers were long and slender, his nails shortly clipped and nicely shaped.

The patient nodded but the woman, whom Georgie assumed was his wife, and who was now back on board the pontoon thanks to the efforts of the crew member, elaborated. 'His doctor said it was angina.'

'Is he on any medication?' Cute guy quizzed the man's wife.

Georgie made a concerted effort to turn her attention back to the contents of the first-aid kit and away from the cute doctor's hands.

'The doctor gave Nigel some tablets.'

'Have you got them with you?'

The wife shook her head. 'We forgot to pack them—they're in our hotel room.'

Fat lot of good they were going to do there, Georgie thought. She looked up from the first-aid kit and caught cute guy's eye. It was obvious from his expression he was thinking along the same lines.

'There's nothing useful in here,' she muttered as she finished searching through the kit. The crewman had returned with a towel but Georgie had another assignment for him now. 'Do you have a medical cupboard that would have any drugs other than mild analgesics? Painkillers,' she clarified, when all she got was a blank look.

He nodded. 'Yes, we've got a sick bay. If you want to come with me, you can see if we've got what you need.'

Georgie stood and quickly followed him along the deck into the small sick room. She grabbed a portable oxygen cylinder that was hooked up against the wall as the crewman unlocked a medicine cupboard. She hunted through the cupboard and found some GTN spray and a mask to use with the oxygen. There wasn't much else that was helpful.

She returned to the back of the pontoon with her meagre supplies. 'Symptoms?' she queried, wanting to know whether the patient's status had changed.

'Pulse rate irregular and possibly slightly elevated,' cute guy said as she squatted beside him. He smelt of salt and sunshine and Georgie could feel the heat of the sun bouncing off him. 'Shortness of breath,' he continued speaking, 'but that could be exercise related. Left-sided chest pain but not extending into his extremities.' He turned to look at her and the movement made his abdominals ripple along his side.

'How long since his symptoms started?' she asked, forcing herself to concentrate.

He glanced at his watch. 'We've been out of the water for four and a half minutes and his pain's no worse.'

'Angina?' she queried.

He nodded in agreement. 'Most probably.'

'I found this.' Georgie held up the spray. 'I think it's our best option.' She expected the doctor to move over and let her administer the spray but he reached out and took it from her. She was a little bit taken aback. She had no idea what sort of doctor this man was but, as a paramedic, she was almost certain she'd have more experience in these situations than him and she wasn't used to playing second fiddle. But she wasn't going to have an argument about it—after all, it was a fairly simple exercise and he'd already given Nigel the spray. All that was left was to monitor him and hope his condition improved.

Georgie saw Nigel's wife waiting anxiously nearby. She swallowed her irritation. Someone needed to talk to the wife. 'I'll call QMERT and put them on alert but hopefully we'll get him stabilised,' she told the doctor as she stood up. 'And I'll explain what's happening to his wife.'

To save time she spoke to a crew member and Nigel's wife together so she only had to explain things once. 'Nigel's symptoms aren't worsening so hopefully it's just a case of angina,' she told them. 'He's been given medication and we'll monitor him for the next ten minutes. If it is angina, we expect his symptoms will have eased considerably in that time.'

'And if they don't? What do we do then?' Nigel's wife asked. 'We're out in the middle of the ocean.'

'I'm going to radio QMERT, that's the Queensland Medical Emergency Retrieval Team.' Georgie kept her voice calm as she wanted to stem the rising panic she could hear in the wife's voice. 'I'll explain the situation and get a helicopter on standby to evacuate him if necessary.' She didn't mention that she worked with QMERT, it wouldn't make any difference to anyone else.

Georgie got a few more details from Nigel's wife and put a call in to the Clinical Coordination centre in Brisbane to advise them of the situation. All calls to QMERT went through Brisbane. It was up to the central command to find the closest available crew from one of the bases located throughout Queensland. It was more than likely that Cairns, which was her base, or the Townsville crew would be put on standby.

She finished the call and returned to the patient. The cute doctor looked up at her with his gunship-grey eyes and Georgie forgot she was annoyed at him.

'He's recovering well, chest pain abating and respirations normal.'

'So you think we're okay to bring him in on the boat?' Georgie asked.

'How long will that take?'

Georgie frowned. Had she misheard him? Hadn't he come out to the reef on the boat? Was his cool grey gaze interfering with her concentration?

'About ninety minutes,' she replied, 'but it's not due to leave for another hour. There's time to alter plans if things change. I've put the QMERT chopper on standby.'

He stood up. 'Can I speak to you over here?' he asked, inclining his head towards the side railing of the pontoon.

Georgie wondered what he couldn't say in front of Nigel and his wife but she nodded anyway. He held out a hand. She reached for him and he clasped his fingers around her wrist to help her to her feet, but when his skin met hers a spark shot through her. It made her catch her breath. It made her heart race. It must have something to do with the adrenaline coursing through her system after the excitement, she thought. He let go of her hand and walked over to the edge of the pontoon, away from Nigel, his wife and the crewman, who was still hovering waiting for any further instructions. Georgie followed him, she didn't think she could do anything else. Her feet seemed to be behaving independently of her brain, following his lead.

He leant on the railing and Georgie could see each bony prominence of his vertebrae where his spine curved as he bent forward.

'Are you happy to monitor him and make that call if necessary?'

Her frown deepened. 'Of course.' She had no problem with that but she wondered why he was handing total patient care over to her.

'I flew out to the reef on a helicopter charter,' he explained, 'and I've just been told it needs to take off as there's another chopper coming in onto the landing pontoon shortly. But I can stay to help monitor Nigel if you like. I need to know what you're comfortable with before I tell him what's happening. I could come back on the catamaran with you if you'd prefer.'

Did he think she couldn't handle things? Was that why he'd offered? He didn't need to do her any favours.

'Thank you but I can manage. I'm used to working in these conditions,' she said as she looked around the pontoon and the expanse of water surrounding it. 'Well, perhaps not these exact conditions, but I'm certainly used to coping outside a hospital environment. If I'm at all concerned I'll call QMERT in. They can do an evacuation from the catamaran if things get really dicey. It's fine. Go.'

Go and let me concentrate. She knew it would be better

if she was left to work on her own. After all, she'd wanted to be in charge.

There was a stretcher fixed alongside the stairs that led to the upper deck, and she instructed the crew to bring it to her as she swapped places with the doctor. She watched him as he gathered his things and boarded the little dinghy that would ferry him across to the helicopter pontoon.

She watched him as he left her to monitor Nigel. That wasn't an issue. She was more than capable. She didn't need his help. She could work more efficiently without the distraction. But as the dinghy pulled away from the pontoon, she wondered where he was from and, as he raised a hand in farewell, she realised she had no way of finding out. She didn't even know his name.

CHAPTER TWO

GEORGIE parked her car beside the airport building that was the headquarters for the Cairns division of QMERT. She climbed out and pulled her white singlet top away from her body, looking for some respite from the heat. A quarter to eight in the morning and the north Queensland humidity was already stifling. She could feel the perspiration gathering between her breasts. She'd been in the tropics for months now but after moving from the cooler climes of Melbourne she still hadn't got used to feeling hot and sticky ninety per cent of the time. But despite the sometimes intolerable humidity she was thoroughly enjoying her secondment to the Queensland Ambulance Service and QMERT.

And the weather wasn't always so oppressive, she reminded herself. It had been remarkably pleasant out on the reef yesterday. It was only on the mainland that she noticed the humidity. The scenery yesterday had been very pleasant too, she recalled with a smile. It had been a pity the cute doctor had left before she'd got his name.

She still hadn't decided whether she was more annoyed or intrigued by him. She had to give him credit for his quick reaction to the crisis yesterday. Nigel had made it safely back to the Cairns hospital and he had the doctor to thank for that. She supposed he'd only been doing what he'd been trained for and she couldn't hold that against him. But, still, she wished she knew who he was.

She'd kept her eyes peeled last night when she'd gone out to dinner with her brother and sister-in-law, hoping she might see him wandering the streets of Cairns, but her search had been fruitless. She shrugged. She'd expected nothing less really, it had been a rather vain hope. But it had been her only hope. The only way she might see him again. More than likely he was just a tourist, just someone passing through Cairns, someone she was never likely to see again. But that idea was strangely disappointing.

She shook her head, trying to clear it. She had other things to think about than a perfect stranger. It was time to go to work. She searched through her bag for an elastic band to tie up her hair. The air was muggy, heavy with moisture, and having her hair hanging halfway down her back was making her feel hotter. She gathered her dark hair into a ponytail that hung in a thick rope between her shoulder blades, picked up her bag and headed for the air-conditioned comfort of the corrugated-iron and weather-board building.

She walked past the helicopter that was the latest addition to the QMERT fleet. The night crew was obviously back at base and she wondered what kind of shift they'd had. She hummed show tunes as she crossed the tarmac, pushed open the door to the base and headed for the communications centre. Comms was always her first port of call as she always wanted to check what was happening.

'Morning, Lou, what have I missed?' she greeted the dispatch officer who was stationed at her desk.

'Nothing much,' was the answer. 'The boys have just got back from an IHT,' Louise went on, using the abbreviation for an inter-hospital transfer, 'but other than that it was pretty quiet overnight.'

Georgie pulled a face, her dark eyes flashing with good humour. She loved the pace and hype of busy days. Flying off in the helicopter to save lives was a huge buzz and while quiet days were good because they meant no one was getting injured, busy days meant the chance to put her skills to use.

'It's not all bad,' Louise added. She knew how Georgie felt about quiet days—everyone on the team felt the same. 'The new doctor starts officially today. Showing him the ropes should keep you out of trouble.'

'That's Josh Wetherly, right? The emergency specialist from Brisbane?' Georgie recalled some details from the bio that had been circulating about him.

Louise nodded. 'His experience looks pretty good on paper but, trust me, he looks even better in real life. I reckon you'll be more than happy to show him around the chopper and maybe even around Cairns.'

Georgie rolled her eyes. She was used to Louise trying to find her a man. Louise and her husband had been married for twenty-five years and she thought everyone deserved the same happiness. Georgie didn't disagree. Her parents were also a fine example of a happy marriage, but she didn't want to be reminded that at twenty-seven years of age people were starting to expect her to settle down. There were still things she wanted to do before she settled down to domestic life and she certainly didn't need another mother figure trying to find her a husband. Her own mother was perfectly capable of that! Besides, at fifty and almost twice her age, Louise's idea of a hot man was not quite the same as Georgie's. It took more than good manners and a nice head of hair to get her attention.

One of the reasons Georgie had moved to Cairns had been to get away from the pressure her family had been putting on her to find a partner but so far her plan wasn't working too well. Her family continued to show a tendency to send eligible bachelors her way and she'd lost count of the number of blind dates she'd been obliged to go on. She didn't need Lou on her case as well. She needed a project, something to occupy her time so she could legitimately say she was too busy to date. Showing Dr Wetherly around Cairns wasn't her idea of a suitable project. She'd have to find something else.

The phone on Louise's desk rang before Georgie could think of a smart retort. She waited for Lou to take the call, knowing it would probably mean a job for the team.

Lou jotted notes as she spoke to the clinical co-ordinator in Brisbane, nearly fourteen hundred kilometres south of their Cairns base. The information the retrieval team received was almost always third hand: the emergency call would be put through to headquarters in Brisbane and, depending on the location of the emergency, the Brisbane co-ordinator would pass the call on to the dispatch clerk in Brisbane, Townsville, Toowoomba or Cairns. They would then pass the information on to the retrieval team. QMERT was responsible for an area extending in a radius a few hundred kilometres around Cairns, including the waters and islands in the Pacific Ocean off the coast of Australia. The Royal Flying Doctor Service took over to the north up to Cape York and further inland into the Outback, while QMERT Townsville covered the area to the south.

Louise hung up the phone and relayed the scant information she had to Georgie. 'A four-month-old baby in respiratory distress. She's in Tully hospital, they've requested an IHT. I'll find Pat—'

'And I'll get changed and track down Dr Wetherly.' Georgie finished Lou's sentence. She knew she had time. Pat, the helicopter pilot on duty, would need to get details about the flight and landing, do his pre-flight checks and refuel if necessary. She only needed a few minutes to get changed and find the new doctor. A job this early in the morning wasn't going to be an ideal introduction for the new recruit on his first day but there was no way around it. She just hoped he was up to the challenge.

She headed for the change rooms to stow her bag and change into the navy and grey jumpsuit that was the retrieval team's uniform. As she pushed open the door and stepped around the privacy wall that screened the room from the corridor she was greeted by the sight of semi-naked men. The QMERT building was not overly large and the change rooms were unisex. There was a central changing area divided by lockers with male and female showers and toilets off to each side, which afforded a little privacy but not a lot.

The night-shift team was changing to go home. Sean, the duty doctor, was towelling his hair after his shower; she recognised his stocky build even though his face was hidden under a towel. And Marty, an intensive care paramedic like herself, was already dressed and was pulling his motorbike helmet from a locker.

'Morning, guys,' she said in greeting.

As Marty stepped away from his locker Georgie could see a third man at the end of the room. He was stripped to the waist, his jumpsuit top hanging on his hips. His back was tanned and smooth, muscular and strangely familiar. She could see two dimples at the base of his spine, just above his waistband, teasing her in a repeat performance. Georgie felt her heart rate increase. It couldn't be, could it?

He was turning around now at the sound of her voice and his abdominals rippled down his side. Did she dare move her gaze higher?

She lifted her eyes. Abdominals and then pectoral muscles came into view followed by full lips that were smiling, and above those a narrow, perfectly straight nose and grey eyes. Gunship grey.

Her eyes widened. Standing in front of her, semi-naked, was the cute doctor from yesterday. All that was missing were the Australian flag board shorts.

He was the new doctor?

She could feel her heart beating in her chest and she imagined everyone else could hear it too in the quiet of the room.

'You're Dr Wetherly?' She broke the silence but didn't apologise for bursting in on him while he was changing. Anyone who was at all self-conscious needed to learn to change in the bathrooms. Besides, she'd been treated to the same spectacular view yesterday and looking at this man's semi-naked body she couldn't think of a single reason why he might need to hide away. She swallowed hard, forcing herself to continue speaking. 'I'm Georgie Carides.' She took a deep breath and tried to relax.

'Please, my name's Josh,' he said as he extended his hand and stepped forward to meet her halfway. He was several inches taller than she was and as he closed the distance between them her gaze fell on his bare chest. Again. It took all her self-control to force her gaze up to his face. But even that was no great hardship. His grey eyes were watching her with amusement and she realised he was still holding his hand out, waiting to shake hers, while she stood there, staring at him. She couldn't believe he was the new doctor.

Quickly she clasped his hand, unprepared for the tingle that shot through her. It was the same reaction she'd experienced yesterday when he'd helped her to her feet on the pontoon. It felt as though he'd triggered a connection in her palm that led straight to her chest. Her breathing was shallow and rapid and her heart was racing. Again. Yesterday she'd put the feeling down to the adrenaline that had been flowing through her but that wasn't the case today. This time she knew it was all Dr Wetherly's doing. Josh.

'It's good to see you again,' he said. He appeared completely unflustered, calm and relaxed, behaving as though he was the old hand, while she felt completely disoriented. He let go of her hand and pulled a grey T-shirt over his head, before slipping his arms into the sleeves of his jumpsuit and zipping it closed. 'Small world.'

'Isn't it?' she replied, able to speak now that he'd let go of her and her breathing had returned to normal.

'You guys know each other?' Marty's voice came from behind her, startling her. She'd forgotten Marty and Sean were there.

'We met yesterday—' she told him.

'But I didn't know who she was.'

'You're in good hands, mate. Georgie's a good operator,' Sean said.

'We're going to be working together?' Josh's grey eyes hadn't left her face. He was watching her intently, almost as though he was committing her face to memory. But why he'd need to do that she had no idea. His gaze was intense and focussed but not obtrusive.

She nodded and remembered what had brought her in here. 'I'm the rostered paramedic today and our first call has just come in. A four-month-old girl in respiratory distress—she's in the Tully hospital but they're concerned her condition is deteriorating. Pat, our pilot, is just getting the flight details. We should be ready to take off in about ten.' That was better. If she concentrated on work, she could block out the image of a bare-chested doctor.

'The chopper's restocked and ready to go,' Marty said as he slammed his locker closed. 'Good luck, Josh.'

'Thanks, guys,' Josh replied as the night crew headed out the door. He turned back to Georgie, watching her with his grey eyes. 'So you drew the short straw.'

Georgie could see flashes of silver in Josh's eyes. The colour was striking. She forced herself to concentrate on speaking. Gazing into his eyes was not terribly professional. 'What do you mean?'

'You get to work with the new guy on his first day.'

'I don't mind,' she said with a grin. 'This way I can get you trained up just how I want.' And she didn't mind. She'd seen his CV and she knew he came with an excellent reputation, although she had expected someone older. Josh looked to be in his early thirties, pretty young for a specialist with his credentials, but that didn't bother her because this time she'd be in charge.

In an effort to stop ogling him, she opened her locker and threw her bag inside. She needed to get changed.

'I'll meet you outside,' Josh said as she slipped off her sandals and stowed them in her locker.

She turned to him and nodded. He was standing very close to her; she could have reached out a hand and touched him but she didn't.

As he stepped away she wondered if he was nervous about her disrobing in front of him? Surely not, she thought. He was a doctor, he'd have seen it all before.

And he'd seen pretty much all of her just yesterday, she recalled. Her cheeks darkened a little as she remembered what she'd been wearing. Her black bikini hadn't seemed revealing out on the pontoon, not when everyone else had been dressed in a similar fashion, but now she felt her outfit yesterday may shown him more than she would have liked. She was glad of her olive complexion. Hopefully he hadn't noticed the blush staining her cheeks.

'See what other info you can get about the job,' she said as she tried to quell her embarrassment. 'Louise should have a contact number for someone at Tully hospital.'

He nodded and said, 'No worries, I'll get onto it.'

He turned and left the change rooms, taking the image of Georgie Carides with him. Hearing her voice today and realising they were to be colleagues had been a surprise. A very pleasant surprise, he thought as he entered the corridor. Working with an attractive woman was always a bonus.

He could remember her features. Her face was round and almost perfectly symmetrical. Her dark hair was pulled back from her face and her widow's peak in the centre of her forehead further highlighted the roundness of her face. Her nose was small and straight and her olive skin smooth and tanned. Her almond-shaped eyes were the colour of chocolate and were accentuated by perfectly shaped black eyebrows. The only splash of colour on her face was the red of her lips.

Her natural demeanour seemed to be quite serious and solemn but when she smiled her whole face changed. Unsmiling, she was striking to look at but when she smiled she was beautiful. Her whole face came to life. Her teeth were brilliantly white against her skin tone and her mouth and eyes and eyebrows all lifted. It wasn't just her lips that smiled, it was everything.

He'd wanted to give her some privacy to get changed but it had been an effort to make himself leave the room. The room was unisex but it seemed wrong to stand around and chat to her while she was changing when they'd only just met. But when he recalled what she'd been wearing yesterday he'd been tempted to stay. He'd seen plenty of her in her black bikini and he could recall every detail.

Despite the fact they'd been working to stabilise a patient, he was able to recollect every one of her curves. The curve of her waist as it had flared out to her hip. The curve of her bottom at the top of her thigh. The curve of her cleavage where the Lycra of her halter-neck top had pushed her breasts together.

He'd known he couldn't stand there talking to her while those images had been flashing through his mind, that wouldn't have been a very professional start to their working relationship. He had no plans to get involved with anyone during his six-month stint; but if there were more women like Georgie Carides in town, his time in Cairns was looking more promising.

Georgie swapped her singlet for a T-shirt with 'Paramedic' stencilled across the back and swapped her skirt for her jumpsuit, before pulling on socks and lacing her boots. Her hands were shaking as she tied her laces. She took a deep breath. Although she'd said she didn't mind working with the new recruit, she was nervous.

But it wasn't Josh that made her nervous. It was her reaction to Josh.

She knew plenty of cute guys but she'd never had the sense that they could affect her physically. She certainly hadn't expected to have such a strong reaction to him. Yesterday she'd put it down to adrenaline but today she knew it was more than that. She'd never experienced an instant, powerful physical attraction to a man and now it had happened twice in a matter of hours. It was unexpected and surprising, pleasant but scary—and it was making her nervous.

She wondered how she was going to be able to work with him. Would they work together smoothly? Would their styles be harmonious? Would she be able to concentrate? Questions buzzed through her mind as she zipped up her overalls. There was no way of knowing all the answers.

She'd have to rely on her skills and expertise. She was an experienced intensive care paramedic; Josh was an experienced emergency specialist. In theory she knew they should be fine. But in reality she was the one with experience in pre-hospital emergency medicine. She was the one who would need to take the lead, which meant she needed to be able to concentrate. Josh was used to working in a well-organised hospital environment and she knew, from her days as an emergency unit nurse, that hospitals were a long way from the chaotic, cramped, hot and dusty locations the emergency retrieval team often worked in. She needed to make sure she kept a cool, calm head. She couldn't afford to be distracted. A lapse in concentration could put her patients at risk. She couldn't afford to get sidetracked by cute doctors.

She closed her locker and headed out.

Josh was waiting. He held the door for her as they left the building and his stride matched hers as they crossed the tarmac and headed for the helicopter.

'Are you feeling okay? Ready for this?' she asked.

She wondered if he was nervous, although he certainly didn't look it. He looked completely at ease. If anything, he looked calmer than she felt.

He nodded his head. 'Don't worry. I'm not a complete novice.'

He'd obviously guessed the reason for her question or knew what she was thinking. It would make her job easier if he had a vague idea of what he was in for. 'This isn't your first retrieval?' she queried.

'I've done a couple of transfers before but no primaries and no S&R.'

The most common retrieval for the QMERT team was an inter-hospital transfer or IHT, which was what they were heading to now. Often, but not always, this was a fairly straightforward exercise and Georgie hoped that would be the case today.

Josh's prior experience of IHTs was a bonus and she was comforted knowing that his confident walk wasn't just window dressing, but, still, it was probably a good thing that their first callout wasn't for a search and rescue.

They were almost at the chopper now and she could see Pat in the pilot's seat, doing his pre-flight checks. Isaac, the air crew officer on duty, was stowing equipment. He closed the final hatch as they approached so it looked as though they were just about ready for take-off. She might just have time to introduce Josh to the rest of the crew but they'd have to check their equipment and run through their procedures in flight. She would have liked a little time to establish some rapport first before they were sent out on a job but, as often happened, the calls dictated their day and they'd just have to get on with it. She prayed it would go smoothly.

'Have you met Pat and Isaac?' she asked.

'Yep, first thing this morning,' he said as he raised a hand in greeting and Isaac nodded an acknowledgement.

'G'day, Georgie, Doc,' Pat greeted them, pointing backwards over his shoulder with his thumb, indicating they should board the chopper.

Georgie let Josh climb in first and she dragged the door shut behind them both, securing it with a flick of the lock. There were four forward-facing seats across the width of the chopper and another two rear-facing seats behind each of the flight deck seats. Josh had taken the third seat across. She could sit beside the door but she preferred one of the middle seats so she slipped into the seat beside him.

'Baptism by fire,' she commented as Josh strapped himself in.

She was relieved to see he was able to shrug into his harness, adjust the straps and snap it closed without difficulty. He seemed comfortable enough in the close confines of the chopper and she knew he'd flown before. Yesterday, in fact. She also knew he would have undergone the escape training course. All the rescue crews had to pass HUET— Helicopter Underwater Escape Training—because a lot of their flying could be over water. So transport wasn't a problem, but what she didn't know was how much medical experience he'd had outside a hospital situation. A few inter-hospital transfers wasn't much.

Pat had started the engine and the rotor blades were spinning. The noise made it impossible to continue a conversation until everyone was wearing headsets. She and Josh both grabbed sets and flicked the comms switch on so they could talk to each other and the air crew.

The chopper was lifting off its trolley. It tilted as it left the ground and the movement threw Georgie against Josh. There wasn't a lot of room to move and she could feel his thigh, firm and muscular, where it rested against hers. His body heat radiated through the fabric of their jumpsuits and into her thigh. She'd never experienced such a visceral reaction to someone before. It was as though her body recognised him despite the fact they were strangers. On some level she knew him. She could feel her knees trembling but she couldn't break the contact. There was nowhere to go.

There wasn't much room to move in the back of the chopper. She often felt as though she only just fitted in between all the medical gear and Josh was several inches taller than she was. He was really jammed in. She was five feet six inches. He'd be six feet at least. The stretcher was locked in place in front of them. It ran the width of the helicopter, from one door to the other, between their seats and those opposite. Josh's knees were crammed between the seat and the stretcher and now he had her practically lying on top of him as well. There was no escape for him, he was well and truly stuck.

'Sorry,' she said through the headset as Pat straightened the chopper and she was able to shift back into an upright position and away from Josh's firm thigh. Perhaps she should have taken a different seat. Squeezed up against him in the back of the chopper, she was a bit too aware of him.

'No worries.' He looked at her and grinned, apparently completely unfazed by the lack of room. Her stomach did a lazy somersault in response to his smile and the look of mischief in his grey eyes made her blush. Her body was overheating, from her thighs to her cheeks. She was stifling and she wondered if she could ask Isaac to turn the air-sconditioning up higher but everyone else looked comfortable enough. She'd just have to put up with feeling as though her cheeks were on fire.

'How did things go with Nigel yesterday?' Josh's voice was cool and relaxed, in sharp contrast to her flustered state. If he'd been surprised to find himself working with her he hadn't shown it, and if their close proximity in the back of the chopper rattled him he wasn't showing any outward signs of that either. Looking at him, one imagined that things were going exactly according to plan. 'Did he get back safely?'

She decided she needed to chill out. She nodded. 'No further dramas,' she said as she filled him in on the outcome of the English tourist's medical emergency from the previous day. 'He was admitted to the Cairns hospital overnight but when I checked on him this morning he'd had an uneventful night and they were expecting to discharge him.'

'The hospital doesn't mind you following up?'

Georgie shook her head. 'As you said, it's a small world.' She shrugged. 'Cairns isn't a big town, everyone seems to know everyone else and that's especially true in the medical field. I think the hospital staff expect us to ring. Most of the QMERT doctors work in the hospital too, and we all like to know what happened to our charges. Will you be doing any shifts at the hospital while you're here?'

He nodded. 'I'll do one or two a week but I'm in Cairns to get as much experience as I can with retrievals, particularly primaries. I imagine it's vastly different from working in a first-class A and E department.'

Georgie finally relaxed. This was her area of expertise and discussing this topic kept her mind focussed. 'You'll find you'll have to strip your medicine back to basics. The principles and the goals are the same, you just won't have the same state-of-the-art equipment at your fingertips or the specialist services you're probably used to. We become everyone from anaesthetist to scout nurse out here.'

'Luckily I like a challenge,' he said. 'So what should we expect when we get to Tully?'

For the remainder of the flight they ran through possible scenarios that might greet them on landing, including the possibility that they might need to intubate the baby. Together they checked the medical kits to make sure they had everything they might need. Small regional hospitals would have standard supplies but they might not always have the less commonly required equipment.

Josh was methodical in his checking but that wasn't surprising. It was a character trait attributable to most of the team—organised, meticulous and logical would describe almost all of them—and by the time they circled over the landing site in Tully Georgie was feeling confident that they would be able to work together comfortably.

She watched out of the window as Pat landed the chopper on the cricket oval. Tully had the highest annual rainfall in Queensland and light drizzle was falling as they climbed out of the helicopter and into the ambulance that was waiting to transport them to the hospital. Within minutes of landing they were walking into the tiny hospital.

The local doctor, who looked like he must only be just out of medical school, gave them a rundown on the patient's condition as they followed him to her bedside. 'Carrie is four months old but she was born eight weeks prem so her adjusted age is nine weeks. She's of Aboriginal descent and this is her third admission for breathing difficulties. The first two admissions we managed to control her and discharge her home with her mum. This time we can't get her oxygen sats up—they're actually falling.'

They were at her bedside now and Georgie and Josh both glanced quickly at the monitors showing Carrie's vital statistics. Her heart rate was 98 beats per minute, low for a baby, and her oxygenation was below 88 per cent. That was dangerously low. The medical staff had a tiny oxygen mask over Carrie's mouth and nose but the baby was listless and her chest was barely moving on inspiration. She was only just breathing.

'What were her oxygen sats when she came in?' Josh asked.

'Ninety two.' Even that was low, and if they hadn't been able to improve her saturation since she got to hospital Carrie was in trouble.

Josh checked the monitor again. Carrie's vital signs were unchanged. 'Right, we need to get some improvement in her vitals. We'll have to intubate to see if we can get her oxygen levels up and we'll have to take her with us back to Cairns. I'll need a straight blade laryngoscope, size one, and a 4.0 endotracheal tube,' Josh told her.

Georgie unzipped the medical kit she'd carried in with her. It included all the items they'd need for intubating an infant. As they'd had no way of knowing whether the hospital would have equipment that was small enough, it had been safest to bring it from the chopper. She passed Josh the items he'd requested and he deftly inserted the tube. Carrie was so sick she didn't resist and the moment Josh was happy with his positioning Georgie taped the tube in place and attached the ambubag. She would need to manually squeeze the air into Carrie's lungs and she'd need to do this all the way back to Cairns. But if it kept Carrie alive she was happy to do it.

As Georgie squeezed the air in they could see the baby's chest rise and fall with each pump. It looked like Josh's intubation had been millimetre perfect. She looked up from the infant and her gaze met his.

She was impressed with his skills—intubating a child of this age was no easy task. 'Nice work,' she said, and was rewarded with one of his heart-stopping smiles. He looked incredibly pleased with himself but not in an arrogant way. His grin was infectious and she had to smile back. Things were good. They'd succeeded. Carrie's oxygen sats and heart rate were climbing. She was stable enough to transport back to Cairns in the chopper. They would manage to keep her alive and get her to specialist care. Their first job together had gone smoothly.

By the time they were ensconced back at the Cairns base after transferring Carrie to the Cairns Hospital, Georgie had almost forgotten it was Josh's first day on the job. She'd ducked across to the Cairns airport terminal building to buy a drink and when she returned she could see Josh chatting to Louise in the comms centre. He was perched on the edge of the desk, one leg swinging lazily, looking quite at home.

Georgie walked slowly towards him, taking a moment to admire the view. His jumpsuit was undone and his grey T-shirt, the colour an identical match to his eyes, hugged his chest. She could imagine the ridge of his abdominals underneath that T-shirt. That image was burned into her memory from the day before. He was rolling a pen through his fingers and his biceps flexed with the movement, drawing her eye to his arms. She could remember how his arms had looked as he'd pulled himself through the water, the sunlight bouncing off his muscles as he'd swum out to the reef. He was an impressive sight.

She was within a few metres before he noticed her but when he looked up he greeted her with a smile. Even though Louise was sitting right beside him Georgie felt as though they were the only two in the building. How could he make her feel as though the rest of the world didn't exist with just one smile?

She was vaguely aware of the phone ringing as she smiled back at him. She forced herself to watch Louise answer the telephone, forced herself to concentrate on what was going on around her.

Louise was scribbling details onto a notepad. 'Male patient, early twenties, he's fallen from the back of a moving vehicle, severe head and chest injuries, possible spinal injuries. He's on a cattle station about a hundred kilometres south-west of here.'

Ten minutes later Georgie was back in the helicopter beside Josh. This time she'd deliberately chosen to leave an empty seat between them. She needed to concentrate. They needed to work out their priorities for when they reached their destination. The anticipated flight time was thirty to forty minutes and every one of those minutes would be spent making sure they had a plan of action so they could hit the ground running. A road ambulance was also on its way but travelling on dirt roads it would take closer to ninety minutes for it to reach the accident site. The QMERT team would be the first team on site. This would be Josh's first primary and Georgie needed to make sure they both had a handle on what they might be facing.

Through the headsets she could hear Pat checking the co-ordinates. They'd flown over the rainforest hinterland and the landscape below them was vast, flat and brown. From this height even the trees appeared two-dimensional, flattening into the dirt. Landmarks were few are far between. Thousands upon thousands of empty miles stretched into the distance, broken only by the occasional hill or river. Homesteads blended into the surroundings and were almost impossible to find unless the sun reflected off a shiny tin roof. They were searching for a couple of isolated vehicles on an unmarked dirt road. A task that was near impossible without the right co-ordinates. It was vital that they find the scene of the accident as quickly as possible. Every minute counted.

Pat had established radio contact with the station hands at the accident site and Georgie heard the radio come to life as a voice, crackly with static, filled their headsets.

'Is somebody there?' Despite the static, Georgie could hear the tremor of panic underneath the words. The station hand continued. 'He's not breathing. What do we do?'

'Can you feel a pulse?' Josh was calm under pressure and Georgie relaxed as her confidence in Josh's medical expertise grew. He hadn't put a foot wrong so far.

The reply came back. 'I think so,' said the station hand.

Georgie glanced at Josh. A more definite response would have been good.

'Can you get his mouth open?' Josh continued to give instructions—keeping them busy would help to rein in any panic. 'Check that he hasn't vomited or that his tongue isn't blocking his airway. If he's vomited, you'll have to try to clear his mouth.'

'His mouth is clear but he's still not breathing.'

'Check his pulse again.'

'I can't feel it!' They could hear panic through the radio.

'You'll have to start CPR,' Josh said. 'Does someone know how to do that?' Despite the urgency of the situation his voice was still calm, his words and tone measured in an effort to decrease any further panic on the ground.

'Yes.'

Pat's voice came through the headsets. 'I can see the vehicles. We'll be on the ground in three minutes.'

'We're almost there,' Georgie emphasised. If they could hear them, if they knew help was close at hand, that would buoy them up. 'Can you hear the chopper?'

'Yes.'

Pat circled the accident. He needed to check the landing site before he guided the chopper down to the ground. As they circled Georgie could see two station hands kneeling in the middle of the dirt track as they performed CPR. Shredded rubber from a blown-out tyre was scattered along the road. The trailer attached to the back of the utility had jackknifed and was resting at an angle. A second utility and a quad bike were standing guard further along the road.

Josh slid the chopper door open the moment Pat gave them the all-clear. Georgie followed him out, running in a crouch to avoid the downdraught from the blades. She carried a medical bag in one hand and an oxygen cylinder in the other. Red dust billowed around them, kicked up by the spinning blades of the chopper. Georgie squinted as she ran in a vain attempt to keep the dust out of her eyes.

As they reached the scene of the accident the two station hands performing CPR stopped, obviously believing that since reinforcements had arrived they weren't required.

'Can you help him? Please, you have to help him,' said one.

'We had a tyre blow-out and Gus was thrown from the back of the ute. I think he landed on his head,' said the other.

'Keep going with the chest compressions while we do a quick assessment,' Josh instructed as he extracted a pair of thin surgical gloves from a pocket in his jumpsuit and pulled them on. 'You're doing fine. Keep going.'

Georgie also pulled on gloves, before kneeling in the red dirt beside Gus. He was lying on his back but there was a depression over his left temple and blood had seeped out of his ear. He must have landed on his head and hit the ground hard enough to fracture his skull. That was not a good start.

Josh was holding Gus's wrist, feeling for a pulse. He looked at Georgie and shook his head. Nothing. He quickly checked inside Gus's mouth, assessing the airway.

'I'll take over now,' he told the station hands, and they didn't argue about relinquishing their role.

Georgie worked with Josh, breathing through a face mask, breathing for Gus, but there was no change. During the flight they'd planned to establish an airway, make sure he had oxygen and get IV access. They hadn't planned on resuscitating him.

Josh continued with chest compressions. Georgie continued breathing. There was no change. He still had no pulse.

'I don't think chest compressions are going to be enough,' Georgie said. It had been more than three minutes and normal CPR procedure was getting them nowhere.

Josh nodded. 'I'll draw up adrenaline.'

On the assumption that doing something was better than nothing and knowing that chest compressions were more important than breathing, Georgie continued pumping Gus's chest while Josh searched through the medical kit. He drew up a syringe and felt for a space between the ribs before he pierced the left side of Gus's chest wall with the needle and depressed the plunger, injecting adrenaline directly into the heart muscle.

Georgie held her breath. Waiting. Her fingers on Gus's carotid artery.

There was a flutter of a pulse.

'We've got him.'

'Get some oxygen into him.'

Georgie started breathing air into Gus again while Josh pulled an endotracheal tube and laryngoscope from the kit. It looked as though they'd be doing another intubation.

Georgie did two breaths. She had Gus's head tipped back slightly and the fingers of her right hand were under his chin, resting over his carotid pulse. His pulse was barely evident. She stopped her breaths and shifted her fingers, searching for a stronger pulse. She couldn't find it.

'Josh, I've lost the pulse.'

CHAPTER THREE

'NO, DAMN it.' Josh turned away from the kit and back to Gus, kneeling over him, checking for a pulse. He trusted Georgie's skill but he needed to double check for his own peace of mind. There was nothing. 'Resuming CPR,' he said as he began chest compressions again in a vain attempt to restart Gus's heart. If the adrenaline hadn't worked he knew it was unlikely anything else he did would have an effect, but he had to do something.

He worked hard for another minute. Another sixty compressions. There was no change.

He felt Georgie's hands over his.

'Josh, stop. His injuries are too massive. He's not going to make it.'

He didn't stop. He couldn't stop. He couldn't lose a patient today. He was in Cairns to get some pre-hospital experience but it was expected that he would be demonstrating his medical skills and performing well. Losing a patient on his first day was not part of his agenda.

He brushed Georgie's hands away and continued. Sixty-one, sixty-two. Another sixty and then sixty more.

'Josh, it's too late,' Georgie insisted. Her hands were back on top of his, stilling his movements. 'It's been too long.'

He listened then. He sat back on his heels, his hands

resting on Gus's chest, Georgie's hands covering his. He could feel her hands shaking. Or maybe it was his. He couldn't tell.

'We've done everything we can,' she told him.

He looked at her and he could see the bleakness of his own expression reflected in her chocolate-brown eyes. He could see she knew exactly how he felt.

'I know,' she said. 'We want to save them all but sometimes we can't. It's just the way it is.'

He rubbed his eyes and the latex of the gloves pulled across his eyelids. He stripped the gloves from his hands and tossed them onto the pile of discarded face masks and syringe wrappings, the detritus of the action. He breathed deeply. He could smell dust and heat and perspiration. He exhaled loudly and breathed in again and this time he could smell honey and cinnamon, an already familiar scent, and he knew it came from Georgie. Sweet and fresh, it competed with the smell of defeat.

The other station hands had moved back, giving Georgie and Josh some room. He looked up at them. They were gathered together, supporting each other. They knew the battle had been lost. He stood and went to them.

'I'm sorry. His injuries were too extensive. Even if you'd been closer to help, if we'd been able to get here faster, even then I doubt there's anything we could have done.' He knew his words would be of little consolation but he didn't want them blaming themselves or wondering if they could have done more. Today was just one day out of hundreds just like it. There would have been many times when someone had travelled in the back of the ute without incident but today Gus's luck had run out.

They stood in silence in the heat of the late afternoon. The bush was still, there was not a breath of wind and even the birds were quiet. Josh knew it was only the heat that was keeping the wild parrots mute but it felt like their silence was in deference to the situation.

In the distance he heard the sound of a vehicle approaching. First one. Then another.

An ambulance pulled up, followed by a police car, their distinctive markings almost obliterated by red dust.

Josh spoke to the policeman. He spoke to the paramedics. He was operating on autopilot. Gus was pronounced dead. His body would be put into the ambulance and transported to the morgue. There was nothing left for him to do here.

Pat and Isaac were helping Georgie load the equipment back into the chopper. He left the police and paramedics to finish up and went to help his team.

'Sorry, mate, tough day,' Pat said as Josh returned to the chopper. Josh appreciated his sentiment. Pat hadn't exaggerated the situation neither had he downplayed it, he'd said all that was necessary with those few words.

Josh climbed into the chopper and started securing the medical kits into position. The empty stretcher in front of his knees was a bleak reminder of what had happened. He unclipped one kit from a seat and strapped it onto the stretcher instead, partially covering the empty expanse. That was better. Less confronting.

The chopper lifted off the ground. As they banked to the east Josh could see the accident scene below them. The paramedics were closing the doors at the rear of the ambulance. The police were still speaking with the station hands. He closed his eyes, blocking out the tableau.

He should be saving lives in a big city hospital, with specialist help at hand and state-of-the-art equipment in place. He should be in control, not shooting adrenaline into a young man's heart on a dirt track out the back of beyond. What a bloody mess.

What the hell was he doing here?

He kept his eyes closed until he knew they were far away from the cattle station. Far away from the ambulance that held Gus's body. When he opened his eyes he kept his face turned to the window, his head turned away from Georgie. He didn't want to make eye contact. He didn't want to have a conversation. Not about what had transpired out in the red dirt. He knew he would have to think about it at some point. He'd have to fill in a medical report. A death certificate. But he didn't want to discuss it yet.

Georgie was quiet. Perhaps she was lost in her own thoughts. Whatever the reason, he was relieved she didn't seem to need to talk. Most women he knew would be attempting to have some sort of discussion, even if it was about nothing. The majority seemed to think that silence was there to be broken. He was pleased Georgie wasn't one of them.

The silence wasn't awkward. He knew she was there and knowing he wasn't alone was somehow comforting. He couldn't see her but he could feel her presence. He could smell her perfume, cinnamon and honey, warm and sweet.

He let the silence continue for the entire trip and it was after six in the evening and night had fallen before Pat started to guide the chopper down to the airport. In the distance Josh could see the lights of Cairns. They were almost home.

Cairns was a beautiful city by day and even more so by night, but it wasn't enough to lighten his mood. They were on their way home while Gus was on his way to the morgue. A young life extinguished. He felt the tension of the day in his shoulders. He sighed, a long, audible exhalation, trying to release the strain in his muscles.

He felt Georgie's hand on his. Her fingers entwined with his in response to his sigh. Her hand connected him to the living. He knew her gesture was meant to give comfort and the warmth of her hand did exactly that. It warmed his entire body. He hadn't realised he was feeling cold but he was now aware of heat suffusing through him, bringing him out of his fog.

'Are you okay?' Georgie asked.

'I will be.'

'We did everything we could,' she said.

'Are you sure?' Today's events made him question his skills. He liked being in control of situations and, while he realised that was sometimes going to be difficult out in the middle of nowhere, what if things went wrong because of him? What if he didn't have what it took to work in this environment? 'It's our job to save lives. I'm no good to anyone if I can't do that.' What if he didn't have what it took to run an emergency department in a big city hospital?

'You said it yourself,' Georgie reminded him, 'Gus's injuries were too extensive. Even if we'd been able to reach him sooner, the outcome wouldn't have been any different. There was nothing else we could do.'

Losing a patient was never easy but Josh knew Georgie was right. He'd said those exact words to the other station hands. He and Georgie had done everything they could. But would others see it that way? He needed to prove himself. He needed to show he could handle working in this environment and losing a patient on day one wasn't an auspicious start.

He'd lost patients before, working in A and E it was inevitable, but today had felt very personal. He knew it was because it had been up to him and Georgie. A team of two when he was used to a team of three or four or ten or however many it took, and having greater numbers took the intimacy out of it. It didn't remove the responsibility but it did lessen the sense of failure.

As Pat guided the chopper down onto the landing trolley Georgie gave his fingers a gentle squeeze. 'Today was a bad day. They're not all like this. It'll be all right.'

He hoped like hell she was right.

Pat switched the engines off. The blades continued their revolutions but even the rhythmic thump-thump of the spinning blades didn't disguise the silence that enveloped the team within the chopper. Georgie unclipped her harness and Josh followed suit.

Georgie leant forwards between the pilots' seats. 'Dinner at my place when we're finished here?'

Josh heard her issue an invitation to Pat and Isaac. He was strangely disappointed not to be included yet there was no rule that said he should be. He was the new kid in town.

Their shift was over but it was their job to restock the supplies ready for the next crew and he knew following a routine would help to focus his thoughts. He got busy unloading the medical equipment they'd used and pretended he hadn't heard Georgie's words.

Georgie climbed out of the chopper and then turned and reached for the kitbags, preparing to carry them back to the QMERT building. 'The guys are coming back to my house for a feed. Would you like to join us?'

Yes, he thought. 'No,' he said, before thinking he'd better elaborate. 'Thanks, but you're not expecting an extra mouth to feed. I'll grab some dinner at the hotel.' He didn't like to feel as though he was imposing.

'Don't be silly. I wasn't expecting to feed Pat and Isaac either but we have a rule that we always have a meal or a drink together if we've had a bad day, kind of an unoffi-

cial debriefing session, and we certainly can't let you finish your very first day with us like this. There's nothing
worse than going home alone with just your thoughts.'

'Are you sure?' After the day they'd had the prospect
of his empty hotel room didn't appeal, neither did the idea
of dinner for one in the hotel's restaurant.

'Positive.'

An evening in Georgie's company would be better than
being alone in his hotel room. Looking at her now, even
though she was wearing her QMERT overalls, which pretty
well covered every square inch of her skin, he could picture her as she had been yesterday, in her black bikini, her
olive skin darkly tanned, her petite figure perfectly pro-
portioned. It seemed wrong, given the circumstances, to
have that vision of her in his head, but he couldn't shake it.
Perhaps he should take himself back to his hotel, he didn't
need any distractions. But even as he had that thought he
heard himself accepting her invitation. 'What can I bring?'

'Nothing. I've got a fridge full of food, I'm always feeding people.'

'She's not kidding, mate,' Isaac interrupted. 'Georgie's
a great cook. Don't ever pass up one of her invitations.'

'I'm Greek,' she said with a shrug. 'It's what we do.' She
smiled at him and her face lit up. It wasn't just her mouth
that smiled, it was everything. Her smile had the power to
make him forget about the day they'd had, just for a moment, and he knew that if he spent more time with her he'd
eventually be able to forget the day for longer than a moment. And that had to be a good thing. He didn't want to
forget about the boy they hadn't been able to save, but he
did want something else to think about and he was more
than happy for that to be Georgie.

'I'm going to have a quick shower here and then you can follow me to my place,' she said. 'Have you got a car?'

He nodded and twenty minutes later he was following her little red car through the streets of Cairns and trying to block out the image in his head of Georgie in the shower. In his mind he could see the water running down between her breasts, her skin glistening wet, slippery and cool. Her long, dark hair was loose, slick and heavy hanging down between her shoulder blades, drawing his eye to the curve of her waist and buttocks. He told himself he was being ridiculous. He hadn't even seen her hair loose, it had been tied back both yesterday and today. He shook his head as he remonstrated silently with himself. He'd known her for barely twenty-four hours, he had to work with her, he had a job to do, he had no plans on starting a relationship. He pictured her in her black swimming costume instead. It was a little bit more demure, but not by much, but at least that picture enabled him to concentrate on navigating the streets.

He pulled into the driveway behind Georgie. Her house was a typical Queenslander. Constructed of weatherboard and raised off the ground, a section of the downstairs had been built in but the main rooms were upstairs. He followed her up the stairs and across the deck into the kitchen. She'd restrained her hair in a plait after her shower and it swung from side to side as she climbed the stairs, catching his eye and reinforcing the fact that her hair was tamed and not streaming down her back. His disappointment was almost palpable.

The house looked far too big for one person. When she'd said earlier that there was nothing worse than going home alone with your thoughts, he'd assumed she'd been speaking from experience. He'd assumed she was single.

But perhaps he'd taken her words out of context, perhaps she'd been talking about him. Did she have someone waiting for her here? 'Are you sharing the house?' he asked.

She shook her head. 'No. I rented a large house because I knew my family would all be visiting and would need somewhere to stay.'

'Visiting from where?'

'Melbourne. I'm from down south originally. I'm almost ten months into a twelve-month secondment to the Queensland Ambulance Service,' she said as she started pulling things out of the fridge. 'In the time I've been here three of my brothers and my parents have all visited. My last lot of visitors headed off to Port Douglas this morning. So you see, I can't share a house with anyone, it wouldn't be fair to subject them to my family.'

Hearing about the number of brothers she had distracted him from the realisation that Georgie wasn't from Queensland and she wasn't going to be here for much longer. 'Three of your brothers! How many have you got?'

'Only four.' She laughed and he knew she was laughing at him. The expression on his face was probably pretty funny. But he was happy to be laughed at, he thought as the sound resonated through him and lifted his spirits. 'I take it from your expression you don't have a big family?' she said as she passed him the salad ingredients, which he put on the counter.

'No, just one brother,' he replied. Who he didn't want to talk about. 'What can I do?' he asked, effectively changing the topic.

She passed him two beers. 'Can you open these for us? And there should be some onions in the pantry,' she said, waving her hand at a cupboard on the opposite side of the kitchen. 'You could chop them for me.' She pulled some meat from the fridge. 'I'll barbecue this. We can have yiros.'

Josh found a bag of onions and by the time he'd turned around from the cupboard Georgie had piled flatbreads next to the lamb and vegetables and had chopping boards, knives and beer glasses at the ready.

Josh twisted the tops of the beers and poured them into two cold, frosted glasses.

'Cheers,' he said as he handed one glass to Georgie.

He sipped his beer as he started chopping the onions. The cold lager quenched his thirst and he could feel the stress of the day ease slightly.

Georgie had slipped out to the deck to light the barbecue but when she returned he had more questions for her. 'What number are you in your family?'

'I'm the baby. And the only girl.'

'Does that make you a tomboy or a pampered princess?'

She picked up the tray of meat and looked at him with one eyebrow raised. 'I'm an intensive care paramedic, you tell me.'

'Tomboy, I guess.'

'You'd think so, wouldn't you? But I wasn't a very good tomboy. My brothers are a lot older than me and I was a bit…' she paused briefly, searching for the right word '…protected. Not pampered, mind, just discouraged from following in the boys' footsteps.'

'How much younger are you?' he asked as he traipsed to and from the kitchen to the deck carrying platters, crockery and food.

'Stephen is the closest in age to me, he's thirty-four so seven years older, the twins are ten years older than me and Tony's two years older than them.'

He couldn't imagine coming from such a large family but he supposed in many ways she'd been like an only child. Her youngest brother, Stephen, was the same age as him and he was keen to know more about her band of brothers, and about her, but the arrival of Pat and Isaac changed the direction of the conversation.

Pat opened more beers for everyone and proposed a toast. 'To Gus.'

They each raised their drink in respect.

'I hope some of his dreams came true. I hope he lived a good life,' Georgie said, touching her glass to Pat's before she turned back to the barbecue to baste the meat.

The aroma of garlic, onions and lamb teased Josh's sense of smell and his stomach rumbled. He moved closer to the barbecue, closer to Georgie, and leant on the railing of the deck.

'Did anyone find out anything more about him?' Josh asked. 'Did he have a wife? Kids?'

Georgie opened her mouth but hesitated before speaking and he saw her flick a glance in Isaac's direction. 'He got married about three months ago, one of the other station hands did tell me that, but I don't know anything further.'

'Poor devil,' Pat chimed in.

'I can't imagine what I would do if I lost Lani like that,' Isaac commented.

'Isaac is getting married in a few weeks and Pat is a jaded, cynical divorcé,' Georgie explained for his benefit.

'And what about you?' Josh asked Georgie. She'd said she lived alone but that didn't mean she didn't have a boyfriend somewhere. In Melbourne, if not here.

Pat laughed. 'It'd be a brave man to take Georgie on,' he said.

'Why is that?'

'She's got four older brothers, that's a lot of pressure for a potential partner to handle,' Pat explained.

'Why do you think I've run away from home?' Georgie asked as she scooped the cooked lamb off the barbecue and onto a platter. 'Isaac's fiancée is a nurse at the hospital.' She turned to Isaac as she placed the platter on the table. 'Josh is going to be doing some shifts there while he's in Cairns, you'll have to introduce him to Lani.'

Josh wondered at the very deliberate change in the direction of the conversation but he had no opportunity to question Georgie as she'd deftly shifted the focus onto him.

'You'll be working in A and E?' Isaac asked. When Josh nodded he continued. 'Lani's in ICU. Let me know when you're doing your first shift and I'll get her to introduce you to a few people.'

'Thanks, mate, I'd appreciate that.'

The conversation slowed as they all assembled and ate the yiros. Eating gave Josh a reason to stop talking, he didn't want to volunteer too much information. It was better to let them all think he was happy to be here and had joined their team at his own instigation. And by the end of the night he found he was actually enjoying their company. They were an easy group, welcoming and relaxed. Perhaps the next six months wouldn't be too onerous.

Especially not if he got to work with Georgie, he thought. His gaze fell on her again as she emerged from the kitchen, carrying yet another platter. Her plait fell over her shoulder as she bent forward to put the plate on the table and Josh had a wild urge to pull the elastic band from the end of her hair and loosen it. She straightened and flicked her plait back behind her shoulder and he had to be content with catching a whiff of her scent as she sat beside him. Cinnamon and honey.

'Who would like coffee and baklava?' she offered.

Baklava. That's exactly what she smelt like. But Josh knew the fragrance he could detect was Georgie and not dessert. He'd been aware of it all day.

Everybody requested dessert and Isaac had several pieces. 'Excellent, thanks, Georgie,' Isaac said as he popped another piece into his mouth.

'I've got a confession to make,' she said. 'My sister-in-law made this.'

'I don't care who made it, it's delicious,' Pat said, his mouth full of the sweet pastry.

Isaac finished another piece and drained his coffee as he stood up. 'Sorry, George, I've got to run. I'm off to collect Lani, she was doing a late shift.'

Pat followed suit. 'I'd better get going too. I'm flying you guys again tomorrow, I need to get a decent sleep.'

Josh stood too but after his initial hesitation to join them for dinner he was now reluctant for the evening to end. His lonely hotel room held even less appeal now than it had a few hours earlier.

'It's okay, Josh, stay and finish your coffee,' Georgie said as she put another piece of baklava on his plate. 'Eat that too 'cos the rest will get sent home with Pat.'

'You're a saint, Georgie,' Pat said as he kissed her cheek.

As Georgie wrapped up the remainder of the baklava and said goodnight to Pat and Isaac, Josh found himself wondering if Pat wasn't just a little bit enamoured with Georgie. If that was the case he then wondered how Georgie felt about Pat. Not that it was any of his business, he thought as he ate another piece of baklava. 'That dinner was delicious, compliments to you and your sister-in-law,' he said when Georgie returned to the table. 'Have you got as many sisters-in-law as you have brothers?'

'Nearly. Alek, one of the twins, isn't married yet.'

'Have all the sisters-in-law visited?'

Georgie shook her head. 'One to come.'

'So you've run away from home and almost all your family have followed.'

Georgie laughed and once again Josh found the sound of her laughter comforting. 'I didn't really run away. Not from my brothers anyway, they're harmless enough.'

He wondered what her reason for being here was. Something in her tone suggested there was more to the story than she was volunteering. What wasn't she telling him?

'So what are you doing here?' he asked.

'Same as you I guess, I came for the experience. In Victoria most people are within reach of a regular ambulance service so there's not nearly as much work for the helicopter team. It's mostly inter-hospital transfers and the occasional multiple-vehicle country accident. The distances in Queensland are so much bigger and the demand for the helicopter units is so much higher I can get twice as much experience in half the time up here,' she explained.

'So this is a career move for you? Work was the draw card?'

Georgie wondered how she should answer that question. The simple answer would be yes, but the honest answer was that she was escaping. Technically, she wasn't running away. She was planning on returning to Melbourne but she had needed to escape for a while. To escape from the life that was being mapped out for her. From her parents or, more correctly, from her parents' plans for her. All her life she'd played the part of dutiful daughter, baby sister or perfect girlfriend and she wanted, needed, a chance to find out who she was while she was on her own, away from the expectations of her family. 'Yes. It really is about maximising my experience in the shortest timeframe.' She went with an edited version of the truth. He didn't need to know more than that.

'And when you're not working? What do you do then?'

'When I'm not being a tour guide and chauffeur for my relatives, you mean?'

He nodded. 'What do you do in your spare time? You were out on the reef yesterday. Do you dive?'

'Was that really only yesterday?' Georgie shook her head in disbelief. It felt like days ago. 'That was me playing tour guide. My brother, Stephen, and his wife, were visiting. They are divers so I went out to spend the day with them. I was actually supposed to do an introductory dive but I chickened out. I had grand intentions of trying new things while I was here in Cairns but it turns out I'm not as adventurous as I thought.'

Josh laughed and his grey eyes flashed silver with amusement. 'Life is for living. You've got to experience it.'

'Believe me, as a paramedic I've seen what can go wrong when people try to experience things. I've decided I'd rather live to a ripe old age.'

'Come on, you must have done something slightly adventurous. You're a Victorian, you must have tried skiing, or have you done any travelling? Bungee-jumping in New Zealand perhaps?'

'I've been to Greece but that's about it,' Georgie said. 'Do you count being lowered from the helicopter by a winch as adventurous?'

'That's a good start.'

'A start! All right, tell me about your wild escapades.'

'What would you like to hear about, diving with Great White sharks in South Africa or heli-skiing in France?'

Georgie could feel herself growing pale just at the thought of those activities. Working as a paramedic, and prior to that as an emergency nurse, Georgie had seen the results of reckless behaviour too many times. There were some things she had no intention of attempting. 'You win. I'm not about to try to compete with that. Don't you realise life is precious?'

'Of course I do, I just don't think we should take it too seriously. We have to enjoy it. I went through a bit of a stage where I tried anything and everything with little regard for safety, but I've calmed down in my old age. Now I look for something middle of the road, somewhere between mundane and illegal but still fun. Could I tempt you to try something like that with me?'

Josh was grinning at her, his expression full of mischief, and Georgie could just imagine what trouble he'd got up to at times. All sorts of ideas flashed through her mind, most of which she wasn't about to share with him, but if he thought he could get her to agree to something dangerous just by smiling at her, he was mistaken. 'Like what?' she countered.

'Sky-diving?'

Not what she'd had in mind. She shook her head. 'No.' Definitely not.

'Scuba-diving?'

'Mmm, unlikely.' She'd hardly jumped at the chance to try diving yesterday. Josh might fancy his chances but she thought it was doubtful.

'White-water rafting?'

That sounded a little better. 'Maybe.'

'Excellent. A definite maybe!'

'That's a "maybe" maybe,' she said with a smile that morphed into a yawn.

'Okay, I'll work on your objections when I see you next but now it looks like it's time to call it a day.' He pushed his chair back from the table and stretched. His T-shirt rode up above the waistband of his jeans, exposing inches of toned abdominal muscles right before Georgie's eyes. She was tempted to reach out and touch him. She could remember how his thigh had felt when she'd fallen against him in the chopper earlier today, hard and warm and muscular, and she wanted to know if the rest of him felt the same. But while she was resisting reaching out to him he had lowered his arms and stepped away to push his chair under the table. 'Thank you for your invitation. You were right. I didn't want to spend the evening alone.'

She'd missed her opportunity. Not that she would have dared take it. Josh was a colleague and that meant he was out of bounds.

'And no one expected you to. I'm glad you came,' she said, remembering just in time to respond to his thanks as she stood and accompanied him down the stairs that led from the deck to the driveway.

'Can I repay your hospitality?' he asked. 'Can I take you out to dinner? I'd offer to cook but until I move into the apartment the hospital has organised for me I'm afraid the meal will have to come from someone else's kitchen.'

'I'd like that, thank you,' she said, meaning every word.

Josh pressed the button on his keyring and his car beeped as it unlocked. 'I'll see you tomorrow, then, and we'll make a date.' He opened the door but before he got in he leant down and kissed her cheek. His lips were soft and warm. She closed her eyes as his lips brushed her skin. 'Thanks again.'

It was just a thank-you kiss, she told herself as she watched him reverse out of her driveway. And his invitation to dinner was just a thank you as well. Josh was a colleague. And that was all he could be.

CHAPTER FOUR

Josh was the first person she saw when she walked into the QMERT building the following morning. Through the viewing window in the wall of the comms room she could see him sitting at a desk, concentrating intently, not aware of her entrance at all. His head was tilted at an angle, he was propping his forehead in one hand, his elbow resting on the tabletop, and his biceps were bulging from the sleeve of his grey T-shirt. She could see the top of his head, his sandy blond hair sticking up in all directions; his face was obscured but she'd seen enough to know it was him. Seen enough to make her pulse race.

She wasn't used to this strange feeling of impatient excitement. She'd spent her life surrounded by men. Growing up, the house had been full of her brothers and their friends and now at work she was often the solitary female so she knew there was nothing special about men in general. She was used to all male company. They were just people. She'd never felt confused by them. Until now.

That was what was unfamiliar to her. Her reaction to him, the strong attraction she felt for someone she'd only known one day. Someone who, for all intents and purposes, was a perfect stranger. But he was someone who could set her skin on fire with one touch. Someone who could send her pulse soaring with one look. While there might be nothing special about most men, she wasn't sure if that description could be applied to Josh. Something about him was playing havoc with her senses. Something about him was constantly drawing her focus and she'd never felt so connected to someone she barely knew.

As she entered the comms room he dropped his pen onto the paperwork spread in front of him and rocked back on his chair. He ran both hands through his hair, a look of exasperation on his face.

'Good morning,' she said.

Georgie was pleased to see his look of frustration was replaced with a smile when he saw her. 'Hi. You have perfect timing,' he said as he retrieved his pen and pushed the papers across the desk towards her. 'Could you read through this and make sure I haven't missed anything?'

She glanced down at the paperwork. It was Josh's report regarding the cattle-station accident and Gus's death. That was what was bothering him. She wasn't surprised. Completing the form would mean reliving yesterday's events. It was a tough thing to do. 'How are you feeling?' she asked.

'I'll feel better once we get the autopsy results.'

'We did everything we could, Josh.'

'I know. I'd just like to have it confirmed by the pathologist's report.'

She sat at the desk and Josh moved his chair closer to hers, looking over her shoulder as she read through his words. He smelt clean and fresh, like peppermint, and she had to concentrate hard to make sense of the report. It was no easy task, reading with an audience, especially one who could distract her just with his scent. Eventually she finished. 'It looks right to me. Shall I witness it for you?'

'Thanks.' Josh passed her his pen and Georgie's heart

skipped a beat as his fingers brushed hers. Once again, just the briefest touch was enough to send a frisson of energy through her.

Get it together, she reprimanded herself. He's just a colleague. No different from anyone else. And she didn't want him to be any different. She didn't want to be attracted to someone. She wanted a break from all that.

But she had to concentrate hard to block him out as they were strapped side by side into the chopper, flying to Ingham for their first job of the day, a little later.

They were on their way to another inter-hospital transfer. The patient, Kevin, had come off second best when his motorbike had slammed into a tree on a wet road. He'd sustained multiple injuries, including spinal fractures and bilateral rib fractures, and his broken ribs had resulted in a flail chest and a haemothorax. He had chest drains in but he was critically injured and needed to be in a specialist unit. Ingham's small hospital wasn't equipped to manage his injuries.

Josh had completed his assessment of Kevin but as they started making preparations for the transfer, Georgie hesitated. Something didn't feel right and she knew neither of them needed another drama today. Not after yesterday's tragedy.

'Wait. I think we should intubate him before we move him to the chopper,' she said.

'Because?' Josh queried.

Because she couldn't cope with a second fatality on their shift in as many days. Because it was better to be safe than sorry.

'It's a two-hundred-kilometre flight back to Cairns,' she said. 'We'll be in the air for over an hour. If something

goes wrong en route, we'll either need to land or try to intubate in mid-air. I don't know about you but I'd rather do
that here.' In her opinion, intubating Kevin now would
decrease the risk involved with the transfer and increase
his chances of survival.

'Sounds reasonable.' Much to her relief, Josh didn't de-
bate her suggestion. 'I'll give him a light anaesthetic so he
doesn't resist the intubation.'

Once again, Josh made the sometimes difficult task
of intubating a patient appear straightforward and Kevin
was sedated, intubated and ready to transfer within a few
minutes.

But ten minutes into the flight their treatment plan
started to unravel. A high-pitched beeping rent the air.
Something had set off the peak pressure alarm on the ventilator.

Georgie was closest to the machine. She checked the
monitor. It was possible that Kevin wasn't getting enough
oxygen. But the screen showed oxygenation at ninety five
per cent, blood pressure 120/60. Both figures were falling but the machine looked to be working okay. It meant
something was going wrong at Kevin's end.

'The ventilator's working—check the drain,' she said
to Josh as she reset the alarm.

Josh was sitting opposite her and the chest drain was
by his knee. He moved it. Nothing flowed out of it.

'It's either blocked or he's got a repeat haemothorax.'

The drain didn't appear blocked but a build-up of air
or blood in Kevin's chest cavity could put pressure on the
tube and prevent it from draining.

Josh removed a scalpel from the open medical kit beside him. The incision for the chest drain was visible on
Kevin's chest wall above his arm. Josh enlarged the inci-

sion and inserted a finger to clear any obstruction in the chest cavity, but still nothing flowed through the drain.

The peak pressure alarm sounded again. The high-pitched noise was loud and intrusive, even against the background noise of the helicopter.

'Oxygen sats at ninety-four. His lips look blue,' Georgie reported. Kevin's condition was deteriorating before their eyes.

'I'll top up his anaesthetic,' Josh said. 'If he's starting to wake, he could be resisting the tube and that could set off the alarm.'

Georgie reset the alarm again while Josh topped up the anaesthetic.

'Pupils equal and reacting.' Georgie checked Kevin's eyes. She couldn't work out what was going on. Kevin was under anaesthetic and he hadn't lapsed into a coma, but his oxygen sats weren't improving and his lips were still blue. The drain wasn't flowing. Nothing was working. What had Josh said? 'Life is for living. You've got to experience it.' If they could save a life today, she was prepared to broaden her horizons and try a new experience. She was prepared to make a deal. 'If we get him through this, I'll go on one of your adrenaline-junkie escapades with you.' The words were out of her mouth before she could really think about what she was saying.

Josh finished injecting the anaesthetic into Kevin's IV and looked across at her with a raised eyebrow. For a moment she thought he was going to give her a chance to take back her impetuous offer but no such luck. 'You're on,' he said.

He looked at the monitor and then back down at Kevin. His concentration was unwavering. 'Right, what's going on with you, mate? I'm going to have to open him up some more.' Kevin's arm was lying alongside his chest. It hadn't prevented Josh from enlarging the incision slightly but he was going to need better access now if he needed to be more invasive. He moved Kevin's arm away from his body and with that slight movement blood began to gush through the drain. 'Would you look at that?'

Georgie could hear the relief in Josh's voice and saw him visibly relax into his seat as he checked the monitor. She followed his gaze. Kevin's blood pressure had quickly risen to 135/70 and his oxygenation was rising too. It looked like the crisis was over but she could still feel the adrenaline coursing through her veins. 'That was close.'

'We were not going to have a repeat of yesterday.' Josh replied. 'Not if I could help it.'

Georgie hoped Josh wasn't going to beat himself up over Gus's death yesterday. Thank goodness they'd managed to pull Kevin through. 'This is a tough gig, Josh. We're often working in difficult conditions with very little information. Things go wrong but luckily for Kevin things weren't worse.'

'Things came pretty close.'

'Yes,' Georgie admitted. 'But he'll make it, thanks to you.'

Josh still didn't look convinced.

Georgie frowned. 'Is something else the matter?'

Josh ran his hands through his hair as he let out a loud sigh. 'I'm not here for the experience alone,' he said. 'I do need exposure to pre-hospital medicine but I also need to show I have the necessary skills for this work. When I leave Cairns I'm hoping to return to Brisbane General as the head of emergency medicine but I was advised to have a stint up here first. I need to show I can work under this kind of pressure. I need to show I can save lives out of a hospital setting. I've already lost one patient and I don't intend to make a habit of it. I need to show I can do this.'

'Don't be too hard on yourself,' Georgie tried to re-assure him. 'You've done an amazing job today. Kevin chose to ride a motorbike in wet and slippery conditions and you've saved his life. It's a good day.'

Josh was nodding. 'You're right. We won this round, didn't we?'

'We sure did,' she agreed. 'But being in this job and see-ing some of the odd decisions people make is why I don't like taking chances.' Now that the drama was over she'd forgotten about the deal she'd made.

'Oh, no. You're not getting out of it that easy.' Josh grinned at her and his grey eyes flashed silver with hu-mour. 'You have a choice to make. Sky-diving, scuba-diving or white-water rafting.'

Inadvertently she'd distracted Josh from his sombre thoughts but now she wondered why on earth she'd made such an impetuous call. 'There's no way I'm voluntarily jumping out of an aeroplane,' she said.

'Okay. On the water or under the water? What's your preference?'

It didn't look as though he was going to let her off the hook. 'Can we toss a coin?'

Josh patted the pockets of his jumpsuit. 'Don't seem to have one on me.' He grabbed an unopened syringe from the medical kit and hid it behind his back. 'Choose a hand,' he told her. 'If you get the syringe, you'll have to learn to scuba-dive.'

She took a deep breath and pointed. 'Left.'

Josh brought his hands to the front and opened both fists. The syringe was in his left palm. Georgie's heart

plummeted. Seeing that syringe reinforced that she really
didn't want to try diving.

'Can we try two out of three?' she pleaded.

Josh grinned at her. 'I guess that means you'd rather go
rafting.'

She nodded. 'I guess so.' As much as she would like to
get out of the deal, she supposed going white-water rafting was a small price to pay in exchange for Kevin's life.
And if she got to spend the day with Josh, she wasn't really about to complain.

A few days passed without Josh mentioning white-water
rafting and Georgie allowed herself to hope for a reprieve.
Today it looked as though she was still in luck. Josh was
doing his first shift at the hospital, which meant he wasn't
at QMERT reminding her about rafting. But it also meant
she was working with Sean.

It was her first shift without Josh since he'd come to
Cairns and it was strange to be working with Sean again.
He was a funny guy with a dry sense of humour and
Georgie enjoyed working with him. He and his wife and
two young children had emigrated from the UK. He was
a good doctor but Georgie missed Josh. She told herself
it was because they'd developed a good working rapport
but she knew that was only half the truth. She and Sean
had a good rapport too, yet she hadn't missed him when
their shifts hadn't coincided.

She enjoyed Josh's company and the buzz she got from
being near him, and that element of excitement was missing today. Normally she would have thought her job was
exciting enough but since Josh had arrived that level had
increased. Even sitting in the lunchroom was more inter-
esting when Josh was there.

She was flicking through the local paper when Louise's voice came through the intercom.

'Georgie, are you there? I've got Josh on the line for you.'

She hurried across the room to pick up the phone. She could feel her heart beating a little bit faster and as she picked up the receiver she felt herself panting. She was out of breath and feeling like she'd sprinted one hundred metres instead of just taking a few steps across the room. She breathed in deeply before she spoke. She didn't want to sound breathless.

'Hi, how's your day going?' she asked.

'Hi, yourself. It's okay, actually,' he replied. 'It hasn't been too busy. I had time to pop in and visit little Carrie to see how she's going.'

Georgie remembered the baby they'd brought back from Tully hospital on their first job together, and wondered if that was the reason for Josh's call. 'How is she?'

'She's doing well. She's had lots of tests done, there's nothing sinister, her chest is obviously just a weakness, most likely a result of her being a premmie, but her mum is expecting the all-clear from the specialist and she'll be taking her home soon.'

'That's good news. It sounds like you're finding your feet.'

'I'm doing okay, but I'm missing you guys. I feel like I'm missing out on the action.' For a brief moment Georgie thought he was feeling the same as her, off balance, but his voice sounded as though he was smiling and she could imagine his grey eyes sparkling as he spoke to her.

'You're not missing anything. It's quiet today and we're sitting around, twiddling our thumbs,' she replied. *And thinking about you.*

'I got the keys to my apartment today,' he told her. 'I've just been around there in my lunch break and although technically it's furnished there are a few things I'll need to get. What are you doing after work?'

'I probably should be going to the gym,' she replied. She tried to get to the gym three times a week; she needed to keep fit in order to cope with the physical demands of her job but at the end of a busy shift she often didn't have the energy. Today seemed like it was going to stay quiet so she should make an effort to exercise, but she wondered about the reason for Josh's call. 'Why?'

'What are you doing after the gym?' he asked. 'Would you come shopping with me? Point me in the right direction for the things I need. I'll buy you dinner afterwards.'

'I'd be happy to help you but I can't tonight.' She didn't have time to fit it all in. She had a previous commitment, one she wished she hadn't made, but it was too late to back out of it now.

'I'll take a rain check, then,' he said before he ended the call, leaving her wishing she hadn't agreed to tonight's blind date with a friend of her brother's.

'How did your date go?' Lou asked the minute Georgie stuck her head into the comms room at the QMERT base the next morning.

'Tedious,' Georgie replied. 'It was about as much fun as going to get my legs waxed. I've decided enough is enough. No more blind dates. No more dating at all. I'm staying single.'

'If you had a proper boyfriend, people would stop trying to set you up on blind dates,' said Louise.

'You stood me up to go out with a complete stranger?' Georgie whirled around when she heard Josh's voice behind her. He stepped into the comms room and closed the door. He leant against Lou's desk and folded his arms across his broad chest. He was clearly waiting for her excuse.

'Sorry, it was a prior commitment, but if it makes you feel better it was a complete disaster,' she told him.

'You didn't tell me you had another option,' Lou reprimanded.

Georgie shrugged. 'Josh wanted me to help him shop for his apartment but I'd already said yes to Costa. I couldn't cancel, my brother would have insisted I reschedule.'

'What has your brother got to do with it?'

'Costa has just been relocated to Cairns. He used to work with my brother Alek, and Alek thought I might like him.'

'Why are your brothers setting up dates for you? What's wrong with you?' Josh's grey eyes sparkled with silver lights as he grinned and baited her.

'Hey, watch it! There's nothing wrong with me!'

'There must be plenty of single men around if you want a boyfriend. What about Marty or Pat?' he continued.

'Don't you start!' she protested. 'Pat's forty! And Marty goes through women like a man possessed. Anyway, I'd have to be completely desperate before I dated a colleague. I've spent far too much time listening to them talk about women to ever want to put myself in the situation where I could be the one they discuss on a Monday morning.' She'd dated a colleague before and she'd hated it when everyone had known their business, sometimes before she'd known it herself. 'Besides, who said I even wanted a boyfriend? I'm perfectly happy on my own.'

'I just thought—'

She jumped in and cut him off. 'You thought you were

helping but I don't need your help and I don't need a boy-friend. What I need is a project. Something to keep me so busy that I can tell my family I don't have time for dating. Actually…' She paused momentarily as a thought occurred to her. 'If you do want to help, you could be my project.'

'What?'

She nodded. 'I can tell my family I need to spend all my free time getting the new doctor up to speed. That might keep them off my back and it'll teach you not to meddle too.' She grinned and both she and Louise laughed at the shocked expression on Josh's face.

He held his hands up in surrender. 'I'm sorry, I didn't mean to give you a hard time. I promise to mind my own business from now on.'

'It's all right, I was just having a bit of fun.'

'Well, in that case, I'm sorry your date was terrible.'

'You don't look sorry,' Georgie argued.

'No?' He shrugged. 'I guess I'm not, seeing as it wasn't my fault. All I can say is you should have come shopping with me instead.' He laughed and Georgie was tempted to agree with him.

'I'll remember that next time,' she said.

'Here, I have something that might cheer you up,' he said. In his hand he held a stack of brochures and he passed them to her.

Every pamphlet had a picture of happy, smiling people wearing lifejackets. Happy, smiling people going white-water rafting. 'Where did these come from?' she asked.

'The tourist information counter in the main terminal building. Were you hoping I'd forget?'

'Yes,' she said. But she wasn't sure if that was true. She'd been planning on trying to avoid it but she had agreed to go. That was the deal.

She opened the top brochure. 'Which one looks good?'

'They're all pretty similar.' Josh took the rest of the pile from her and shuffled through it. He passed one brochure back to her. 'The girl at the tourist counter recommended this one. They've been around for a long time and have a good safety record. And it's on the Tully River, which has proper rapids.'

Georgie flicked through the brochure. 'What does that mean exactly?'

'It means you'll feel like you've done something challenging.'

Georgie pointed to the half-day option, 'So this one you think, "The River Challenge"?'

'No, that's for kids,' he said with a smile, almost daring her to argue. 'This is the one I think we should do.' He pointed to the full-day option.

'But that says "thrilling", not challenging.'

'I know. Sounds fun, doesn't it?' He was still grinning at her, his grey eyes flashing with amusement.

She raised one eyebrow in response as she read from the brochure. '"Level Three and Four rapids." That sounds okay if they're classed out of ten, not so fun if they're classed out of five. How are rapids rated?'

'Out of six.'

'Six!'

'It's okay. Only grade-six rapids have the warning "Danger to life or limb" so by the process of elimination that should mean that grades three and four are pretty safe.'

'Hmm.'

Josh wrapped his arm around her shoulders. 'I won't let anything happen to you, I promise.'

Georgie jumped when he touched her. She reacted as though she'd touched something hot when she hadn't expected to and that was how she felt, as though she'd been zapped by electricity. Why did he affect her like this? She needed to get away. She needed some distance, some perspective.

She stepped out of his embrace. 'We'd better go and get changed so we're ready if we get called out,' she said as she hurried to the change rooms.

But this wasn't one of her best ideas. In fact, it was downright idiotic. Because, of course, Josh followed her and the first things he did was open his locker and strip off his shirt. There was nowhere to hide in the unisex change rooms. Nowhere she could go to avoid Josh. And if she found it difficult to ignore her attraction to him when he was fully clothed, it was almost impossible to ignore it when he was standing beside her half-naked.

She put her bag in her locker, hiding behind the door to avoid ogling Josh's washboard abs. Not that it made any difference. She was perfectly capable of remembering what his body looked like: the image of him in his board shorts out on the reef was permanently imprinted on her brain.

'So are you doing anything on Saturday?' he asked. 'I know we're both rostered off.'

She pretended to be searching in her locker, looking for something. She found her hairbrush. That would do. 'Saturday? I don't have any plans.' She pulled her hairbrush out and turned away from Josh to look in the mirror and brush her ponytail but realised she could still see him in the reflection. He was pulling another T-shirt over his head.

'Excellent. Shall I ring the rafting company and book us on a trip this weekend?' he said as he tugged his shirt down to his waist.

Josh took his overalls from his locker and Georgie realised he was about to drop his shorts. Her breathing was suddenly shallow and she needed to look away. 'Okay. I guess I don't have an excuse not to do it. A deal is a deal.' At the moment she'd say anything just to get him out of the locker room so she could get her hormones under control. Her heart was beating like crazy and her mouth was dry. Her senses were fully charged. Why didn't she feel like that when she went on these blind dates?

She put her hairbrush away and plaited her ponytail, keeping her face hidden, using delay tactics until she was certain Josh had finished getting changed. Suddenly she wasn't sure how sensible this plan was, she'd be spending the day with Josh on the river and he'd be wearing next to nothing if the pictures on the brochure were anything to go by. She wasn't sure how she'd cope with that but it was too late to back out now.

'Come on, it'll be fun,' he said as he closed his locker. 'I'm sure I can be better company than your date last night.'

Once she heard his locker-door slam shut she dared to look again. He was dressed now and her breathing was under control again. She didn't doubt she'd enjoy Josh's company more than her blind date but she wasn't about to tell him that. It was bad enough that he seemed to know the direction of her thoughts. 'And if you're not?' She laughed.

'Then you get to choose the next adventure,' he said as he bent down to tie his bootlaces.

Once Josh left the change room Georgie collapsed onto the bench that ran in front of the lockers. She needed a moment to get her head together. She had to work out a way to cope with the feelings Josh evoked in her. She had to work out a way to get her responses under control when he was around.

CHAPTER FIVE

GEORGIE spent all the free time she had over the next few days cooking. Cooking normally helped her to clear her head but it wasn't having its usual calming effect this time. She alternated between trying to keep her mind off Josh and trying to work out why she was so affected by him so she could figure out how she was going to deal with it. But when he arrived to collect her for the drive to Tully she still hadn't come up with a solution.

He was wearing a grey polo shirt and camel shorts. He had good legs for shorts, muscular without being bulky. She glanced over at him where he sat in the driver's seat. His thighs where she could see them emerging from his shorts were tanned and covered with light, sandy blond hair. Strong and masculine.

She should have kept her eyes to herself because now she had to sit on her hands to stop herself from reaching out to touch him.

She concentrated hard to hold normal conversation as she tried to work out what it was about him that stirred her senses. She felt alive, alert and aroused. She realised he made her feel like a woman. It wasn't necessarily because of the way he treated her but more in the way she responded to him, to his masculinity. She was totally aware of him and, in response, she became aware of her own desires.

She'd have to accept that was how it was and deal with it. Ignore it. She certainly wouldn't act on it. She was taking a break from dating and she certainly wasn't about to date a colleague.

She managed to keep her hands to herself and her hormones in check until they reached the meeting point for the white-water rafting company. They left their car at the end point of their ride and were taken upriver by bus. At the launch site they were kitted out with lifejackets, aqua shoes and helmets. Josh took off his T-shirt and stood before her in his board shorts before he put the lifejacket on over his bare chest. Getting through that display without licking her lips was test number one. Test number two was when he helped her fasten the chin strap on her helmet and his fingers brushed against her throat, sending her heart rate soaring. She swallowed but managed not to hyperventilate. So far, so good. She hoped she'd get through the rest of the day as easily.

'I thought you said this was safe?' she said as she straightened her helmet and flicked her plait over her shoulder.

'It's just a precaution,' he replied. 'The company has an impeccable safety record. I checked.' He reached out to help straighten her helmet and her heart skipped a beat. 'You'll have fun, I promise.'

Georgie looked around at their group and suppressed a smile. The helmets they had to wear were most unflattering but she guessed she looked as bad as everyone else. The participants had been divided into four small groups and she and Josh followed their guide as he led them away for the safety briefing.

Their group, like the others, mainly consisted of young backpackers, but fortunately most had enough command of the English language to be able to understand the instructions. Once they'd covered the basics regarding the commands, how and when to paddle or not to paddle and how to approach the rapids, they were allocated a position in the inflatable raft. Their guide, Darryl, sat in the rear, Josh was given the front position and Georgie found herself given a spot towards the back of the raft near Darryl. That wasn't quite where she wanted to be but she knew the raft need to be balanced and they couldn't choose their own positions.

Before they launched their raft Darryl instructed them to practise their war cry.

'Our what?' Georgie asked.

'Our war cry,' Darryl explained. 'Each raft has their own war cry. There are spots on the river where we compete to get to the next set of rapids and our war cry is part of the challenge,' he explained before he let loose with his catch cry. 'All for one…'

'And one for all,' his team responded.

From along the bank the other teams responded with their own cries and the bush reverberated with noise.

'You didn't warn me about this,' Georgie muttered to Josh.

He laughed. 'What's the matter? It's just a bit of fun. Just think of it as a team-building exercise.' Georgie's response was one raised eyebrow. 'You must have done things like this before?' he said. 'What about when you went to Greece, did you join any backpacker tours? Some companies are notorious for these types of stunts.'

'I went to Greece with my cousin and we stayed with relatives. I was barely allowed out of the house without a chaperone, so there's no way I would have been permitted to go off with a group of random twenty-somethings.' She looked at the backpackers sitting all around her in the raft and thought how different her overseas experience was from theirs. But it was what it was.

'In that case, you'll just have to trust me,' Josh was saying. 'Let yourself go and yell, it's quite empowering.' To prove his point, he joined in with the rest of their group in a raucous 'And one for all' following Darryl's next command as they pushed off the bank and entered the water. Georgie had no option but to do as he said. The only way out of there was downriver and to reach the end they had to work together. She dug her paddle into the water, let go of her inhibitions and yelled with the best of them. Her reward was a big thumbs-up from Josh and a huge smile. The effort was worth it and made her determined to enjoy herself.

From her vantage point she could see Josh working hard, digging his paddle into the water, pulling strongly, his biceps flexing with the effort. He looked completely at ease. It was obviously something he'd done before and he seemed to relish the activity. She could imagine Josh alongside her brothers—they would enjoy rafting too. They were always on the go, always challenging each other to silly contests, always active. Josh was a lot like them, full of the joy of life.

She kept Josh in the corner of her vision as she concentrated on paddling and following Darryl's instructions. The section of the river they negotiated before lunch was relatively easy but they were still soaked when they stopped for a barbecue on the river bank. They dried out as they devoured the burgers but once they'd eaten Josh suggested taking another dip in the water.

'We've just eaten. What if I get cramp and drown?' Georgie protested.

'I'll save you.' Josh grinned as he reached for her hand and pulled her to her feet. 'But if you don't trust me, put your life jacket back on and we'll just float about.'

Georgie picked up her jacket and slipped her arms into it. The river was wide and shallow in this spot and some rocks had formed a natural pool, cutting into the main channel. Georgie waded into the pool and floated on her back, drifting with the current.

Josh floated beside her. He turned his head and grinned at her, his grey eyes flashing silver. 'This is the life.'

She had to agree with him. This was perfect. There were no demands on her, there was nothing else she should be doing, and that was an unusual state of affairs. She was completely relaxed. And she had Josh to thank for that. She could be herself with him. He had no preconceptions about her. No knowledge of her as part of her large family. No knowledge of her as someone's daughter or sister or girlfriend. He was spending time with her because he'd chosen to and she was enjoying his company. But all too soon they were called from the water and directed to climb back into the raft for the post-lunch trip.

Georgie's confidence had increased and she was loving every minute of the experience. She laughed and yelled and occasionally screamed and she was still grinning and yelling encouragement as they approached the final rapid.

She couldn't believe how quickly the day had flown by. On the other side of this last rapid was the car park and kiosk that marked the end point of the day's excursion. One rapid remained to negotiate before the day was over. She couldn't believe how much fun she'd had. She'd expected to be totally out of her comfort zone, her sheltered upbringing and girls' school education hadn't prepared her for this. Perhaps she was really an adrenaline junkie. Perhaps, thanks to Josh, she'd discovered something about herself today.

They were neck and neck with one of the other rafts as they headed towards the final, narrow opening.

'Paddle hard, all for one,' Darryl yelled at them.

'And one for all,' they responded as they dug their oars into the water and tried to inch their nose in front of the other raft.

'Left side only,' was the next command, and those sitting on the right took their paddles out of the water, but their reaction time was slow and the other raft shot past them, taking first place into the final rapid.

As they emerged from the rapid in the wake of the first raft they could see the victors celebrating downstream. They had their paddles raised above their heads and were chanting their war cry. In the excitement of the celebration one boy stood up and his movement unbalanced the vessel. Because everyone had their hands and paddles in the air, no one was holding onto the ropes that ran around the inflated sides of the raft. As it tipped three rafters fell overboard into the river.

The raft righted itself as the weight distribution corrected and continued to drift down the river. Two heads emerged quickly from the water and those boys struck out for the raft where eager hands waited to pull them back on board.

The river wasn't particularly deep and the water here was relatively calm but the third boy hadn't reappeared. They all scanned the water, searching for him.

There. Georgie saw the red of the boy's lifejacket pop up behind a boulder. She pointed in his direction as she saw him trying to grab hold of the rock but the boulder was smooth and slippery with no purchase.

'I'm going in,' Georgie heard Josh yell to Darryl even as he was already slipping over the edge of the raft and into the river.

'What the—?'

Georgie heard the confusion in Darryl's tone. He was sitting near her, and she turned to explain to him. 'It's okay, he's a doctor—an emergency specialist.' She had every confidence in Josh's ability to get the situation under control. She'd seen him do it before. In fact, watching him swim away from her now gave her a sense of déjà vu. There was something immensely attractive about a man who didn't back away from a challenge, a man who was prepared to leap to the rescue and who had the skills to pull it off.

He'd reached the boy now. She could see Josh talking to him and, as Darryl and the other guide steered their rafts into the bank, Josh floated the boy on his back and pulled him to the shore but not out of the water.

'We've got trained first aiders, I'll get one from the office,' the guide from the other raft called out to them as Darryl gave orders for disembarkation from his raft.

Georgie was agitated as she waited for the others to climb ashore before her. As soon as she was able to, she hurried off to assist Josh, though she knew he was perfectly capable of managing on his own. There was no doubting his skill and medical expertise. She couldn't believe she'd joked about having to help him get up to speed with pre-hospital emergency medicine, he was totally in control of the situation, but she wanted to help. She wanted to be a part of it. It wasn't in her nature to be a spectator in these situations.

'Hi.' He didn't waste time with pleasantries. 'We need to get him out of the water but we'll need to be careful. I suspect he has fractured ribs and he's twisted his knee. There doesn't appear to be any spinal damage. His name is Ulrich.'

One of the rafting company's employees arrived with a first-aid kit and a stretcher. Together Georgie and Josh rolled the boy onto the stretcher and with the help of the guides lifted him onto the bank.

Josh unclipped the boy's lifejacket. The jackets were cushioned at the front and back but along the sides, under the arms, the fabric was only thin. Georgie could see a large bruise already forming under the boy's left armpit. Ulrich grimaced in pain as Josh moved his arm but told them it was his chest that was sore.

Josh undid his own life jacket now that they were out of the water and slid it from his body. Georgie knew he'd want to get rid of its cumbersome bulk to give him freedom of movement.

He was bare-chested, his back tanned and smooth as he leant forward and extracted a stethoscope from the medical kit. He bent over the boy and placed the stethoscope on the boy's chest. 'Can you try to breathe in through your nose and out through your mouth for me?' he asked the boy. Ulrich did as he was asked but complained when he attempted a deep breath. He spoke perfect English but Georgie could detect an accent, possibly German, which fitted with his name.

'I know it hurts but try once more for me,' Josh instructed as he moved the bulb of the stethoscope.

'Equal air entry,' he said to Georgie. With fractured ribs she knew Josh would have been concerned about a pneumothorax but equal air sounds meant that was one thing the boy had escaped.

'He's not going to be going anywhere in a bus, you'll need to call an ambulance to take him to Tully hospital.' Josh was speaking to the rafting guide. He was issuing instructions, taking control of the situation, as Georgie had known he would, and everyone was running around doing his bidding, happy to have someone take responsibility.

Georgie helped Josh to sit the boy up so they could remove his wet lifejacket. She then carefully dried his upper body with a towel before covering him with a space blanket to keep him warm. Satisfied that the boy was able to breathe and hadn't sustained any serious chest trauma, Josh moved his attention to the boy's knee.

'It looks as though you've just twisted your knee. Nothing's broken,' he announced as he finished his examination. Darryl arrived at that moment with the news that the ambulance had been called but would take half an hour to reach them. The boy's friends trailed in Darryl's wake.

'Do you want anything for pain relief?' Josh asked Ulrich. A thirty-minute wait with fractured ribs would seem like a long time. When Ulrich nodded Josh searched the rafting company's medical kit. 'There's nothing really suitable, or strong enough, that won't interfere with the paramedics when they arrive,' he said to Georgie. 'In my car is a medical bag and there should be an analgesic inhaler in there. Do you think you could get my keys from our locker and find it?' Josh turned back to Ulrich. 'You don't have any medical conditions, do you? You're not diabetic?'

Ulrich shook his head and Georgie went to find their things and retrieve the car keys. She was familiar with these inhalers. They were carried in all the ambulances for short-term pain relief, and she found the box and slotted the cylinder into the bright green inhaler and returned to Josh.

Ulrich seemed much more comfortable once he'd self-administered the analgesic and the wait for the local paramedics became easier to bear. One of his friends travelled in the ambulance with him and Georgie and Josh stood side by side and watched as the ambulance made its way down the road towards Tully.

'I suppose that's the end of our foray into uncharted waters for you, then?' Josh asked her. 'You won't believe me next time I tell you something's safe.'

Georgie laughed. 'I'm pretty sure things wouldn't have gone haywire if Ulrich had kept his seat. He's only got himself to blame.'

'You haven't written me off altogether, then?'

'Not completely, but whether or not you get a second chance will depend on what you have in mind.'

'How about dinner? If we leave now we'll be back in Cairns in time for me to take you out somewhere.'

'Are you okay to drive all the way? You're not too tired?' It was a two-hour trip back to Cairns, a long way at the end of a busy day.

'Would you rather stay in Tully overnight?'

'No!' Georgie panicked. 'I was just going to offer to share the driving.'

The two of them, staying overnight in Tully. Together! Not that he'd actually suggested they spend the night together but she knew her resistance would be minimal at best if she found herself alone with Josh, away from home, overnight. Staying in Tully would only complicate matters. She needed to rein in her crazy fantasies.

'We're heading home, then?' he asked.

She nodded. Spending a couple of hours in a car with Josh would be enough to test her willpower and she thought even that might be a struggle. She couldn't be expected to stay away overnight with him and behave.

'All right,' Josh continued, 'let's head off so we can shower and you can choose somewhere for dinner. You will have dinner with me?'

Did she want to? She wasn't tired after the day of rafting. Adrenaline was still coursing through her system and if she was honest she'd admit she didn't want the day to end. Dinner would help to stretch out the day. 'Dinner would be lovely.'

Josh's grey eyes gleamed as he smiled at her and despite the streaks of dust and dirt on his face he looked fresh and alert, not in the least bit exhausted. Georgie wasn't sure where he got all his energy from but his smile was enough to give her a second wind and she looked forward to dinner with eager anticipation.

He took her hand as they walked to the car. His touch made her skin tingle. It felt alive, as though she could breathe through her pores. She felt as though she was floating and it was several moments before she even wondered about his easy, casual manner. She shouldn't be holding his hand but it felt so natural and so good she didn't want to let go.

On the drive back to Cairns Josh kept glancing at her even as he was driving and he would occasionally reach over to touch her arm or her knee as he talked. His touch was enough to keep the adrenaline coursing through her system and she was on the edge of her seat by the time they reached Cairns.

She hurried through her shower once he dropped her

home. She was keen for their time together to continue. He was good company, he knew how to enjoy himself and he made her feel attractive, intelligent and amusing.

Which was exactly why she should keep her distance, she knew she should. She was supposed to be using this time in Cairns to find her independence, to find her own identity, and she couldn't do that if she was spending time with someone else.

So in an effort to attempt to keep Josh in the box marked 'colleague' she chose The Sandbar on the esplanade for dinner. It was a new restaurant and bar, not far from the hospital, and Josh's apartment, and it was super-trendy and busy so there was little danger of an intimate dinner for two. Georgie figured there was safety in numbers and she knew if she was going to be able to resist Josh she needed to avoid being alone with him. Every time she was alone all she wanted to do was touch him and taste him but she knew there was no point.

The bar was busy, as Georgie had hoped, but she hadn't counted on it being so busy that they wouldn't be able to get a table in the restaurant.

'If you don't have a reservation then I'm sorry but we're fully booked,' the hostess told her when she requested a table.

Josh intervened.

'If you could manage to swing it, I'd really appreciate it.' He focussed intently on the hostess and Georgie knew she'd be feeling like the only woman in the room. She knew that feeling all too well herself. Then Josh played his trump card. He smiled at her and Georgie saw the hostess cave in.

'I'll see what I can do. Come this way,' she said as she

led them to a table on the very edge of a balcony overlooking the Cairns foreshore.

Josh held Georgie's chair for her as she sat. He ordered drinks for them and then proposed a toast.

'To new experiences.'

'Thank you for organising the rafting,' Georgie said as she joined in the toast. 'I really did enjoy it. I think maybe I am an adrenaline junkie in disguise.'

Josh laughed. 'Of course you are—you're a paramedic. I just can't believe it's taken you all this time to discover that side of you. What were your brothers doing when you were growing up? Why weren't you out with them, pushing boundaries?'

'I'm so much younger than them they didn't want me tagging along after them and my parents certainly didn't encourage it. I was, am, a good Greek daughter. I spent my time in the kitchen with my mum and Nonna. I wasn't out climbing trees and terrorising the neighbourhood with the boys. But after today I think I might be a little more adventurous.'

'Sky-diving?'

'Still unlikely.' She laughed. 'I know I told you I came to Cairns for the career experience but it was also my chance to try to discover who I am, away from the perceptions and expectations of my family, and today I learnt a bit about myself. I tested myself physically and I survived. I even enjoyed it, so thank you.'

'It was my pleasure.'

The waitress brought their order but as soon as they were alone again Josh continued the theme of the previous conversation. 'I'm intrigued. How do your family see you? Is their version very different to the one I see?'

Georgie shrugged. 'I'm the baby, the only girl with four

big brothers. They all think I need looking after. That's why they're all looking for a partner for me, they see that as part of their responsibility, making sure I'm taken care of.'

'They're still searching for boyfriends for you? I thought you were going to tell them you're happy being single?'

'I haven't said anything yet. It's not that I mind the idea of marriage,' she explained. 'I'm just not ready for it. I need to work out who I am first. I just hope I can do that before my time here is up and I find myself back in Melbourne.'

'You're braver than I am. The idea of marriage frightens the life out of me.'

'Why?'

'Spending your life with one person, that takes a lot of commitment, a lot of trust. I think it's a lot to ask. A lot to expect.'

She smiled. 'Don't let Isaac hear your opinions. Their wedding is only a fortnight away.'

'I'm not against marriage for other people,' Josh clarified. 'It's just not for me.'

'Why not?'

'You're lucky to come from a stable, supportive family background. That immediately gives you a different perspective. Naturally you think the institution of marriage is a good one. Not everyone is as fortunate.'

Her family was immensely important to her and she couldn't imagine feeling differently, but it was clear that Josh didn't have the same rosy view of family life. She wanted to know more, she was desperate to know more, but something about Josh's tone stopped her from questioning him. Before she could think of another topic of conversation to break the awkward silence that had fallen, the waitress came to clear their plates.

The trade-off for securing a table for dinner was that they needed to vacate the restaurant by nine o'clock for another booking. Georgie still wasn't ready for the day to end; she didn't think she ever would be, but because she'd parked her car at Josh's apartment the day stretched further still. They walked along the esplanade together.

It was a beautiful North Queensland evening, warm and humid, but once the sun had set the humidity became pleasant rather than stifling. Josh took her hand as they crossed the street and instantly Georgie felt her temperature rise even further. His hand was warm and the heat, his heat, flooded her body. Their steps were unhurried but still she felt they reached her car all too soon.

Things had changed today. Despite her best intentions, her awareness of Josh had increased and her resistance was weakening. Every glance, every touch, every smile had gone straight to the heart of her, making her pulse race, her stomach flutter and her nerves spark. She wasn't sure exactly what had happened, she just knew that she wasn't ready for the day to be over. She wasn't ready to say goodbye.

She raised herself up on her toes and kissed his cheek. Her lips pressed against his skin, so close to his mouth that if he'd turned his head a few millimetres she would have kissed his lips.

'Would you like to come up for coffee?' His voice was soft and she could feel his words brush her cheek in little puffs of air.

She hesitated, running the different scenarios through her head, letting her imagination take flight before she replied. 'I really need to get home, I'm working tomorrow.' It had nothing to do with tomorrow, it was all about her lack of resistance to Josh. A coffee could mean so many different things. She'd learnt to take risks today but she didn't think she was ready for another one quite so soon.

'It was just a coffee.' He was smiling at her and his grey eyes were full of amusement.

'Stop doing that!'

'Doing what?' Now his eyes were a picture of innocence.

'Reading my thoughts.'

'Let me see if I read them correctly.' He leant towards her.

He was so close she could feel the heat radiating from him. Their faces were inches apart. He moved his head towards her, closing the gap.

Was he going to kiss her?

He stayed where he was for what seemed like for ever. How could he remain so still?

He was watching her, studying her, and then he moved another fraction closer, his head tilted slightly to one side.

Georgie shut her eyes as she waited for the caress she was sure was coming.

Josh's lips brushed over hers, the gentlest of touches, so soft she wondered if it was nothing more than her imagination. His mouth met hers again. His touch was firmer this time, more definite. Her lips parted involuntarily and she tasted him. He tasted of mint and she heard herself moan as his tongue explored her mouth. The outside world receded; it was condensed into this one spot, this one man.

CHAPTER SIX

HER heart raced in her chest and she could feel every beat as Josh's lips covered hers. She closed her eyes, succumbing to his touch. She opened her mouth and Josh caressed her tongue. She felt her nipples peak in response as he explored her mouth. His hand was on her bare arm and she could feel the heat of his fingers on her skin. She wanted his hand on her breast but she didn't dare move it there. She pressed herself against his chest instead as she kissed him back. Where was the harm in that?

Her skin was on fire as Josh ran his fingers up her arm. She melted against him. She was aware of nothing else except the sensation of being fully alive. She wanted for nothing except Josh.

She felt his hand move to her back. Her skin was bare between the straps of her sundress and her flesh burned under his touch. She felt her nipples harden further as all her senses came to life and a line of fire spread from her stomach to her groin. She deepened the kiss, wanting to lose herself in Josh, but a car horn tooting shattered the silence, interrupting the moment and making her jump. Her eyes flew open as Josh straightened up. Too late, she remembered where they were, standing beside her car in the middle of the street, behaving like a couple of hormone-fuelled teenagers. Her heart was racing in her chest and her breaths were shallow. She could hear herself panting.

Josh was studying her face as if committing each of her features to memory. His fingers trailed down the side of her cheek, sending a shiver of desire through her.

'Now would you like to come up to my apartment?'

She hesitated. The kiss was magical but it couldn't lead anywhere. Hadn't he made it clear at dinner he wasn't looking for commitment? It would be a one-night stand. That wasn't what she wanted.

She pulled back, breaking their connection. 'I can't.'

'Why not?'

'It's a bad idea.'

'It was just a kiss.'

Just a kiss! Maybe to him, but it had set her world on fire and she knew she couldn't be trusted if she followed him to his apartment. No, this was definitely a bad idea. 'You're a colleague. You're off limits.'

'Are you sure?'

She nodded. She couldn't speak.

'Okay. But let me know if you change your mind. No strings attached.'

No strings attached. It wasn't her style but it was tempting.

If he could play it cool, so could she. She smiled, striving for a casual tone, and said, 'I'll get back to you,' as she pushed the remote on her car keys and unlocked the door.

He bent his head and kissed her softly on her mouth, a brief brush of his lips, a gentle goodbye kiss, but her reaction was every bit as strong as when he'd kissed her more thoroughly. She used every ounce of willpower to make herself get into her car and drive away. But she watched him in her rearview mirror as he stood in the street and she knew she wouldn't be able to avoid him or pretend he didn't exist. She knew she couldn't pretend she wasn't attracted to him and she suspected he would become her forbidden apple, a temptation too strong to resist. One way or another she would need to get him out of her system.

Josh had got to work early and was chatting to Louise when they saw Georgie struggling through the door, carrying two large baking trays. She pushed the door open with her hip and nodded in their direction as she headed for the QMERT kitchen.

Louise watched her go before she turned to Josh and said, 'Something's bothering her.'

Josh wondered how on earth Louise had figured that out. Georgie had seemed perfectly okay to him. In fact, she'd seemed perfectly okay for the past few days, ever since he'd kissed her. He, on the other hand, had been completely rattled. Despite what he'd told Georgie, their kiss had rocked his world. It hadn't been 'just a kiss'. It had shocked him, surprised him, to his core. The moment he'd kissed her he'd had the sensation that he'd been waiting all his life to find her, all his life to have that kiss, and ever since then he'd been wondering how to persuade her to date him. What was the difference between him and any of the blind dates she was prepared to go on? The only difference he could see was that they already knew they had chemistry. But she refused to date a colleague and she'd refused to discuss it any further and he had no idea what he could do about that.

But why did Louise think something was wrong? What had he missed? What did Louise see that he didn't?

'How do you know something's wrong?' he asked.

'She's been cooking.'

Josh frowned. As far as he could tell, Georgie was always cooking. 'Don't forget we're all going to her place this weekend for Pat's birthday. Maybe she's run out of room in her fridge.' To his ears that sounded like a perfectly reasonable explanation.

'I'm telling you, something's bothering her. Go and find out what's wrong.' Lou glared at him and he half expected her to shove him out the door.

'Okay, okay, I'm going,' he said, fighting the urge to laugh. With a sharp salute in Lou's direction he followed Georgie into the kitchen.

Her back was to him as she slid the baking trays into the fridge. He dragged his eyes off her rounded backside as she stood up and turned around.

'Hi. Is everything okay?' he asked.

'I guess.'

Josh felt his heart drop to his stomach. She wasn't sounding like her normal chirpy self. Something was wrong. He wondered if he could fix it.

He crossed the room and put his hand on her arm, connecting them. 'What is it?'

'My parents arrive tomorrow.'

'I thought that would be good news.' In the time he'd known her she'd only had nice things to say about her parents and she seemed more than happy to have visitors.

She nodded. 'But they're meeting up with some friends here too.'

'And?'

'These friends have three sons.' She paused. 'Three single sons.'

'Let me guess, they're your next string of blind dates?' he smiled.

'It's not quite that bad. I don't think the boys are coming, but my parents think it's time for me to settle down and they're getting desperate. If it doesn't look like I'm going to find my own husband, I think they're not averse to helping me.'

'An arranged marriage?'

'That's not very twenty-first century,' she said, and finally he saw her smile. 'I don't think they'd call it that but they seem happy enough to send a few eligible bachelors my way. Or the bachelors' parents.'

'Why haven't you told them you're happy being single?'

'Because that's easier said than done. You haven't met my parents. That excuse would only work for so long and then they'd feel obliged to "help" me again.'

'Well, tell them you've already got a boyfriend.'

'Josh, they're coming to Cairns, they're coming to visit.' Georgie sighed. Hadn't he been listening? 'They'll expect to meet my fictitious boyfriend. What do I do about that?'

'Introduce me.'

'You? Why?'

He shrugged. 'You have a problem, that's one solution. I'll be your surrogate boyfriend. It'll give you your freedom back. Your parents can stop setting you up. It'll take the pressure off you.'

It wasn't a bad idea—in fact, she rather liked the sound of it—but she knew she liked the sound of it for all the wrong reasons. 'You don't want to do that. The experience could be a bit traumatic.'

'That doesn't matter,' he said. 'How long are your parents staying? A week? I can keep the charade going for that long.'

'Thanks for the offer but I wouldn't subject you to that.' She smiled and added, 'It's for your own protection.'

'What does that mean?'

'My last relationship ended because of my parents. Trust me, you do not want that level of expectation.'

'Didn't they approve?'

'No, quite the opposite. They loved Peter. So much that they wanted him to join our family. They started asking when we were going to settle down, offering to help us buy a house. Peter decided he wasn't ready for that commitment and headed for the hills. If you told my parents that's what happened, they'd be horrified. I don't think they're aware of what they did, but I don't want to subject each and every boyfriend to the same treatment. I don't want someone forced to marry me.'

'That's why I'm the answer to your problems. There'll be no forcing me to marry anyone! I'm offering my services and I guarantee I can handle parental pressure.'

She wished he was the answer to her problems but she doubted it was that easy. It was his fault she'd spent hours in the kitchen cooking, trying to clear her head. Her parents' expectations were nothing to cope with compared to her reaction to Josh. If she'd relived the kiss they'd shared once, she'd relived it a hundred times. She'd never spent so much time obsessing over a man, let alone one she barely knew, but she couldn't get that kiss out of her mind. She could remember how he'd tasted and felt and how the kiss had made her blood flow like molten gold and warmed her insides. For every second the kiss had lasted she'd spent as many hours thinking about what she should do, but when Josh walked into the kitchen she still hadn't made up her mind. Just the sight of him got her all flustered again. Her heartbeat kicked up a notch and her skin tingled when his fingers caressed her arm.

She shook her head. Her parents were definitely the least of her problems.

'They'd know something was up. They wouldn't be expecting you.'

'What does that mean?'

'You're not Greek.'

'You're kidding? You have to date Greek men?'

She shrugged. 'Pretty much.'

'Surely you've dated men who aren't Greek before?'

'Yes,' she admitted, 'but I've never seen the need to introduce them to my parents. It's never been anything serious and it would just make everyone uncomfortable. I don't need a pretend boyfriend. I don't even need a real one. I don't need to be rescued but I appreciate your offer.'

He shrugged. 'Okay, but let me know if you change your mind. I'm happy to help.'

'Thanks, but I'll manage. I'd better go and get changed.'

She appreciated his offer but it wasn't one she could imagine accepting. As if the kiss wasn't enough for her to ignore, now she had to ignore the image in her head of Josh as her boyfriend. The idea was delicious. He was delicious. But therein lay the danger. He was offering to be a fake boyfriend and she knew she might have trouble remembering that.

No. She was positive she could handle having her parents' friends here. Surely that would be easier than handling Josh. But knowing she had his support gave her some comfort.

Twenty-four hours later Josh was surprised to receive a frantic phone call from Georgie. Her parents had landed in Cairns that morning and he hadn't expected to hear from her at all today.

'Josh, it's me. Can you talk?'

'Why are you whispering?'

'I don't want my parents to hear. I have a favour to ask you. Remember when you offered to be my surrogate boyfriend?'

'Yes.'

'Does your offer still stand?'

'Why?'

'Mum has just told me that Con and Anastasia, the friends with the three sons, were making noises about bringing one of them up to Cairns to meet me. I kind of panicked, I'm definitely not ready to be set up by two sets of parents, so I took your advice. I told them I have a boyfriend and now they expect to meet him tomorrow at Pat's birthday barbecue!'

'And you want me to be your boyfriend?'

'Just for a week or so. Unless you've got any other ideas? Please?'

He had no intention of refusing, especially as it had been his idea in the first place. 'All right.' He was happy to do it, not least because he knew there would be some enjoyable perks to accompany the position of Georgie's boyfriend. 'I'll come over a bit early tomorrow and you can introduce me to your folks.'

'Thank you. You're a lifesaver. I owe you.'

Josh kept his word, arriving half an hour earlier than the other guests, and Georgie tried to get her heart to slow down and stop its frantic pounding. She was nervous and anxious. She hoped their plan wasn't a disaster.

He was carrying a large cardboard box, which he deposited on the kitchen table before kissing Georgie. His spontaneity startled her and she could feel her mother's eyes watching every move.

'Relax,' Josh whispered, and Georgie willed herself to

stay calm. She knew Josh was keeping up appearances and she needed to do the same.

She introduced him to her parents, George and Sofia, and Josh pulled gifts out of the box, champagne for Georgie and flowers for Sofia, and then he set about helping with last-minute preparations, setting up the bar, putting out glasses, turning on the barbecue. He obviously remembered his way around the kitchen, he looked right at home, and his casual assistance lent authenticity to their charade.

When their QMERT friends began arriving, Georgie introduced them to her parents as Josh slipped into the role of host. As she watched Josh pouring drinks and handing around nibbles, Georgie realised she hadn't properly thought through their story.

What would happen if one of their colleagues alerted her parents to their fabrication? What would happen if her parents found out about their deception? What would their colleagues think? If she'd known she'd worry so much, she would have thought of a different plan.

She pulled Josh aside to ask him what they should do, only to find he'd already filled Louise in on their scheme and she'd told the others. Their secret was safe.

But the one thing she hadn't thought about was physical contact. Josh was very demonstrative and she realised she hadn't given this side of things any consideration. She didn't want to appear cool and aloof but she jumped every time he touched her. Which was often. Every brush of his fingers, every touch of his hand sent her pulse racing, and she grew more and more self-conscious.

Eventually, when she thought she was going to go crazy, she dragged him aside again and begged him to stop.

'Don't think you're overdoing it just a little?' she asked.

'Overdoing what?'

'The touching, the kissing, the looks.'

'The "looks"?'

He was laughing at her now. 'Stop it,' she said, trying to glare at him, but he'd made her smile. 'I think you've convinced my parents enough for one day.'

'Don't be a spoilsport, I'm enjoying myself.' He reached for her hand and hooked his fingers through hers. 'This is what people do when they're in a new relationship, when they can't get enough of each other. Before it all goes pear-shaped. Don't you remember a time when you couldn't keep your hands to yourself?' He brought her hand to his lips and kissed her fingers. Georgie had to clamp her lips together to stop herself from sighing out loud. 'I'm making sure we look authentic,' he said. 'I'm having fun.'

'I think you're having too much fun. Can you try keeping your hands to yourself? Please.'

'That's the first time I've had that request,' he said just before he leant forward and kissed her lips. It was just a quick kiss, timed to perfection so she couldn't resist or complain, and then he winked at her. 'I'll do my best.'

He walked away then and left her standing, rooted to the spot, looking after him as he did another round of the party, topping up people's drinks.

She took a deep breath. Her fingers were still warm from his touch and her lips were still tingling from his kiss. She needed to relax.

She went to find her glass. Perhaps another drink would help.

She finished her drink and tried to forget about Josh but she couldn't help wondering whether she'd made a mistake by asking him to do her this favour. She couldn't help wondering if it was all going to end in tears.

But the rest of the afternoon went smoothly. Her father was enjoying himself, mingling with the guests, but Sofia was spending most of her time in the kitchen. Georgie tried to get her to leave the dishes and go outside to enjoy the party, but she resisted.

'I'm happy in here and everyone pops in eventually either for more food or on the way to the bathroom. I'm fine,' she said as she started to assemble coffee cups and saucers on the kitchen table. 'So Josh is the one who took you white-water rafting?'

Georgie nodded in reply.

'I thought you weren't going to date co-workers after what happened with Peter,' Sofia said.

'Peter was a paramedic, Josh is a doctor.' It was all semantics but Georgie could hardly tell her mother it was irrelevant because it was only a charade. Fortunately Sofia had moved on to more important matters.

'His surname is Wetherly?' she asked. 'He's not Greek, then?'

Georgie suppressed a smile. 'No, Mum, he's not.'

'Well, your father seems to like him anyway.'

She looked across the deck to the barbecue, where Josh and her father were deep in conversation. She realised then it was too late to change her mind. Josh was doing her this favour and it was working. Her parents liked him and hopefully he'd buy her some time.

She wondered if she should rescue Josh but before she had a chance, guests began to say their farewells and she didn't get a moment alone with Josh until everyone had left, the dishes were done and her parents had gone to lie down.

Georgie made more coffee and took it out to the deck

to Josh. 'Thank you for your help,' she said as she handed him a cup.

'My pleasure,' he replied. 'It went well. Pat enjoyed himself. It was a really nice thing to do for him.'

'He gets a bit lonely, I think. I wish he would find someone, I'm sure he'd like the companionship.'

'You're not planning on matchmaking, are you?'

Georgie shook her head. 'No. He says he's happy on his own and I'm the last person who'd interfere in that case. I hate that interference myself.' She sipped her coffee and asked the question she'd been dying to know the answer to. 'What were you talking about with my dad?'

'Your ex-boyfriend, Peter.'

'Peter! What about him?'

'Your dad was just saying that it was good to see you happy again after Peter broke your heart.'

'What? He didn't break my heart.'

Josh held his hands in the air. 'Don't shoot the messenger. They were your dad's words, not mine.'

'That's probably my fault,' she admitted.

'How so?'

'After Peter and I broke up I pretended to be more distraught than I actually was because it gave me a reason to escape Melbourne. I wanted to take the twelve-month posting up here but Dad would have argued against it—his single daughter moving to the other end of the country—but he gave in when I said it would help me to get over Peter. We worked together. He was—is—a paramedic too, and I over-emphasised the discomfort I felt at work after we broke up. But my move wasn't so much to do with Peter as it was to do with me. I wanted a chance to find my own identity, away from being a daughter, a sister or a girlfriend. This move was about a journey of self-discovery.'

'You can handle going back to your old job? Even though Peter is married?'

'He wasn't married when I went out with him. He got married three months later.'

'Sorry, that's not what I meant, but I thought he broke it off with you because he wasn't ready for a commitment?'

'That's what he said, but it turns out he just didn't want to commit to me.'

'And you're okay with that?'

'Yes, perfectly okay. Despite what my parents were hoping for, I didn't want to marry him either.'

'You weren't in love with him?'

'No, and he didn't break my heart. I'm twenty-seven years old and still waiting to fall in love,' she said as she finished her coffee and took a piece of birthday cake from the plate in front of her. 'Have you ever been in love?'

'Yes,' he said.

Georgie was surprised at the wave of disappointment that flowed through her when she heard his answer. She wasn't sure what she'd expected him to say, he was thirty-four years old so it would be unrealistic to think he'd never been in love, but she hadn't realised she'd hoped he was in the same romantically barren situation as her.

'Was it a long time ago?'

He nodded.

'Was it the loveliest thing in the world?' She sighed. Despite being in no hurry to get married, she did want to experience her own very traditional, romanticised idea of being in love.

'Yes and no. I gave her my heart but it ended badly.'

'What happened?' She asked the question before she realised it might not be something Josh wanted to talk about.

'She was killed in a car accident.'

'Oh, Josh, I'm so sorry.'

Georgie felt mortified, as though she'd had the wind knocked out of her. She was so shocked she could barely talk. She sat in silence for a moment and then remembered he'd told her that that he didn't plan on marrying. 'Was she your soul mate? Is that why you said you won't marry?'

'No.' He was shaking his head. 'We were engaged but a few months before the wedding she came to me and said there was something she needed to tell me. It turned out she'd been having an affair. She told me because she was worried I'd find out anyway. I think if she thought she could keep it a secret she would have. We had a huge fight. That wasn't unusual, we had lots of ups and downs and usually I gave in, but not this day.' He paused slightly and Georgie wondered how long ago this had happened. It was obvious it still affected him deeply. 'I couldn't believe she'd behaved that way. I told her it was over, the engagement, us, everything. I told her I didn't want to see her again. I should never have let her get in the car but I didn't stop her and then she was dead. And it was my fault.'

'You weren't to know what would happen.'

'Maybe not but I should have stopped her. She was upset when she left, she was in no state to drive, but I was so angry I let her go.'

'When was this?'

'Eight years ago.'

'You're still blaming yourself?'

'No, eventually I realised that a lot of what had happened was beyond my control but it took me a long time to process it all and it made me think differently about relationships. I decided that I needed to be in control of my life and being in a relationship, to me, seemed to require giving up control. When my parents were still married there was a lot of arguing in our house, lots of yelling and screaming, lots of crying, lots of broken promises. I thought that was how families were. But to keep things together, someone always gives in. Tricia and I had a similar pattern but I was the one backing down. I didn't want to live like that again. I didn't want to be one of those people who spend their life fighting and arguing. I promised myself I wouldn't solve problems that way.'

'And have you changed?'

'I hope so but I don't really know. I avoid serious relationships, I don't want to put myself in that position again. I don't want to lose control. That's why I'm the perfect fake boyfriend—you know I won't fall in love with you and make things difficult.' He finished his coffee. 'But now it's time for me to go.' He stood and came around to her chair. He leant over her and kissed her softly on the lips. Georgie was surprised again, thinking this time it was a spontaneous gesture on Josh's part, but that was before he explained himself. 'Kiss me back, your mum is watching.'

He pulled her to her feet and tipped her face up to his. Georgie closed her eyes and waited for his lips to meet hers. His mouth brushed across hers very gently before he deepened the kiss. She tried to pretend she wasn't enjoying the experience but as his tongue teased her lips apart she sighed and opened her mouth and she knew she'd just given him part of her heart.

CHAPTER SEVEN

GEORGIE had seen Josh every day for the past week, at work or after work or both. He was playing the role of the perfect boyfriend perfectly. Her parents thought he was fantastic and Georgie had to keep reminding herself that he was acting. His acting skills were beginning to rival his medical skills.

She was dressing for Lani and Isaac's wedding but it was taking her twice as long as usual. Her hands shook as she zipped up her dress, as she applied her makeup, and they were still shaking as she tried to slide a silver clip into her hair to keep it out of her eyes.

Josh was coming to collect her to take her to the wedding and no matter how many times she told herself otherwise it felt like she was waiting to go on a real date. She was full of nervous anticipation and she was finding it hard to keep a clear head.

He had everyone convinced that he and Georgie were a serious item. If he hadn't told her about Tricia, even she might believe there was a chance he could feel something for her. But Georgie had the impression that Josh was quite content living his solitary life and was not planning on giving it up. But if she thought she had a chance to change his mind, would she take it?

Josh arrived just as she finally got the hairclip into

place. Her breath caught in her throat when she saw him
standing before her. He was wearing a light grey suit with
a white shirt and he looked divine. The suit fitted his broad
shoulders perfectly, the cut was exact, and Georgie guessed
it had been tailor-made for him. The colour of the suit was
a perfect match for his grey eyes.

'You look beautiful.' She thought he was reading her
mind again before she realised he was complimenting her.

'Thank you,' she said as she smiled at him.

'You both look gorgeous,' Sofia gushed. 'Let me take
a photo before you go.'

Georgie took her camera from her handbag and handed
it to her mother. Josh wrapped his arm around her waist
as she stood beside him and her stomach did a lazy somersault of desire. As she posed for the photo she reminded
herself not to forget it was all make-believe. She was worried that the invisible line between friendship and something more was disappearing. She'd have to be careful to
make sure she didn't blur the boundaries between their
pretend relationship and their real one.

The wedding and reception were being held in one
venue, the yacht club overlooking the Cairns marina,
and there were plenty of guests already assembled when
Georgie and Josh arrived. Isaac was mingling with the
crowd, showing no sign of pre-wedding nerves as he
waited for his bride, but Georgie only had eyes for Josh.

She'd felt a million dollars when she'd walked into the
room on Josh's arm and that feeling stayed with her even
when they became separated as they mixed and chatted
with other guests while they waited for the ceremony to
start. But even when he was on the opposite side of the
room she had no difficulty finding him. It seemed she

could find him through osmosis, almost as though she could channel his energy and feel where he was.

He was chatting to Marty but he must have felt her gaze. He looked across at her and winked and as the music started for the ceremony he made his way back to her side. The guests began taking their seats and with his hand resting lightly in the small of her back Josh guided her towards two empty chairs. As they sat he removed his hand from her back and held her hand instead. She thought she should tell him he didn't need to, her parents weren't there to see, but because he'd never listened to her before and because she was enjoying the contact she kept quiet.

Josh's attentiveness didn't waver throughout the evening. They were seated together at a table with their QMERT colleagues and even though they all knew the story behind their 'date' Josh continued to play his part. He held her chair for her, kept her water and champagne glasses filled and constantly touched her knee or arm to get her attention. Each touch of his hand made her blush and she was finding it difficult to concentrate on the conversation as his touch was so distracting. As Isaac led Lani onto the dance floor for the bridal waltz Georgie finally decided to let Josh off the hook.

'It's okay, Josh, everyone knows it's just pretend, you don't need to worry about me.'

'I don't mind,' he replied. 'It's easier to stay in character.' He leant back as he spoke and rested his arm across the back of her chair, brushing his forearm against her bare shoulder. 'I think it's becoming a habit.'

Georgie wasn't sure if she liked the sound of that but she didn't argue any further, content to sit and enjoy his company, and if he was happy to continue playing his role she wasn't going to stop him. But as other guests joined the bride and groom on the dance floor, Josh stood. He leaned over her shoulder and his voice was soft in her ear as he asked, 'Would you dance with me?'

She looked back at him and smiled. 'Of course.'

Josh pulled Georgie's chair out for her and smiled when she slipped her hand into his and let him lead her onto the dance floor. He'd been waiting for this moment all night. Waiting for an excuse to have her in his arms.

She was beautiful. He'd grown so accustomed to seeing her in her work overalls that seeing her in a formal dress was a revelation. It was as if he'd met her for the first time all over again. All evening he'd found himself distracted. Distracted by her and distracted by the sequins shimmering on her silver dress.

He took her in his arms and her cinnamon and honey scent wafted over him. He wondered if he'd just made a mistake. Would he be able to dance with her in his arms? He feared he might suddenly discover he had two left feet. But then she looked up at him, her dark eyes luminous, her lashes thick and long, and his feet began to move of their own accord as he lost himself in the depths of her eyes.

The band was playing a waltz and he pulled her in closer, letting the music wash over them. His right hand rested at the base of her spine, his left held her fingers. She fitted perfectly within his embrace. Her heels gave her enough extra height to make her the perfect dance partner for him and he guided her around the floor, his arm wrapped around her waist, her head just below his. Every time he breathed in he inhaled her perfume and he knew the scent of cinnamon and honey would always remind him of her.

Her dress clung to her curves. Its neckline was demure

but the exposed skin on her arms was smooth and soft and delightful. Her hair was pulled back on one side and caught in a silver clip but it cascaded down her back in soft curls and all night he'd been longing to run his hands through it, to feel its weight in his palms. On the dance floor he could slide his hand under her hair and as far as he was concerned that was the next best thing.

He knew he was supposed to be playing a role but it was becoming more and more difficult to remember that. Her scent, her red-lipped smile and her soft velvet skin were becoming part of him and he had to fight to recall that their relationship was just a pretence. It was starting to feel real.

Georgie was getting under his skin. It was dangerous. He should be wary but he was positive he could keep things under control. He hadn't made a mistake so far. What was the harm in satisfying their desires? He'd promised not to fall in love; he hadn't promised not to try to seduce her.

He was sure the attraction wasn't one-sided but he had to make certain. He bent his head to hers, burying his face among the soft curls of her hair, and whispered, 'You look amazing.'

He was pleased to see he was able to make her blush. If he hadn't been so close to her he wouldn't have noticed the deepening colour of her cheeks. It was hard to see with her olive skin, but from a few inches away there was no disguising it.

'Thank you.' She smiled and her eyes sparkled and her teeth were bright against her dark red lips.

The song ended and the band began to play a more up-tempo tune. Josh couldn't keep Georgie in his arms but he wasn't ready to let her go. He led her onto the balcony overlooking the marina. It was his chance to get her alone, away from their colleagues. There was something he wanted to ask her.

'What are you doing after the wedding? Am I taking you home or would you come home with me?'

'Why?' She looked up at him and her eyes were twin pools of midnight, inky black and shining.

He knew this was dangerous. If she came home with him he would be mixing physical intimacy with emotional intimacy and that was something he didn't do. He should stop now, before it was too late. He should leave her alone, but as he looked at her in his arms he knew he wouldn't. He couldn't. He liked the way he felt when she was with him.

It had been a long time since he'd had a relationship that wasn't just about sex. It was dangerous but something about Georgie made him want to try it.

'Let me show you something.' He took her hand and pulled her close. The moment he touched her he could feel her soul. He could see her react to him. Her face was like an open book—every thought flashed across it and he knew his touch stirred her in the same way hers stirred him. He placed her hand over his heart. They were alone on the balcony but he wouldn't have cared if there was a room full of onlookers. Her hand was cool through his thin shirt. 'Can you feel my heart beating?' She nodded. 'Its rhythm is your rhythm. We have a spark. I want you to imagine how we could make each other feel. There is something real between us. It's not all make-believe. Don't ignore it. Don't fight it.'

'What do you want me to do?' Her voice was a whisper.

'Come home with me. Explore our connection, see where it takes us. Don't deny yourself that pleasure.' His heart throbbed with longing where it beat under the touch of her palm. He lifted her hand from his chest and kissed her fingers, slowly, deliberately, one by one, drawing out the moment of intimacy. Her eyelids fluttered closed and he knew she was thinking about his proposal. 'We can have a night to remember.'

He bent his head. He had one last chance to convince her. He put his fingers under her chin and gently tipped her head up. She didn't open her eyes and she didn't resist. His lips met hers. Her mouth was soft, warm, pliant. She moaned a little as he teased her lips apart. His tongue darted inside her mouth and she welcomed him, opening to him. He had one hand behind her back and he pulled her in closer, deepening the kiss. Her hands slid up his back and pressed through the thin fabric of his shirt. Her breasts were flattened against his chest. He could feel her nipples through her dress, hard and erect against his body, and he knew their attraction was mutual.

She was holding onto him as tightly as he was embracing her. Her hips pushed into his groin and he knew she must be able to feel his response to her touch. He let her kiss him back. Let her feel their connection.

'Come home with me,' he repeated.

'No.' She was shaking her head. Her soft, black curls bounced around her shoulders and cascaded down her back, distracting him. 'I'm not denying we have chemistry but I see no point in complicating things. This is make-believe. We are make-believe. Remember?' She gave a slight shrug that sent the sequins on her dress shimmering again.

'I remember. But it's only one night, it doesn't need to change anything. There's nothing to worry about. Nothing to be afraid of. No strings attached.'

Before he could beg, plead, argue or cajole any further,

they were interrupted by the master of ceremonies. He was summoning everybody to the dance floor to say farewell to the bride and groom.

'I'm sorry, Josh, one-night stands aren't my thing.'

Georgie pulled her hand from his and moved away. It appeared the discussion was over.

He watched her go.

At least one of them had the sense to fight this attraction. He'd been mad to propose the idea.

He let her go. He couldn't have followed her even if he'd wanted to. He needed to wait for his desire to abate. It was several moments before he was able to leave the balcony, by which time the women had gathered around the edge of the dance floor ready for the traditional tossing of the wedding bouquet. He threaded his way through the throng to the peace and quiet of the far side of the room, away from the women, away from Georgie. But from the opposite side of the room he had a clear line of sight to where she stood. She was right in the centre of the crowd, surrounded by other women.

Lani turned her back to the female guests and lofted the bouquet over her head. The bouquet hit Georgie solidly in the chest. It was a natural reflex to catch it.

She could feel everyone's eyes on her but she could feel one pair in particular. Across the dance floor a pair of gunship-grey eyes watched her as she caught Lani's flowers. Over the delicate bouquet of frangipani flowers she met his gaze.

She stood still, holding the bouquet, as Josh turned and raised one eyebrow.

She wanted to go to him but she held her ground. She couldn't give in.

She had no doubt they would have had a night to remember and even though she could imagine in minute detail how the night would have proceeded, she couldn't do it. She was afraid she wouldn't be happy with just one night, and it could be nothing more.

He'd offered her sex with no strings attached but that was the trouble. She couldn't trust herself to handle that. It would be like playing with fire and she knew she'd be the one to get burnt.

They were too different. He was a confirmed bachelor, focussed solely on his career with no strong family ties and no plans to ever settle down. She wanted to fall in love, she wanted to be married one day, she wanted a family of her own. Their backgrounds, their views on life and love, they were all different. She wished for the chance to get him to open his heart but she didn't think she was up to the challenge. He wasn't going to change for her or anybody else.

She wished she could have gone home with him. She wished he was offering her more than one night but that wasn't going to happen.

He'd told her there was nothing to be afraid of. But he was wrong. She was afraid of getting her heart broken and in her mind that was plenty. He had promised not to fall in love. She'd made no such pledge.

She didn't think she could.

I could have danced all night and still have danced some more. Georgie couldn't remember the right words but it didn't matter, she knew exactly how Eliza Doolittle had felt.

She climbed the steps leading to her deck and twirled around, reliving the feeling of being in Josh's arms, of being swept around the dance floor. Since the moment the music had begun she'd imagined how it would feel to be in his embrace but her imagination hadn't been able to capture the delight; the sensation of floating on air, the warmth of his hand where it had rested in the small of her back, the firmness of his shoulder muscles under her fingers or the soft brush of his breath as his words had caressed her cheek.

She could have quite happily stayed in his arms until the sun came up. But she would have been a fool to take that option. A fool to open herself up to those feelings. She'd have to be content with the memories. And if that was all she was going to have, she was determined to hold onto them.

She held the bouquet of frangipani flowers in one hand as she opened the back door. She was still humming the tune as she walked into the kitchen.

'You sound as though you had a good night.' Sofia's voice greeted her as she closed the door.

'Mum! What are you doing up?'

'Your father can't sleep. I got up to make him a warm drink and now I'm wide awake so I thought I'd wait up for you. How was the wedding?'

'It was lovely.' Georgie sighed. 'Isaac and Lani were so happy and their mood was infectious. Lani looked gorgeous. I took more photos,' she said as she put the bouquet on the table and removed her camera from her evening bag. 'Would you like to see?' Georgie had planned to come home and take her memories of Josh to bed with her as some form of comfort but she couldn't ignore her mother.

They sat together at the table as Georgie scrolled through the photos. There were several of Lani and Isaac exchanging vows and several more pictures of the QMERT team, which Georgie had taken during dinner, and a couple of Isaac and Lani during the bridal waltz. Georgie thought they were the last photos but her mum continued to go forward and the next photo was one of her with Josh. She must have left her camera on the table when he'd asked her to dance and, unbeknown to her, someone had picked it up and snapped a picture.

She was wrapped in his arms as they danced. He was smiling down at her as she gazed up at him. To anyone who didn't know better, they looked like a couple in love. The camera had captured a moment in time when they had been unaware of anything or anyone else around them. They looked like they were in their own little world and Georgie realised that's how Josh made her feel. In his company she was content. She didn't want for anything else when he was with her. Thank goodness she hadn't gone back to his apartment tonight. Seeing the expression on her face in the photograph, she knew now she was in big trouble. She'd have to watch herself. She was falling under his spell.

'That's a lovely photo, I didn't realise it was quite so serious between you two.' Her mum employed her favourite tactic, make a comment sound like a question and see what information was forthcoming, but Georgie recognised the technique and kept quiet. She wasn't going to give her mother anything to speculate about; she'd learned long ago how to play that game. Besides, she didn't know what she could say.

After what seemed like a short lifetime her mum gave up. 'I'll just go and check on your dad. I'll be back in a minute.'

Georgie put her camera away while her mum was out

of the room and took the opportunity to change the subject when she returned. 'Is he okay?'

'He's asleep. He hasn't been sleeping well recently so that's good.'

'Is something the matter?' Georgie frowned. She hadn't noticed anything.

'He's been very tired lately. He's blaming the lack of sleep but what I don't understand is why he isn't sleeping well. He's not worried about anything, he's relaxed, but he says he finds it hard to breathe.'

Now that her mother had mentioned it, Georgie remembered that her parents had been having afternoon rests, her dad especially, which was something he'd never done before, but Georgie had just assumed it was because he was on holiday and could lie down. Now she wondered what she'd been missing. 'Has he complained of shortness of breath at any other times? With activity? Have you noticed anything?'

Sofia shook her head.

'Has he been to the doctor?' Georgie asked.

'He's made an appointment for when we get home from this trip.' Sofia paused. 'Perhaps it's been bothering him more than he's let on,' she mused, 'especially if he's made a doctor's appointment. You know what he's like about going to the doctor.'

'Has he got any other symptoms?'

Sofia frowned. 'Like what?'

'Chest pain, dizziness, that sort of thing?' Georgie was worried. Her paramedic training made her assume the worst, even though she hadn't actually noticed any worrying signs herself.

'No. He reckons it's just old age. He's been talking about

getting old a lot lately. I think that's why he's keen to see you settled down.'

And with those words Georgie had to rein in her fantasies once more. On her way home from the wedding she'd imagined what would have happened if she'd gone home with Josh. Now that she knew what it was like to be in his arms, what it was like to feel as though they were the only two people who existed, her imagination had been able to conjure up all sorts of fantasies.

She'd imagined the touch of his fingers on her knee as they sat in the taxi, the warmth of his hand as he led her into his building, the heat that emanated from him as he pulled her against him in the lift, the taste of his lips when he closed his apartment door and kissed her, the breeze over her bare skin as he lifted her dress over her head, and finally the look in his eyes as he took her to his bed.

She could sleep with Josh to satisfy her curiosity and desire but nothing more would come of it. She remembered the photo of them dancing and she knew she wouldn't be able to sleep with him without exposing herself to heartache, she would be leaving herself wide open. She'd never had a one-night stand and she wasn't going to start now.

Maybe she should put a stop to this fake relationship before she got any more involved. Before it was too late.

CHAPTER EIGHT

GEORGIE was flat out for the next couple of days and it had nothing to do with work. She'd spent a pleasant day with her parents following Isaac's wedding, although she found herself watching her dad carefully, looking for any sign that he was unwell. Her parents were only in their mid-sixties and it was the first time she'd really thought about them getting old. Her dad was semi-retired; he was a builder and he'd worked hard and always been in good physical shape, but perhaps the years had taken their toll on him. It wouldn't be unusual. But Georgie had never imagined her life without her parents. Keeping a close eye on him while trying not to make him aware of her attention was difficult but thankfully she didn't see anything that concerned her.

Con and Anastasia arrived the next day and Georgie found herself playing tour guide to not one elderly couple but two. She'd organised to take them up to Kuranda, a town in the rainforest hinterland inland from Cairns. Travelling by a combination of cable car and old steam train, it was an extremely touristy thing to do but Con and Anastasia seemed to enjoy the outing and were appreciative of the effort Georgie had made.

But the combination of looking for anything untoward with her father's health and being a shining example of a perfect daughter meant she was exhausted by the end of the day and she was looking forward to returning to work.

Until she got there.

The first thing she saw on the noticeboard in the kitchen was photos of Isaac and Lani's wedding. That was fine, except that when she got closer to the board she saw that most of the photos were of her with Josh. Lou was in the kitchen, making herself a coffee, and Georgie knew she was watching her, waiting to see her reaction.

'Who put these up?' she asked.

Lou stirred milk into her coffee. 'Marty. He's taking bets on whether your relationship with Josh is happening for real now.'

'He's doing what?'

'He seems to think that you and Josh are dating seriously now.'

'And what about everyone else? What do they think?' She'd been off work for two days and this was what had happened? She couldn't believe what she was hearing.

'I think they'd be quite happy to believe it. You do make a good couple.'

'Not you as well, Lou?'

'Don't worry, I haven't put any money on you either way, I value my life too much.'

That was why this whole fake relationship was a dumb idea. She didn't want to be gossiped about. She'd conveniently forgotten all the reasons why she hadn't wanted to do this but Lou was rapidly reminding her. 'What about Josh? What has he said?'

'He said nothing's going on but it seems most people are choosing not to believe him.'

Georgie was mortified. 'Is he working today?' She had to find him.

Lou was nodding. 'He came in just before you. He should be in the change room.'

Georgie didn't bother saying goodbye to Lou, she bolted for the change room and hoped and prayed she'd find Josh alone. He was just coming out as she got there. She grabbed him by the arm. 'Can I talk to you? Somewhere private?'

'Sure. What's this about?' he asked as she dragged him outside. She took him around the QMERT building, on the opposite side to the helicopters—that way she was pretty sure they wouldn't be interrupted.

'Do you know what Marty's doing?'

'Running a book?' He nodded. 'Yeah, I know. Pretty funny, don't you think?'

'No, I don't think.'

He was frowning now. 'What's the matter?'

'This is just what I didn't want, people gossiping about me. This is why dating a colleague is a bad idea.'

'Fair enough, except we're not dating.'

'We know that but it seems everyone else thinks otherwise. All because I caught the stupid bouquet.'

Josh didn't think that was why people were talking. He'd seen the photos. He'd seen the way they'd looked when they'd been dancing together. Even in a photo their chemistry was obvious. It wasn't surprising that people were putting two and two together and he couldn't blame them for jumping to conclusions. He knew he and Georgie were acting the part convincingly, so much so that they were also in danger of believing the illusion.

'So what do you want to do about it?

'We should just cancel the whole thing. It was a dumb idea in the first place.'

'And what will you tell your folks?'

Georgie shrugged. 'I'll think of something.'

'No. We may as well keep going. How much longer are your parents in town for?'

'Three days.'

'And their friends are here too now, aren't they?'

Georgie nodded.

'I think we should stick with the plan. Everyone here will draw their own conclusions anyway. I don't think they'll believe we've called it off for a minute if they don't want to.'

'Are you sure you don't mind?'

'That people think we're getting down and dirty?' He grinned.

'No! Are you sure you don't mind being a surrogate boyfriend for a little bit longer?'

'It's fine. It's probably only a matter of one more dinner and everything will go back to normal.' Georgie's parents would leave and this would all come to an end then. But until then he needed to remind her, remind them both, that this wasn't real. Could never be real.

'If you like, I can tell Marty and the others exactly why I'm the perfect fake boyfriend. I can tell them why I'm never getting married, why I won't commit.'

'You're going to tell them about Tricia?'

He was positive he could make everyone believe it was all a show, Georgie included, but he needed to tell her his whole story.

'There's more to it than what I've told you. The others don't need to hear the whole story but I think you do.' It would ensure she wouldn't imagine their relationship to be anything other than the charade it had started out to be.

'My parents got divorced when I was a teenager. My dad worked for a big international corporation and he travelled a lot. Mum was bored, and lonely too, I suppose, and she had a few affairs. I think my father turned a blind eye the first few times and despite lots of fighting they managed to stay together, but I guess at one point he decided not to accept it and they split up. My brother and I were sent to boarding school. Dad was still travelling and I think Mum either didn't want the responsibility of looking after us or the reminder of what she'd done to the family so she chose a new life. Scott, my brother, was…' he paused and corrected himself '…is a couple of years older than me. He was the only constant in my life. I depended on him, trusted him, and that was pretty significant because trusting people wasn't something that came naturally to me. When I started dating I always expected my girlfriends to either leave me or betray me. I was always suspicious and that wasn't conducive to healthy relationships. I can't remember now whether I chose to trust Tricia or whether she convinced me but, in my mind, she was my first serious, committed relationship until she betrayed me. But her betrayal wasn't the worst of it. It was Scott's betrayal that almost destroyed me.'

'Scott's?'

Josh nodded. 'Tricia had been sleeping with Scott. That's what we were fighting about when she drove off, when she was killed.' He paused and took a deep breath. He never discussed the incident that had changed his life and made him into the man he was, the man who couldn't commit, but Georgie needed to hear this. She needed to understand him.

'She'd been having an affair with your brother?' Georgie's dark eyes were wide with surprise. 'How could they do that to you?'

'I don't know. I couldn't understand it and I certainly couldn't accept it. Scott and I were always very competitive, as I think most brothers are, but I never expected him to steal my fiancée. He was my big brother. I thought he'd look out for me. I thought we'd look out for each other, but I was wrong. I went a little bit crazy after that. I took time off university, went travelling, looking for the most dangerous activities and situations I could find, the more outrageous the better. I was feeling sorry for myself, testing my own mortality, trying to decide if life was worth living.'

'And you decided it was?'

'Yes, but I promised myself I'd never put myself in a situation like that again, so I concentrated on work and avoided my brother and relationships in general.'

'Do you see your brother now?'

He shook his head. 'No. My experience of relationships has all been about arguing, fighting and betrayal. That's why I don't plan on getting married. I have nothing left in me to give anyone. If I can't trust, what's the point? But I can tell everyone about Tricia. That'll give them something else to gossip about instead.'

'No.' Georgie shook her head. Three days, that's all it was. She could manage three more days. 'You don't need to tell them about Tricia. I'd rather let everyone jump to conclusions for a few more days than make you divulge your secrets.' Marty could take bets but she wouldn't give him any more fodder for gossip. 'My parents will be gone soon and this will all be over. If you can manage one more dinner, that'll keep my parents happy and then things will be back to normal.'

Only two more days now, she thought the next morning as she parked her car outside the QMERT building, but even so she found herself automatically searching for Josh's car as she locked hers. Just thinking about seeing him again made her heart race.

Georgie disagreed about his assessment that he had nothing to give but she knew it wasn't her place to say so. He was doing her a favour; he hadn't asked her to interfere in his life. In two days there would be no need to have any extra contact with Josh.

She'd let herself get carried away with their charade but hearing Josh's story had reminded her of the truth. She suspected that's why he'd told her and she knew she had to keep her feelings under control. She had to remember their relationship wasn't going anywhere. Had to remember they didn't actually have a relationship and they definitely didn't have a future.

She waited for her heart rate to return to normal, waited until she was sure she could behave normally around Josh, before she gathered her things and went into work, only to find he was doing a shift at the hospital. But at least with him out of the way she knew she'd be able to keep her mind on her job.

But he wasn't completely out of contact. The crew was on their second run of the day, a routine inter-hospital transfer, when Louise patched a phone call through to the chopper.

'Georgie, I have an urgent phone call for you. It's Josh.'

Louise's message immediately sent her into a spin. She wondered what Josh could possibly want that would require him to go to the trouble of tracking her down in the chopper.

'Josh, what's up?'

'Where are you guys?'

His tone was short, abrupt even. His phone manner left a lot to be desired but as the call was coming through the helicopter radio she gave him the benefit of the doubt. Maybe it was because he knew everyone in the chopper could hear the conversation through their headsets.

'We're heading to Dimbulah,' she told him.

'You're on your way there now?'

'Yes, we're about twenty minutes east of town.'

'I have something I need to tell you.' He paused very slightly and Georgie frowned. There was complete silence through the radio and it felt as though minutes had passed before she heard his next words. 'Everyone is okay but your father has just been brought into Emergency with chest pain.'

Immediately Georgie recalled her father's shortness of breath. 'Is he having a heart attack?' Why hadn't she insisted that he have a check-up with a doctor while he was in Cairns? Why had she been content for him to wait until he got home to Melbourne? Even though she'd seen no sign of any problems she still berated herself. Her mother had told her of the episodes—why had she ignored her?

'We're running tests now,' he said.

'It'll be a few hours before I'm back in Cairns. How serious is this?' She could hear the panic in her voice. Was there more that Josh wasn't telling her?

'It's okay, Georgie, you can relax. We've got things under control.' Hearing him say her name calmed her nerves. He sounded so assured and confident. He'd tell her straight, wouldn't he? 'If I thought it was critical I'd tell you,' he continued. Even over the radio it seemed as though he could follow her thoughts. 'The ECG isn't showing any signs of cardiac arrhythmia but we'll keep testing until we find out what's going on. I'll take care of him but come in when you get back.'

She breathed out, concentrating on expelling the air,

releasing the tension. If Josh said he'd take care of things she trusted him to do just that. 'Have you seen Mum? Is she okay?'

'She seems to be. She's with Con and Anastasia.' He knew who they were and now he'd met them, but it was still strange to hear him mention her parents' friends. It was as though they had no secrets, as though he knew all the intimate details of her life, but fortunately he didn't disclose anything further. He hadn't forgotten that the rest of the crew could hear their entire conversation. 'Don't worry, everything will be all right. I'll keep you up to date. See you when you get back.'

'Thanks, Josh.'

She worked hard to keep her focus and concentration on the job and fortunately the IHT was straightforward and the return to Cairns went smoothly. Josh phoned with another update as they were returning to Cairns. Her father's condition had stabilised and he'd been transferred to one of the cardiology beds, and this news helped to settle her nerves.

It was nearing the end of her shift when the chopper landed opposite the hospital to transfer their patient. Sean suggested that Georgie stay behind and she gratefully accepted.

'Pat and I will get your car back to you somehow,' he said. 'And Louise can call Marty and see if he can come in a bit early in case we need a paramedic. Don't worry about us, go and see your dad.'

She didn't need to be asked twice. She and Sean transferred their patient to the hospital but Georgie didn't return to the chopper, heading instead for the cardiology ward. Her mum was in a chair beside her father but Georgie was pleased to see there were no other visitors. Con and Anastasia must have returned to their hotel.

'Dad! How are you feeling?' she asked as she kissed both her parents.

'Completely fine,' George said. 'If I wasn't hooked up to these monitors I'd walk out of here. It was just a bit of indigestion, I'm sure of it.'

'You don't have any pain? Any discomfort?'

'None. I feel like a fraud.'

Georgie's gaze flicked to the monitor. According to the figures George was okay. His oxygen sats, blood pressure and heart rate were all within normal limits. But that didn't explain why he'd been admitted.

'Tell me what happened this morning.'

'Your mother and I had breakfast with Con and Anastasia and then we went for a walk along the esplanade so they could have a look around Cairns. I had a bit of chest pain, which I'm sure was indigestion—'

'There was a bit more to it than that, George,' Sofia interrupted her husband. 'You felt a bit dizzy too.'

'I'm not used to the heat, that's all,' George insisted. 'I didn't have any arm pain or anything else.'

Sofia ignored him and turned to her daughter. 'We were right by the hospital so, in view of his other recent complaints about shortness of breath, I thought he should get checked out.'

'That was the right thing to do,' Georgie responded. With chest pain, dizziness and a history of shortness of breath, it was no surprise her father had been admitted to the cardiology ward. There was definitely something abnormal going on. 'What have the doctors told you? What have they found?'

'I think they said the major arteries are okay but they're going to do more tests tomorrow.'

Movement in the doorway distracted George, and Georgie turned to see what, or who, her father was looking at.

It was Josh.

'Hello, you're here,' he said as he entered the room, and with those few words he managed to make it sound as though he'd been counting the minutes until she arrived. He made it sound as though he'd missed her.

His eyes locked with hers and he smiled. His grey eyes sparkled silver and his smile said he was there for her. His dark blond hair was sticking up and he had a slight shadow of beard darkening his jaw. He looked good. She smiled in return and took a step towards him before she hesitated. She wasn't sure how she should be behaving. But Josh didn't hesitate. He stepped forward and took her in his arms.

'What are you doing?' she whispered.

He leant down and his lips pressed against her hair. 'I'm comforting you, I'm supposed to be your boyfriend, remember?'

She closed her eyes as she hugged him back, savouring the feel of him, the solid, dependable sense of wellbeing he gave her. They'd had no physical contact since the wedding, since she'd turned down his invitation to go home with him, and she'd missed it. Being in his arms gave her a sense of belonging, which was silly because she didn't belong to him, but that was how he made her feel.

'You have perfect timing. Dad's a bit vague with the details. Can you give me a bit more information?' she asked as she stepped backwards, out of his embrace.

Josh was nodding. 'He's had several tests today and the

results in most of them were normal but the echocardio-gram showed a problem with the mitral valve.'

'You left out that bit of information, Dad,' Georgie reprimanded her father.

'Josh interrupted,' he countered.

'The cardiologist will do some more tests tomorrow to see how serious the problem is. I'll give you a heads up, George, just so you don't get any nasty surprises, but you may need surgery.'

'I thought my arteries were fine and I didn't have a heart attack. Why would I need surgery?'

'The valves in your heart regulate the blood flow. If they're not opening or closing properly, you get insufficient blood pumped around your body and your heart will work harder to compensate for it. That stresses your heart and can lead to a heart attack down the track,' Josh explained. He kept the details simple and Georgie knew her parents would be able to follow his summary. 'The breathlessness and dizziness you've already experienced can be symptomatic of heart disease. But the severity of the symptoms doesn't always indicate the severity of the disease so the cardiologist will investigate further, and that's why I've said you may need surgery. It's a possibility, that's all. Does that make sense?' Josh waited for everyone's agreement before continuing. 'Now George needs to rest and I'm sure you two need to eat,' he said, preparing to bustle them out.

'Well, if you think it's okay to leave him?' Sofia was deferring to Josh.

'You don't need to worry. You can come back in the morning,' he told her.

Her mother turned to Georgie. 'I guess it would be okay

to go home. Anastasia offered to cook dinner for us. She's at your house. I hope you don't mind.'

'I don't mind,' she said.

'Have you finished work for the day, Josh?' Sofia asked. 'Would you like to join us?'

Josh looked at Georgie. She tried to keep her face blank; she knew how well he could read her mind. She gave him just the tiniest shake of her head and then held her breath as she waited for his reply. She doubted her parents would be leaving in three days as originally planned and, if that was the case, Josh was going to have to continue to play the part of her boyfriend for a bit longer. But she needed time to digest this thought, they probably both did, and if she was going to survive until her parents left and life returned to normal, she needed to keep everyone in their own little compartments. Which meant only seeing Josh when absolutely necessary. Which meant not tonight.

'Thanks,' he said in response to Sofia's invitation, 'but I've got some other things I need to take care of. I'll catch up with you all again tomorrow. I'm back at QMERT then, but if you have any questions about what's happening speak to the staff here, and if you need further clarification don't hesitate to call me.' He turned to Georgie. 'Are you working tomorrow?'

She nodded and let out the breath she'd been holding.

'I'll see you then,' he said before he left the room.

'Josh?' Georgie called out to him and he turned, stopping in the corridor. She left the room and took a few steps towards him. She reached out, putting one hand on his arm. It was a reflex movement but the moment she touched the bare skin of his forearm and felt the tingle of awareness race through her she realised what she'd done and removed her hand quickly, as though it had been burnt.

'Thank you for taking care of my parents today. Knowing you were here helped when I was stuck out in the chopper.'

He glanced down at his arm, at the spot where her hand had touched him, and when he looked at her his eyes were dark grey, darker than she'd ever seen them before and unfathomable. 'Don't mention it. It was my pleasure. I'll see you tomorrow.'

'Mum and Dad might be here for a bit longer, depending on what dad's tests show. You were expecting to be my surrogate boyfriend for only a couple more days. What do you want to do, what do we say?'

'Don't worry. I'm happy to do this for as long as you need. I won't let you down,' he said. Then he was gone with just a brief nod of his head.

Georgie watched him disappear along the corridor, wondering if he was okay. He seemed upset. She wished she could read his mind as easily as he read hers. She had no idea what could be wrong. She stood looking after him as she tried to figure it out and then realised that nothing was wrong with Josh, something was wrong with her. She was feeling let down because he hadn't kissed her goodbye. She'd come to expect it. But no one had been watching so why should he kiss her?

Her mum joined her and Georgie let her distract her from Josh as they headed for the lifts. 'How are you coping, Mum? This must have come as a bit of a shock.'

'It was quite frightening, not knowing what was wrong. Your dad makes it sound like nothing but, believe me, he looked dreadful. He went quite grey and I thought he wasn't going to make it into the hospital. Thank goodness for Josh,' she said as the lift doors slid open and they stepped inside. 'He was fabulous. He was so good to me, to both of us. He kept checking on me, making sure I knew what was happening. He's quite something, isn't he?'

Georgie kept her gaze averted, avoiding eye contact. She didn't want her mother to read her opinion of Josh on her face, that wouldn't do. Her mother was going to take the news badly when Georgie and Josh had their inevitable 'breakup' and she didn't need her mother to know how much she really liked him—that would only make things harder. 'Mmm,' she replied, hoping that some sort of response would be all that was expected before her mother continued talking.

'I wouldn't have coped nearly so well without him,' Sofia added. 'It's a pity he couldn't join us for dinner.'

Sofia's chatter kept them occupied until they reached the taxi rank and climbed into a cab for the short trip home. Once there, conversation flowed easily between Sofia, Anastasia and Con, and Georgie wasn't required to contribute much at all, which suited her. The others made excuses for her, assuming she must be tired after such a long, exhausting and emotional day, but the reality was that she was quite happy to sit quietly and think about Josh. About how smoothly he'd taken care of all of them, her included. He'd single-handedly turned what could have been an extremely scary, stressful situation into something that seemed manageable. She'd seen his calm, confident approach when they'd worked together but to be on the receiving end of his bedside manner really made her aware of his compassion and ability to read a situation. It appeared that being able to read her mind wasn't his only talent. Her mother was obviously totally impressed by him and it wasn't difficult to see why.

The next few days were a whirlwind of activity, all revolving around her family. The cardiologist determined that George had a diseased mitral valve, which was more serious than his symptoms indicated. He advised George not to fly and advocated immediate valve-replacement surgery, which sent Sofia and Georgie into a spin. In the space of a couple of days George had gone from a fit and active man to one who required heart surgery.

Georgie didn't have many opportunities to think about Josh and their fake relationship, she was too busy concentrating on what her parents needed, but Josh didn't disappear. He worked quietly and tirelessly in the background, taking care of the little tasks that didn't seem important in the bigger picture but still needed to get done. Georgie hadn't asked him to help out but he seemed to be able to sense when things needed to be taken care of, and he did it without any prompting and without seeming to expect any thanks. He was just Josh, doing the things no one else had the time or energy for. He organised for Marty to swap shifts with Georgie so she could keep Sofia company while George was in surgery. He replenished the food in her fridge, filled her car with petrol and even managed to get George and Sofia's flights home to Melbourne changed. Georgie didn't know how he did that, considering he wasn't family, but Louise told her that Josh had gone across to the airport terminal in his QMERT uniform with 'Doctor' embroidered on the chest and had charmed the customer service officer into doing his bidding.

It must have been a female on the counter at the time, Georgie thought, but just picturing the scene made her smile. She didn't care how he'd managed it, she was just grateful for his help. It meant one less thing for her to worry about.

In fact, with Josh's help she found she had very little to worry about. Nothing was too much trouble for him. And it wasn't just Georgie he was taking care of.

He was constantly popping into the hospital to check on her father too. They'd started a regular evening game of backgammon to pass the time and he even helped to entertain Con and Anastasia. His efforts with them gave Georgie more time to spend time with her parents and it was another one of the selfless gestures that benefited her.

She couldn't believe she'd initially wanted to keep their contact to a bare minimum. She now wondered how she would have managed at all over the past few days without his help.

Five days after her dad's surgery Josh and Georgie were in the chopper, heading to Cooktown, two hundred kilometres north of Cairns. Georgie was tired. It had been a stressful few days and while her dad was making a good recovery she was feeling emotionally drained, even with all Josh's help. She'd been trying to keep several balls in the air—updating her brothers, looking after her mother and Con and Anastasia, plus keeping on top of dad's medical condition and working—but Josh had been effectively holding down two jobs and helping her, while somehow managing to remain his usual upbeat, enthusiastic self. Typically for an emergency doctor, he seemed to thrive on challenges. She wasn't quite sure how he'd managed it, but it left her feeling a little incompetent. But things were slowly getting back to normal. Con and Anastasia were leaving today and then it was just a matter of waiting for her dad to recover enough to head home to Melbourne. And then her life would return to normal and she and Josh would go their separate ways.

Georgie didn't actually want to think about that so in an effort to keep her mind occupied with other things she immersed herself in checking the medical kits. She told herself it was imperative that she know exactly what they were carrying, but the reality was that if she kept her head down she didn't need to watch Josh and she knew that's what she would do. It was far safer to sort through the medical kits, even though they didn't need sorting, but she could feel Josh watching her as she worked.

'You've checked that kit three times. Are you going to tell me what's on your mind?' he asked.

'You mean you don't know?' She'd become so used to Josh being able to read her thoughts that to hear him ask her what was wrong was a surprise.

He laughed and the sound cheered her up. 'I could guess but it would be quicker if you told me.'

Georgie flicked the communication switch on her headset to the 'Off' position. She didn't need Pat and Isaac listening to this conversation.

'I'm not sure if I'm ready to go back to Melbourne.'

Josh switched his headset off too before he answered. 'Why don't you stay in Cairns?'

'My parents expect me home and I promised I'd go back at the end of my twelve months. I've always done the right thing but I'm not sure I'm ready to go back to being the Georgie I was when I left. I've changed but I don't know if I've changed enough to avoid slipping back into the role of the dutiful daughter.'

'You'll be all right,' he replied. 'The Georgie I knew first isn't so different from the Georgie I see now. Being you parents' daughter has shaped you into the person you are, someone who embraces other people wholeheartedly and without reservation or judgement. Someone who is compassionate, unselfish, loyal and strong. There is nothing about you that you should want to change.'

'You think I'm strong?'

Josh nodded. 'And capable and confident.'

'I haven't felt very capable this past week. I don't know how I would have managed without your help.'

'You would have been perfectly fine. I didn't do anything you couldn't have done. Have faith in yourself. You can do anything you want to do, be anyone you want to be. Here or in Melbourne.'

Georgie wanted to ask Josh what else he saw in her. What could he see that she couldn't? But Isaac was leaning back between the seats, pointing at his headset, signalling to them to switch their communication on. They flicked the comms switches and Pat's voice came through their headsets. 'There's some rough weather coming—make sure you're buckled in nice and tight.'

The sun disappeared as Georgie checked her harness and the cabin was cast into semi-darkness. They were over the ocean, heading east away from Cooktown and the Queensland coast. They were searching for a yacht, and were planning to evacuate a sixty-year-old woman who'd slipped and fallen and had a suspected broken leg.

Georgie looked out of the window, lost in her thoughts. Josh saw someone who was strong and confident. She wondered how much of that was due to his influence. She didn't think she would have been nearly as capable over the past week without his help. But perhaps the Georgie she was discovering was those things. She just hoped she could continue to be that person once she was back in Melbourne. Once she was without Josh.

'We should get a visual on the yacht in the next five minutes,' Pat said and as they approached the location they'd been given Isaac, Georgie and Josh all began scanning the ocean for the sailing boat. Away to the west Georgie saw a mass of dark clouds, chasing them over the ocean. The storm was heading their way and she hoped they could outrun it or find the yacht before the bad weather hit.

Ten minutes passed and there was no sign of the yacht. Not one boat could be seen.

'This is Victor Hotel Romeo Hotel Sierra to QMERT Cairns, do you read me?' Pat radioed Louise.

'This is QMERT Cairns, go ahead, Pat.'

'Can we check those coordinates please? I'm overhead now and there's no sign of a yacht.'

Louise read out the coordinates she had been given.

'Confirm that's our current location,' Pat said. 'But, I repeat, I do not have a visual on the yacht. Can you confirm with the vessel and get back to us?'

The clouds were closing in quickly now as Pat circled the chopper over choppy seas while they waited for Louise to confirm the yacht's position.

'QMERT Cairns to Victor Hotel Romeo Hotel Sierra.'

'Go ahead, Lou.'

'I have new coordinates for you, they read them out incorrectly.' Louise relayed the new location and Isaac repeated the coordinates back to her.

'That's thirty nautical miles north-north-west of where we are,' Pat said. 'Please confirm our ETA of fifteen minutes with the vessel and remind them to have their medical assistance flag flying for identification.'

'Will do,' Louise replied.

'This extra flying is going to make fuel pretty tight and the weather's not going to help as we'll be heading into the storm. We'll have to assess the situation when we find the vessel and determine if we can do a safe evacuation.' Pat filled the crew in. Being out over the ocean in bad weather when they were low on fuel was certainly not an ideal position to be in.

'We'll need to be ready to go as quickly as possible,' Georgie told Josh. 'We're not going to have the luxury of time.'

Isaac would lower them to the yacht on a winch. One would go with the stretcher and the medical kits, the other would follow. It was always a tricky manoeuvre as there were so many variables and the weather was only going to complicate matters. They would need to move quickly. 'Let's get the kits strapped onto the stretcher.'

Isaac spotted the yacht on their starboard side as Georgie and Josh finished arranging the equipment. Pat did a flyover and Georgie and Josh peered out the windows.

The sails had all been lowered in preparation for the storm, which had made the yacht more difficult to locate but gave them a good view of the deck. A woman was lying on the lower section of the deck at the foot of a short flight of stairs. They'd expected her to be in the cabin but this was preferable as access was easier. A man was squatting beside her, waving to the chopper.

'I'll go down alone. It'll be faster to evacuate if we only need to do one retrieval,' Josh said.

If only one of them went, it would mean two winch operations instead of four, something that would save precious time.

'That sounds sensible,' Georgie agreed, 'but can you manage to get the patient onto the stretcher on your own?' If the diagnosis was correct and the woman had suffered a broken leg, there was no great need for both of them to attend. The issue wasn't the medical care but the transferring of the woman.

'I should be fine but if it's difficult, her partner will have to lend a hand. If I find things are more complicated than we expected, I'll call you down then.'

Georgie shrugged. 'Okay.'

Isaac was out of his seat and had climbed into the rear of the chopper. He attached all three of them to safety lines.

'The wind is picking up and the forecast is for increasing wind speeds ahead of the storm so we're only going to get one shot at this,' Pat said.

Isaac slid the door open and the wind buffeted them inside the chopper.

'Your call, Josh,' Isaac said.

Georgie watched Josh's face. It was up to him whether he wanted to attempt this evacuation or whether he thought it was too dangerous. His expression was calm, his grey eyes steady and he didn't hesitate.

'Let's do this.'

Josh fastened himself into the harness and together Isaac and Georgie hooked him and the stretcher to the winch before disengaging him from the chopper's safety line.

Isaac directed Pat above the yacht. Pat was flying blind. In order to lower Josh directly onto the yacht, he had to position the chopper above it, meaning he couldn't see either the yacht or Josh on the winch. Isaac became his eyes; he was in charge of the descent. He swung Josh out of the chopper and waited for his signal before he pressed the button and the winch began to lower its load. Josh's head disappeared from view and Georgie watched as he dropped towards the sea.

Georgie was nervous. The yacht looked tiny, bobbing about on the waves beneath them. The sea was rough and it was a difficult exercise; trying to manoeuvre a heavy

load on a wire suspended from a moving object onto a
moving target was no easy task in calm seas, let alone in
rough conditions. Georgie didn't like being in a situation
where she had no control. She would have preferred to
have been the one going down to the yacht rather than the
one sitting, watching and waiting. If she was occupied she
wouldn't have time to think of the danger.

Isaac slowed the winch down, trying to get his timing
right. He had to lower Josh carefully to avoid crashing
him onto the deck if the boat was lifted up on the peak of
a wave.

Georgie saw Josh's feet touch the deck, saw him take his
weight but then the deck fell away from him as the yacht
fell into a trough. Josh was suspended again, his weight
hanging on the winch line.

His feet touched the deck for a second time but the
yacht tipped. Georgie saw Josh lose his footing and her
heart was in her throat as he slipped and fell to his knees.
For a second she forgot Josh was securely attached to the
chopper, for a second she could imagine him sliding off
the yacht into the sea, but then the yacht levelled out and
he was on his feet.

He was on the deck now. He'd laid the stretcher out beside him as he knelt and waited for the winch line to give
him some slack before unfastening the hook from the strap
around his chest. He gave Isaac the signal and Isaac began
to pull the cable in as he gave Pat the all-clear to move
away, Josh didn't need the downdraught from the chopper
to add to the already difficult conditions.

Pat guided the chopper far enough away to avoid the
downdraught but close enough to still have visual contact. Georgie could see Josh working quickly, taking ob-

servations, talking to the woman's companion, assessing the situation. She wished she'd been able to go with him. Having two of them there would have made his job easier, but the extra time used might have been critical. Neither the weather nor their fuel situation was on their side.

Josh was putting a canula in the woman's vein and, Georgie assumed, giving her something for pain. They had radio communication but there was no need to use it. The others were of no assistance while they were in the chopper but Georgie still wished he'd say something. The silence was making her uneasy.

She saw him quickly splint the woman's leg before rolling her onto her side to get her onto the stretcher. He was working flat out. There was no time to wait for the pain relief to take effect, they needed to get her evacuated and get away from there before the storm hit.

Josh had fastened the straps on the stretcher and was repacking the medical kit. He was kneeling on the deck, his knees spread wide for stability. The woman's partner was bending over the stretcher but was supporting himself against the cabin wall with one hand. The waves had picked up and it seemed he could no longer keep his feet without support.

Josh crawled around to the top of the stretcher to fasten the protective cage over the woman's face. He was kneeling at her head, reaching for the cage, when a rogue wave slammed into the side of the yacht. The vessel was thrown onto its port side and anything that wasn't tied down went sliding across the deck. Including the stretcher. And Josh.

Georgie watched as though it was happening in slow motion. She saw the woman's partner fall forward, slamming onto the deck. She saw the stretcher sliding towards the sea. She saw Josh's hand on the side of the metal cage.

'Josh!' she yelled, but she was too late. The stretcher had collided with the edge of the deck, trapping Josh's hand. The weight of the stretcher pinned him in place.

CHAPTER NINE

'JOSH!'

Georgie didn't know why she was yelling. There was nothing she could do.

Josh was trapped, pinned between the stretcher and the edge of the deck. She could see him trying to pull the stretcher away from the edge but with only one free hand he couldn't apply enough pressure.

The seconds seemed like hours. He needed help. He needed her. She should have been there.

In reality it was only moments before the wave subsided and the yacht righted itself, but the stretcher still didn't move. Josh was still trapped. Georgie could see him trying to shift the weight of it by moving from one leg to the other but because he was kneeling he couldn't get enough force. If the stretcher hadn't been loaded it wouldn't have been a problem, but he had close to one hundred kilograms pinning him to the side of the yacht. He needed help.

What was the other man doing? Georgie looked across the deck. The other man was on his knees and there was blood pouring down his face from a gash on his forehead.

'Isaac, I need to get down there now!' Georgie grabbed a second harness as Pat brought the chopper back over the yacht and Isaac organised the winch.

'Josh, I'm coming down.'

The wind whistled in her ears and her eyes watered as Isaac lowered her to the yacht. She narrowed her eyes, peering down to see how Josh was faring. The waves were tossing the yacht about but the movement of the boat had finally enabled Josh to push the stretcher off his hand. By the time Georgie reached the deck he had locked the protective head cage into place over the stretcher.

'Are you okay?' Georgie asked.

'Yes, I'm fine.' He nodded as he answered, emphasising his point. 'Can you see to Brian?'

The woman's companion, Brian, was now sitting on the deck, looking quite dazed. Blood was still streaming from a cut above his left eye but on examination he didn't seem concussed. Georgie opened a medical kit, looking for swabs, and was cleaning the wound to assess how to treat it when Pat spoke to them from the helicopter.

'Decision time, guys. We've got about fifteen minutes before we need to be heading back for fuel. I can leave now and come back for you but the storm is going to complicate matters. There's no guarantee I'll be able to get back or that we'll be able to get you off the boat. Are you ready to load up now and get out of here?'

Georgie checked Brian again. His head wound wasn't deep, she could see to it on board the chopper but to do so would mean leaving an unmanned yacht bobbing on the Pacific Ocean. Another option was treating Brian and leaving him behind on his own, on a yacht in the middle of a storm. A third option was for one of them to stay behind with Brian.

She looked over at Josh. He was looking pale and she knew he was hurt too. If one of them stayed behind, it would have to be her. She didn't like option two or three.

'I agree we need to get everyone on board the chopper now but what do we do with the yacht?' she asked.

Pat answered. 'I'll alert the coastguard, they'll come out and tow the yacht back.'

'All right,' Georgie replied. 'Let's get going.'

Quickly she taped a dressing over Brian's wound as a temporary fix as she explained to him what was going to happen. She told him to keep some pressure on it and went to help Josh. Isaac was lowering the winch cable and Georgie could see Josh trying to grab it with one hand. Somehow he'd managed to secure one medical kit to the stretcher but he was protecting his left hand, holding it against his chest.

Concern flooded through her. Was he badly injured?

She reached out to him, careful to make sure she didn't knock him off balance. 'Do you need some help? What have you done?'

'I'm okay. It's only a knock to my fingers. We'll worry about it later.'

She didn't have time to argue but she knew he was hurt, which meant they were going to do this evacuation her way. 'You take Brian up first—he's just got a nasty gash on his forehead that'll need stitching—and I'll come up next with the stretcher.'

Josh nodded, surprising her with his easy acquiescence. 'This is Meredith, fractured NOF, no LOC, no other injuries.' Josh gave Georgie a basic summary of Meredith's condition as Georgie fixed a harness around Brian and strapped him to Josh. Isaac winched them to safety and Georgie tried not to watch them every inch of the way.

She attached herself to the stretcher and waited for Isaac to lower the cable for Meredith and herself. Finally, he dragged them into the chopper and the moment they were inside Pat turned for the coast.

Georgie secured the stretcher and she could see Isaac helping to secure Brian and Josh. She wanted to check Josh but he couldn't be her priority. She checked Meredith's vital signs. Her BP and heart rate were slightly elevated but within acceptable limits and her oxygen sats were normal. When she was satisfied that Meredith's condition was stable she attended to Brian. Then, and only then, could she see to Josh.

'Your turn,' she said.

'I'm okay. It's just a couple of fingers.'

He was right, it was only a couple of fingers, but Georgie knew it could have been worse, much worse, and she'd hated the feeling of helplessness and fear that had overcome her. Josh had been in danger and there'd been nothing she could do about it.

'We should have both gone down to the yacht in the first place,' she said, still convinced that somehow she would have been able to keep him safe.

'It was an accident, you couldn't have stopped it,' he replied, still reading her thoughts. She wouldn't have thought she'd smile again today but hearing him voice the words that were in her head made her think everything would be okay.

He was sitting opposite her. She stretched out her hand, reaching for his. He didn't argue any further. He held his left arm out to her. The third, fourth and fifth fingers were already blue and swollen.

'Can you make a fist?' she asked.

He shook his head. 'No.'

She applied gentle pressure across the phalanges of his middle finger. Josh grimaced as she touched the intermediate phalanx. She got the same reaction on his fourth finger.

'Two broken bones, I suspect. Do you want something for the pain?' It had to be hurting regardless of what he told her.

He shook his head. 'No. I don't want anything affecting my judgement. Not while we've got patients on board.'

Georgie could have argued that being in pain could just as easily cloud his judgement but she knew that wasn't the same. 'Okay. I'll strap your fingers for you for now but you'll need to get an X-ray when we get home.'

Josh surrendered his hand again and let Georgie tape his fingers together.

'Georgie?' Pat's voice came through their headsets.

'Yes, Pat.'

'Our fuel's pretty tight. We're going to have to refuel in Cooktown and then head home. Are our patients okay for that?'

'Yes, all three are stable,' Georgie replied with a smile.

It took a long time to get home. Their shift had well and truly ended by then, but fortunately there were no further emergencies. When Pat landed at the hospital Georgie saw an opportunity to get Josh to the radiology department.

'Do you want to go into the hospital? Get your fingers X-rayed before we head to The Sandbar for today's post-mortem?'

He shook his head and made no move to follow the hospital gurneys. 'I'll come back after we knock off.'

'I'll take you, then,' Georgie offered. She wanted to make sure he got seen to. She hadn't been able to prevent the injury but she was going to ensure that he was properly taken care of now. 'I'm going to see Dad before I head to the bar. Mum was going to pick me up but if I drive your car it'll save her the trip.' Georgie knew that if she made it sound as though Josh would be doing someone else a favour he'd be more likely to acquiesce.

Her argument worked and she drove Josh from the QMERT base back to the hospital and delivered him to the radiology department before heading to the cardiology wing.

'Is everything all right, Georgina? You looked exhausted,' Sofia asked her as she entered her father's room.

'Yes, I'm fine,' she told her parents as she kissed them both. 'We just had a rather dramatic day at work,' she said, and proceeded to fill them in on the day's events.

'Do you think this is the right job for you, darling? It sounds terribly dangerous,' Sofia asked once Georgie had finished.

Her parents hadn't loved the idea when she'd told them she was going to retrain as a paramedic and quit nursing, although they had eventually got used to it, but Georgie knew they still had concerns. But ninety per cent of the time the job was routine and risk-free and Georgie loved it. She had no plans to give it up, not even once she was married with kids. But today she'd been frightened, not for herself but watching Josh and being unable to help him had been terrifying. But she didn't tell her parents of her fears neither did she tell them about running low on fuel. The worst hadn't happened, they'd made it home safely, and there was no reason to scare them with hypothetical situations. She was tempted to cross her fingers as she told them, 'I wasn't in any danger today.'

'Well, I'm relieved to hear that,' Sofia said.

Georgie kept her visit brief. She wanted to get to The Sandbar, and she was eager to check on Josh.

Sofia was staying at the hospital to keep George company in Josh's absence but she walked with Georgie to the exit. 'The surgeon had some good news today, darling. He's hoping to discharge your father the day after tomorrow. Dad would like to get home to Melbourne as soon as possible to recuperate there and the surgeon expects to give him medical clearance to fly a day after discharge. Which brings me to a favour I want to ask of you?'

Georgie listened, knowing she was going to agree, but there was one thing she needed to do before she granted her mother's request. And she'd have to do it quickly, as soon as an opportunity presented itself, or perhaps she'd have to create the opportunity. She ran through the possibilities in her head as she walked along the esplanade to The Sandbar.

Josh had beaten her there. He was talking to Isaac and laughing, looking like he didn't have a care in the world. As Georgie watched them, Isaac finished his drink and headed to the bar. Josh was alone.

She went to him. 'How's your hand?'

'Your diagnosis was one hundred per cent correct. Two broken fingers.'

'Are they sore?'

'Not now. I've taken something for that.'

'Are you able to work or do you need some time off?'

'I'm fine. I'm going to go into the physio department tomorrow and get a proper splint made. That should take care of things while they heal. It's no big deal.'

No big deal. He had been lucky to escape with just two broken fingers. Georgie remembered how she'd felt as the yacht had tipped on its side. She'd been terrified it was going to go over. Terrified it was about to drop Josh into the ocean. She had no idea whether capsizing a boat was easy to do, she hadn't had much experience with boats, but she did know she'd never been as frightened as she had been then.

It was time to face facts. There was no point denying that Josh sent her crazy with desire. That the touch of his hand sent her hormones wild, that his smile made her heart race or that his kisses made her want to leap into bed with him. She did. And sometimes it felt like it was all she could think about. She wanted Josh and if she didn't do something about it now, tonight, she was going to miss her opportunity. She hadn't forgotten how it felt to be in his embrace and she was having a hard time letting that memory go.

The team was celebrating the safe evacuation and return to Cairns but to Georgie tonight was about more than that. Tonight was about Josh.

'You haven't got a drink. Can I get you something?' he asked, seeing her empty hands.

It was now or never. 'That depends,' she said.

'On what?'

'On whether or not you're ready to go home.'

Josh looked at his watch. His left hand and fingers, what she could see of them where they emerged from the strapping, were swollen and bruised. 'But you just got here and it's still early,' he said.

'I know. But I thought I'd come home with you.' She looked up at him through her lashes and gave him a half-smile. She saw him read between the lines.

'Just the two of us?' he asked.

She licked her lips and smiled fully now. 'I thought that might be fun,' she said.

'Why now?'

Had she missed her chance already? Had he changed his mind? Given up?

'I'm tired of trying to fight this attraction,' she admitted. 'It's not going away. Pretending it doesn't exist hasn't worked. Ignoring it hasn't worked. I can't pretend I don't want you. I want to know what it's like to make love with you. I want to know how it feels. I've never seen the point in spending just one night with someone but it was so hard today, watching you in danger, and I realised that one chance, one night, is all I might have, and I know I'll regret it if I don't take it.'

'Are you sure?'

'This is what I want. No strings. No promises. Just this night.'

'But—'

'I know our relationship is an illusion,' she interrupted. 'I know it's not real and I don't expect a real relationship but you were right, our chemistry is real and all I'm asking for is just one night. You've taught me to take chances. You've given me the confidence to try new things. This is something I want. But if you're not feeling up to it…?' She let the question tail off into thin air.

Josh grinned at her, his grey eyes shining with excitement. 'A couple of busted fingers won't slow me down.' He drained his drink in one swallow and put his glass on a table. 'Ready when you are.'

'Down, boy.' Georgie laughed. 'Meet me out the front in five minutes. I don't want everyone to see us leaving together. They don't need any more fuel added to the fire of speculation.'

Georgie went to the ladies' bathroom to freshen up. Beside the hand dryer, directly opposite the door, was a condom vending machine. It was the first thing she saw as she walked in. She crossed the room and stood in front of it. She studied it. Was she really going to do this?

It would just be one night, she told herself. It didn't have to change anything.

She couldn't deny she'd spent many hours imagining just what it would be like. There was nothing stopping her. Nothing would change except she would know how it felt to let Josh love her.

She turned to her right and looked in the mirror. Her eyes were dark and shining. Her cheeks were flushed and her lips were bright red. Her blood vessels were dilating in anticipation. She wanted this.

She searched her purse for coins and inserted them into the machine. She twisted the knob and caught the little packet as the machine dispensed it and she stashed it in her handbag. She wanted this more than she'd wanted anything in a long time.

She left the bathroom and went to meet Josh.

He was waiting under a palm tree, leaning against the trunk looking calm and relaxed. She was a bundle of nerves. It had been a long time since she'd been intimate with a man, but she wasn't apprehensive. She was excited. She reached for his right hand and pulled him away from the tree.

'Are—?'

'Shh.' Georgie pressed her fingers against his lips. She didn't want to talk, she didn't want a discussion, she just wanted to get to Josh's apartment and make love.

Josh had left his car at the hospital and they didn't speak as they walked. The heat from Josh's hand was searing her palm, threatening to ignite her entire body. She could imagine how his hands would feel running over her naked skin, how her body would respond to his touch.

He pressed the button for the lift and Georgie was grateful he lived so close to The Sandbar. She didn't think she could make it much further. He held the door for her and followed her into the empty lift, pushing the button for the seventh floor on his way past. She stood in the corner and pulled him to her. She wasn't going to wait any longer. This was part of her fantasy. This was what tonight was about, satisfying her curiosity and their desire.

She reached her arm up and cupped her hand around the back of his head, guiding his mouth to hers. She kissed him hard and he kissed her back. His hands were on her hips, holding her to him. Her hands were behind his head, keeping him with her.

She felt the lift stop, heard the doors open. She didn't care if more people were getting into the lift, she didn't care if they were surrounded, she had no space in her head for thoughts of anyone else.

Josh was holding her hand, pulling her out of the lift. They were at the seventh floor. He unlocked his apartment door and they turned left, heading for the bedroom, not pretending this was about anything more than desire, lust and longing.

Georgie dropped her bag on the bed and went straight back into Josh's arms. She ran her hands under his shirt. She trailed her fingernails lightly over his skin and heard him moan. She grabbed the bottom of his shirt and pulled it over his head, exposing his flat, toned stomach. He started to undo his belt but Georgie stopped him.

'Let me,' she said. It would be difficult for him to undress with three fingers strapped together, though not impossible, but Georgie wanted the pleasure of doing it. She undid his belt and snapped open the button on his pants before sliding the zip down. She could feel the hard bulge of his erection pressing into her, straining to get free.

Josh stepped out of his shoes, not bothering to untie the

laces, as she pushed his trousers to the floor. His pants joined his shoes and shirt in an untidy heap. He was naked except for his boxer shorts. Georgie looked him over.

He was glorious.

CHAPTER TEN

HE GRINNED at her and raised one eyebrow. In reply she put a hand on his smooth, broad chest and pushed him backwards until the bed bumped the back of his knees and made him sit. It was his turn to wait for her now.

She picked up her bag and opened it. Retrieving the condom, she placed it on the bedside table. Josh watched every move she made.

She stepped back from the bed. Out of his reach. He could watch but he couldn't touch. She wanted to tease him. She reached for the zip at the side of her dress and undid it slowly. She slipped one strap from her shoulder and then the other and let the dress fall to the floor. Josh's eyes were dark grey now, all traces of silver vanishing as he watched and waited for her.

She reached her hands behind her back and unhooked her bra, sliding it along her arms and dropping it to the floor. She lifted her hand to pull the elastic from her hair.

'Let me do that.' Josh's voice was husky with desire. Lust coated his words, making them so heavy they barely made it past his lips.

Georgie dropped her hand, leaving her hair restrained. She slid her underwear from her hips and went to him. She was completely naked but she didn't feel exposed. She felt powerful.

She sat on the bed beside him. He reached for her with his right hand, running it up her arm. His fingers rested at the nape of her neck before he flicked her plait over her left shoulder and pulled the elastic from her hair. He wound his fingers through her hair, loosening the plait as he spread her hair out, letting it fall over her shoulders before burying his face in it.

His thumb rested on her jaw. It was warm and soft, his pressure gentle. He ran his thumb along the line of her jaw and then replaced it with his lips. He kissed her neck, her collarbone and the hollow at the base of her throat.

His fingers blazed a trail across her body that his mouth followed. Down from her throat to her sternum, over her breast to one nipple. His fingers flicked over the nipple, already peaked and hard. His mouth followed, covering it, sucking, licking and tasting.

He pulled her backwards onto the bed.

She reached for his boxer shorts and pulled them from his waist. His erection sprang free, pressing against her stomach.

His fingers were stroking the inside of her thigh. She parted her legs and his fingers slid inside her, into her warm, moist centre. His thumb rolled over her most sensitive spot, making her gasp. He kissed her breast, sucking at her nipple as his thumb teased her. She arched her back, pushing her hips and breasts towards him, wanting more, letting him take her to a peak of desire.

Still she wanted more. She needed more.

She rolled towards him and pushed him flat onto his back. She sat up and straddled his hips. His erection rose between them, trapped between their groins. Georgie stretched across him, reaching for the condom, and her breasts hung above his face. He lifted his head, taking her breast into his mouth once more. She closed her eyes as she gave herself up to the sensations shooting through her as his tongue flicked over her nipple. Every part of her responded to his touch. Her body came alive under his fingers and his lips and her skin burned where their bodies met.

She felt for the condom, finding it with her fingers. She picked it up and lifted herself clear of Josh, pulling her breast from his lips. Air flowed over her nipple, the cool temperature contrasting with the heat of his mouth. She opened the condom and rolled it onto him. Her fingers encircled his shaft as she smoothed out the sheath.

She put her hands either side of his head and kept her eyes on his face as she lifted herself up and took him inside her. His eyelids closed and she watched him breathe in deeply as her flesh encased him, joining them together.

She filled herself with his length before lifting her weight from him and letting him take control. His thumbs were on the front of her hips, his fingers behind her pelvis as he guided her up and down, matching her rhythm to his thrusts, each movement bringing her closer to climax.

She liked this position. She liked being able to watch him, she liked being able to see him getting closer and closer to release. His eyes were closed, hiding their silver flecks, but his lips were parted, his breathing was rapid and shallow, his thrusts getting faster.

She spread her knees, letting him in deeper inside her until she had taken all of him. Her body was flooded with heat. Every nerve ending was crying out for his touch. 'Now, Josh. Now.'

He opened his eyes and his grey gaze locked with hers as he took her to the top of the peak.

Her body started to quiver and she watched him as he

too shuddered. He closed his eyes, threw his head back and thrust into her, claiming her as they climaxed together.

When they were spent she lay on him, covering his body with hers. Their skin felt warm and flushed from their effort and they were both panting as he wrapped his arms around her back, holding her to him. She could feel his heart beating under her chest. She could feel it as its rhythm slowed, gradually returning to normal.

'Wow.'

Josh's prediction had been right. Their chemistry made for amazing sex. Georgie had never been so overwhelmed by an experience. It was a pity she wasn't going to be able to get used to it.

'Wow indeed,' he said as he kissed her shoulder. 'Do you think we could improve on that with practice?'

Georgie laughed. 'I'm not sure it gets much better than that.'

'Give me a minute and we'll see.'

A minute! She needed longer to recover than that. 'I can't stay. Mum was expecting me home after dinner.'

'We haven't had dinner,' he said.

'She doesn't know that.'

Josh's fingers were running along her spine and Georgie would have been more than happy to stay right where she was. But that wasn't part of her plan. She didn't want to go, she wanted to spend the night in Josh's arms and forget about the world, but she couldn't stay. The longer she stayed, the harder it would be to make herself leave.

Tonight was about the present. It was a once-in-a-lifetime opportunity. They didn't have a future. She would have her memories but she wouldn't have Josh.

God, she was a fool, she thought later as she climbed into her own bed. Her sheets were cold and clean. They smelt of detergent and sunshine but she wanted them to smell of Josh. She never should have slept with him. Now she had to walk away from the best sex of her life.

But it shouldn't matter. Great sex was just great sex. She could appreciate it for what it was and move on. Great sex wasn't a basis for a lasting relationship and that was what she wanted, the one thing Josh couldn't give her.

She was looking for a relationship based on respect, shared values and companionship, not on great sex; but she knew that, at the moment, she'd trade respect and shared values for another night with Josh.

Josh wasn't at work the following day as he had a physio appointment but he arrived at the hospital for his regular game of backgammon with her father just as she was leaving. He was waiting for her in the corridor.

He was wearing jeans and a green T-shirt, his hair was spiky and he looked just as he'd looked last night when she'd left him all rumpled in his bed. The only difference was that he was dressed and the fingers of his left hand were encased in a splint.

He was smiling at her. She wanted to tell him to stop, it was messing with her equilibrium and with her resolve, but she couldn't speak—her mouth was dry, her knees were weak and her heart was racing. Her body reacted even before her brain had fully registered that he was there. Last night couldn't be repeated. They wouldn't share another night. She'd have to get over it but her body seemed to have other ideas.

'Hi. I was hoping I'd catch you here.' He stepped towards her and reached for her hand. His eyes were dark grey but as their hands touched she saw silver flecks flash in his irises like little lightning strikes and she felt the flash race through her. 'Can you sneak away tonight?' he asked.

No, she meant to say, but when she opened her mouth to speak that wasn't the word that came out. 'Yes,' she said.

'My place? Eight-thirty?'

She nodded and tried to tell herself that when she got there she'd explain why she couldn't stay, why they couldn't have another night. But then Josh leant forward and kissed her lips and she felt her resolve crumble into a pool of rampant desire.

She smelt of cinnamon and honey. He closed his eyes and savoured her scent as he kissed her in the hospital corridor. In ninety minutes she would be in his arms once again but first he had an appointment to keep.

'Evening, George,' he said as he entered the room. George was sitting out of bed, looking a picture of health, but the room was bare. The flowers, cards and magazines that had been cluttering all the horizontal surfaces of his room and giving it some personality were gone. 'What's going on?' he asked as he looked around.

'I'm being discharged in the morning,' George explained.

'That's great news.'

George was nodding. 'I'll be glad to get home, that's for sure. This wasn't how I planned to spend my holiday. Not that I'm complaining, it could have been a lot worse, it could have been my last one.' George stood and crossed to the table and picked up a small case that was lying there. It was his backgammon set and it was the only personal item that hadn't already been packed away. 'Have you got time for one final game?'

'Of course,' Josh said, 'but I'll warn you now, this time I'm going to win.'

George laughed. 'Give it your best shot, but if you couldn't beat me when I was medicated up to my eyeballs following surgery, I don't fancy your chances now.' He flipped the catches on the case and opened it out, quickly positioning the checkers. They sat on the edge of the bed, the table between them, and started to play. As had become their habit, Josh went first.

'You've been given medical clearance to fly?' he asked as he shook his dice in their cup and rolled them out.

'Yep. I had another echocardiogram today and a stress test and apparently it's all looking like it should. I've got my piece of paper and the flights are all booked. I was a bit nervous about flying but the specialist says it's fine and Georgie's coming home with us.'

Josh was about to move his checkers but he hesitated. 'Georgie's going with you?'

George was watching the board, waiting for Josh's move, but he looked up quickly. 'She hasn't told you?'

Josh shook his head, afraid to hear what George would say next.

'She's taking holidays and coming home.' George threw his dice as he spoke.

Josh didn't like the sound of that. 'So she's coming back?'

'I'm not sure. You'd have to ask her,' George said as he moved his checkers. 'What are your plans? You're only in Cairns temporarily too, I understand. What's next for you?'

Josh wondered if it was a deliberate change in the direction of conversation. Was there more George wasn't telling him? But George had always called a spade a spade and Josh couldn't imagine him keeping something from him now. 'I'm waiting to hear about an appointment at Brisbane General,' he answered.

'For what position?'

'Head of Emergency.'

'That sounds important.'

'I've been working towards a position like this for years. As you can imagine, they don't come up all that often. The current head of emergency suggested I come to Cairns to get some more experience in emergency retrievals. He's due to retire when I finish here and I'm hoping to be able to step into his role. That's where I'm headed.'

'You've no plans to come to Melbourne?' George asked.

Josh shook his head, aware that George was watching him closely. 'No.'

'Georgie knows of your career plan?'

'She does,' Josh replied, thinking that he'd at least been honest with her about his future direction. He wondered when, or if, she was going to tell him about her departure and whether or not she was planning on returning.

'Well, if you ever find yourself in Melbourne, be sure to come and see us,' George said as he moved his last checker into the home position, victorious in yet another game of backgammon. 'You'll always be welcome.'

It was close to midnight and Josh knew Georgie would be going home soon. All evening he'd been waiting for her to tell him about her plans to return to Melbourne but she'd said nothing. Not before or after they'd made love. They were lying in his bed, naked. He knew his bed would feel cold and empty when she left. She was tucked in against his shoulder. He had his arm around her and the top of her head was resting under his chin. Her skin was soft under his hand and he was surrounded by the scent of honey and cinnamon. He closed his eyes and let her scent invade his senses. He could get used to this.

No. He didn't want to get used to this. That was a dangerous thought.

He needed to keep his defences up. He had to get on with his future. He couldn't get caught up in Georgie. Her parents would be returning to Melbourne and his life would return to normal. While he had enjoyed this interlude, it was only ever going to be temporary. That was their arrangement and that was the way he operated. He would keep his memories but he would move on.

He opened his eyes and moved his head slightly so that Georgie's head was no longer under his chin, trying to avoid her scent of honey and cinnamon so he could concentrate. 'Your dad told me he's going to be discharged tomorrow. That's good news.'

She nodded.

'And you're going home with them?' Josh asked, even though he already knew the answer. What he didn't know was what would happen next and it seemed that unless he asked, he was never going to find out.

'He wants to go home to Melbourne to recuperate but he's nervous about flying. They've asked me to fly with them,' she explained.

'When will you be back?'

'I'm not coming back.'

Josh frowned and wondered if that's what George had been keeping from him. 'What do you mean? You've still got another month on your contract.'

'I've applied to take annual leave. We leave the day after tomorrow.'

He'd known she was leaving, just as he was, but he

hadn't expected it to be so soon. He'd thought she'd come back, give them time to say their goodbyes. He was ready to move on but he hadn't expected to start the process tonight.

He tried to be pleased. He should be pleased. Surely this was a good thing.

Georgie was lying in Josh's arms. She'd hoped to resist him but it had been impossible to forego her one last opportunity. He'd opened his apartment door for her and kissed her senseless before he'd started undressing her with his eyes, and she known then she'd end up here, naked, in his bed. He hadn't needed to say a word. In fact, he hadn't spoken, he'd just looked at her and her heart had pounded so hard in her chest she'd thought it would explode. Her hands had been shaking as he'd held them and pulled her to him. She'd stepped into his arms and kissed him, followed him to his bed and made love to him. Now she was lying in his arms, her head nestled in the curve of his shoulder, her cheek resting on his bare chest, her ear pressed against his heart, listening to it beating.

His words vibrated in his chest when he spoke, reverberating under her ear. It wasn't quite where she'd planned to have the conversation about leaving Cairns, leaving him, but he'd opened the discussion and she couldn't put it off any longer. She didn't have any more time.

'I've applied to take annual leave. We leave the day after tomorrow.' Accompanying her parents on the flight back to Melbourne was the favour her mum had asked of her and it had given her the perfect escape clause. And she was going to take it. She knew she had to get away from Josh quickly before it became impossible. She was going to Melbourne and she wasn't coming back. She'd decided that the way to get over Josh was to have a quick, clean break.

'So that's it? You're leaving now?'

'It's only a bit earlier than I'd planned. It's not going to make any difference in the scheme of things.'

She wanted Josh to tell her that it would make a difference to him. She wanted him to ask her to come back. Or not to go. But of course he didn't. She was a fool to hope for that. He didn't want a relationship, he'd told her that. 'Your life can return to normal. No more pretending,' she said.

'I thought…'

'What?'

He shook his head and she could feel his shoulders shaking with the movement. 'Never mind.' He paused briefly and she was left wondering what he'd been going to say. 'So what was last night all about? And tonight?' he asked.

'It was about you. Us.' She shrugged. 'Your philosophy has rubbed off on me. I was being adventurous. This was sex with no strings attached. That was what you wanted.'

He didn't argue.

She wished he would.

But he didn't protest and as she lay in his arms she knew he would keep quiet. He wasn't going to beg her to stay.

What on earth had she expected? Had she thought he was going to tell her he loved her and he couldn't live without her?

She'd made a mess of everything. She should have left him alone. She should never have crossed the invisible line they'd drawn. But she hadn't been able to resist.

The old Georgie would have resisted. The old Georgie hadn't had casual sex but she knew that was also true of the new Georgie. She was kidding herself if she thought going to bed with Josh could be considered casual sex. She'd known exactly what she was doing. The question was, why had she done it? Why had she crossed that invisible line?

And she knew the answer too. She'd crossed the line both physically and emotionally.

She'd fallen in love with him.

She had come to Cairns to find her independence. To find herself. She hadn't expected to fall in love but that's what had happened. She had begun the process of her metamorphosis from dutiful daughter to independent woman; she'd engineered the move away from home; and Josh had helped her to complete it. He'd helped to complete her. She was now the person she wanted to be but would she be able to continue to be that person without Josh by her side?

She would have to do it, she thought, she had no other option. But that meant the sooner she got away from here the better, before she lost herself in Josh.

She was leaving for Melbourne tomorrow. Part of her couldn't believe it. She knew she would find it hard to leave but she had no other option. She'd told everyone of her decision and nothing had happened to change her mind. Or, more specifically, no one had tried to convince her to stay.

Her last shift with QMERT was an ordinary day. She was working with Sean and they were called out for a couple of routine inter-hospital transfers, nothing dramatic, nothing difficult. Without realising it, she'd shared her last shift with Josh the day they'd evacuated Meredith and Brian from the yacht off the coast of Cooktown. But she would see him tonight. She was on her way to The Sandbar for her farewell dinner and drinks, and Josh would join them there after his hospital shift.

This was going to be the last time she saw him and she was determined to put on a happy face. She was trying to be brave. Trying to pretend she was happy to be going home. Pretending she was ready. Pretending she didn't mind that he hadn't asked her to stay. Or come back.

Pretending she hadn't fallen in love.

But, of course, nothing in the world of emergency medicine ever went to plan when she needed it to.

Her mobile rang as she walked into the bar and Josh's name appeared on her screen. As she answered she could hear sirens in the street. This was only going to be bad news.

'Georgie, it's me. I've been held up. There's been a fire at one of the backpacker hostels and it's all hands on deck while we wait to see what the ambos bring us. I have no idea yet how bad it is or how long I'll be.'

Disappointment surged through her but there was nothing she could do. 'It's okay.'

'I'm sorry. I really wanted to be there.'

'I understand, Josh. I know how it goes. Hopefully we'll see you later.'

She would have a drink with her other colleagues but Josh was the one she really wanted to see. The night dragged from that point on.

She waited and waited but Josh didn't show. She checked her mobile phone constantly but it was hours before she heard it beep, signalling a text message. She pulled it out of her handbag.

Can't get away. Working at QMERT 2mro, will c u at terminal.

'Is something wrong?' Louise was standing beside her. 'You've been looking at your phone every five minutes.'

'Everything's fine,' she lied. 'That was Josh, he's still at the hospital. I was waiting to see him, to say goodbye, but if he's not going to make it I think I might go home. There are still some things I need to do before we leave tomorrow.' That wasn't true either. She'd packed and the removalists had collected her boxes and her car. All she had to do was get up and go to the airport but she didn't want to be at the bar any longer without Josh.

'I'll give you a lift home,' Louise offered. 'It's past my bedtime too.'

Louise drove down the esplanade and along the sea-front. 'We're going to miss you,' she said as she drove. 'You've been a breath of fresh air around the place.'

'I'm going to miss all of you too. I've loved my time here,' Georgie replied, but her heart was heavy with the knowledge that there was one person she was going to miss most.

'Why don't you come back?' Louise asked as they passed the hospital.

Georgie couldn't help looking through the emergency entrance, hoping for a glimpse of Josh, but of course she saw nothing except for a couple of paramedics standing by their ambulance. Her heart ached in her chest, knowing that Josh was just a few metres from her but unreachable.

'Because there's nothing for me here,' she answered. Josh was leaving too, there was nothing to bring her back to Cairns. She sighed with longing and the sound escaped from her and broke the silence.

Louise slowed the car and turned her head to watch Georgie. 'Did you want to go in and say goodbye?'

Georgie looked at her, wondering how much she thought she knew. 'No, he'll be busy.'

'I'm sure he'll stop for you.'

Georgie didn't think so. She shook her head.

'Have you told him how you feel?'

Georgie heard her own sharp intake of breath. 'What do you mean?'

'Marty was right about the two of you, wasn't he? Your relationship isn't pretend any more,' Lou said. 'Does Josh know how you feel?'

Georgie didn't bother denying Lou's assessment but she wasn't about to announce it to everyone and especially not to Josh. 'No. And I won't tell him.'

'What if he feels the same way? What if both of you are too stubborn to be the first to admit your feelings?'

She wished she was brave enough to take that chance but although she was more confident than she'd been a year ago, she wasn't that brave. 'He has a totally different view of it. He doesn't want a proper relationship.'

'He's a man,' Lou scoffed with the voice of experience. 'I doubt he has any idea what he really wants. You need to tell him.'

'No.'

Louise turned the corner and the hospital receded into the distance. 'Have you thought about moving to Brisbane? You'd get a job there.'

Georgie shook her head again.

'Why not?'

'Because Josh hasn't asked me to.' She knew it wouldn't take more than that to get her to pack her bags and move again. All he had to do was ask. But that wasn't going to happen. 'It's okay, Lou, I'm okay,' she said before her friend felt she had to offer counselling. 'Josh and I had a deal. This whole thing was make-believe, I just forgot that temporarily.'

To her relief Louise didn't question her further. She probably realised that Georgie had a point. No matter what she or Louise thought, there wasn't anything they could do to change the situation. It was what it was. Life would go on. Without Josh.

Georgie had made it through her last night in Cairns by consoling herself with the idea she'd see Josh at the airport before she left. He'd told her he'd get across to the airport terminal. She wanted to know she would see him one last time, it would make it easier to leave, but as the taxi drove her and her parents along the entry road she saw the helicopter taking off from the QMERT base. Her heart sank in her chest. Josh would be on board, on his way to an emergency, which meant he wouldn't be meeting her at the terminal. He wouldn't be saying goodbye.

Disappointment and frustration left a bitter taste in her mouth. She'd prepared herself to say goodbye but she hadn't prepared herself not to.

Perhaps it was for the best, she thought as she started piling luggage onto the trolley. There was always the danger that if she saw him again she might just tell him she'd fallen in love with him. And there was no need for him to know that. It was better this way. She needed to move on.

CHAPTER ELEVEN

IT WAS a glorious spring day in Melbourne. One of those perfect days that made up for the many bleak, grey wintry days the city seemed to exist on. Or perhaps that was her perception. In the two months since Georgie had been back in Melbourne every day had seemed grey and wintry.

Today was her parents' fortieth wedding anniversary, a day her parents had been looking forward to celebrating, but she was having trouble mustering up any enthusiasm. She was pleased for her parents but every time a wedding was mentioned it just served to remind her of her own situation.

She was still single but dating, and for the past few weeks had been seeing Con and Anastasia's son Michael. She knew Michael was more into the whole idea than she was and it was getting to the stage where she'd have to do something about that. She knew everyone was hoping for some sort of announcement and while he was nice enough they had no chemistry, no spark. Maybe that would come, but all she could think of was the instant connection she'd had with Josh. He'd been a perfect stranger yet they'd had an immediate, physical attraction, an awareness, a connection, and it hadn't dissipated. If she was honest, it was still overpowering her, making everything else seem paler, less significant, weaker.

She couldn't bring herself to get excited about anything at the moment. Least of all Michael. But that wasn't his fault. She wanted Josh and she couldn't imagine wanting anyone else the same way.

Georgie knew she should be focussing on her future. Josh was history. She hadn't heard from him since she'd arrived back in Melbourne but it was proving impossible to forget about him.

'Are you looking forward to dinner tonight?' Sofia asked her as they sat at the hairdresser together. The official party that had originally been planned to celebrate the anniversary had been replaced with a small dinner for the immediate family due to George's surgery. The big celebration would now take place in two weeks' time but Sofia had decided that a family dinner was enough of an occasion to warrant a trip to the beautician and the hair salon.

Georgie looked across at her mother. Today was such a special occasion for her that she would have to try, at least, to pretend to be happy. 'Of course.'

'Are you sure you don't want to invite Michael? You know he's welcome.'

'I'm positive. It will be nice to have dinner with just the family. I feel like I still haven't caught up with all the boys properly since I got home from Cairns,' Georgie said, making excuses. 'Michael doesn't need to come.'

She could feel her mother's watchful gaze on her but she avoided eye contact. 'How are things going with him?'

'Fine.'

'What does that mean exactly?'

Georgie didn't need to look at her mother to know she'd raised her eyebrows and was giving her a questioning look. 'Fine means fine. It means there are no problems, no dramas. There's no anything really.' She sighed.

There was a brief silence and Georgie knew her mother was weighing up her next words. 'Can I ask you a question? When you picture your own fortieth wedding anniversary, who do you see by your side?'

Georgie didn't respond. She didn't know what to say. How honest to be.

Sofia didn't wait for an answer. 'It's not Michael, is it?'

Georgie shook her head.

'Is it Josh?' Sofia asked.

She risked a glance at her mother. 'Why do you ask?'

'For the twenty-seven years that I've been lucky enough to be your mother I've never seen you look like you do when Josh is around. You glow from within, as though something about him gives you an extra boost, makes you complete. Are you in love with him?'

Georgie swallowed hard. 'It doesn't matter if I am. We don't have a future together.'

'What makes you say that?'

'He doesn't want to get married. He doesn't want a relationship. His future is about his career.' Hot tears gathered in her eyes as she remembered that Josh hadn't chosen her. 'His dream is to be head of the emergency team at Brisbane General. His dream isn't me.'

'Have you heard from him?'

Georgie shook her head.

'It's going to make it difficult for you to find someone while you're still in love with Josh.'

'I'll get over him.' She was not going to admit to her mother that she was right. It wasn't going to do her any good to acknowledge her feelings. She wished she was brave enough to admit she loved him, but the confidence that Josh had seen in her, the confidence he believed she had, seemed to have forsaken her. Somehow he'd helped her believe in herself. 'I don't want to spend the rest of my life alone. I'm sure you and Dad can find someone for me, seeing as I haven't done a very good job of that myself. Maybe an arranged marriage isn't such a bad idea. It worked for you.'

'Ours was a slightly different proposition.'

Georgie frowned. 'What do you mean?'

'Our families came to Australia from the same village in Greece. Your father and I practically grew up together, but when we fell in love we decided the best way to ensure that we were able to get married was to let your grandparents believe they were arranging our marriage.'

'You fell in love and then got married?' This version of the story was different from the one Georgie had grown up hearing.

Sofia was nodding. 'Your father sowed the seeds of the idea and then we let our parents work it out. That arrangement suited everybody. We all got what we wanted. Your grandparents believed they had final approval and your dad and I got each other. Your father wants to see you settled and happy but we don't want you getting married because we think it's the right thing for you to do. We would never encourage you to marry someone you don't love. We want you to be happy.'

Georgie wanted to be happy again too, but right now she was miserable. She wanted to feel complete but she knew that was impossible. She'd gone to Cairns on a mission to find herself. The irony was Josh had helped her to discover her true self, but she couldn't maintain it without him. She needed him. Part of her had remained behind with Josh and she knew she'd never be complete again without him.

Josh took the coffee pot off the stove as he tried not to think about the free Saturday that stretched emptily in front of him. It was the first free day he'd had in the past eighteen since he'd moved back to Brisbane General to take up his new position as Head of Emergency. The role had been offered to him earlier than expected and he'd jumped at the chance. Not only was it the job he wanted but it gave him a reason to leave Cairns.

He'd thought leaving Cairns was the answer. He'd thought it would help him get his life back in control. After all, taking up this position meant he was achieving his goals. And leaving Cairns should help him to forget about Georgie. It would remove him from everything they had in common, from all the familiar places they'd shared. But, of course, he took his memories with him and even taking on the new job didn't keep him busy enough to forget about her.

Last weekend he'd chosen to spend his days at the hospital, finding his feet, he'd told himself, rather than spending the days alone. His own company wasn't something he normally minded but he wasn't particularly enjoying his solitude at the moment. He wasn't particularly enjoying anything.

He thought about what he'd shared with Georgie—sex with no strings attached. It was what he'd asked for and what he'd been given, but it hadn't been the answer either. Too late he'd discovered that it wasn't what he truly wanted. He wanted the strings. He missed the strings.

The phone rang, interrupting his sombre thoughts. He recognised the QMERT Cairns number as he answered.

'Hi, Josh, it's Lou. How are you? How's Brisbane? How's the new job?' In typical Lou fashion she barely paused for breath.

'Good.'

There was silence. Josh had expected her to jump straight in with her next question but she was obviously waiting for him to elaborate and he had nothing more to say. The job was good, it was everything he'd expected, but it wasn't enough. He had the job he wanted but he didn't have the girl. And he wasn't about to tell Louise that.

'I've got some mail here for you.'

Louise had his forwarding address. Why was she ringing to tell him about random mail?

'It's from Georgie's parents,' she said. 'I got one too. It's an invitation to their fortieth wedding anniversary celebrations. I'll send it down to you.'

'Thanks. When's the party?'

'In two weeks,' Lou said. 'But why did they send the invitation here? Don't they know you're in Brisbane? Haven't you spoken to Georgie?'

Ah, her phone call made more sense now. 'No. Why would I have?'

'I just thought you might have called to tell her you'd got the job and were back in Brisbane. I'm sure she would be pleased for you.'

'Have you spoken to her?' he asked. Maybe Louise could tell him what he wanted to know. 'Is she—?' He cut himself off. He couldn't ask the questions he wanted to. Is she seeing anyone? Is she happy? It wasn't up to Louise to tell him the answers. Lou was right, he should have called Georgie himself. But he couldn't do that. Somehow that would feel as if he'd be losing control. He changed his words. 'Is she enjoying being back in Melbourne?'

'I think she's taking some time to settle back in. You should call her, tell her you'll go down to Melbourne for the party.'

'No. I don't think I will.'

'Why not? I thought you'd want to catch up with her. I still don't understand why you let her go.'

'Because I'm not the man she's looking for. I'm not what she needs.'

'Did she tell you that?' He could hear the surprise in Lou's voice.

'No. She didn't need to. I'm not cut out for relationships, for commitment. I'm no good at it.'

'What a load of rubbish. You've obviously just never been in the right relationship.'

'My relationships always end in disaster. She's better off without me.'

'There's always the chance that the two of you would be better off together than apart. Georgie wants someone to love. What if that someone was you? Have you thought about that? Unless, of course, you're happy alone?'

No, he wasn't happy, he thought as he hung up the phone, but being alone meant having complete control over his life.

But he didn't feel like he was in control of anything. His career was supposed to be all he needed but it was no longer enough.

He missed her.

He wanted to know how she was. He wanted to hear about her day. He wanted to be able to come home and share his day with her.

But he had his reasons for not calling. He'd been speaking the truth when he'd told Lou he was no good at relationships. Georgie wanted a happy ending and she wasn't going to get it from him. It was better for him to be miserable and alone than to make Georgie miserable.

But he missed her.

And she wasn't coming back. She was hundreds of miles away from him. Waiting for someone else to sweep her off her feet.

The realisation hit him that this was it. This was going to be his life. Georgie wasn't coming back to him. He hadn't really imagined what his life was going to be like without her. He couldn't imagine it.

But what if she loved him like he loved her? What then?

He loved her.

He was an idiot.

He loved her.

Why hadn't he realised that?

Why did love always make such a fool of him?

The first time he'd been in love, Tricia and his brother had made a fool of him. This time he was doing it without help from anyone else. But this time it wasn't too late. Or so he hoped. He loved Georgie and this time he had a chance to change the outcome.

Georgie wanted to fall in love. What if she could love him? What if she did love him?

He stirred his coffee as an idea took hold. He figured he had one last chance. He was supposed to thrive on challenges, wasn't he? He'd taught himself to see challenges in a positive light and this might be his biggest challenge yet. He wasn't going to let it beat him. It wasn't over. He had one last chance and he had to take it.

Josh paced nervously in front of the lounge room fireplace. He'd spent the entire flight from Brisbane to Melbourne rehearsing what he'd say, only to arrive in Melbourne to find Georgie wasn't home. He had left Brisbane after speaking to Lou, once he'd made his decision he hadn't waited, but apparently he'd arrived on the actual day of George and Sofia's fortieth wedding anniversary and Georgie was at the hairdresser with her mother.

Despite his timing, George was pleased, but not overly surprised, to see him. Apparently he and Sofia had been discussing him and trying to work out how to entice him to Melbourne—hence the invitation to the forthcoming anniversary celebrations. His early arrival was greeted with enthusiasm, particularly when Josh explained why he'd appeared on their doorstep.

Now all that remained was to see if Georgie was similarly enthusiastic. If their chemistry was as powerful as he remembered. If she loved him like he loved her. If he could persuade her to follow her heart.

He and George heard the garage door opening, signalling the return of Georgie and her mother. George left Josh in the lounge and would send Georgie in on a pretext without alerting her to the fact that Josh was waiting.

Josh froze as he heard the doorhandle turning. He held his breath as he waited to see who was coming into the room.

Her scent reached him first.

Honey and cinnamon. It washed over him in a wave of memories.

The fireplace where he stood was on the same side of the room as the door and he knew she hadn't noticed him yet, so he took a moment just to look at her. Her tan had faded since she'd been away from the tropical Queensland sun, but her skin was still smooth and golden and her hair was still glossy and thick. It wasn't constrained but hung in a thick, straight shiny sheath over her shoulders.

She still hadn't noticed him but he'd seen her now and his feet were moving without direction from him, taking him towards her.

Georgie opened the lounge room door to retrieve her father's glasses. Movement to her left made her jump. There was someone in the room. There was someone moving towards her.

'Josh?' For a moment she wondered if her imagination was playing tricks on her. He'd been in her thoughts so much. Was she now starting to have visions? But it was him, in her parents' lounge room. His familiar gait, his familiar figure, his broad shoulders, his spiky sandy blond hair, it was definitely him.

He smiled at her and the silver flecks sparkled in his grey eyes. Her heart skipped a beat and she was halfway across the room, meeting him in the middle, halfway into his arms, before she remembered she didn't have the right to be there any more.

She stopped in her tracks. 'What are you doing here?'

She'd spent the afternoon talking about him and now he was here. In her house. This made no sense.

He didn't share her hesitation. In two strides he'd closed the remaining distance between them. 'I came to see you,' he said as he gathered her in his arms. She clung to him. It felt so good to be back in his embrace. She could feel his heart beating next to hers, echoing the rhythm.

She looked up, turning her head to him, lifting her mouth to his, and that was all it took for Josh to claim her. His lips covered hers, hungrily, passionately. There was nothing soft and gentle about this kiss. It released all the longing that had built up in the days they'd been separated. This kiss brought them home.

It left her feeling light-headed and weak-kneed and, as usual, Josh could read her thoughts. He took her hand and led her to a sofa.

'Why are you here?' Georgie couldn't remember if she'd asked him that or if he'd already told her. Her thoughts were completely chaotic and confused.

'I didn't get to say goodbye.'

'You came all the way to Melbourne to say goodbye?'

'No. I came all the way to Melbourne because I couldn't say goodbye. I don't want to say goodbye. I came to see you because there are some things I need to know.'

He was still holding her hand. His touch sent shivers of desire through her and made it impossible for her to speak. She sat beside him, mute with surprise.

He leant forward and lifted her hair in his palm, burying his face in it and inhaling deeply. Georgie closed her eyes as she felt his breath on her neck. Her heart was pounding in her chest and she could feel herself leaning in towards him, yearning for his touch. 'I remember your scent perfectly,' he said. 'And I needed to know if our chemistry was real or whether my memory has been deceiving me. Can I still read your thoughts? Do you miss me like I've missed you?'

'You've missed me?'

He nodded. 'Every minute of every day.' He reached up again and tucked her hair behind her ear. 'And I have to know, have you missed me too or has Michael made you forget all about me?'

'You know about Michael?'

Josh nodded. 'Your father told me. Does he make you happy? Is he the one for you? If he is, I'll leave now. You just have to tell me.'

His arrival had totally confused her but she did know one thing. She shook her head. 'Michael isn't for me.' This was her chance to be honest with Josh. Something had brought him to Melbourne, to her. She wanted no regrets. 'There's no spark,' she said. 'Before I met you I thought it didn't matter but now I think I need more. I want more. I want passion, excitement, exhilaration, all those things I said weren't important. I want fireworks and everything that goes with them. I want to fall in love.'

'Do you think you could love me?'

She wasn't sure she was planning on being that honest. Did Josh need to know her heart already belonged to him? She hesitated but Josh didn't wait for her reply.

'I came to ask you to marry me.'

'Marry you?' Georgie couldn't understand what was happening. She felt as though she was watching a movie of someone else's life but she'd missed the beginning. 'But you don't want to get married.'

'I didn't want to but I've changed my mind. You've changed my mind.'

Georgie was more confused than ever. 'What happened to the man who was focussing on his career? Who didn't need relationships?'

'I have the job I wanted and it's fantastic, but it's not enough. It's challenging, it's rewarding, it's keeping me busy. At the end of the day I don't want to go home, but that's not because I can't bear to leave work—it's because I don't want to go home and find that you're not there. There's more to my future than my career. You are my future. I want you. I need you.'

Georgie waited but the words she longed to hear didn't come. If he didn't love her then what was he doing here?

'Are you sure I'm not just the next challenge in your life?'

He frowned and the silver flecks in his eyes darkened to grey. 'What do you mean?'

'You thrive on challenges. You set yourself a goal and when you achieve it you need a new goal. For the past eight years that goal has been your career. Now that box is ticked. You've avoided relationships ever since Tricia died and now that your career is on track suddenly you're ready to get married?' She didn't want to be his next challenge. This wasn't what she'd been dreaming of. 'Are you sure this is what you want? Have you really thought about this?'

'This is not about Tricia,' Josh argued. 'It hasn't been about her for a long time. When she died I lost two relationships, one with her and one with my brother, and I admit it did change my view of the world. I made a decision to put my energy into my studies and my career. I wanted to concentrate on things I could have some degree of control over. I decided not to invest time and energy into relationships but that was a conscious decision. I recovered a long time ago but, until recently, I haven't had any reason to change my mind about relationships. Until I met you.

'You have opened my eyes and opened my heart. Everything has changed for me since I met you. I tried to tell myself it was Cairns affecting me, making me see things differently, but it wasn't. It was you. You showed me how to let people back into my life. I had closed myself off and you opened me up.

'The night before you left Cairns I could have made it to The Sandbar but I chose not to. I was afraid I might not be able to say goodbye. I didn't want you to go but I couldn't ask you to stay because I was afraid of what that might mean. I was scared that I might fall in love. I didn't realise I'd already fallen in love with you.'

He loved her.

'You do challenge me but you are not a challenge. You challenged the way I saw myself and you made me reassess my life. I can't ignore my feelings. I can't pretend I want to be alone any more. Everything is better when you are with me. I am better.' He got off the couch and knelt beside her on one knee. 'I want to share my life with you.' He picked up her hand. 'I know you. You exist here...'

he touched their hands to his forehead '…and here…' He touched their hands to his heart. 'You're part of me,' he said as he kissed her hand. 'I love you, Georgie, and I want you to be my wife. Will you marry me?'

He loved her and he wanted her to be his wife.

But could she marry him? There was so much they'd never discussed, so many differences. But were they big enough to stop her from having the one thing she wanted?

'What is it? What's wrong?' he asked, and she could hear the worry in his voice. She needed to find a way to make this work. He loved her and she was determined to make sure they got their hearts' desires.

'My parents—'

'Want you to be happy,' Josh interrupted. 'Your father has given us his blessing. He's told me the decision is yours.'

'He has?'

Josh nodded. 'Your father is on our side and you can let me worry about your mother.'

Georgie knew he'd have no problem there. She smiled at him. She knew exactly how her mother felt about Josh and if her parents were prepared to give their blessing she knew she could have what her heart desired. 'My mother thinks the only thing wrong with you is that you don't want to get married. Now she'll believe you're perfect.'

Josh grinned and his eyes flashed silver again. 'So that just leaves you. Do you love me?'

Georgie nodded. 'I've only ever loved you.' She never would have believed that she could love someone so completely. 'I've been waiting for you my whole life.'

'And will you marry me?'

'Do you trust me with your heart?' She had to know he could trust her to love him completely and only him. 'Do

you believe I will love, honour and keep you? When I say
you are the only man for me, do you know that I mean it?'
She had to know that he didn't doubt her words, that he
believed her promises.

Josh nodded. 'I know how you feel about your family.
If you love me and if you will marry me and make me part
of your family, that's all I need. You are all I need. I have
faith in you and me. I trust in us.'

'And you realise what you're getting yourself into?' she
asked. She had to be sure. 'A big Greek family and everything that goes along with that?'

'Why do you think we're going to live in Brisbane?' He
was smiling at her but he'd never looked more serious. He
held both her hands, holding her to him. 'I promise to keep
a spare room ready for your family and to fly your parents
up to visit whenever they want. I will immerse myself in
all of it if you'll marry me.'

She had seen how he'd cared for her parents. She'd seen
how he'd looked after her. She trusted him. She loved him.
She belonged to him. They belonged to each other. Fate
had brought them together and she knew he'd keep his
promises. She knew he'd do anything for her, just as she
would for him.

'I love you more than I ever imagined it was possible to
love someone,' she told him. 'I will marry you. I am yours.
Now and for ever.' She leant forward and kissed him, sealing their commitment, sealing their love. 'I love you now
and I promise I will love you just as much on our fortieth
wedding anniversary and on every one before and after.'

EPILOGUE

JOSH saw his wife as she came out of the house and crossed the grass. Her hair was loose, caught behind her ear on one side with a clip, and he thought how amazing it was he never grew tired of watching her. He couldn't believe how much his life had changed in the past two years. How fortunate he was.

He crossed the lawn and went to meet her. Georgie smiled at him as she saw him approaching and his heart swelled with love and satisfaction. 'Is she asleep?'

She nodded and her hair swung in a thick, glossy curtain around her shoulders.

He slid his arm under the heavy sheath of her hair and pulled her close to him, breathing in her scent of cinnamon and honey.

'I can't believe our daughter is one year old already,' he said as he hugged her.

'I know. Soon she'll be running after her cousins and getting into all sorts of mischief.'

Josh looked over to the pool where most of Georgie's nieces and nephews were mucking about. Her parents were keeping a watchful eye on their grandchildren and her brothers and sisters-in-law were scattered around the garden, having all travelled up from Melbourne to celebrate the baby's birthday. Despite Georgie living in Brisbane, her family kept in touch and they all made a special effort to get together for big celebrations. But Josh knew that, for his daughter, seeing her cousins on an irregular basis was no match for growing up surrounded by family.

'Do you miss Melbourne or are you happy here?' he asked.

Georgie took his hand from her shoulders and held it. 'Come with me.' She smiled at him. 'I want to show you something.' She led him into the house. 'I don't miss Melbourne. Sometimes I miss my family,' she admitted, 'especially after we've had weekends like this, but I have you and I have our family.'

She opened the door to their daughter's room and led him to Alexandra's cot. Alexandra was lying on her back, arms thrown wide, spread-eagled in her favourite position, clutching one of her soft toys in her chubby fingers. Georgie stood in front of him and wrapped his arms around her waist, resting them on her stomach. 'I have everything I want right here.'

Josh rested his chin on the top of his wife's head as he watched his sleeping daughter. This was another vision he'd never grow tired of. 'What about Alexandra? Do you think we're depriving her of her cousins and grandparents?'

'She'll be okay. Don't forget, she won't know anything different,' Georgie assured him. 'We'll just have to have a big family ourselves so the kids can keep each other company.'

'More kids?' He raised an eyebrow. 'Should we start today?' he asked with a grin.

Georgie laughed. 'We've already started,' she said as she squeezed his fingers and turned her head to smile at him. 'I'm nine weeks pregnant.'

'What? You are?'

Georgie nodded. She'd planned to tell him the news when her family had all returned to Melbourne as she'd wanted it to be just between them for a while, but once she'd had a positive pregnancy test she'd found it very difficult to keep the news from Josh. She knew that if she didn't tell him soon, he'd guess. His ability to read her thoughts hadn't diminished since they'd married but, for once, if the stunned look on his face was anything to go by, she'd managed to surprise him this time. 'Is that okay? Not too much to deal with?'

'Are you kidding?' His eyes were shining silver and he was grinning like the Cheshire cat. 'Being married to you, being a father, has been the best thing that's ever happened to me. Adding to our family can only make things better,' he said as he smoothed his fingers over her stomach. 'It's fantastic news.'

The gentle pressure of his fingers sent a shiver of desire through Georgie. She'd never imagined she could love someone so completely. She turned to face him, careful to stay within his embrace. 'I love you. Thank you for sharing your life with me.'

'Our life together is still only just beginning,' he said as he bent his head and kissed her softly on the lips. 'I am going to love you for ever.'

And as he claimed her lips a second time there was not a trace of doubt in her mind that he would do just that. She had everything she'd ever wished for.

* * * * *

THE NURSE'S
NOT-SO-SECRET
SCANDAL

BY
WENDY S. MARCUS

All the characters in this book have no existence outside the imagination of the author, and have no relation whatsoever to anyone bearing the same name or names. They are not even distantly inspired by any individual known or unknown to the author, and all the incidents are pure invention.

All Rights Reserved including the right of reproduction in whole or in part in any form. This edition is published by arrangement with Harlequin Enterprises II BV/S.à.r.l. The text of this publication or any part thereof may not be reproduced or transmitted in any form or by any means, electronic or mechanical, including photocopying, recording, storage in an information retrieval system, or otherwise, without the written permission of the publisher.

This book is sold subject to the condition that it shall not, by way of trade or otherwise, be lent, resold, hired out or otherwise circulated without the prior consent of the publisher in any form of binding or cover other than that in which it is published and without a similar condition including this condition being imposed on the subsequent purchaser.

® and TM are trademarks owned and used by the trademark owner and/or its licensee. Trademarks marked with ® are registered with the United Kingdom Patent Office and/or the Office for Harmonisation in the Internal Market and in other countries.

First published in Great Britain 2012
by Mills & Boon, an imprint of Harlequin (UK) Limited.
Harlequin (UK) Limited, Eton House, 18-24 Paradise Road,
Richmond, Surrey TW9 1SR

© Wendy S. Marcus 2012

ISBN: 978 0 263 89164 5

Harlequin (UK) policy is to use papers that are natural, renewable and recyclable products and made from wood grown in sustainable forests. The logging and manufacturing process conform to the legal environmental regulations of the country of origin.

Printed and bound in Spain
by Blackprint CPI, Barcelona

Dear Reader

This is the third and final (at least for now) book in my *Madrin Memorial Hospital* series: Roxie's story. If you're unfamiliar with the first two books, please check out Book One, Allison's story, WHEN ONE NIGHT ISN'T ENOUGH, and Book Two, Victoria's story, ONCE A GOOD GIRL…

For me, a story builds from a few random ideas—usually jotted down on napkins, receipts, and/or scraps of paper that clutter my pocketbook and desk. After I come up with a few key scenes, and figure out the basics of what I want to happen in the beginning, middle and end, I start to flesh out my characters.

This is my favourite part of the writing process. Beyond their physical characteristics, I delve into their pasts. I create their personalities and mannerisms, their goals and motivations. And the more time I spend with them, the more real they become—to the point where they often take on a life of their own, sending my story in a direction different from the one I'd originally intended.

All three women in this series had difficult childhoods, and had to overcome many obstacles on their way to becoming strong, self-sufficient, professional young nurses. I'm happy to have helped each of them find their happily-ever-after.

As I put the final touches on Roxie's story I realised how much I'm going to miss spending my days (and nights) with my friends at Madrin Memorial Hospital. I hope you've enjoyed reading Allison, Victoria and Roxie's stories as much as I've enjoyed writing them.

I love to hear from readers. Please visit me at www.WendySMarcus.com

Wishing you all good things.

Wendy S. Marcus

**Praise for
Wendy S. Marcus:**

'Readers are bound to feel empathy
for both the hero and heroine. Each has a uniquely
disastrous past, and these complications help to
make the moment when Jared and Allison are able to
give their hearts to the other all the more touching.'
—*RT Book Reviews* on
WHEN ONE NIGHT ISN'T ENOUGH, (4 stars)

Dedication:

This book is dedicated to my dear neighbors,
Grisel DeLoe and D. David Dick, two of my biggest
supporters, and a heck of a lot of fun to celebrate with.
(Although after my 4 star *RT Book Reviews* celebration
I had some trouble getting started the next day!)
I love you both. And if you try to sell your house
I may have to resort to vandalism. You have been warned!

With special thanks to:

Grisel and her sister, Ivette Vazquez,
who answered my last-minute cries for help
with some Spanish translations. Your e-mails made me
laugh out loud. Even at three in the morning.
You are one hysterical woman. Any mistakes are my own.

My editor, Flo Nicoll, who encourages me,
puts up with me and always pushes me to do my best.
I am so lucky to have you.

My wonderful friends, old and new, who have
purchased my books, written reviews, and/or attended
my book signings. You know who you are.

And to my husband and children for loving me,
cooking for me and making me laugh. (And for
not saying one negative word when I spent a weekend
in my pajamas and didn't shower for almost
three whole days while under deadline to finish this book.)

CHAPTER ONE

"It's not Roxie," 5E head nurse Victoria Forley insisted. The tiny brunette slammed the file in her hand onto her old metal desk. "She's one of my best nurses, and a dear friend. I trust her implicitly. This is absolutely ridiculous."

"Calm down, honey," her fiancé, Dr. Kyle Karlinsky, said as he wrapped his large arm around her narrow shoulders. "We'll figure it out."

Ryan "Fig" Figelstein leaned against the door frame of Victoria's fifth-floor office, watching the cozy scene. An observer. An outsider in his best friend's new life.

Kyle shot over the look that more often than not got Fig into some kind of trouble and added, "And Fig will help us."

"Ooohhh, no." Fig held up both hands. "Come see where I work, you said, just for a few minutes." Kyle knew how much Fig hated hospitals. The smells. The sounds. The isolation and deprivation. He staved off a shudder.

"You okay?" Kyle asked, studying him, able to read Fig better than anyone.

"Yeah." Fig pushed off the door frame and took a step into the tiny office. "So what's your idea?" he asked to get the focus off of him.

"You're here another week, right?" Kyle asked.

"That's the plan."

"It's perfect." Kyle rubbed his hands together.

Perfect would be them leaving the hospital. Now. Perfect would be an end to his mother's constant telephone calls and ploys for his attention. Perfect would be some sense of normalcy in a life that was feeling increasingly out of his control.

"You hire on here. As the unit clerk."

"Are you…?"

Before he could get out the word *crazy* Kyle added, "Just hear me out." His voice took on that placating tone he used every time he set out to convince Fig to do something he didn't want to do. Kyle removed his arm from Victoria and set his full attention on Fig. "You answer the phone, respond to the call bells, direct visitors."

"It takes more than that…" Victoria started.

"And he watches Roxie and the narcotic cabinet," Kyle added to silence her. "Each time she or someone else accesses it he'll call you."

"You're brilliant," Victoria said to Kyle with a big grin. Then she turned to Fig. "You have to take the job," she pleaded. "Each day I have a different temp circulating through. I need a person I can trust to keep an eye on Roxie. Something's going on. She's been forgetful and distracted. She doesn't have her normal spunk."

Signs of drug abuse. Fig glanced at Kyle.

Victoria caught him. "She's not on drugs. Please," she said, looking up at Fig in that way women do when they have no intention of accepting no for an answer.

"I work with computers." And he was damn good at it. In demand even. "I have a job."

"But you can work anywhere," Kyle pointed out, oh, so helpfully.

"I'm not a big fan of sick people," he admitted. Some deep-seated fears were not easy to get past. "And I know nothing about being a unit clerk in a hospital." Frankly, the thought of spending twelve captive hours in one left him cold and clammy.

"You're not expected to have any physical contact with the patients. And I'll train you myself," Victoria said. "I'll help out as much as I can and I'll tell my nurses to pitch in, too. The narcotic cabinet is in a locked room right behind the desk where you'll be sitting. All you need to do is report any suspicious behavior and I'll check the Demerol count."

"I've got an idea," Fig said. "If you're so certain Roxie had nothing to do with the missing drugs, why don't you tell her what's up and ask her if she knows anything?" Fig preferred the straightforward approach, hated when people danced around an issue.

"Normally I would, and as her friend I want to." Victoria looked torn. "But my job requires I remain objective and investigate the matter fully. Which is what I'm trying to do. Please say you'll help me."

"We can spend more time together." Kyle smiled. "And you'll be earning nine dollars an hour to boot."

Like Fig needed the money. "Seriously," Kyle said. "This means a lot to Victoria so it means a lot to me. You're here. You're impartial. You have no vested interest in Roxie's guilt or innocence."

Now, that wasn't entirely true. In the few hours he'd spent with her at last week's Employee of the Month dinner to honor Kyle, Fig found Roxie to be a total hoot. He liked her. Really liked her. And would rather not participate in any activity that may turn out to be detrimental to her well-being. Not to mention after pulling a no-show for their date Friday night, Fig was not looking forward to Roxie setting eyes on his alive self. The woman had a sharp wit and, per her own admission, an even sharper temper.

But then Kyle added, "I trust you, my closest friend, to help prove Roxie's innocence."

And Fig was sunk. Over the past eight years—since rooming with Kyle at the physical rehab after his "accident"—Kyle had been like a brother, building Fig's confidence and helping him through the most difficult time in his life. How could he say no to the man who'd improved his quality of life to the point it felt worth living?

"I know I'm going to regret this," Fig conceded.

"So you'll do it?" Victoria asked, cautiously optimistic.

"Yeah."

"I'll call Human Resources." She picked up the phone. "You can start tomorrow."

Terrific. For the next week Fig was stuck in the Podunk town of Madrin Falls in upstate New York—where he couldn't even get a decent cup of coffee—filling in for the unit clerk on a busy medical-surgical floor at Madrin Memorial Hospital. What did he know about being a clerk? Nothing. But he'd seen enough of them in action to have a pretty good idea of what he'd need to do. And honestly, he was a college-educated professional. How hard could it be?

The next morning at the God-awful hour of way the hell too early, Fig set his two cups of cafeteria "coffee" on the table in the 5E nursing lounge and caught a glimpse of his reflection in the huge window. Obviously the hospital didn't have many six-foot-four-inch unit clerks on staff, because the drab tan uniform jacket they expected him to wear fit like a bolero jacket with three-quarter sleeves.

He peeled it off and tossed it onto a chair. He jogged in place to work off some of his jitters. "You are not a patient," he started his pep talk. "At the end of the day you get to go home." He jumped three times and stretched out each shoulder. "You can do this."

"Well, lookey here. All alone and talking to yourself. Psych ward's on the fourth floor."

He recognized the voice instantly. Roxie Morano. He turned to face her, so as not to leave his back open to attack. Purely precautionary.

"Jeez, woman." He held his arm up to shield his eyes. "You're an assault to early-morning vision." While she wore the lavender scrubs that identified her as 5E nursing staff, she'd chosen a long-sleeve white turtleneck covered in small multicolored stars to go underneath her top. About a dozen colorful cartoon character pins adorned her left breast pocket—which covered an appealing, rounded breast. Red rectangular-framed glasses hung from a purple chain around her neck that tangled with the lime-green cord from which her chunky yellow pen hung. A bright red scrub jacket with bold pink, yellow and blue hearts lay draped over her arm. Farther down she had on red clogs that clashed with a few inches of exposed orange, green and yellow striped socks. Up on her head her kinky cream soda curls were pulled back in a thick, bright orange hair band.

Beyond the distraction of color, Fig took a moment to absorb the beauty of her smooth, tan skin, her warm brown eyes—that looked heavy with exhaustion rather than light with laughter like they'd been on the night they'd met—and the lusciousness of her perfect-for-him body.

"If it isn't Ryan—my friends call me Fig—Figelstein." She walked toward him. "I thought the deal was if you survived the week we'd head out to dinner to celebrate, *Ryan*."

Okay. He got the emphasis she placed on *Ryan*. Point

received. He'd have to work to earn back her favor. An effort well worth the anticipated payoff. Her. Naked. In his bed. Which, based on the heated attraction zipping and zapping between them last week, was where they'd been headed. If only someone else had been available to babysit Victoria's son after the dinner. If only he hadn't missed their date.

"When you didn't come," she continued, "I said a prayer, just like I'd promised. I even contemplated attending church on Sunday, and what a ruckus that would have caused." She stalked toward him. "And here you are." She looked him up and down. "Fit as a fiddle."

Her cell phone rang. She looked at the number, let out a frustrated breath and turned away. "What?" she snapped into the device. "I told you no. My answer won't change." She listened. "Fine. Do what you have to do." She slipped the phone back into her breast pocket and turned to him. "So, *Ryan.* I can't begin to imagine what's transpired to make a self-proclaimed computer genius, such as yourself, stoop to the role of hospital clerical worker."

"Anything to get close to you," he said. "So I could apologize for missing our date. Please, we're friends. Call me Fig." Only his mother called him Ryan, because she flat out refused to call him anything else. Ryan represented his old self. The child homeschooled because of his medical conditions, brainwashed to fear the world around him, the tentative, lonely teenager who lacked confidence and had no real friends. Fig—the nickname chosen by Kyle—fit his new and improved self. A man of character who chose to embrace life rather than hide from it, to experience life rather than watch others have all the fun.

With raised eyebrows and a taunting head tilt Roxie asked, "You think we're friends, *Ryan?* I beg to differ."

She walked past him to a row of lockers and set to working the combination dial of the one on the end.

Fig took a step back so he could see inside, but she blocked the contents with her body.

He hated the position Victoria had put him in. While he liked watching Roxie—her butt, for example, which filled out the back of her scrub pants in all of its pleasing roundness, with not one panty line—*watching* her for anything other than his own personal enjoyment felt sneaky and underhanded. Two things Fig was not.

"You see, *Ryan,* my friends don't lie to me or leave me waiting without so much as a telephone call to say that something came up or they'd received a better offer."

"I didn't…" No way she'd understand what having a mother like his was like. He didn't want to talk about that night, just wanted to put it behind him. "I'm sorry."

"Yes, *Ryan.* You are. Because you missed out on a good time."

No doubt he had. For sure he would have much rather been with her than where he'd wound up.

"Such a pity." After pushing her huge purple purse and a lunch sack into her locker, she pulled out a hot-pink stethoscope, popped a piece of gum into her mouth and closed the door. The next thing he knew she had her chest pressed to his and was leaning in close to his ear to whisper, "I'd put on my crotchless panties and peekaboo bra especially for you."

He pulled her bottom half close. Could not stop himself. "I sure wish I'd been there to see them." And enjoy them. He drew in her sensual scent. God help him he wanted her. While Kyle liked his women small, Fig liked 'em tall and thin. Just like Roxie. He went for full body contact—skin to skin from head to toe.

At first she stood rigid, looking away from him. He

slid his hands up her sides, teased the outer curve of each breast. She reacted, an infinitesimal softening, a barely noticeable exhalation, both of which he may have missed if he wasn't so attuned to her. "You want me," he observed.

"To move your hands," she replied.

He did. To her upper back where he proceeded to hug her close. Her cell phone rang.

Dag-nab-it. He released her.

She took a step back—still not looking at him—set her stethoscope on the table and pulled out her phone to check the screen.

Fig forced himself to stop thinking about how good she'd felt pressed against him, how much he wanted to see her beautifully formed body in nothing but some sexy, barely there undergarments, and resumed focus on his mission—to determine if Roxie was the one responsible for 5E's missing Demerol. While his brain made a smooth transition, his body was not so easily redirected.

Roxie returned the phone to her pocket without answering it, and, with a deep breath, she turned and headed for the door like she'd forgotten all about him. "Hey," he called after her, holding up her stethoscope.

Seeing it, she snapped two fingers. "Right. I'll be needing that."

When she grabbed it he held on and waited for her to look him in the eye, making note that hers were bloodshot—damn. "I'm sorry you had to sit home on a Friday night because of me."

She laughed. "Don't kid yourself, *Ryan*. There are plenty of men who enjoy my company." She stared him down. "Really enjoy it. And just because you weren't up for a good time doesn't mean I didn't have one." She yanked the stethoscope from his hand. Over her shoulder she said,

"For the record, I never sit home on Friday or Saturday nights. Ever."

Her phone buzzed.

She retrieved it and looked at the screen. "I hate men." She glared at him. "I'm done with the lot of you. Every single one. So tell your kind to stay the hell away from me if they value their man-parts." Then she slammed out the door.

Fig waited, wanting a little distance between Roxie and his man-parts. At least for now. He smiled, taking her words as more of a challenge than a warning.

Roxie burst out of the lounge, her heart pounding, rage coursing through her system. She looked at the text message, again: "It's done." *"¡Coño!"* And the colossal jerk had sent her the link. She eyed the darkened hallway of even-numbered rooms, wondering if she had the strength to hurl the phone hard enough to break through the reinforced glass window at the far end. The way she felt? Probably. But what would that solve?

The video was out there for anyone with a computer to see. Her friends. Her coworkers. Her family. Of course Roxie would shrug it off, make like she didn't care. But she did. What went on in private between two consenting adults was supposed to be just that. Private. The thought of people watching, knowing, sat like a pregnant hippo on her chest.

Deep breath in. Deep breath out.

"The Lord doesn't give us more than we can handle." Roxie whispered her mantra of the past ten years and leaned her back against the wall, wishing He didn't have so much confidence in her.

Each time she thought things couldn't get worse something inevitably happened to prove her wrong. She slipped her hand into the pocket of her scrub coat and wrapped her fingers around the three cartridges of injectable Demerol. At least that she could fix before anyone found out.

Or so she'd thought until she reached the nurses' station at the center of the H-shaped unit and froze. What was Victoria doing at work so early? And why was *she* verifying the narcotic count with the night shift? The hippo gave birth to twins that landed heavily on her gut and set off a tumultuous, acidic churn. There'd be no hiding her stupidity now. Victoria was going to be livid.

"You okay?" Fig stopped beside her, standing way too close. She took the opportunity to draw on his calm and confidence to rejuvenate her dwindling supply.

"Just fine." Always fine. Fine. Fine. Fine. Roxie hoped if she said it enough it would turn out to be true.

"You're looking pale."

"We Latinos don't pale," she snapped. Not like him. Did the man ever get out in the sun? She looked up at the strong features of his handsome face and the rounded smoothness of his enticingly bald head. Actually had to look up. How often did that happen? At just under six feet, Roxie was usually the tallest person in the room. Aside from the fact she'd had a terrible day with her mom and had been really looking forward to their night out, his height played a small part in why she'd been so angry about being stood up. In search of the perfect shoes to wear on their date, actual heels, Roxie had torn through dozens of stores, had spent hours looking. Did he have any idea how difficult it'd been to find a pair of hot-pink glossy patent-leather peep-toe platform pumps? In a size thirteen? When would she ever have another opportunity to wear them?

"Hey, Rox," one of the night nurses called out from room 504. "Would you help me out? I need to get home on time today."

"Sure thing." Roxie glanced at the schedule board across from the nurses' station to confirm her assignment. District one. As usual. Even-numbered rooms 502–508. Eight beds. Two empty, awaiting new admission post-ops. One pre-op due in the operating room at 7:30 a.m. She glanced at the clock, 6:45, then turned to Fig. "When Victoria's done would you tell her I need to speak with her? It's important."

"My first official unit-clerk task." He lifted his pad and pen and wrote something down. "I'm on it."

Then Roxie got to work, assisted her colleague, took a quick report and sent her pre-op patient off to the O.R. On her morning round each of her patients had a problem. Pain. High blood pressure. Low blood pressure. Hypoglycemia. Constipation. Fever. An infiltrated IV. And two saturated dressings.

Finally, by 11:00 a.m. she had everyone settled and could take a quick break for some much-needed sustenance. Only, on her way to the nurses' lounge she met up with a recovery room nurse pushing a sleeping patient in her direction. "You're supposed to call first," Roxie said.

"I did," the plump nurse at the head of the stretcher said. "The guy who answered said to come on up."

Roxie glared at Fig. "The floor nurse gives approval to accept patients from the recovery room. Not you," she told him.

"Oops. Duly noted," Fig answered, making a note on his stupid pad. "It won't happen again."

She eyed the girth of her new patient and looked back over to Fig. "Make yourself useful. Come help us transfer this patient to her bed." May as well see if those muscles worked as good as they looked.

Fig stood, something strangely uncertain in his expression.

"No," Victoria said from behind him. "He's here as a

unit clerk. The only contact he's to have with patients is from behind this desk."

What the...?

Roxie's stomach growled. She didn't have time for this nonsense. "All available hands to 502A," she called out. "Chop-chop, ladies. My blood sugar is starting to drop." That was sure to get their attention. No one wanted a cranky Roxie around.

With the recovery room nurse's help Roxie lined the stretcher up next to the bed and locked the wheels on both. "Welcome to 5E, Mrs. Flynn," she said to her new patient. "My name is Roxie Morano and I'll be your nurse until seven o'clock this evening." She raised the bed so it was the same height as the stretcher, transferred the bag of IV fluid to the bed pole and placed the catheter drainage bag by the patient's feet so it didn't pull during transfer. As the recovery room nurse gave report, Roxie checked the patient's right-sided chest dressing, which was covered by a surgical bra, and inspected the drains and tubing.

"Fifty-nine-year-old, morbidly obese female. Status post right-sided modified radical mastectomy."

Roxie noted the drainage in each of the two bulbs, labeled R1 and R2, to establish a baseline and pulled her report sheet—which contained pertinent information on each of her patients—from her pocket. She unfolded the paper and set it on the over-the-bed table. In the blank box reserved for room 502A she wrote in the patient's name and diagnosis, last set of vitals and time of last dose of pain medication. Then she jotted down her observations. Patient arousable to verbal stimuli. Catheter draining clear yellow urine. Dressing clean, dry and intact. Drains to self-suction with scant red drainage in each. IV infusing to left forearm.

When Victoria and Ali—her other best friend and the

nurse working in the district next to hers—arrived to help, Roxie directed, "One on the stretcher side, one over here by me." She stood on the side of the bed, at the patient's upper body, so she'd be responsible for pulling the heaviest part of her. As her colleagues got into position Roxie spoke to her patient. "We're going to slide you onto the bed, Mrs. Flynn."

The groggy woman nodded in understanding.

"Keep your hands at your sides and let us do all the work," Roxie instructed.

Each staff member grabbed a hunk of the bottom sheet.

"Everyone ready?" Roxie locked eyes with each woman. Just last week a patient on 4B fell between the stretcher and the bed during a transfer, suffering a severe hip fracture as a result. Not on Roxie's watch. "On my count of three. One. Two. Three."

Using every bit of strength she possessed, Roxie pulled. If the grunts around her meant anything, her coworkers were giving it all they had, too. Yet the patient barely budged.

Fig entered the room.

Victoria told him to leave.

"What kind of man would I be if I let four lovely ladies struggle when I could help?"

"Are you sure?" Victoria asked, handing him a pair of latex gloves from the box on the wall.

"Scoot over." He squeezed between Roxie and Ali, bumping Roxie's hip with his as he did. "Now tell me what to do," he said as he put on the gloves.

"Ball the sheet like this." Roxie showed him her hands. "Tight."

He took the sheet in his large hands. She remembered how they'd felt on her body, holding her just a few hours earlier, and realized how much she'd like to feel them again—and in more places. She shook her head to clear her thoughts.

"And on the count of three," she continued, "we pull and they—" she motioned to the women on the other side of the stretcher with her chin "—push."

"Got it," Fig said, testing his grip on the sheet, looking so cute in his concentration.

"Everyone ready?" Roxie asked again and waited for each woman and Fig to respond in the affirmative. "On my count of three. One. Two. Three."

Again Roxie pulled as hard as she could, and this time the patient slid toward her like she was on plastic liner slick with baby oil.

"Wow. You *are* a strong one," Roxie said to Fig.

He smiled, a genuinely pleased smile, and winked. "Remember that." He moved closer on his way to discard his gloves in the trash can and whispered, "Dream about it."

"As if any part of you registers with my subconscious." Especially not his head—in the dream where she was a cat sleeping curled around it. Or his fair skin—in the dream where they'd lounged by a pool and she'd rubbed him with suntan lotion—repeatedly—to protect him from the harsh rays of the sun. Or his laugh, or the teasing twinkle in his green eyes, or the contagious smile that brightened his handsome face.

Something about him had made her feel safe, like she could let her guard down. Thank goodness she hadn't. He also made her want...things she didn't usually crave without a couple of beers on board. Was it his slow, laid-back demeanor and quiet confidence? His quick, dry sense of humor? His build—a perfect complement to her large frame? His distinctive look or his air of reserved power?

Whatever it was, it gave her an unsettling schoolgirl crush sort of feeling. And Roxie didn't like it. In her experience men were unreliable, opportunistic and good for one thing only—sex. Add in emotion and the fun factor took a nosedive.

"Thank you, everyone," she said.

Fig didn't move.

"Back to work, you," she said, using her hands to shoo him along. "I hear a phone ringing."

He turned his back to the patient and leaned toward her. "Your mom called," he said quietly. "She sounded upset."

Last night had been particularly difficult. Roxie hated to leave for work this morning but what else could she do? They both depended on her income.

"She said she couldn't find the knobs for the stove," he added.

Duh. Because last week she hadn't turned off a burner, which caused the macaroni and cheese she'd made to burn and spew the smoke that prompted their obnoxious, constantly complaining neighbor to call the fire department. Which was the reason every damn thing in her not-so-terrific life had gone from "barely tolerable but afloat" to "she's taking on water!" fast approaching "she's going down. Abandon ship."

"There's a perfectly logical explanation for that," Roxie said. "Which is none of your business. Next time tell her to call my cell." She turned to her patient.

Fig reached for her arm to stop her. "She told me she'd tried but you didn't answer," he whispered.

What? Roxie always answered *Mami*'s calls. She patted her breast pocket. Empty. Jammed her hands into both scrub coat pockets, rummaged through their contents. Bandage scissors. Alcohol prep pads. Tape. Three injectable Demerol cartridges. Damn it, she needed to get in to talk to Victoria. Two paperclips. Three pens. A box of thermometer probes. A roll of candies. And a breakfast bar she hadn't had time to eat.

No phone.

She yanked her hands out so fast something went flying. A pen? It rolled under the bedside stand. She'd get it later. "Shoot. Where the heck did I leave my phone?" *Mami* panicked if she couldn't reach her. How long had it been since she'd called?

Roxie bent to look under the bed.

"Hot-pink with crystals, right?" Fig asked.

"Yeah."

"I'll keep an eye out for it."

"Thanks."

"And you got these." He handed her some slips of pink paper from his pocket.

She looked at the male names on each of six message slips. So they'd seen the video. Perverts. She ripped the papers in half and tossed them in the trash. "Anything else?" she asked, losing patience, wanting to get finished admitting her patient so she could call home then find her phone. Which contained that link she should have deleted upon receipt.

"You okay?"

"I'm fine." Always fine. Fine. Fine. Fine.

After getting her new patient settled Roxie took a minute to use a phone at the nurses' station. *"Hola, Mami."*

She started to cry.

"No. Please don't cry. You don't need the stove. I left you a sandwich in the refrigerator."

"I want to make hard-boiled eggs," her mother said.

"It's egg salad. Your favorite."

"Que buena hija. You're a good daughter."

"*Gracias*. Look, I have to get back to work. I misplaced my phone. If you need me call the floor and Fig will get me."

Nothing.

"Okay, *Mami*?"

"Okay," she said, her mouth full. "It's good. I was hungry."

Roxie smiled. "Be careful getting back to bed. I'll come straight home after work." She hung up the phone, dropped her head and let out a sigh of relief.

When she looked up her eyes met Fig's. "If my mom calls back…"

"I'll come find you," he finished.

"Thanks." Her stomach growled.

"Go eat. If any of your patients buzz I'll have Ali or Victoria check on them."

"I think I will." She stood. Swayed. Grabbed on to the counter to steady herself at the same time Fig reached for her. "Wow. Looks like the tank is empty. Time to refuel."

"Is that all it is?" Fig asked, looking concerned. And… suspect?

"Do you have any idea how many calories it takes to run this body?" she asked. "I skipped breakfast this morning. And, thanks to you, worked through my break." She lifted a shaky hand to flatten her hair. "I'm fine." Always fine. Fine. Fine. Fine.

"I'll walk you to the lounge," Fig offered.

She pulled her elbow out of his loose hold. "Don't be ridiculous." She exited the nurses' station, her head feeling disconcertingly foggy. Maintaining focus on the lounge door, she took deep breaths, concentrated on each step and willed her body to continue moving forward. Passing out at work would not be a good thing.

Two bottles of chocolate milk and two bologna-and-cheese sandwiches on rye later, Roxie felt back to her usual self. And ready to tackle Victoria before returning to her patients.

Just outside the open door to Victoria's office, Roxie heard Fig talking. "You have your proof right there," he said. "You asked me to watch her and I did. She showed up to work with bloodshot eyes, forgot her stethoscope in the nurses' lounge and misplaced her phone—which the pharmacy tech found in the med cart."

A flush of anger heated Roxie's skin. Fig was reporting her activities to Victoria, who had asked him to watch her? Why?

"And she almost passed out at the nurses' station not fifteen minutes ago," he went on. "I think it's time to switch your focus from trying to find Roxie innocent to figuring out a way to help her out of this mess."

Find Roxie innocent of what? Help her out of what mess? Exactly how much did they know about what was going on in her life? She walked into the office and with narrowed eyes looked from Victoria—sitting behind her desk, prim and professional—to Fig, looking all relaxed in the one chair across from Victoria. "What mess might that be?" she asked Fig. "And you hired him to watch me?" she asked Victoria. "Why?"

Victoria looked down at her desk at a lone cartridge of injectable Demerol.

Roxie slid her hand into her pocket and found only two of the three that had been there earlier.

Not good.

CHAPTER TWO

ROXIE withdrew her hand from her pocket and held out what Fig assumed were the other two missing doses of Demerol in her palm. He admired her calm.

"I was planning to tell you today. I asked Fig to relay the message I needed to talk to you." She looked over at him.

He nodded.

Apparently Victoria didn't care. She looked up at Roxie. "You altered the narcotic count," she accused.

"Yes." Roxie hung her head. "But I can explain."

"You altered the narcotic count," Victoria said again. A bit louder this time. "There is no explanation to justify what you did. This is grounds for termination, you know. And there's not a thing I can do to help you. This will follow you around, Roxie. You could lose your nursing license. What were you thinking?"

"Whoa." Panic flashed in Roxie's eyes. "Can't we keep this between us?"

"No, we can't keep this between us," Victoria snapped. "Because someone or a group of someones have been tampering with the narcotic-distribution system in the hospital. A pharmacist identified the inaccurate count as part of a hospital-wide investigation."

That was a pretty important chunk of information she'd neglected to share.

Roxie looked ready to collapse.

Fig stood. "Here." He motioned to his chair. "Sit."

"Why, thank you," she said sarcastically, looking ready to show her appreciation by slamming him into the wall and jamming her knee into his groin. "If you'd have come to me," she hissed under her breath as she moved past him, "instead of tattling to the boss I could have fixed this."

"No, you couldn't have," Victoria said. "And don't be mad at Fig. He only did what I asked him to do."

"A rare thing, a man who does what you ask him to," Roxie said to Victoria. "Lucky me you found one."

Fig felt like the low-life informant who'd deceived a friend. Because, in essence, he had.

"Tell me what happened," Victoria said.

"Does he need to be here?" Roxie asked.

No he didn't. Fig stepped toward the door, welcoming the chance to escape.

"Yes," Victoria said. He stopped. "As an impartial witness to our conversation."

Great. There was that word *impartial* again. The more he heard it, the more he realized he wasn't impartial at all. He wanted to help Roxie, wanted to erase the anger, frustration and sadness he'd noticed in her expression since early that morning, and bring back the fun-loving woman with the beautiful smile and infectious laugh from the night they'd first met.

"Fine," Roxie said, not looking at him. "The attending suspects my patient in 508B is a malingerer probably addicted to his pain meds. He reports intractable back pain yet all his diagnostic testing since admission has been negative or within normal limits. Every time the doctor tries to change over from IM Demerol to oral pain meds, the patient balks and is on the call bell every five minutes. Mention detox and he turns irate and verbally abusive."

"I'm aware of the situation," Victoria said.

"Late Friday night the doctor ordered the patient's doses of IM Demerol to be alternated with a placebo of IM sterile normal saline. The next morning—when I came on duty—it didn't take the patient long to figure it out and demand to see the syringe before I injected him. So I kept a Demerol cartridge in my pocket to show him. Then, each time he was scheduled to receive the placebo, I switched it out at the last second. It was not easy to do, I tell you."

"And you forgot to put the Demerol back," Victoria said.

Roxie nodded. "Luckily—" she looked between him and Victoria with sad eyes "—or unluckily, as it turns out, I was assigned to narcotic count Saturday night."

"But incoming shift is supposed to count and outgoing shift records."

"I can be very persuasive when I want to be." Her lips twitched into a tiny hint of a smile. "Anyway, I knew the Demerol was in my scrub jacket, which was out at the desk at the time. I increased the number in the box of Demerol by one, planning to return it before I left. Then my mother called." Roxie let out a breath. "And I had to rush home. Sunday morning I was running late, and I bolted out of the house, leaving it safely tucked away in my dresser."

"So you altered the count again."

"What else could I do?"

"How about talk to me?" Victoria asked, her anger evident. "Warn me the count was off so I wasn't completely blindsided."

"I'm sorry. I screwed up."

"How did you wind up with the other two?" Victoria asked without acknowledging Roxie's apology.

"More of the same. I was rushing. Then they got misplaced."

"You *misplaced* three doses of Demerol?"

"No." Roxie shook her head. "Only two." Like that made it okay. "The third," she went on, "was my mistake. I'd thought it was a normal saline in my pocket, but it turned out to be a Demerol."

"What is going on with you?" Victoria yelled.

Roxie shrugged and looked down at her lap.

Both women sat in silence until Roxie asked, "What happens now? Should I finish my shift or clean out my locker and head home?"

"Let me talk to the director and explain what happened. You returned the missing meds. Maybe…"

Fig interrupted. "Just to play devil's advocate for a second." He moved out of Roxie's reach, which was no small feat in the tiny office. "How do we know there's actual Demerol in those things and she didn't refill them with water?"

Rage flared in Roxie's eyes. She jumped up from her chair, whipped a plastic contraption from her pocket and grabbed the fluid-filled cartridges from Victoria's desk. "How about I inject all three of them into your lily-white gluteus maximus and you can vouch for their potency right before you lapse into a coma?" She inserted one of the cylinders into the injection device and took a step toward him.

"Stop it, Roxie." Tiny Victoria launched herself between them. "This isn't helping."

"But maybe it will make me feel better," she said. Then she looked at Fig. Challenging him. "You want to know for sure what's in this syringe?" She held it up, speaking slow and calm. "Drop your pants."

"The hospital is investigating medication tampering." Fig held Roxie's arms to keep her away from him. "Those cartridges left the hospital. I'm just posing the potential for substitution that any good investigator would acknowledge," he defended his question.

"He's right," Victoria agreed.

Roxie backed down and surprised him by starting to laugh. Not a happy laugh. Rather the kind of laugh that happens when things are so bad if you don't laugh you'll cry. He knew it well.

Roxie collapsed into the chair, tears streaming down her cheeks. "The irony is too much." She could barely get the words out. "I tell that idiot no." She took a deep breath, blotted her eyes with a tissue Victoria handed her and started to laugh some more. "I get blackmailed. I still say no, so he posts the video on some porn site." She laughed even harder. "And I'm accused of tampering with narcotics, and I'm getting fired, anyway." The laughing was so loud people up and down the hallway outside had to be wondering what was going on.

"Wait a minute," Fig said, remembering Roxie's phone conversation from earlier that morning. *I told you no. My answer won't change. Fine. Do what you have to do.* "Someone's blackmailing you?"

"Not anymore." The thought seemed to sober her. She inhaled deeply then exhaled as if trying to blow out any lingering giggles. "And it's all your fault." She gave him the stink eye.

What? "*My* fault?"

"If you'd have taken me out on Friday night like you were supposed to, I wouldn't have gone home with Johnny-the-jerk, who, come to find out, had his bedroom outfitted with cameras so he could videotape our little interlude."

"Who is Johnny-the-jerk?" Victoria asked.

"I'm guessing he's somehow involved with the hospital's drug tampering problem because after the deed was done—" she looked at Fig and emphasized "—*twice,* he used his tape to try to coerce me into substituting his bootlegged pills for real narcotics. He said the packaging was almost identical and no one would know. I told him *I* would know and I wouldn't do it."

"You mean you can identify him?" Victoria asked.

"I'm guessing you can, too, if you check out our video." Victoria recoiled.

At least Fig could help with that. Computers were his thing. Audio. Video. Programing. Networking. Hacking. You name it. If there's a way to track this guy, to catch him and make him pay, Fig could do it. "Do you have the link?" he asked Roxie.

"On my cell phone, wherever that is."

Fig reached into his pocket and handed it to her. She pressed a few buttons and held up the screen to him. "May I use your computer?" he asked Victoria.

"To go to a pornography website?" She paled. "Use my laptop." She took it out of her briefcase, placed it on her desk and booted it up. Then she stood so Fig could take her chair.

He typed in the link. A few seconds later Roxie's voice called out through the speakers. "Harder," she demanded. Fig fumbled to find the volume. "Yeah, baby. That's how I like it."

Just as he'd thought, Roxie was as take-charge in the bedroom as she appeared to be in every other aspect of her life. It'd take a strong man to stay in control. Anticipation of the challenge excited him.

Until the slam of Victoria's office door reminded him where he was.

"Do you have to be so loud?" Victoria chastised Roxie.

Fig didn't mind loud as long as the volume was attached to moans and screams of delight.

"Did you honestly think I'd be quiet in the bedroom?" she asked with a hint of a playful smile.

Fig muted the computer. "Twenty-seven minutes," he commented about the length of the video, giving a nod of approval.

"Not my best night," Roxie joked.

Fig relaxed a bit.

"Almost eighty thousand views in the six hours your video's been up on this site."

"Delinquents, all of them," Roxie said, standing up and walking over to stand beside him. "What are all those people doing home during the day? Shouldn't they be working?"

"Degenerates is more like it," Victoria said, looking uncomfortable. "Can you make out the man's face?" she asked Fig.

"Five stars," he noted instead, impressed.

"I bet you're regretting standing me up on Friday night." Roxie nudged his shoulder with her hip.

More than he regretted just about anything else.

"Standing her up? You didn't tell her what happened?" Victoria asked.

"No." And Victoria had better not say anything, either.

"Tell me what?" Roxie asked.

The last thing he wanted her thinking was he was some sort of pansy mama's boy, running home every time she called. "Nothing," Fig said and flashed Victoria a "keep quiet" look.

"But…"

"Woo wee," Roxie cut Victoria off. She leaned in close to the laptop. "I look good on screen."

Yes, she did. And since she didn't seem at all upset about the video, Fig commented, too. "You have an amazing ass."

Victoria sucked in an affronted breath.

"It's one of my best features," Roxie replied proudly. She had quite a few other mighty-fine features. Fig tilted his head to get a better look at one, watched her lift her long, smooth leg. No way. She couldn't possibly… She did.

"You liking what you see?" Roxie's voice turned sexy. Alluring.

Heck yeah! But Fig thought it best not to mention how much.

As if Roxie knew, she bent close to his ear and whispered, "Then I suggest you download my video so you can watch it over and over. Because that's as close as you'll ever get to sampling my goodies, you creep."

Shut. Down.

"For heaven's sake, Roxie," Victoria said. "A man taped you having sex and loaded it onto the internet. Without your consent. And you're standing there, watching yourself as if you're okay with it. You should be outraged. Shut it off, Fig."

"And what good would my outrage do?" Roxie asked. "The video is out there. And from the number of messages I've received today, people around town have seen it. There's nothing I can do. Heck, if I can't get another nursing job, maybe I'll use it as an audition tape." She turned to Fig. "Can you make me a copy?"

"You can't be serious," Victoria said.

"I'm totally serious," Roxie said, turning somber. "You may think you know me but all you know is the part of me I allow you to see. So let me share this. At the age of fourteen I gave my virginity to the owner of the superette down the street from our home to pay off our account when my mother had no money. That may have been the first time I used my body to barter, but it certainly wasn't the last. I'm a survivor. I do what I have to do."

Based on Victoria's look of complete and utter shock, she'd had no idea. Just how close were they? Roxie's defiant stance made Fig wonder if she shared her deepest, darkest secrets with anyone.

He couldn't stand the thought of lecherous men using a young Roxie who was desperate for food. He felt sick. Yet despite her experiences she still managed to enjoy life, with a wonderful sense of humor and a vivacious spirit he envied. "The man's face is blurred out," Fig said, to change the subject.

"Trust me," Roxie said. "I know who he is. And as soon as I find him you'll know who he is, too. Tell the E.R. to be on the lookout for a white male, around five feet ten inches tall, two hundred and twenty pounds, who will be arriving most likely after midnight, sometime in the next week. If things go as planned he'll be unconscious with severe facial trauma and both testicles rammed so far up into his pelvic cavity he'll require the skilled hands of surgeon to set him back to rights."

"You need to stay away from him," Victoria urged. "He's probably dangerous."

"No more dangerous than a pissed-off Puerto Rican with a grudge. So what's your call, Vic?" Roxie stood tall. Proud. "If you're going to fire me, do it now. Otherwise I need to get back to my patients."

"Let me talk to the director," Victoria replied. "Finish out your shift. You're out on vacation for the next week due to return on Wednesday. Hopefully I'll have everything worked out by then."

"Thanks," Roxie said to Victoria. "I really am sorry about all this."

"Me, too."

After Roxie left, Victoria asked Fig, "Can you take down the video?"

"I'll need to use my own computer, but yeah. I'm sure I can."

"Do you think it's up on more than one site?"

"If it is, I'll find it."

"She's going to go after that man," Victoria said.

"I'll keep an eye on her." Fig stood. He owed her that much. "I need to get back to work, too."

"Now that we know what happened you don't have to stay on here," Victoria said.

"I know. But I'll finish out my shift."

Roxie pulled her red Scion onto the short, bumpy, part-gravel, part-concrete patch that served as her driveway, turned off the engine and leaned back in her leather seat. The tiny house she shared with *Mami* held not one good memory, and yet, rather than filling her with excitement, the prospect of being forced to live somewhere else filled her with dread—mostly because *Mami* would not handle the change well. Dull blue paint, faded, chipped black shutters—one hanging askew—and overgrown, half-dead landscaping told the world this was not a happy place. The moss growing on the roof, the saggy porch and the collection of other people's discarded stuff that overflowed into the side yard added to the dilapidated appearance.

Oh, to have her own home to return to after a hard day's work. To live a stress-free, clutter-free, mother-free existence where the only person she was responsible for was herself. To be able to open a beer, actually sit down on the living room sofa and watch some mind-numbing television.

Her cell phone rang. She dug into her huge purse on the seat beside her and looked at the screen. The hospital. She let out a breath. What did she forget? Or was it Victoria calling to tell Roxie her fate? "Hello."

"Hey," Fig said. "You ran out of here before I could give you the message from your brother."

No need to ask which one. Only Ernesto, the one closest to her in age, took the time for an occasional phone call. But, "He called the hospital?"

"No. Your cell phone. While I had it. I thought it might be your mom so I answered it."

Well, surprise, surprise. A nice gesture.

"He, uh—" Fig hesitated "—sounded angry."

What did he have to be angry about? She was the one desperately trying to reach him for over a week with no response.

"I think—" Fig hesitated again.

"Just spit it out already," Roxie said.

"I think he may have seen your video."

Not Ernesto. He'd be the last one she'd expect to...

"I'm sorry, Rox. I got tied up. I'm on my way home now, and I'll take it down as soon as I get there."

Help. From an unexpected source. "Thanks."

"You doing anything tonight?" he asked. "I thought maybe we could..."

"If I decide I need sex you're unlucky number thirteen on my list."

"I'm not calling for sex. Just dinner. I want to explain..."

Roxie noticed the bags on the front porch. "No." She sat up. "She didn't."

"What?" Fig asked.

"I've got to go." Roxie ended the call then pushed open the car door, lunged out and slammed it shut. "Not again." She stormed across the patchy grass and packed dirt of the small front yard, whipped out her key and tried to open the door. Met resistance. Shouldered it open just wide enough to squeeze through. "I told you we need to keep the doorway clear," she yelled in frustration.

Behind the door her mother had stowed five white garbage bags filled with clothes. Roxie picked each up and hurled them, one at a time, into the depths of what used to be the family room, bringing the junk piled in the far corner up to chest level.

"This is crazy!" Roxie screamed. "Why are the bags back on the porch?" Two huge black garbage bags, filled to capacity, put out at the curb for the sanitation service to pick up that morning. Two bags of trash that were no longer adding to the safety hazards of their home. A mere speck of progress in cleaning out the house. Derailed. "And I told you to stop accepting used clothing from the church." A total of five bags that she saw. But who knew if her mother had more stashed somewhere?

"*Deja de gritar.* Stop yelling," *Mami* said, shuffling slowly, carefully along the narrow pathway from the back of the house to the kitchen, the clutter on either side of her hip-high.

"Do you understand what happens if the fire marshal doesn't see a noticeable improvement in our living conditions? He'll condemn this house as unfit for human habitation. If we don't sort through this junk—like I've been trying to get you to do for years—he's going to do it. We'll be forced to leave. I can't afford a mortgage payment and a rent payment. We have one lousy week left. One week." An impossible time frame to sort through years of accumulation. The two bags she'd managed to drag to the curb had taken at least a dozen hours of encouragement and convincing to get her mother to part with her treasured possessions. And now, not only were they back, but she'd accepted five more.

"I won't leave my house." Her mother stood tall despite her slightly hunched shoulders, looked vaguely formidable despite her frailty and washed-out floral housedress.

"These are my things. *Tus hermanos vendrán*. Your brothers will come. You'll see."

Not one of her four brothers had visited "the den of crazy" in the fifteen years since the last one had moved out, leaving Roxie—her mother's unsuccessful attempt to save her failing marriage—to care for her mother, the house and herself, on her own, since the age of ten.

"If they think it's unsafe for you to go on living here—" and what normal person wouldn't? "—they will *make* you leave." The interior looked like a huge refuse heap, with only the tops of long-standing, partially collapsed piles available to view. Children's clothes, toys, magazines and books—for the grandchildren her mother had never met. Housewares—for the daughters-in-law who shunned her. Newspapers—to wrap the castaway finds for safe transport when her sons returned home to finally accept their *mami*'s gifts of love.

Too little. Too late.

And while the brothers, who'd never had time for their way-younger sister, continued to rebel against the past and focus on their futures, Roxie lived an ant-farm existence, maneuvering along paths she maintained daily, leading from the front door to the kitchen, two of the three bedrooms and the bathroom. Seven years ago she'd closed the door to the third bedroom—so cluttered with junk it was unsafe to enter—and to her knowledge, the door hadn't been opened since.

"They'll physically remove you, *Mami*." When she refused and fought, like Roxie knew she would, what then? Would she get hurt? Have a heart attack? Get a free trip to the psych ward over at Madrin Memorial?

Maybe that's what she needed. Maybe the firemen alerting the fire marshal and health department to the state of their home was exactly what *Mami* needed to finally deal with her hoarding and allow Roxie to clean more than the bathroom and kitchen counters.

"Lo siento," Mami said, wringing her hands. "I'm sorry. But I couldn't find the stuffed frog for little Daniel. I thought maybe it was in one of the trash bags."

"It's in the dryer," Roxie said. "It needed to be washed. Remember?"

Mami looked down at her hands.

No. She didn't remember. Which was another reason Roxie needed to clean out the house. If *Mami's* health continued to deteriorate, soon she'd need someone to supervise her while Roxie was at work. Whereever she happened to be working. If she was working.

She had to work. And she'd need a good job to continue to support the two of them and pay for the house and an attendant and the cleaning crew she'd put off hiring, worried the stress of strangers in their home would be too much for *Mami*.

But they were running out of time. *"Mami.* We need help. We can't do this on our own," she broached the topic. "There's a…"

"No."

"Please. Be reasonable." It was the same argument every time. "We can't continue to live like this." Existing was more like it. *Mami* had no friends except for some women from the church, a bunch of enablers who inventoried the donated items and contacted her to see what she "needed."

Roxie couldn't entertain, spent the hours at home confined to her bedroom—the only clean, orderly room in the house because she dead-bolted the door whenever she left—unless she was supervising her mom's shower, cajoling her to sort and clean or cooking the meals they ate on wooden TV trays surrounded by Roxie's hepa filters which just barely neutralized the odor of decay, and God knew what else, that lingered outside her door.

"*Lo siento,*" *Mami* said again, this time with a sniffle. "I'm sorry."

Great. Roxie felt like a big bully. She'd made her mother cry. She stepped over a small stack of magazines and skirted around a laundry basket that held dozens of her mom's favorite frogs to reach her. "I'm sorry, too." For yelling, for forgetting, albeit momentarily, that hoarding was a mental illness and not laziness or purposeful behavior meant to upset Roxie. She pulled the only family member who really mattered to her into a hug. "It'll all work out, *Mami.*" Although how it would, she had no idea.

"I'll do better," *Mami* said. "After dinner. We can try again."

It was always later or tomorrow. Any time but right now.

"We can do it. We don't need a bunch of strangers in here." *Mami* scanned the devastation that had once been a large eat-in kitchen, family room and dining room, and sighed. "It's overwhelming."

"One area at a time," Roxie said, taking *Mami's* hand and leading her along the path through the kitchen. "You decide, like on the television show. We'll continue with our piles. One for each of the boys and their families. And one for...*Papi.*" She nearly choked on the word. "But you'll have to let me box it all up and mail it."

"No. They need to come. I want to see them to show them."

They weren't going to come. *Mami's* ex-husband—who Roxie referred to as such because he refused to accept she was his daughter—had remarried years ago. As for her brothers, the only one she had any semblance of a relationship with was Ernesto—if you considered an annual birthday telephone call and occasional requests for money a relationship—and he hadn't come home any of the other times she'd asked him to, so she didn't hold out much hope he'd suddenly developed a conscience.

"Let's eat," Roxie said, changing the subject. She'd had about all the confrontation she could handle for one day.

Despite her moratorium on men, by Thursday night, forced by the frustration of *Mami* refusing to clean and annoyance at the number and tone of the messages piling up on her cell phone in relation to her video, the neon-pink and fluorescent-orange walls of Roxie's bedroom seemed to squeeze in on her. And under the weight of worry about where they'd go when forced to leave their home and what would happen if she lost her job, her bright sunshine-yellow ceiling seemed to sag until she felt it just might smother her. Roxie needed to get out, to mingle and occupy her mind so she'd stop obsessing about things outside of her control.

"Shake it off." Roxie shook out her arms and legs then rotated her neck. "Nothing you can do about it." Play it cool. She slid each foot into a flat gold-colored sandal that showed off her bright pink self-manicured toenails to perfection. "Nothing bothers Roxie Morano." She walked over to the dresser and inserted a large gold hoop earring into each earlobe. Then she stood tall and evaluated her reflection in the full-length mirror angled high on her wall.

Denim mini hugging tight to her curves. She swiveled to get a look at her butt. Check.

Legs smooth and lotioned to an enticing sheen. Check.

Hair a mass of loose, wild curls lending a carefree, untamed appearance. Check.

Tube top—in an attention-getting hot-pink—accentuating each of her womanly assets. Check and check.

Roxie was ready to go. A quick peek to make sure her mother was sleeping, and she went outside to wait for the cab, antsy to get find-the-humor-in-anything drunk, psyched to lose herself in some make-me-forget-how-much-my-life-sucks-at-the-moment sex. Preferably of the un-videotaped variety.

Outside the heavy wooden doors to O'Halloran's Bar, one of three bars in town, and the preferred drinking and bar food eating establishment for the majority of Madrin Memorial employees, Roxie hesitated. While the music from the jukebox beckoned her, she sought fortification in the vibration of the bass and swayed her hips to the slow rhythmic beat.

She could do this. So what if the people inside had watched her video, had seen her naked and wild with passion? At least they hadn't seen the worst of it. She let out a breath, determined to enjoy this night. Tomorrow she'd deal with Johnny's new threat.

"You don't have to go in there," a male voice said from behind her.

For a split second she stiffened, until she recognized it as Fig's voice.

"We can go someplace else. Maybe talk a bit more about what we're going to do to each other when we get naked."

Like they'd passed the time at the employee recognition dinner last week. "You see that's where we differ." She turned and gave him the once-over, noting his loose-fitting, expensive-looking jeans, long-sleeve white tee, black leather vest and black ascot cap. Damn it if he didn't smell even better than he looked. "I like the doing more than I like the talking." She reached for the handle on the door. "And I'm not one to hide out because of a little controversy."

"Then allow me." He pushed one hand past hers and opened the door. The other he set at her low back and, applying a gentle pressure, eased her inside.

Just as the song on the jukebox ended. The bar went quiet. All eyes turned on her. Roxie hesitated.

Fig leaned in close, his chest pressed to her back, his palm flat on her belly. "Time to muster up some moxie, Roxie," he whispered. "Every woman in this bar is wishing she had a body as gorgeous as yours, and every man is wishing he had your long, beautiful legs clamped around his butt."

Roxie relaxed. Smiled even. "Does that include you?" She allowed herself to be led to the large wooden bar.

"Nah." He assisted her up onto a stool, even though she didn't need assistance then slid onto the stool beside her. He looked up, locked a pair of dreamy green eyes with hers and added, "My wish involves them wrapped around my head."

Hell-o! An excited tingle started—there—and flared out to her periphery. Roxie came dangerously close to grabbing him by the arm and dragging him off to someplace more private. So she could grant a little wish fulfillment. Because with men there was a Polly Pocket–size window of opportunity between "I want to make you feel so good" and "me, me, me." But, "So that's why you're here? Sex?" Making him no better than the rest of her post-pornographic-video fan club. Too busy to bother with an official date, too cheap to shell out some bucks on dinner and a movie, but ready to get naked at the first opportunity. The slug.

"I'm here because Victoria's worried you're heading down a dangerous path."

"Ah. How sweet." Not. "And she sent her does-what-he's-asked-to-do lackey to stop me?" Roxie stood. "Well, thanks anyway, but I don't need a keeper." She didn't need anyone.

"I beg to differ." He caught her by a belt loop on her skirt as she tried to walk away. "Sit down," he said quietly, but it was an order all the same.

Not likely. "Who do you think…?"

"I can tie a cherry stem in a knot using only my tongue and teeth," he said, calm as can be. The randomness of his comment caught her off guard. Intrigued, Roxie stopped.

"In eight seconds," he added with a slow, confident smile.

He was too cocky for his own good. "Triple B," she called the bartender. "The usual for me. My friend would like something with a cherry in it."

"I guess that leaves you out," Raunchy Rob from Radiology called from the other side of the bar. The guy next to him laughed.

"Ha-ha," Roxie said. Idiot.

Fig stood, looking ready to do some damage. "Apologize to the lady," he demanded.

"What?" Rob asked. "I was only having some fun. You know I love you, Roxie." He snickered. "Even more so on my computer screen." He elbowed the loser next to him. They both chuckled.

Fig took off.

Now it was Roxie holding *him* by the belt loop in a futile attempt to slow him down. "Don't." The man was a plow horse. She was the plow, her sandals absolutely no help in the traction department. "Oh, look," she tried. "Our drinks. Time to prove your oral dexterity." Fig kept on going. "For heaven's sake, apologize, Rob. Or I'll tell everyone…" about his stubby little pecker. What a miserable night that'd been.

"I'm sorry." Rob hopped off his stool and backed across the dance floor. "I'm sorry. Hell, Roxie. Call him off."

CHAPTER THREE

Flirty banter and sarcastic teasing aside, Fig refused to stand by and do nothing when a poor excuse for a man flat-out disrespected a lady. Especially one he considered a friend, whether or not she considered him a friend in return. When the loud mouth pleaded out an apology then scurried away, Fig stopped. "Anyone else have anything to say?" he asked the now quiet crowd. He stood tall, his arms at his sides, prepared to fight, hoping he didn't have to.

Because he had plans for later tonight and they didn't include a visit to the emergency room.

No one spoke.

Good.

Gradually the bar's patrons resumed their conversations and turned back to their pool and dart games. Time to take Roxie's mind off her quest for vengeance and convince her to leave. With him.

"My hero," Roxie teased from beside him. She looked down at the wood floor and nudged a small drink umbrella with the toe of her delicate gold sandal. "But if you're looking to protect my honor, I'm afraid you're at least ten years too late. I've had sex with—" she scanned the crowd "—at least half the men in here tonight. I bet the other half have watched me doing the videotaped hoochie coochie probably with their hands down their pants." She shrugged. "I'm not proud of it. But I'm not ashamed, either. It is what it is. I am who I am."

He appreciated her honesty. "I like who you are."

She smiled up at him. "Because you want me to wrap my legs around your head."

"Hey. Don't knock it." He matched her grin. "I'll make sure you enjoy yourself as much as I do." Turned out Fig had a real knack for pleasuring women. He may have hit the sex scene later than most, but according to several very reliable sources he'd surpassed the competition in the oral sex arena.

Two positives to come out of months and months spent as a patient in the hospital:

Patience. From waiting for the nurses to bring his medication, waiting to get strong enough to walk to the bathroom on his own, to get healthy enough to return home. Women seemed to like his unhurried approach to foreplay.

Chivalry. From the hours and hours of black-and-white classic movies his mother watched at his bedside. When he'd pretended to be asleep so she'd stop fussing over him. When he'd vowed if he survived long enough, got big and strong and lucky enough to find a woman who didn't think he was a sickly, hairless freak, he'd treat her like a princess. In his early twenties he'd learned as much as they touted equality, women liked to be treated special, to be protected, cared for and respected. As much as they wanted independence, they liked a man to take charge.

With that thought in mind, Fig caught Roxie around the waist, pulled her close. "Dance with me."

Roxie settled her body flush with his and clasped her hands behind his neck. "Since you *asked* so nicely."

Fig rested his hands on her hips, his cheek to her mane of soft, lightly perfumed curls, and swayed in time with the slow beat, loving the closeness, the feel of her. But he needed Roxie to understand. "About our date."

She leaned back to look at him. "You mean the one I got all dressed up for? The one I'd been looking forward to all week? The one you didn't bother to show up for?"

"That's the one." He pulled her back against his body and held her there. "I had a family emergency and had to run home for the weekend. Can we leave it at that as long as you know I didn't get a better offer, because there's no place I would have rather been than with you that night? And if there was any way I could have gotten to you I would have? I should have called." But he'd been enraged that his mother had manipulated him. Again. For the absolute last time. "I'm sorry."

"And…" Roxie said.

"I'm sorry for what went down at the hospital. I had no idea the investigation was hospital wide. Victoria asked me to help prove your innocence, and that's what I'd intended to do."

"A-a-and?"

And what? Fig had no idea.

"And you're going to make it up to me."

"Yes." Most definitely. "And I'm going to make it up to you." Tonight. All night long. Fig slid his hands into her back pockets and eased her hips closer, putting her in contact with his growing arousal, making his intentions clear. They'd had quite a tempting flirtation going last weekend, and Fig was eager to back up his words with a little action.

Roxie turned her head, her mouth on his ear, her breath warm and moist. "By taking off your cap so I can feel your head."

The head wearing the hat was not the head he wanted her hands on at the moment. He leaned back so he could face her. "You want to…"

She nodded. "Feel your head," she said, looking up at him. "It looks so soft."

What was it with women and a bald-headed men? Far from being the turn-off he'd once thought it to be, they loved it, asked to caress it and pet it. Holding Roxie in place with his left arm at her low back, Fig pulled off his cap. Holding it, his right hand joined his left and he said, "Feel away."

She slid both hands up the back of his neck to the top of his head. For as loud and in-your-face as Roxie could be, she had a gentle touch, skimming lightly across his flesh. Fig wanted to bury his face in her hair, close his eyes and enjoy every second of it.

Total loser that he was, a simple caress from Roxie was capable of turning him to mush. Like on his twenty-first birthday, when he'd undressed Kyle's gift—one of the always-looking-for-a-good-time Stavardi twins—and almost didn't last long enough to lose his virginity. Luckily he'd had enough presence of mind to put his mentor's sage advice into action: take control. Focus on the woman. Always satisfy your partner—multiple times when possible—before allowing yourself to come. That last one had taken some time to master. But he was nothing if not a good student, committed and willing to practice, often, until he'd gotten it right. After a few months his confidence grew and word got around and he'd never again needed Kyle's help to attract women.

Fig slid his hands back into the pockets covering Roxie's nicely rounded butt. He'd already taken control. Now he'd focus on the woman. "Nice," he said.

"Yeah," she muttered on a sigh, her hands still exploring. "Soooo, is the rest of you this enticingly smooth and hair-free?" she asked.

He smiled. "If you're a really good girl maybe you'll get to find out," he teased.

"Oh, I'm good."

From the snippet of her video he'd watched in Victoria's office, he'd lay odds she was much better than good. His cell phone vibrated in his front pocket.

Roxie rubbed against it. "Me likey."

"You're a kook," he joked, ignoring the call. Less than a minute later, it vibrated again. His mother's typical pattern. Call incessantly until he picked up. Call the local police if he didn't answer within an hour.

Tomorrow he'd get a new number.

"You'd better answer that," Roxie said when the phone buzzed a third time. "Not that I'm not enjoying all the activity down there, but it may be important."

He reached into his pocket to retrieve his phone and checked the caller. Sure enough. Still holding Roxie, he answered the call. "Hi, Mom. I'm fine. Goodbye," he said. And put the phone away.

It buzzed again.

"Talk to your mom," Roxie said, starting to pull away.

"I'm not ready to let you go." Fig held on. "We were in the middle of discussing how good you are." A topic he'd like to address in detail as a prelude to the demonstration portion of the evening.

"Our drinks are getting warm." She pushed on his chest and he released her. "I promise to save you a dance for later."

Save him a dance? He intended to have all of her dances. Back at the bar an open bottle of beer and three shot glasses filled with a dark amber liquid awaited Roxie. A Shirley Temple with a long-stemmed maraschino cherry awaited him.

Fig reached under the bar, squirted a dollop of hand

sanitizer in his palm and cleaned his hands. That done, he removed the stem from the cherry—regretting having mentioned his unusual skill—and wiped it with his napkin. He lifted the glass, toasted the bartender, who smiled, and returned it to the bar without taking a sip. Last night they'd joked around for a couple of hours while Fig had waited to see if Roxie would show up. After serving Fig his third bottle of water—unopened—the bartender had offered him a shot of anything, on the house. Fig had refused and shared he no longer drank alcohol—thus the Shirley Temple.

He'd tried living life under an alcoholic haze through which his situation passed as acceptable. As a result the abuse had gone on years longer than it should have. Because he wasn't clearheaded enough to notice it. Because it took Kyle almost dying for him to figure it out.

Roxie tossed back a shot.

The bartender, who she called Triple B—for Big Burly Bartender—came over to tell her which man had purchased each shot for her. And to bring Fig a bottle of water—unopened.

Roxie looked at it with disgust. "You want one?" She held up a shot glass.

"No. I'm good."

She tossed back the second one.

Fig recognized Roxie's need to get drunk. Fast. More to escape and forget than embark on a little giddy, uninhibited fun. Been there, done that. "Did you drive tonight?"

"Nah." She followed the shot with a swig of beer. Then smiled. "I'm sure someone will be willing to give me a ride home."

When alcohol rendered her inhibitions ineffective. "I'll drive you home," he said. Even if he had to drag her out by her hair while swinging Triple B's behind-the-bar baseball bat back and forth to hold off the predators.

She lifted her third shot, smiled at some blond-haired schlub who blew her a kiss and finished that one off. "Don't you dare ruin my fun, figlet. Go call your mother."

Figlet. His man-parts shriveled in response. Roxie turned to face the man sitting on the other side of her and began to chat, effectively dismissing him. He took the opportunity to dial his mom. When she picked up he said, "I'm fine, Mom. Now's not a good time to talk. I'll call you tomorrow."

He caught Roxie watching him out of the corner of her eye. "I'm on a date," he answered when his mom shot off a question about why it was so noisy.

"Oh, you think this is a date?" Roxie asked, her head tilted to the side and both eyebrows raised.

He smiled. "No. She's not a nice Jewish girl," he answered his mom.

Roxie harrumphed and brought her bottle of beer to her lips.

"She's a nice Latina girl," he clarified.

She smiled around the opening.

"Yes. They do have beautiful complexions." He drew a figure eight on the warm, bare skin of Roxie's upper back. She shivered.

"Okay, Mom," Fig said when she told him to be careful.

"Always," he agreed when she told him to use protection.

"Never," he denied when she reminded him not to kiss his date on the mouth—because the human mouth was the dirtiest part of the body and kissing transmitted disease.

And, "I will," he agreed when she told him to have fun (but not too much), get a good night's sleep (after he got rid of the shiksa) and to call her tomorrow (so she'd know he'd survived the night). He disconnected the call without saying what needed to be said. That he was twenty-six years old and she needed to find a hobby or something else to occupy her time.

To which she would have replied, "You can't turn off being a mother, Ryan. Especially to a sick son who you've given up your own life to care for and homeschool." Certain he would have given up his own life if not for his mom's steadfast love and encouragement when he was young, Fig indulged her. He'd even forgiven her. But he'd reached his limit of guilt and manipulation. If they were going to have any type of relationship from here on, it'd be on his terms. Which he planned to lay out for her the next time they met face-to-face. Not in a bar, with Roxie listening in.

"Your mom sounded disappointed that you're hanging out with a shiksa. Good luck finding a nice Jewish girl here at O'Halloran's. Don't look so surprised." Roxie shrugged and looked down into her third shot glass. "Mom and I used to clean for a Jewish family up on the hill. I heard what they said."

"Maybe I don't want a nice Jewish girl," Fig said, leaning in, trying to make eye contact.

She bumped him with her shoulder. "You and me are like matzo balls and hot sauce. We don't mix."

Fig disagreed. The potent chemistry he and Roxie shared was a perfect mix. "What do you know about matzo balls?"

"Sometimes we helped Mrs. Klein prepare and serve at Rosh Hashanah and Passover. I'll have you know I can make a chicken soup so tasty and a matzo ball so light and fluffy your mom would weep."

"Maybe I like my matzo balls as hot and spicy as I like my women."

This time Roxie laughed. "I'm out of your league."

"Maybe this will change your mind." Fig lifted the cherry stem and held out his expensive watch. "Time me."

She counted him down. "Five. Four…"

He placed the stem between his teeth.

"One," Roxie said and stared at his lips.

Fig maneuvered the stem with his tongue. Twisted it, shoved it and…*voilà!* He spit the knotted stem into his palm.

Roxie looked down at the watch. And swallowed. "Eight seconds."

He leaned in close. "Imagine what a few minutes of that would feel like." Her expression softened. Ah, yes. He had her. Atta girl. Imagine him going down…

The tall man with blond hair came up beside Roxie. "Come on, hot stuff," he said, grabbing her arm. "They're playing our song."

"Born to be Wild."

Roxie looked torn—for all of five seconds. "Go home," she said. "I'll tell Victoria you did your best." Then she hopped off her stool and led scruffy surfer dude to the dance floor.

As if Victoria's concern was the only reason he'd come to the bar.

"She's headed for trouble with that one," Triple B commented. "Even more than with the last loser she paired herself off with."

Fig stiffened. "The last loser." The videographer. "You know him? What he did?"

Triple B nodded as he picked up a glass and started drying it with a towel. "He started coming in a few weeks ago. Always after midnight." He set down the glass and picked up another. "Him and a shifty-looking sidekick. They moved through the crowd. Zeroed in on a certain woman and started buying rounds of drinks until they practically had to carry her out." He slammed the glass on the bar. "What could I do? The women didn't protest. They didn't ask for help. The next time they come in here…"

"You call *me*," Fig said. He removed his business card from his wallet and handed it to the bartender. "Anytime."

For the next hour Fig listened to an increasingly loud, slurring, laughing Roxie sing—if you could call it that— along with the jukebox. He watched the enticing gyration of her hips and the bounce of her pleasing breasts as she danced and stumbled from one groping partner to the next, only resting long enough to do a shot or chug down a constant supply of beer, a fresh drink purchased by her many admirers before she'd completely finished the one before it. He kept an eye on the time and waited for the right opportunity to claim the dance she'd promised him so he could entice her away from the bar. Before midnight.

It happened in an instant. Roxie pushed the blond guy away. Fig made it to the dance floor just in time to hear him say, "Come on, baby. Double your pleasure," as he threaded his right arm through Roxie's, and another man, who could have passed for his twin, did the same on the other side. Their execution practiced. Effective. They led Roxie to the door.

"I don't do tag team, fellas," Roxie said, looking at each. "If you don't…"

"A real man doesn't need help to pleasure a woman," Fig said, coming to a stop directly in front of Roxie. The men halted. Roxie didn't.

"Right on, figlet," she said just before she collided with his chest.

He caught her and held her upright as he leaned in close

to her ear. "There are two of them and only one of me. It'd help if you talked me up, not down."

She stepped back. "I mean, Big Fig," she corrected. "Big *Bad* Fig," she emphasized. It would have been more effective if her tone had been less mocking.

"How about that dance?" he asked, holding out his hand. Cautious. Not sure how the duo once again flanking Roxie would respond.

"Ta ta." She dismissed them with a flippant wave. "It's been fun."

"I don't think so," one said at the same time the other said, "Not after all the money…"

"Triple B," Fig called out to the bartender. "Add their tab to mine." He motioned between the two men. "If they make their way back to the bar in the next ten seconds, tack on whatever they drink for the rest of the night." He turned to both men. "It's the only offer on the table, gentlemen." He pushed back his shoulders and widened his stance. "The lady's with me."

"How absolutely caveman of you," Roxie said with a grin. "I think I like it."

They all did.

The scruffier of the two men looked Fig up and down. Fig had about six inches on him. With a curse he returned to the bar. After a brief hesitation, the other one followed.

"Come on." He held open his arms. "You promised me a dance."

The music playing had a raucous beat.

"I'm tired," Roxie admitted.

"Too tired for a slow dance?"

She swayed on her feet. "I'm all hot and sweaty," she said.

Fig closed the distance between them and pulled her

close. "Next time I want to be the one to make you all hot and sweaty."

She rested her head on his shoulder and followed his lead, leaning heavily. "I like that idea," she said as her hands snaked up his arms and the back of his neck, coming to rest on his head. "Nice," she said on an exhalation as she caressed him.

Nice indeed.

After the second song Fig thought there was a distinct possibility Roxie had fallen asleep. "Hey," he said, rubbing her back. "I'm going to take you home now."

"To *your* home."

Well, Kyle's condo since it was where Fig was staying while in town since Kyle had all but moved in with Victoria. That'd been the plan, anyway. Before he'd seen Roxie consume enough alcohol to fell a lumberjack. The first time he hankied her panky he wanted her fully alert, capable of consent and of remembering their encounter—so she'd stop calling him figlet.

Unlike his lesser male counterparts, Fig did not take advantage of intoxicated women.

"Come on, hot sauce," he said, giving no indication he'd be taking her directly home to her house. It was eleven forty-four and he didn't have time for an argument.

"Sure thing, matzo ball," she said with a giggle. "You know you kind of look like a matzo ball."

"Is that your idea of a compliment?" he asked, leading her to the bar so he could settle up with Triple B and get his cap.

"I like matzo balls," she said defensively.

At least that was a start.

During the walk across the parking lot, the fresh air rejuvenated Roxie. Made her ache with want. Excitement started to build. For sex. For a wipe-my-mind-clean orgasm and the blessed satiated calm that followed.

After all of Fig's big talk last week, he had better deliver.

Uh-oh. "You know what they say about men and expensive sports cars," Roxie said when he brought her to an uber-fancy silver Corvette.

He spun her around so fast her head kept going. Before she knew what'd happened he had her pinned to the side of said fancy sports car. Then he grabbed her ass, lifted her left leg behind the knee and ground his zipper against the dampening cotton lining of her undies. "Ya know..." he said.

If Roxie were a smidgen less intoxicated and a bit more coordinated she would have jumped up, wrapped her other leg around him and hung there. His yin to her yang.

"...one day soon," he continued, "you are going to owe me a huge—" he held her tight and ground his erection against the very place she wanted him "—and when I say huge I mean *huge*—apology."

Before she could make sense of the "someday soon" time frame, he pulled away, opened the door and helped her in. "I feel like my butt's dragging on the ground," she said when he pulled onto the open road.

"Close your eyes," he suggested.

She did and felt the car accelerate. The power. The speed. She loved it. Until the car started to spin. Bad idea. She opened them back up and focused in on the hula girl on the dashboard.

"You okay?" Fig asked. The electric window to her right opened. The cool night air blew through her hair. She felt wild and free. And gassy. She burped. Her attempt to quickly cover her mouth wound up an awkward smack in the nose. "Sorry." She waited for his censure, for his condemnation for how drunk she was.

Instead he burped, too. "Now *that* feels better," he said.

Smiling, Roxie relaxed into the welcoming soft leather seat. Until she noticed they were headed toward her house, not Kyle's condo. "Hey," she said. "We're supposed to be going to your place." To rip each other's clothes off. To have sex like wild wildebeests out on the Serengeti. "So you'd best pull a U-ey and get us going in the right direction." She hoped the walls of Kyle's condo had sufficient soundproofing between his unit and the ones next door.

"I'm taking you home, Roxie. To your house."

"Oh, hell no." Roxie sat up. "I have until three."

She could see Fig's smile in the light from the speedometer. "What happens to you at three?"

Mami started prowling around. Roxie's brief opportunity to play at carefreeness ended and she returned to her hellish existence inside the walls of the childhood home she hated.

"I am *muy caliente* for you, figlet," she tried, leaning across the center console to slip her tongue in his ear while she ran her hand from his knee up the inside of his thigh.

He covered her hand with his and stopped her, mere inches from her destination. "What's with the figlet?" he asked, moving her hand to her own thigh. "You keep calling me that and I doubt I'll get turned on enough to put out the flame atop a birthday candle much less take on the blaze you've got going."

"Fine." Roxie crossed her arms over her chest and stared out the window. "If we're not going to have sex then take me back to the bar," she said, feeling tense from a potent mix of anger, frustration and lust churning inside her.

"Why?" Fig asked. "So you can find someone else to screw you?"

He made it sound immoral. "What's wrong with two people having sex? Finding enjoyment and satisfaction in each other's bodies?"

"That's exactly the reason we're not going to have sex tonight," he said, sounding a little pissed off himself. "When we're together—and notice I say *when* not *if*—" he glanced at her then looked back at the road "—it will be because we both want each other, not because any member of the opposite sex will do."

And to Roxie's utter disgust she started to cry. "How could you do this to me?" she wailed. "You have no idea…" she sobbed. "I need…"

"I know what you need, honey," he said, placing his cool palm on her thigh. "When I get you settled into your bed I'll take care of you."

If the thought of him seeing the inside of her home hadn't sent her into a panic, she may have had more time to think about how sweet he sounded just then. "You are not coming into my house." She wiped at her wet eyes with the back of her hand. "I don't want you anywhere near my house." She reached for the handle to open the car door. "Let me out here." She tried to yank on it.

Fig slammed on the brakes and grabbed her hand. "Are you insane?" He swerved the car onto the shoulder of the road.

"Why can't anything go the way I want it to?" She fought Fig. "Why do you do what Victoria asks and not what I ask?" She opened the door, hauled herself out and screamed up at the starless sky. "Is one night of fun too much to ask for? One freakin' night?" She turned and pounded toward her house.

"Where are you going?" Fig asked.

As if it weren't clear by the direction she was headed. "Home," she snapped. "That's where you want me to go, right? So that's where I'm going. To *my* home. Where *you* are not welcome," she screamed. "Good. Night." Although why she'd wished him a good night when hers was getting suckier by the second—because of him—was a mystery. May his tire pick up a nail on the way home and he be greeted with a flat first thing in the morning. Four flats. "If you won't do it for me," she yelled at the sky, "do it because he deserves it."

"Who deserves what?" Fig jogged after her.

"You'd better not leave your precious car unattended in this neighborhood. You'll come back to find all your tires missing."

That'll do, Roxie thought as she turned the corner onto her road. The darkness enveloped her. She'd walked this route hundreds of times, didn't need light to see where she was going. Unfortunately Fig didn't know enough to step over the hose Mr. Victor kept laid out across the sidewalk to drain his sump pump into the sewer grate.

"Damn it," Fig said in the midst of trying to keep himself from falling to the ground.

Roxie smiled, wishing she could have seen it.

"Any more hazards I should be aware of?" he asked from beside her.

"I think I heard the sound of your windshield shattering. Probably vandals. You'd better go check it out."

"It's only a car. It can be replaced."

Roxie stopped short. Fig bumped into her. Three more houses and she'd be home. It was time to put an end to this nonsense. "See that light up ahead? That's my house. I am certain I can make it there unassisted." Because her anger had sobered her up but good.

"I don't mind walking you." He took her arm in his.

Daring man. "Well, I mind." She yanked herself free.

"Let me take you out tomorrow," Fig said. "Or better

yet, come to my place. I'll cook you a delicious meal. Tell me what you like. I'm up for anything."

"I choose O'Halloran's. Without you. So I can get drunk and go home with someone who's up to the task of giving me what I want."

"Oh, I'll give you what you want and more," Fig said. "When you're sober."

"Sex is more fun when I'm drunk." Which worked for her, since that's the only time she ever wanted it. Until she'd met Fig.

He turned to her, his face so close she felt his breath on her cheek. "Then you're not doing it with the right men."

Her phone rang. She pulled it out of the front pocket of her skirt and looked at the lit display. *Mami*. She whipped it open. "What's wrong?" It was just after midnight. *Mami* always slept until at least 3:00 a.m.

"I smell smoke," *Mami* said, coughing.

Roxie sniffed the air.

And ran.

Her sandals slapped the broken-up sidewalk. The bottoms of her feet stung. She didn't stop. This was all her fault. The fire marshal had warned the house was unsafe. A fire hazard. But *Mami* had clutched at her chest and grabbed for her sublingual nitroglycerin tablets when Roxie broached the subject of living someplace else, even temporarily.

Fig called out behind her.

Roxie didn't answer. She should have done more, tried harder. Now *Mami* would pay the price for her failure. She tore up the front lawn. Thick, dark gray smoke billowed from the open kitchen window. Roxie jammed her hand in her front pocket to get her key and took the front steps all three at once.

"Wait," Fig yelled.

Roxie inserted the key in the lock.

Fig tackled her. "I said wait."

"My mother's in there," Roxie yelled. "Get off of me." She struggled beneath him.

He tightened his hold. "I called the fire department. They'll be here in a minute."

But they wouldn't be able to locate her amongst the clutter. Only Roxie knew the path to the back bedroom, what she needed to skirt around and climb over. Only Roxie knew where *Mami* would be, huddled near the edge of her mattress, her bed all but taken over by dolls and clothing she worked to repair, and beloved mementos of her life with her husband.

"You don't understand." She fought with every bit of strength she had and managed to turn onto her back.

"Stop it," Fig said. "You're going to hurt yourself."

Roxie didn't care about herself. Tears leaked from her eyes. "Only I can get to her. I have to get her."

"You're not thinking clearly."

She was thinking clearly enough to know he was stronger than her and had the advantage of being on top of her, and the only thing she could do to escape him was knee him in the balls as soon as the opportunity presented itself.

Which is what she did.

Fig sucked in a breath and forgot about her for the few seconds it took to push him away. She felt a moment's remorse at the sight of him lying on his side in the fetal position, before she opened the door.

A huge blast of heat and smoke greeted her. When it dissipated she yelled, "*Mami,* I'm coming." Then she headed into the darkness.

CHAPTER FOUR

"ARE you insane?" Fig yelled at Roxie for the second time that night as she removed the oxygen mask, again, and coughed. Black soot stained her face—especially beneath her nostrils—and clothes. "You could have been killed."

While he'd writhed in pain on the front porch, on the verge of vomiting, and struggling to breathe. Incapacitated. Helpless. Two conditions he'd decided long ago he'd rather die than ever experience again.

But she'd done it. Gotten herself and her mother out of the house right as the fire trucks had arrived. At least he'd managed to force himself upright, albeit hunched over, to help her the last few feet so he didn't come off like a total loser.

"I'm sorry," she said, her voice gravelly from smoke inhalation, her words muffled by the oxygen mask.

Not as sorry as she was going to be. Because once he got her alone he was going to spank her bare backside until it was a bright cherry-red for doing what she'd done.

He shifted his stance, the ache in his balls accompanied by a deep pressure low in his gut. Terrific.

"I told you this would happen, young lady," an older man wearing a red windbreaker with the words "Fire Marshal" in black across the chest said. "But did you listen? No. You thought you knew better than I did and look what happened. Your mother could have been badly burned or killed, and it would have been all your fault."

Fig waited for Roxie to put the condescending windbag in his place. But she sat in the back of the ambulance, her feet dangling, looking utterly devastated.

"Hold on there." Fig jumped to her defense. "If, in your professional opinion, this house was a fire hazard and Roxie and her mom were in imminent danger, then it was your duty to enforce whatever fire codes you have in this town and evacuate the premises. Any less speaks of negligence on your part which makes this situation your fault, not Roxie's."

"I recommended she leave," the old man said, losing some of his initial bluster.

"You gave me two weeks to clean it up," Roxie spoke.

Clean up what? Fig wondered.

"More than half that time has elapsed and it looks as if you haven't done a blessed thing."

She lowered her head.

"This isn't helping," Fig pointed out. "Do you know what started the fire?"

"We can't be sure until our investigation is complete. And all the junk inside the house is hindering our efforts." He turned to Roxie. "I don't know how you could live in those deplorable conditions."

Deplorable conditions? Fig wondered. Roxie looked over his shoulder, her expression one of mortification. "*Ay Dios mio!* Do they have to do that?"

Fig turned to see firemen dragging piles of stuff and bulging garbage bags out of the house, dumping them on the front lawn.

"We can't take a chance any smoldering ash will reignite," the fire marshal said. "And my men need room to move around in there."

Roxie closed her eyes. "I want to go to the hospital to see *Mami*."

"You're going to the hospital to get yourself checked out," Fig insisted, tired of arguing with her.

"I don't need…" More coughing.

"She's ready to go," Fig called to the paramedic.

The fire marshal handed Roxie a paper. "I warned you if I didn't see a noticeable improvement I'd take action. As of this minute you are officially ordered to vacate the premises."

"Great timing," Fig said to the old man. "I bet you'd recommend she up her fire insurance coverage right about now, too, huh?"

He turned in a huff and left.

"What about my things?" Roxie called after him. "And *Mami*'s things?"

"We'll worry about that in the morning," Fig said. "I'll meet you at the hospital."

Fig glanced at the passenger seat, where a subdued Roxie reclined. He had so many questions about the condition of her house, the bags and piles of what looked like trash that firefighter after firefighter had carried into her front yard. Whose were they, and why were they inside the house? It was beyond belief, the polar opposite of his neat, orderly, obsessively clean existence.

He pushed the sight out of his mind. It didn't matter. Regardless of her situation at home, tonight she was a friend in need of a place to stay.

"You can drop me at a motel," she said sullenly, facing away from him.

"I didn't convince you to leave your mom in the capable hands of the CCU staff so I could drop you at a motel. You're coming home with me."

"*Now* you'll bring me to your place?"

He smiled, relieved she sounded a bit more like the spunky woman he was growing to like a little more each minute he spent with her. Until she added, "Right. I get it. You wanted me sober. Well, tough luck. I'm not in the mood."

"So the only reason I would bring you home with me is for sex? I couldn't possibly have the least bit of compassion for a woman left homeless by fire, for a friend who's worried about her mother? I couldn't possibly be a decent enough guy to think maybe after the night you've had you wouldn't want to be left alone in an impersonal motel room? Thanks for the compliment."

"I don't even have a change of clothes," she muttered in reply.

"I can put up with you walking around naked. I'll even join in if it makes you feel more comfortable." He watched for her response.

She turned to face him and graced him with her first smile since their argument in his car. "Opportunist."

He smiled back. "If I have to, I'm sure I can rustle you up a clean T-shirt and boxer shorts."

"Thanks," she said.

"For you? Anytime."

"Only for me?" she asked, her voice teasing. "'Cause you kind of come off like a rescues-damsels-in-distress kind of guy."

Not really, more because he didn't get out all that much than he minded doing it. "We're here." Fig pulled into the parking lot and parked in Kyle's spot.

Up in the condo, Roxie collapsed on the old sofa. "I stink like smoke. But I'm too tired to shower."

It was fast approaching five in the morning. Fig was exhausted, too. "I'll help you." Fig held out his hand. "Come."

"If only it were that easy," Roxie quipped.

"Woman, you have sex on the brain."

"It's an affliction." She placed her hand in his, and he pulled her up. "Brought on by drunkenness."

"But you're not drunk now," Fig pointed out, moving to stand in front of her, as close as he could without touching her. The room heated. Or maybe it was just him.

"No." She swallowed, but maintained eye contact. "I most definitely am not drunk now."

Fig eased his fingertips up the side of her neck, slowly, stopping to cup the area just below her ear. "So what do you think is causing it?"

She leaned into his touch and closed her eyes. "This wanting a guy—without an alcohol inducement—is new territory for me," she admitted.

Good. Fig liked to explore new territory. "Come," he said quietly. "I'll get you set up for your shower."

She covered his hand with hers. "Will you join me?" she asked.

God help him, he wanted to. But, "Not tonight." She'd been through too much, may not be thinking clearly.

"But I…"

He covered her lips with his index finger. "Shhh. I'm trying to do the right thing here." He could remember only one other time when doing the right thing was this difficult.

Based on the appearance of her home, when Roxie exited the bathroom, Fig expected to find it trashed. Instead what he found surprised him. If he wasn't mistaken, she'd left it cleaner than when she'd entered. There was not one hair in the tub, sink or on the floor. And with her head full of thick curls it defied logic to chalk it up to pure coincidence. The mirror and counter and even the tub looked like she'd toweled them dry.

Why did she pay such close attention to the cleanliness of his home and so little to her own?

As the tepid water sluiced down his body, Fig half hoped Roxie was only pretending to be asleep when he'd checked on her and that she'd join him. He'd done the right thing in turning her away. But if she persisted—and he'd left the door unlocked, hoping she would—he'd take what she offered—he was, after all, only human—and give her triple the pleasure in return. Because he wanted to lose himself in her as much as she wanted to lose herself in him.

To his overwhelming disappointment, he began and ended his shower alone.

After toweling off Fig peeked into Kyle's bedroom again to find Roxie still asleep, her beautiful face peaceful, her lovely body resting uncovered on top of the comforter. The pull to join her on the bed, to cuddle in behind her and hold her through the night, was strong. He fought it, and in an act of willpower akin to walking away from a genie offering three life-changing wishes, Fig headed for the couch.

The somewhat stinky couch with a rogue spring that made sleep impossible, as it turned out. Which was why he was awake when Roxie padded to the kitchen, quietly took a glass from the cabinet and filled it with tap water.

"You okay?" he asked, sitting up to look at her over the back of the couch. She had an exotic beauty her wild hair and men's underclothes couldn't diminish.

"Sorry," Roxie said. "I tried not to wake you. Bad dream."

"You want to talk about it?"

"Not really. I'd rather forget about it." She pulled out a chair and sat at the table.

Fig joined her.

"I never thanked you for taking down my video." She took a sip of water.

He'd done a lot more than that. "Who told you?"

"Victoria." She smiled. "Boy, did you tick her off."

Because, while he'd deleted "Roxie Loves Coxie" from four pornographic websites, he'd left the links and attached something that would make people in this town think twice before they tried to exploit one of their own again.

"I have to say I'm touched. No one has ever spread a malicious virus on my behalf before. Malicious gossip, yes. But a computer virus? Never. Did you see the line at Frankie's Computer Fix yesterday?" She smiled again. He loved her smile, sometimes teasing, sometimes flirty, sometimes happy and fun. All the time exquisitely beautiful in the way it lit up her face.

Inconvenience them. Teach them a lesson. It's what he'd intended. "Failing to consider that employees at the hospital might try to access your video while on duty was an oversight."

"That locked up computers in the lab, Radiology and Engineering." She laughed.

On which he'd spent hours of his day yesterday working with the hospital's IT department to correct.

"I especially liked the hot-pink-and-black flashing 'Pervert' that filled the screens of the affected computers. Nice touch."

Fig crossed his arm over his midsection and bowed. "I aim to please."

Roxie stilled.

They sat in a charged silence, staring at each other until Fig asked, "You hungry?" just to get the conversation started again.

Roxie placed her elbows on the table and said, "Depends

on what you're offering." She slapped her hand over her mouth. "What is wrong with me?"

"Simple human attraction. You want me," he added with a big, satisfied smile. And he wanted her right back, the proof—presently tenting his boxer shorts—impossible to hide.

"So," Roxie said, not denying it as she stood. "What do you think I should do about this attraction?"

Lick me... Ride me. "Whatever you'd like." Fig aimed for aloof. But leaned back in his chair and opened his legs, inviting her in.

She RSVP'd in the affirmative by kneeling at his feet, reaching between his thighs and cupping him. "How are the boys?"

Fine. "In need of a little attention."

"Can I tell you how sorry I am…"

"I'd rather you show me."

She met his eyes then lowered her head. And kissed him—right where he most wanted to be kissed. "My, my," she said, setting him free. "You are not at all a figlet, are you?"

No, he wasn't. "And you owe me…" he prompted her.

She looked up at him, her eyes twinkling with laughter. "A *huge,* and I mean *huge,* apology."

Without further hesitation—thank you, thank you, thank you—she slid her mouth onto him and took him deep.

"Apology accepted," he choked out, barely capable of speech at the feel of every millimeter of his aroused flesh tightly encased in Roxie's luxurious silkiness. She released him. Then swallowed him down again, and again and again in rapid succession.

"My God." She wasn't kidding when she'd touted her skill. Or maybe he'd gone too long without, avoiding the challenges of having a woman in his life, even short-term. Either way, another couple of moves like that one and he'd be finished for the night. He plowed his fingers into her hair, gently guiding her, slowing her, taking back control.

Roxie did not relinquish it easily. "That's it," he said, lifting her head, holding her firm when she tried to go back for more. "It's my turn." And to do it the way he wanted to, Fig needed her in his bed. Naked. "Come on." He leaned forward, scooped her up and carried her toward the bedroom.

"Big *and* strong," Roxie said, wrapping her arms around his neck. "Maybe my luck is finally changing."

"Baby," Fig said, then kissed her neck. "In about half an hour you're going to feel like the luckiest woman in the world."

Roxie hoped he meant it. Fig certainly had length and girth in his favor. Whether he knew how to use them remained to be seen. He placed her on the bed. Calm. Unhurried. Time to pick up the pace. Roxie grabbed the hem of his navy tee, planning to whip it over his head.

He stopped her. "I'd rather you didn't."

"I want to see you," she said. "Feel your skin next to mine."

"When it's dark."

The early-morning sun was already peeking through the curtains. "Then I won't be able to see you, will I?" Roxie asked.

"Exactly." He smiled and eased his weight on top of her, moved his mouth to her ear and said, "You smell so good."

"Why?" she asked in reference to why he wouldn't allow her to remove his shirt.

"It must be your natural scent. Because I used the same soap as you, and I don't smell near as scrumptious."

"I meant…"

"I know what you meant." He shimmied down her body. "You have the most amazing breasts." He cupped one and, while fondling its nipple, sucked on the tip of her other breast through her T-shirt. At the sheer pleasure of it, Roxie decided to let her request to see his chest drop. For now. When he lifted her shirt over her head, she didn't argue. When he slid the boxer shorts he'd loaned her down her legs, she welcomed the cool air on her heated skin, welcomed his slow, confident touch.

"You're bare, too," he said in awe and brushed his fingers across her mons.

Too? The image she conjured excited her. Would he let her see? In her momentary distraction, Roxie wasn't aware Fig had opened her thighs and maneuvered himself between them. Until he kissed her. There. And rubbed his soft lips along hers.

"Lift your legs," he instructed.

She did, opening for him, eagerly awaiting his next touch.

"Like this." He closed them and turned her on her side. How did he plan to…?

Whack.

His hand connected with her backside. Hard.

"What the heck…?" She certainly hadn't expected that.

Whack.

He spanked her again.

Why was he holding her down? Did he think she wouldn't like it? Was he planning to do more than a little spanking? She tried to wiggle free, wanted to discuss boundaries.

Whack.

It felt so good.

"Don't you ever knee me in the groin again," he said.

What? He was disciplining her for real? She almost laughed.

Whack.

"And if I do?" she challenged. Hoping for more.

Whack.

Yessssssss!

"I'll do a lot worse than a few smacks on the behind." An excited tingle spread from her invigorated right butt cheek to her core. She trembled.

He noticed. "Damn it, Roxie." He removed the hand holding her down. "You're enjoying this, aren't you?"

She smiled but didn't let him see. "Please, sir. May I have another?"

"Well, that takes all the fun out of trying to teach you a lesson," he said.

"Maybe for you."

"Time for plan B," he said, spreading her thighs and settling himself between them once again.

"What might plan B entail?" Roxie asked, hoping she'd enjoy it as much as plan A, liking Fig's attempt to control her in the bedroom. *Attempt* being the operative word. Since the age of sixteen, no male had ever mastered Roxie. And no man would.

"I'm going to make you beg," Fig said.

Not likely.

"I'm going to drive you so wild with lust you'll do anything, promise me anything to let you come."

"*Let* me?" He had to be kidding.

He licked up the seam of her sex until he reached it, the epicenter of her sexual being. And he set to work. Like he'd read her instruction manual from cover to cover, he did everything right, ultimately robbing her of her capacity for speech. And since she'd started enjoying sex, Roxie couldn't remember that ever happening before. All she had to do was think it—harder—to the right—faster—deeper—don't stop—and he obeyed. They were of one mind. In sync. Absolute perfection. Her breathing heavy, she rocked beneath the onslaught. So close. Almost there. Ready, oh, so ready to explode. To release every bit of frustration with her mother, guilt over the fire and fear for the future.

Then the connection broke.

"Don't stop," she commanded, gripping his head in her hands, trying to steer him. "Higher." She could feel it building. Could taste it and smell it. "Please."

"I told you I'd make you beg."

Damn him.

He flicked his tongue in rapid little strokes. Side to side. Oh, yes! He exhaled, his breath heating her. The sensation grew again. This was it. Roxie braced herself. Ready. Finally.

He stopped.

"Say it," he said.

As if she had any clue what the heck he was talking about. "More licking. Less talking." She wanted action, not dissertation.

"I won't ever kick, knee, squeeze or touch, with intent to do harm, Fig's boys, as you call them," he said, holding perfectly still about six inches away from where he should be using his lips and tongue for far more important things than talking.

Roxie couldn't wait. Needed more. Now. She reached down between her legs to take care of herself.

"I don't think so," Fig said. Balancing on one elbow, he took both her wrists in one hand and stopped her.

"Your danglers are safe. Okay?" Roxie panted. "From

this moment forward, the only reason I will ever touch them is to worship them and slather them with my affection. Now back to work."

He chuckled.

"Pleeaassee." Roxie did, in fact, beg.

Fig did not make her wait. Good man. Super-terrific-talented man. And just so he could enjoy himself, too, Roxie wrapped her legs around his head. Just like he'd wanted.

"You are an oral sex phenomenon," Roxie said, lying on her back, her body limp, still tingling from the after-effects of the fiercest orgasms—yes, as in plural—of recent memory. Maybe ever.

"We're not done," Fig, who lay beside her, caressing her and, although she didn't think it possible so soon, arousing her all over again, whispered seductively. "I am nowhere near done with you." His tongue traced the inner rim of her ear.

"What's your fancy?" Roxie asked. "Top. Bottom. Standing. Sitting. Dressed. Undressed."

Fig rolled on top of her, his arousal hard and heavy. He lifted his shirt and pressed his naked chest to hers. Smooth and muscled. So good.

"Me likey." Roxie massaged the bare skin of his back while holding him close. "Kiss me," she said, wanting to taste him, to experience his luscious mouth in a new way.

He kissed her ear and the enchanting cove beneath it. He moved on to her neck and chin. He hesitated.

"Kiss me." She lifted her head to meet him halfway… and her lips connected with his cheek. Why?

Fig didn't give her time to ponder. He slid his hand between her legs and plunged his fingers inside of her. Shallow at first. Then deeper. Over and over. Each time the heel of his hand rubbed and teased and increased her stimulation exponentially. An accomplished multitasker, he used his mouth to lavish attention on her breasts.

Roxie's mind went blank. Again. Her only thought. More. "I need more," she said, rocking her hips, meeting each of his thrusts. "You." She thrust one last glorious time. "Inside." She pulled him on top of her. "Me." She tugged at his boxers. He lifted. She yanked them down.

His bare flesh met hers.

She let out a breath. "You feel so good."

"So do you." He went up on his arms, looked down at her, and rubbed her sex with the length of his, in long, lazy strokes. All too soon he rolled off of her.

"No." She made a grab for him.

"Patience, my sweet."

Aroused and wanting, the word *patience* did not exist in her vocabulary at the moment.

He reached for a condom from a drawer beside the bed and held it out to Roxie. "Care to do the honors?"

Heck yeah. She took it. "You mean they make them this big?" she asked. Because, hello, Fig had a package every man of her intimate acquaintance would envy and any woman who swung toward heterosexual would kill to have inside her. Roxie opened the wrapper and tossed it to the floor.

He smiled. "I have to special-order them."

He sounded serious, but mischief danced in his eyes.

"But do you know how to wield such a fine instrument?" She rolled the condom into place, praying he did.

"Why don't you tell me?" With a jerk of his hips, he rested at her entrance. "You ready?" He dipped inside. A sample. A tease.

So ready. Like she'd been waiting for this moment—for him—all her life. "Impress me," she challenged.

Boy, oh, boy, did he. Fig didn't rush, his style more finesse than frenzy. Thorough and thoughtful. It worked. He watched her as he slid in and out of her body. Intense. Controlled. Like her satisfaction mattered. Like she mattered.

And, well what d'ya know? Roxie—a "sprint to the finish so we can do it again" kind of gal—relished each slow, sensual stroke. He kept her on the sublime edge, an optimum place to languish.

Then she saw it. A hitch in his facade. He thrust deep and closed his eyes. Stiffened, but not in orgasm. More like trying to regain charge of himself. Sweet man.

"Don't hold back," Roxie said, clamping her legs around his butt, locking him to her and setting a pounding pace. "I'm there. I'm ready."

Fig let out a breath, collapsed on top of her and buried his head in the side of her neck.

"Let yourself go," she said, in between panting breaths.

"My God," he said, reverence in his tone. "You are amazing."

Roxie liked the sound of that.

"I don't want to hurt you," he said.

"You can't." At least not as a result of sex. But she was growing to like him. A little too much. And with that came the probability he'd hurt her at some point. If she gave him a chance. But she wouldn't think of that now. Not while he filled her so completely and held her like he never wanted to let her go.

"I can't stop," Fig said. "I'm going to…"

"Me, too," Roxie answered. And she did. Again. But this time, it was so much better, the experience so much more powerful, because Fig accompanied her, his heated breath coming in spurts and moans against her neck, his body rigid and twitching, a comforting weight on top of her.

She felt a connection that transcended sex.

He didn't roll off of her when he was done. He didn't say something crass like, "You are one hell of a lay, Ronnie." "That's Roxie." "Sorry, honey." He didn't head for the bathroom and return carrying her clothes. He didn't offer to call her a cab or stretch and tell her how early he had to get up in the morning.

He simply lay there, nestled within her, twirling his fingers in her hair.

After a while he said, "I don't want to move. Ever."

Neither did Roxie. "No reason to." She cuddled him close. Perfectly content.

"I must be crushing you."

"I'm made of sturdy stuff." At least on the outside. Inside? Not so much.

Roxie's cell phone rang from the kitchen. She didn't want to answer, didn't want to deal with Johnny or the hospital. But it could be *Mami*. Was it too much to ask for a few minutes to enjoy some postcoital bliss? For a few peaceful, undisturbed minutes where the outside world, her problems and responsibilities didn't intrude? "I, uh, need…"

Fig lifted off of her and rolled to the side. "Go."

Roxie ran to the kitchen. "Hello," she said into the phone without looking at the display.

"Where are you?" Victoria asked, sounding frantic. "Why didn't you call me?"

"Everything happened so fast. Then it was too late."

"I am always there for you," Victoria said quietly. "No matter the time. We're friends."

Maybe Roxie didn't want her "friend" witnessing yet another of her screwups. "Fig was with me."

Victoria said nothing.

"How did you find out?" Roxie asked.

"Haven't you seen the newspaper?"

"*¡Coño!*" Roxie closed her eyes and leaned against the wall. Now everyone would know. "It happened at midnight. How did it make the paper?"

"I don't know but there are pictures." She paused as if considering what to say next. She settled on, "And an interview with the fire marshal. Roxie, I had no idea. What can I do to help?"

"There's nothing you can do. Nothing anyone can do. I've got to go."

"Wait," Victoria said. "I visited your mom. It occurred to me in all the years I've known you, I've never met her."

Because *Mami* didn't like strangers and rarely left the house except to go to the doctor or church. "How is she?" Roxie asked, feeling guilty that while she was enjoying herself with Fig, her mother was lying alone in a hospital bed.

"She's stable. No reports of chest pain through the night. But she's hypertensive and anxious. She's asking for you."

"I'll get there as soon as I can."

"She wants you to bring her glasses," Victoria said. "She said you keep a spare pair in your room."

Because *Mami* kept misplacing her pair in the mess. "I will." Roxie hesitated. "Thanks." And she disconnected the call.

"Everything okay?" Fig asked, handing her a navy bathrobe.

"*Mami*'s asking for me. I've got to go. Would you drop me at my house so I can pick up my car?" And sneak in to get some clothes and *Mami*'s glasses.

Fig offered her another tee and a pair of sweatpants. They left five minutes later.

What Roxie saw when Fig pulled up to park across the street from her house was reminiscent of the newsfeed from coverage of a natural disaster. Debris littered her yard to the point there was barely any visible grass. Bags and boxes and piles of *Mami*'s "treasures" in all their broken, stained, waterlogged splendor tossed out for all to see. And there were plenty of lookers, their faces a mix of awe and revulsion.

Roxie hung her head. She should have done more, pushed harder, been more assertive in getting *Mami* to accept therapy—even though she'd made it clear she did not want or need it. Roxie should have snuck out to a Dumpster under cover of darkness and gotten rid of the bags as fast as *Mami* took them in. But even though it didn't look like *Mami* could possibly know what she had and where, she did. And when she wanted something in particular, she went looking for it. Heaven help Roxie if she didn't find it.

No one but a daughter forced to assume the caregiver role of her mentally ill mother could possibly understand the delicate balance necessary to keep the peace or how truly difficult it was to assert any type of authority over the woman who raised you. Over the years, during many a heated argument, *Mami* had threatened to kick Roxie out of "her" house.

Then who would have taken care of her? So Roxie'd resigned herself to doing the little *Mami* allowed her. It wasn't near enough.

Fig put his hand on her thigh. "I'll come in with you."

"No. I don't need you to come with me," Roxie said, taking a deep breath and bolstering up her courage. She opened the car door and climbed out.

Fig did the same. "I want to."

"You one of those gawkers who can't stay away from a catastrophe?"

He ignored her and simply walked around the car to stand next to her. "There's the fire marshal," he pointed out.

"Oh goodie. One of my favorite people." *Favorite* as in top-five people she'd love to go a few rounds with in a no-holds-barred matchup.

"I'm going to talk to him." Fig took her hand and led her across the street.

At the edge of the driveway Roxie removed her hand from his. "I'll wait here." As soon as Fig had the fire marshal distracted, she slipped into the house, not wanting him to see the magnitude of her mother's hoarding or to know the extent of Roxie's failure to get control of the situation, failure as a daughter responsible for the care of her mother.

Despite the open windows, the pungent smell of smoke and char lingered. All the clutter from the entryway, kitchen and hallway was gone. Just like that. Simply and easily removed. While she'd spent years unsuccessfully trying to coax *Mami* to allow her to do it.

It felt odd to see the expanse of linoleum, had been years since she could walk through her house unencumbered. Roxie refused to look at the kitchen, the focal point of the blaze. She didn't want to know the extent of the damage. Not yet. Instead she walked down the hallway without having to turn to the side to squeeze past the two dollhouses and piles of towels and children's books that'd been stacked hip high prior to the fire. *Mami*'s room looked the same. Untouched. Horrific. Shameful.

"It's hard to believe she actually lives in there," Fig said, standing close, looking over her shoulder.

"I asked you not to come with me. Do I need to call Victoria to have *her* ask you in order for you to listen?"

"By my recollection, you didn't ask, you ordered. I don't

respond well to being told what to do," Fig said. "Where do *you* sleep?"

Since she needed to get *Mami*'s glasses and change her clothes anyway, Roxie slid past him, took the key from her pocket and unlocked her door.

"You have a dead bolt on your bedroom door?" he asked. Incredulous.

The lock was the only reason her room remained immaculate, exactly the way she'd left it.

"I'm trying to understand," Fig said, his words tight, "how you can let a house get this overrun with…stuff without making any attempt to clean it."

Without making an attempt to clean it? Roxie went rigid. She cleaned it every single day. The bathroom and the kitchen, the pathways and hallway. She argued with *Mami*, every single day, to get her to part with her things, to let Roxie sort through the piles and throw away what wasn't worth saving. But *Mami* would cry and yell and clutch her heart. No one could possibly understand how hard she'd tried, day after day, year after year, to clean this house that had become the absolute bane of her existence.

"And how a daughter can allow her mother to live in such filth while she lives in this beautiful room," he added.

"*Allow?* You think I *allow* my mother to live in filth? That I have any control over what she does and how she lives?"

"The fire marshal said he's seen this before. He knows of a therapist." He held a business card out to Roxie. "Maybe she can help."

"*Me?* You think *I* need therapy? My God." This was not to be believed. "You think this mess is *my* doing? You think *I'm* the hoarder? That I'm the reason we live like this? Get out," she screamed. "Get the hell out of my house."

CHAPTER FIVE

THE fire marshal had painted a grim picture of Roxie, using words like *neglect, abuse* and *Adult Protective Services.* Fig refused to believe the jaded man's claims. Roxie was too kind and caring. But people never suspected his mother was capable of what she'd done, either. So for a few seconds, when Fig experienced the sharp contrast of Roxie's beautiful room in relation to the rest of the house, Fig allowed doubt to creep in, considered the possibility maybe he'd misjudged her. Unchecked, an accompanying rage at a person in power mistreating someone dependent upon them overtook his good sense and he'd lashed out.

But the look in her eyes confirmed what he should have known.

He'd made a terrible mistake.

Beyond her anger he saw hurt and disappointment, a deep sadness, and if Fig wasn't mistaken, there was a bit of hysteria there, too. Good thing they weren't standing in the kitchen, where death by—insert sharp object here—would have been a distinct possibility. "Calm down," he said, using his most placating tone. "I didn't mean…"

"You want calm?" Roxie yelled, slamming open her closet door to expose two rows of neatly hung clothing on equally spaced hangers. Pants with the pants. Shirts with the shirts. All sorted by color. "Well, you're not going to find it here," she continued. "You won't find anything here because this house is an abso-frigging-lute disaster area." She yanked a pair of pants off of a hanger. "And of course this mess is all *my* fault because *I'm* a hoarder. The fire marshal thinks it. You think it. After the article in the newspaper—which I have yet to see for myself—I bet the entire town thinks it." She bent down to pick up a pair of bright orange flip-flops from the neat rows of shoes on the closet floor. Sneakers with sneakers. Sandals with sandals. And so on.

"I didn't say…"

"You want calm?" she screamed again. "Then stay away from me because I am chock-full of crazy." She pulled on a drawer so hard it flew out of the dresser. She dumped its contents on the bed, sorted through what turned out to be dozens of pairs of skimpy panties and plucked out a zebra-striped thong.

Then, right there in front of him, she pushed down the sweatpants and boxers he'd loaned her, stepped out and handed them to him.

"I'm a loon. A hoarder. I live like this because I like it. I neglect and abuse my mother. Because that's just the type of low-life, uncaring daughter I am." She untangled her thong then jammed one foot followed by the other into the leg openings. "Oh," she added. "Let us not forget—" she yanked up the panties "—I'm a porn star. And a drug dealer. Come on, Fig. What else? What other terrible things can we come up with?"

Her upset seared the outer walls of his heart. But at the same time he knew Roxie needed this release, this chance to purge the bad. She'd feel better when it was over. How he'd fare remained to be seen.

She pulled on her pants. "Slut. Alcoholic." Tears streamed down her cheeks. "Illegitimate—because my *papi* denies I'm his. And why the hell are you still here?" she yelled. "Oh." She whipped the T-shirt she'd borrowed over her head and threw it at him. "You have your clothes. Now go."

She had beautiful, smooth, tan skin and pert, rounded breasts. The inner curve of the left one bore his love bite. He smiled at the memory of putting it there.

"What's so funny? You enjoying the show?" She hauled out another drawer and dumped its contents on the bed. Bras this time. In an impressive array of colors and patterns. She sorted through until she found the one that matched the panties and slipped it on.

"I hate this house." She snapped an orange-and-white-striped shirt off of a hanger. "I hate this town." She pulled it over her head. "And I hate you." She glared at him.

"I'm sorry…" Fig tried.

"Agreed." She moved to the mirror and ran a pick through her hair. "Now take your sorry self someplace else."

"Roxie, I shouldn't have…" he added.

"I shouldn't have, either." She ran an eyeliner pencil under each eye and applied some clear lip gloss. "But I've learned my lesson." She grabbed a pair of eyeglasses and a set of keys from the top of her dresser and stepped toward the door.

Fig stopped her. "Wait." She stood defiant, looking away from him. "I didn't say you were a hoarder," he said calmly. "I don't believe you're a slut or an alcoholic or an abusive/neglectful daughter. And I know you're not a drug dealer or a porn star."

He noted the tiniest hint of softening in her posture.

"I didn't say you need therapy, but from the condition of this house, someone does. I was only trying to help."

"The last thing I need is some judgmental, do-gooder

pity. I don't need or want your help. And I don't need or want you." She pulled away and darted for the door. "Goodbye, Fig."

"Roxie. Wait," Fig called out and went after her.

She halted.

Not because he'd called her.

She stood completely still, staring into the charred remains of her kitchen. The entire room would need to be gutted and rebuilt.

Fig walked up beside her.

"I wish this house and everything in it had burned to the ground last night," she said quietly.

"Maybe, while your mom's in the hospital, we can bring in Dumpsters and get rid of everything," Fig suggested.

She glared at him. "If it was as easy as bringing in Dumpsters and throwing everything out, don't you think I'd have done that by now? You really don't think much of me, do you?" She turned toward the door.

Fig reached for her arm. Again. "Please," he said. "Help me to understand. When did it start? How did it get this bad?"

Roxie let out a breath and looked down at the floor. "Apparently it started after *Mami*'s husband—my alleged *papi*—left her, before I was born. She refused to get rid of his stuff and continued to buy him clothes and presents, anticipating his return. Growing up, it was like he still lived here. His slippers rested on the floor in front of his recliner—" she pointed into the mounds of junk in the far corner of what may have been a family room at one time "—which is over there somewhere." She laughed. "For all I know they're probably still there." She paused. "His favorite coffee mug—from the manufacturer of his favorite bowling ball—sat next to the coffeepot. His winter coat hung in the closet. Come to think of it, that's probably still there, too."

"She was trying to hold on to her life before he'd left," Fig surmised.

"She paid more attention to the past than she did to the present. Which is why my brothers got out of here first chance they got."

"Leaving you behind."

She nodded. "Then *Mami* started doing the same for each of them. Buying things—with money she didn't have—in an attempt to entice them home to visit."

Which was why Roxie wound up sleeping with a grocer for food. Fig's initial reaction was the woman needed some sense pounded into her. But he knew, from experience, the complex challenge of dealing with a mentally ill mother.

"When she'd spent down all her savings and the money she'd gotten from refinancing the mortgage on the house, she started asking for donations of clothing, housewares and children's toys from the church."

"How old were you when your brothers left home?"

"The youngest one moved out when I was ten. That's when stuff really started to pile up. I tried—" she sniffed "—to stop her. To throw things out. But I was a kid and she can get mean and aggressive."

Fig put his arm around her shoulders and directed her back to her bedroom, the only place clean enough for them to sit down. "Tell me why the fire marshal thinks *you're* the hoarder."

Roxie shrugged. "When he came to the house after the first fire…"

"The first fire?"

Roxie nodded. "*Mami*'s been getting more forgetful. A week ago she burned her lunch, which is why I removed the knobs from the stove. It was more smoke than anything." She waved it off. "Anyway, *Mami* refused to speak to him. She wouldn't leave her room. She just sat there, looking down at her feet, fidgeting, rocking." She looked up at him. "She does that when she gets stressed. *Mami* doesn't like strangers in her home."

They entered Roxie's room.

"*Mami* started rubbing her chest in the way she does when her angina is coming on. I did what I had to do to get the men to leave. I took responsibility and said I'd clean out the house."

Roxie sat on her bed, lifted one of her drawers onto her lap and started to fill it with her bras. "He gave me two weeks."

Two weeks? It'd take at least a dozen people working day and night to clean out the house in two weeks. No wonder she'd been preoccupied at work. Fig sat next to her, lifted the other drawer onto his lap and said, "Let me help you."

Roxie smirked. "Can't pass up an opportunity to paw at my panties, can you?"

Fig smiled. "Guilty." He got to work. "Why do you stay?" he asked, knowing the answer.

Roxie shrugged. "She's my mom. She has her problems, but deep down I know she loves me. And I love her."

He understood completely.

"When I graduated high school I thought about leaving, like my brothers had. But then who would have shopped and cooked and cleaned up around here? I know it doesn't look like I do anything, but I keep the kitchen counter clear so I have room to prepare our meals. I keep the refrigerator clean and do the dishes. I maintain the paths so *Mami* doesn't trip and fall and I keep the clutter out of the bathroom. It takes a lot more time and effort than you'd think."

"I'm sure it does."

She looked at him askance. "She doesn't work. Hasn't worked since I got my first job at sixteen. Her health is deteriorating. What would happen to her if I left?"

She'd become a ward of the state, and they'd have to deal with her. But Roxie was too good a daughter to let that happen. "She's lucky to have you."

"Yeah. Yeah." Roxie downplayed her worth, stood and replaced her drawer in her dresser. Fig replaced the one beside it.

"So what happens now?" Fig asked.

Roxie held up a pair of glasses. "Now I go to the hospital to check on *Mami* and give her her glasses."

"I mean what are you going to do about the house and the mess outside? Oh, and I forgot to mention, the fire marshal said upon inspection this morning, the house is structurally sound. You can't return to live here, but you can come and go between the hours of nine and five as long as you don't use any electricity."

At least that was something.

"Where will you stay?" Fig asked. "Where will your mom stay when she's released from the hospital?"

"I'll work it out." She stood. Everything always worked out. Somehow. "No need to worry about me."

"You're welcome to stay at my place. I'll take the couch." But he'd rather not.

"What fun would that be?"

Thank you! "Or I could make myself available for stress relief after a long, hard day."

"Or at the start of one." She smiled back.

"Anytime," Fig clarified and meant it.

"What about right now? What if I were to say 'I want you now. Hard and fast and I'm in charge.' What then?"

Fig stood up, walked to the door, closed and locked

it. It'd be unrealistic to expect to control a woman with Roxie's passion every time. Part of focusing on the woman involved knowing when she needed to take the lead.

"Just like that?" Roxie asked. "I say I want sex, you drop your pants and we go at it?"

If that's what she needed. "I know how you feel, Roxie."

She laughed. "How could you possibly know how I'm feeling?"

"Because I've been there."

"Where exactly is *there?*"

"Living with a mother who cared more about herself and her needs than she did mine. Living the life she'd created for me rather than my own life. Feeling let down and angry and betrayed by my family. Feeling my life was going nowhere but too tired to fight for what I wanted."

After a few moments of silence, she said, "Which hits home the fact you know a lot more about me than I know about you. I want three questions, and you have to answer honestly."

"I'd rather you use me for sex."

She smiled playfully. "We can make them strip questions, you know, since the door's already locked."

All he'd have to do was answer three simple questions to get her naked. "Your bra and panties count as undergarments. That's one item of clothing."

"Fine. When we first met and I asked you out to dinner, why did you say you were dying of cancer?"

"Because my medical history usually freaks people out. But you looked like you could handle it. So I made a joke to see how you'd react."

"For the record, jokes are supposed to be funny. That wasn't. You'd do better with a different approach."

"You handled it just fine."

"Well, I'm not your typical woman, am I?"

No, she wasn't. "Is that your second question?" He smiled. "Because you need to take off your shirt before I'll answer another one."

"No, that's not my second question," she grumbled as she lifted her shirt over her head to expose her well-endowed, zebra-print-bra-covered breasts.

"Is your medical history the reason you're so pale and have no hair?"

"Childhood leukemia. In and out of remission. Radiation therapy. Chemotherapy. Bone-marrow transplantation resulting in permanent remission but accompanied by permanent alopecia—but I'd like to point out, freak that I am, I somehow retained my eyebrows and eyelashes." Both of which he bleached to a pale blond or they looked odd on his pigment-challenged face. "I'm pale because I grew up the boy in the proverbial bubble. I rarely went outside except to go to the doctor or the hospital. I developed indoor interests that I continue to enjoy as an adult."

Roxie looked sad. This time for him.

"None of that, sweetheart," he said, hating pity. "Now give up your pants."

She smiled as she stood. "Pushy, pushy." She shimmied out of her cargo pants. Lord help him, she had a beautiful body. Tall and slender yet rounded in all the right spots. A body he dreamed about and would no doubt continue to dream about long after he returned home.

He reached for her.

"Nuh, uh, uh." She wagged a finger between them. "I have one more question."

"Well, spit it out. You expect too much if you think me capable of sitting politely when you are looking so good and so naked and all I have to do is extend my arm this much to touch you." He poked her on the shoulder.

She reached behind her back, undid her bra and flung it at him. "To sweeten the pot."

"This last one must be a doozy." He eyed her breasts, imagined each one filling his palm. "Go ahead. I'm ready."

"Why wouldn't you take off your shirt for me this morning?"

Fig let out a breath and tried to think of a way to get out of answering. But the determined look on Roxie's face left no doubt if he didn't answer they would not be having sex. If he wanted Roxie, and, oh, did he want Roxie, he'd have to explain. Or he could simply go ahead and show her. Roxie was different. Maybe the sight of his torso wouldn't appall her like it had the few women he'd shared it with.

He reached for the bottom hem of his tee.

Roxie could not believe her eyes and, yes, could not stop her mouth from dropping open in surprise. "You're…" The words wouldn't come.

Fig stood there, staring back at her, looking vulnerable and so uncomfortable under her perusal.

"I have scars and…I'll put my shirt back on."

Roxie ripped it from his hands and tossed it over her shoulder. "From now on," she said, stepping close enough to touch him, "when we're together, I want you shirtless." She traced some of the outlines with her finger. "*You* are a thing of beauty, a colorful canvas to be ogled and appreciated, not hidden."

Brilliantly colored, professionally crafted tattoos, interwoven with scrolls on which motivational proverbs were expertly written, covered his chest and shoulders to the point they obliterated his pallor. Yet no hint of this amazing profusion of color extended past the short sleeves or neckline of his T-shirt. Which made her wonder, "Your legs?"

He nodded. "I needed some color."

Roxie dropped her hands to the button of his pants. "I am a huge fan of color." She had his pants down to his ankles in a matter of seconds. A realistic-looking python, surrounded by various shades of brilliant-green foliage, circled his left thigh. The tail of a fire-breathing red dragon, set against a mountain of rock, circled his right. Both tattoos ended just above his knee. "Why do you hide them?"

Fig shrugged. "Tattoo art is not an acceptable form of expression among my business associates, friends and family."

"Then you need to find some new people to hang around with." He was…beautiful and so different than he appeared at first sight.

"There's one more," Fig said, sounding hesitant. "On my back."

"Let me see. Let me see." Roxie rubbed her hands in anticipation.

He took his sweet time showing her. But when he did… Roxie sucked in a breath. Absolutely magnificent.

"It's a phoenix," Fig explained.

A beautifully drawn, intricately detailed phoenix rising up from flames. Reborn. The image filled Fig's back, the mythical bird's plumage inked in vibrant reds, oranges and golds. Its wings extended, spanning his shoulders.

"You're awful quiet." He turned his head to try to look at her. "I chose a phoenix because each time the doctors had thought I wouldn't make it, I pulled through, came back from the dead in a sense."

Roxie set her palms to his skin and caressed the bird. Felt something up by its beak. Stopped.

"I was in a car accident," Fig said. "I received over a hundred and seventeen stiches."

"I'm so sorry."

"Don't be." He turned to face her. "It's how I met Kyle. In rehab." He lifted her hand to his left upper chest. Another scar. "This one's from the portacath the doctors inserted for my chemo."

Roxie kissed it.

Her phone rang.

Not now. She dropped her forehead to his chest. He kissed the top of her head. "You'd better answer that," he said.

Most men would have told her not to answer it. But Fig understood. "I know. But I don't want to." They'd each shared a part of themselves. Things she hadn't shared with another person. And Roxie got the impression Fig didn't share his tattoos with many people, either. Yet he'd shared them with her. She felt so close to him right now and didn't want it to end. But the call could be from *Mami*. Roxie picked up the phone and checked the voice mail. *Mami* asked, "Where are you? What's taking so long? I can't see the TV up close without my glasses."

"I have to go," Roxie told Fig.

"I know," Fig answered, pulling up his pants.

"Tonight?" Roxie asked. She'd make this interruption up to him then.

"Most definitely."

After helping Roxie pack a small duffel and bag up some clothes to wash, Roxie let Fig drive her to the hospital. Yes, she could have driven herself. But then he wouldn't be holding her hand and she wouldn't be feeling so…happily content.

"If your mom wasn't in the picture," Fig said, "where would you be living? What would you be doing?"

"I stopped wishing for a different life years ago." She never understood people who wasted their time pining for a life they couldn't have. Better to accept the life you did have and make the best of it.

He squeezed her hand. "Humor me."

Okay. "Tightrope walker traveling with the circus. Roller Derby queen. Llama farmer."

"Come on, Roxie."

"All right. I'd still be a nurse because I love it. But I wouldn't live anywhere near Madrin Falls. This town holds very few happy memories for me." She looked over at him. "Although today increased the count by two."

He smiled. "I'm glad."

"I think I'd like to live someplace warm. In a condo by the beach. Where I could parade around in skimpy bathing suits and sip iced drinks beside a pool every day if I felt like it."

"I'd risk blistering sunburns to come and watch you parade around in those skimpy bathing suits."

"Well, I'd rub you from head to toe with SPF 50—" just like in her dream "—to protect your beautiful skin. And I'd invest in a huge beach umbrella." Wouldn't that be fun. The two of them. Hot days at the beach. Hotter nights. Together. Naked.

"Honey, you'd better let me apply my own sunscreen or we'll be spending more time indoors than out."

Fig veered onto the hospital drive and reality slammed back into the forefront. There was no condo, no beach and no iced drinks by the pool in Roxie's immediate future.

At the block of elevators in the lobby, Roxie pushed three for the CCU. Fig pushed five. Roxie looked up at him.

"I have an appointment," he said. "Do you want me to meet you over in CCU when I'm done? Or should I wait in the lobby?"

Who could he possibly have an appointment with on the

fifth floor? Victoria? She studied him, but he gave nothing away. Was there some meeting—that she apparently was not privy to—where her future at Madrin Memorial was to be decided? And if that were the case, why hadn't Fig told her?

"It's nothing important." He pulled her close and kissed the top of her head. "I'll miss you," he whispered.

Although it was hard to fathom, she felt a pang of loss at their separation, too.

"Hola, Mami." Roxie channeled good cheer as she entered the single-bedded room, noting the wires emerging from beneath her mother's hospital gown winding up to the cardiac monitor flashing on the wall. Heart rate eighty-two. Normal sinus rhythm. Good.

"I have no privacy here," *Mami* complained, motioning to the glass half of the wall overlooking the nurses' station. "I want to go home."

"According to your nurse, the doctor wants to keep you for at least another day so you can have a few more respiratory treatments." Which gave Roxie one more day to figure out what to do with *Mami* after discharge.

"I don't want to stay." She sat up, slid her legs over the side of the bed and started to push off. "Stop," Roxie said, rushing to the other side of the bed and holding *Mami* by the shoulders. "At the moment, our home is uninhabitable." The fire marshal had his scrawling signature on an official paper saying so.

"What does that mean?" *Mami* suddenly looked very old and weak in that big hospital bed.

"Lie back down." Roxie got her propped up on her pillows and tucked the covers around her. "It means we can't live in the house until we clean it enough that the fire marshal says it's not a safety hazard for you to live there." And until Roxie settled with the insurance company—who had deemed two fires in two weeks suspicious—so she could replace the kitchen.

"It's *my* house."

Technically it was Roxie's house since *Mami* signed it over to her when she'd turned eighteen—to keep her creditors from going after it.

"Where will we go?" *Mami* clutched her chest. Roxie detected an arrhythmic change in the blip of the cardiac monitor. "*Ay Dios mio*. What will happen to us? To all our things?"

"Calm down," Roxie said, caressing her thinning gray hair. "We are going to be fine. I'll take care of everything." Like she always did.

"It's already taken care of." Fig entered the room. "Victoria's offered to have your mom stay at her house."

What? "That's where you went? To talk to Victoria?" Fig nodded.

"Why didn't you tell me?"

"Because you would have told me not to."

He was right. Roxie didn't like imposing on her friends.

"Who are you?" *Mami* asked Fig.

"The name's Fig." He held out his hand. She took it. Hesitantly. "I'm a friend of Roxie's."

"You're so pale."

"*Mami!*"

"You need to eat some meat. I want to cook you a steak."

The woman in the bed looked like her mother, but that last comment had Roxie questioning her true identity. "You haven't cooked a steak in over ten years." Hadn't cooked much of anything besides macaroni and cheese, grilled cheese and canned soup.

"Because I haven't had a man around to cook for." So the daughter who took care of her day after day didn't rate a delicious steak dinner. Good to know.

"I'm sorry, but I don't eat meat, Mrs. Morano."

Come to think of it, she hadn't seen him eat much of anything.

"Which is why you're so pale," *Mami* said.

No, he wasn't. Not really. He was bright and colorful and she loved that he kept it secret from the world, yet shared it with her. "We were talking about Victoria."

"Is that the nice young lady who visited me this morning? A tiny thing with black hair?"

Roxie couldn't believe she remembered. "That's her."

"We can both stay there?"

"No," Fig answered. "I'm afraid she only has space for one. But you'll have your own room and television and there's a full bath just down the hall."

"I couldn't…" *Mami* started. "I want to stay with Roxie. Where will you be?" she asked.

Fig raised one of his bleached brows.

"With a friend," Roxie said, avoiding eye contact. *Mami* still preached the importance of Roxie remaining chaste for her future husband. Like any man in this town would marry her after the life she'd lived to date—and with her hoarding mother in tow. "She has a small place. Only one bedroom." At least that last part was true.

"She's very nice to take you into such cramped quarters," Fig commented with a smirk.

"More like desperate for company," Roxie said. "She's kind of an oddball. I actually feel a little sorry for her."

"You'd really be helping Victoria," Fig said, ignoring her last comment. "School's out and she could use some help keeping an eye on her son until summer camp starts, and if you're there long enough, maybe after camp."

Mami's face lit up. "How old is the boy?"

"Nine," Roxie answered. "But I don't think…" She wasn't well, mentally or physically.

"That's the same age as Angelo." One of the many grandchildren they'd seen only in Christmas card photos. "I'll do it," *Mami* said, looking happier than Roxie had seen her in years.

But still. "You're not up to babysitting." She could barely take care of herself.

"May I speak with you in private?" Fig asked.

What was he up to? Roxie followed him out into the hallway.

"Victoria wants to do this," he said, taking her hand. "She said when she visited your mother this morning she'd perked up at the mention of Jake—" Victoria's son "—and she thought if we could convince your mom she'll be helping out with Jake, it may sway her decision. Victoria assured me she will make sure both your mom and Jake are well supervised and safe."

Safe was good. "But she'd be taking Kyle's room." Since Victoria wouldn't let her fiancé sleep upstairs with her until they were officially married.

"Kyle loves the idea of giving up his room. And having you and me at his condo so Victoria has no choice but to welcome him in her bed."

"Did she agree to that?" Because it wasn't like her friend to stray from a plan.

"Not yet. But she will."

"You two are such schemers." Who had grossly underestimated Victoria's resolve.

"Kyle gets to sleep with Victoria. Your mom has a place to stay until we get the house cleaned out and fixed up. It's a win-win."

We. Roxie'd done so much on her own, for so long, was so tired… She almost collapsed against him at the word *we*.

"Come on. We need to talk to your mom about the house."

There it was again. *We.* Although, "I think we should wait. She's not strong enough."

"She looks strong enough to me. If I'm wrong, there are plenty of doctors and nurses who will swarm the room at the first sign of trouble."

"Maybe I should talk to her in private."

"Maybe having someone else in on the conversation will help."

It was worth a try. "But if it upsets her—" like Roxie anticipated it would "—we drop it."

"Let's play it by ear." Fig led her back into the room.

"*Mami,* we need to talk about what we're going to do with all the…stuff that's accumulated in the house over the years."

She clamped her lips together and glanced nervously at Fig.

"I think you're a truly special lady for working so hard to acquire things for your boys," Fig said. "But we need to find a way to get all the clothing and toys to them so they can put it to good use."

Mami relaxed. Roxie could have kissed Fig.

"My boys need to come home. So I can show them everything I have for them."

"I'll make a deal with you, Mrs. Morano. If you work with Roxie and me and a few of our friends to sort through all the items in your house and divide them into what goes to which son, I promise to get your boys to come and pick it all up personally."

Not "I promise to try" or "I promise to do my best," but "I promise to get your boys to come." As if Roxie hadn't been trying to do just that for years. What the heck made him think he'd succeed when she couldn't? Roxie swung from wanting to kiss him to wanting to snap his neck.

"May I speak with you outside?" Once there she turned on him. "What the heck were you thinking?"

"Trust me," he said.

"The words 'I promise' and 'trust me' coming out of a man's mouth don't mean a whole hell of a lot to me. But when you say 'I promise' to my mother, she'll believe you, and I won't stand by and see her hurt and disappointed when you can't deliver." Like she'd been all the times Roxie had thought her brothers would finally come through for *her* after they'd spewed their worthless "trust mes" and "I promises."

"Well, you can believe them when they come from me." Roxie started to say something but he cut her off. "I have a plan. I'm sure it will work."

CHAPTER SIX

AFTER they left the hospital, Fig made Roxie breakfast back at the condo. Then they took advantage of having her house to themselves to do some preliminary cleanup.

"I think there's a push broom in here somewhere," Roxie said, crawling across a mound of bulging plastic garbage bags into the far corner of what he'd learned was the family room.

Fig walked down the hall. "What's behind this door?" He tried the knob.

"No!" Roxie yelled. "Don't go in there."

But he'd already shouldered open a space large enough for him to stick his head inside. Unbelievable. Bags and boxes and loose…stuff were piled from floor to ceiling in every corner, chest high up to the window on the far wall, sloping down to thigh high around the door. Dust motes hung in the air, illuminated by the sunlight. Based on the dank smell and the layer of dust covering everything, that door hadn't been opened in years. He sneezed.

"Step away from that door," Roxie ordered, awkwardly trying to hurry to flat, stable ground.

"This door?" Fig pushed on it again in an attempt to create an opening big enough for him to squeeze through. When he succeeded, he slipped inside. As soon as he released his hold on it, under the weight of more bulging white garbage bags stuffed with clothes, the door promptly slammed behind him.

Roxie knocked. "Are you okay?"

"Afraid I was sucked inside by the monster behind the door?"

"Ha-ha. Open up."

"Easier said than done." He bent to lift some bags to toss them away to make room. Only, each time he moved one, something or things slid into its place. He sneezed again.

"Please tell me you're not allergic to dust," Roxie said through the door. "I told you to buy yourself a mask when we picked up the work gloves and cleaning supplies."

He hadn't wanted to insult her by wearing a mask in her home. The gloves, however—two pairs—were a necessity. A few minutes later he had enough of an area cleared to fully open the door.

Roxie walked in, her eyes wide. "Holy cow."

"How long has it been since you've been in here?"

"Seven years."

Fig climbed up on two stacks of old newspapers to survey the mess from a higher vantage point.

"Articles from Dad's bowling wins and the boys' sporting events," Roxy said.

He picked his way deeper into the room, climbed over an old red metal tricycle. Something tilted beneath him. He started to slide and caught hold of the head on a life-size plastic Santa to steady himself.

"Be careful," Roxie cautioned. "Where are you going?"

"To open the window to get some fresh air in here."

He climbed higher, slower, the piles more unstable. To the left he noticed a softball-sized hole in the corner where the ceiling met the outer wall. He pointed. "I think you may have something living in here." He scanned the room for movement, but seeing none he continued on.

"I'm going to get my broom," Roxie said. "Just in case," she called out from the hallway.

Fig came across some old *Playboy* magazines, and like any red-blooded heterosexual male, he paused to look through one.

"What's that?" Roxie asked.

He turned the magazine to the side and opened the centerfold. "Yowza!"

"What is it with men and nudie pictures? The sooner we get done, the sooner you can have the real thing. Now get crack-a-lackin'. We only have a few hours until we have to vacate the premises for the night."

With the incentive of having Roxie again, soon, Fig tossed the mag and made haste. Something on his right moved. A globe started to roll, revealing a... *"Raccooooon!"*

Fig backpedaled to avoid its vicious fangs, turned and ran.

Roxie started up the incline, her broom overhead. "Ee-yah," she yelled like some warrior cry to battle and half ran, half climbed toward him, whacking the broom in the vicinity of the vermin. His fierce protector.

Fig leaped over the tricycle, well, at least he tried to. Unfortunately his foot caught on something, and he came down hard on his right wrist. Damn, that hurt. He struggled to stand. Something gave way beneath him and he was going down again. This time backward, all the way to the carpet below. Oomph. On impact, all the air left his lungs. Papers and clothes and God only knew what else piled on top of him.

"Fig?" Roxie called out.

He couldn't answer.

"You'd better not be fooling around," Roxie threatened.

He moved something off his face and tried to suck in a breath.

"Holy crap," Roxie said. "I can see the headlines now. 'Man Smothered to Death in Hoarding House after Raccoon Attack.'"

With all the debris closing in around him, it felt like a distinct possibility. He tried to relax, to remain calm while he waited for his lungs to regain function.

A hand plowed through his covering and touched his face. "Nod if you're okay."

He did.

"Thank God. We've got to get you out of there. That raccoon may have friends or babies. There may be a whole network of tunnels down there."

Shoot. He hadn't thought of that. Fig forced in a breath and elbowed some space around him so he could move. If nothing else, the commotion should keep the critters away.

He felt Roxie lifting things off of him from above.

He moved something off his belly. Pain shot from his right wrist up his arm. Not good. "Oh. Look," he said, eyeing the object. "An old-style toy car garage. I used to have one of these." He'd played with it for hours at a time, loved that toy.

"You think you could focus on getting out of there? I refuse to take responsibility for you getting bitten by anything while you're reminiscing about your childhood."

Right. The raccoon.

Fig managed to sit up and pop his head out. Ahhhh. Fresh—well, fresher than down below—air.

"Hey, there, handsome," Roxie said with a smile.

She held out her hand to him.

He took it. With his right hand. Big mistake. Excruciating pain. "Ow. Ow. Ow. Let go."

"What's wrong?"

"I twisted my wrist. Nothing serious." He reached up with his other hand. She tugged and he stood.

"Let me see."

"It's nothing."

"Now."

He held out his wrist. It hung in an unnatural position. She cupped it gently. "This doesn't look good." She ran a finger—oh, so lightly—over a lump forming on his lower forearm just before his wrist. "I'm taking you to the hospital for an X-ray."

Fig stepped back. "Oh, no, you're not. It's not broken. I am not going to the emergency room." As a patient. Ever again. A cold chill washed over him.

"Oh, yes, you are," Roxie said. Determined. "Right after I figure out where that raccoon went."

She was a persistent pain in the patoot. Fig sat at the bottom of the stretcher, his jeans and sneakers still on, but a hospital gown replaced his T-shirt. At least she'd gotten him a small private room with a window to the outside.

"So tell me again why you ran?" she asked innocently.

"Because raccoons have rabies."

Roxie held up the realistic-looking stuffed animal that'd turned out to be the cause of his current predicament. "Only the live ones," she said with a smile.

"That thing was moving," he insisted.

"Only in your imagination."

"He looked up at me."

"With glass eyes." Roxie snickered. "Probably manufactured in China." She full out laughed.

"Go ahead. Get it all out. I'm glad you find this so amusing."

Roxie struggled to catch her breath. "Raccoooooon," she imitated him, tears leaking out of her eyes.

"Get out," Fig said but without heat because he didn't really want her to leave. She kept him occupied, so he didn't spend all his time thinking about the antiseptic hospital smell. The cool, functional room. The stretcher. The coarse sheets. And the feeling of pending incarceration that accompanied them.

"I'm sorry." Roxie walked to the counter by the sink and plucked two tissues from the box. "Really." She blotted the inner corner of each eye. "I'm sorry. It's just not every day someone I know fractures a bone trying to escape a stuffie." She turned away, her shoulders bouncing in silent laughter.

"Yes. Please. Let's focus on the outcome of this fiasco. Fractured right distal radius." He held up his damaged appendage. "In need of surgical repair. I'm right-hand dominant. I work on computers for a living." So what if he wasn't involved in any high-priority projects at the moment and he had enough money—thank you, Grandma Rose—that he didn't have to work another day in his life if he didn't want to? Having his right arm incapacitated was going to be a major inconvenience.

"Excuse me. Don't you go looking for sympathy now, Mr. It's-not-broken-I'm-not-going-to-the-emergency-room."

"See. This is why I didn't want to come. It's like taking the car to a mechanic. They always find something wrong."

"Hello. There is something wrong. You have a broken bone."

"I don't want to be here." He didn't want surgery, didn't

want Roxie to feel like she had to take care of him. He wanted to be taking care of her, helping to get her house in order.

"I know." She walked over to the stretcher and took his good hand in hers.

"So joke time is finally over?"

Roxie nodded. "But the next time I see a raccoon you can bet it'll start up all over again."

At least she wasn't looking at him with sympathy and fawning all over him.

"I can't wait."

Dr. Jared Padget, Roxie's friend and the E.R. doc on duty, entered the room. He pointed at the stuffed raccoon propped up on the over-the-bed table. "That the little guy who caused all this trouble?"

"Yeah. Wasn't it nice of Roxie to bring it to the hospital with us?" Fig asked, picking up the culprit with his left hand and lobbing it into the plastic trash container. Swish. Two points.

"Hey," Roxie said. "You're going to have to explain to *Mami* why her favorite stuffed raccoon's gone missing."

"She loves it so much she kept it locked in a room for seven years?"

"You may find it hard to believe she knows exactly what she has, but she does."

"I've got good news and bad news," Dr. Padget interjected. "Which do you want first?"

No bad news. Fig's skin started to prickle. His heart started to pound. This is how it happened. You go in for one thing and they find something else. Mass on the lung. Out-of-whack blood count. We need to admit him. The air felt too thick to reach his lungs.

"You okay?" Roxie asked, looking down at his hand with concern, which was when he realized he had such a tight grip on her, the tips of her fingers had turned a deep red.

He eased up but didn't release her. Couldn't. He swallowed. "Good news first, please."

"Dr. Rosen agreed to take you on," Dr. Padget said to Fig. "As a professional courtesy to Miz Roxie." He inclined his head in Roxie's direction. "You're scheduled for surgery at four-thirty this afternoon."

"Four-thirty?" Fig looked at his watch. "That's in three hours." What the heck was he supposed to do locked in this room for three more friggin' hours? "Please tell me I can leave and come back."

"We're not busy. It's easier if you sit tight and we'll send you up when the O.R. is ready for you."

"Easier for who?" He wanted to leave. To get in his car and drive as far as he could on whatever gas he had in the tank. Because filling up left-handed would be awkward. Damn. "Is that the bad news? That I'm stuck here?"

Dr. Padget glanced at Roxie. "Uh, no."

Great.

"Based on your mechanism of injury and your past medical history, I suspect, and Dr. Rosen concurs, that you may be suffering from some degree of osteoporosis as a long-term effect of your childhood cancer treatment."

Fig stiffened. Osteoporosis was an old-lady disease, wasn't it? Was he destined for a back hump like his grandmother? "What does that mean?"

"That you may, and we won't know for certain until we do a bone density test, have a decrease in skeletal bone mass that puts you at an increased risk for bone fractures. It would explain why a young, strong, seemingly healthy man sustained your severity of injury from a relatively minor fall."

"What does a bone density test entail?" Fig asked. Long,

thick needles, no doubt. He remembered them well. And pain. Lots of pain. Nausea threatened.

"A simple X-ray. Or more technically, a dual energy X-ray absorption or DEXA scan."

Fig exhaled.

Roxie squeezed his hand. "It doesn't have to be done today, right?" she asked.

"No," Dr. Padget said. "But soon. Depending on the test result, your primary doctor may want to start you on a combined medication and exercise regimen to slow down the bone loss and decrease your risk of additional fractures."

"I'll take care of it as soon as I get home."

When the door closed behind Dr. Padget, Roxie said, "Not a big fan of hospitals, are you?"

Fig shook his head. "I've spent way too much time in them over the years. You sure you can't slip me out for an hour or two? I need a shower. I feel all grungy." Caked with dust and scented with mildew. If nothing else, at least he could wash his hands. Fig stood and walked to the sink, reached for the handle. "Damn it." Pain stabbed through his right wrist and forearm.

"That's why Dr. P. doesn't want you out and about. Bang your wrist and you risk increasing the displacement of your fracture." Roxie shut off the water. "Let me get your nurse to give you some pain medication."

"No," he snapped. He would not take anything that would alter his cognitive function. *Roxie isn't your mother,* his rational self attempted to make him see reason. But so far Kyle was the only one who'd been able to earn Fig's trust. And that'd taken years.

"My, you're a cranky patient. Sit." She tried to guide him back to the stretcher.

He stood firm. "I'd rather stand." Tall and proud and

healthy. Not wounded and weak, or dependent and vulnerable. A victim.

"Give me a few minutes. I've got to run and get some things then I'll be back to get you all settled and you can relax until surgery."

Relax. Fat chance.

In Roxie's absence, Fig paced, holding his right elbow bent and his hand elevated or it started to throb. Three steps to the window. Pivot. Three steps to the door. Pivot. Repeat. And with each forward progression he asked himself, *What am I going to do about Roxie?*

Having her sleep over when she had no place else to go and so he could take care of her was okay, but having her puttering around Kyle's condo when he wasn't up to watching her and keeping in charge of her was something else entirely.

So far the issue of her preparing food for him hadn't come up. Was it too much to hope Roxie didn't like to cook? His stomach tightened. She wouldn't understand. He'd no doubt hurt her feelings, and she didn't need him adding to her current aggravation. He liked her, but he needed to keep things casual. Friends only—preferably friends who only had sex—nothing more. He'd found that to be the easiest way to conceal his…issues. Unfortunately, most women didn't buy into the arrangement for long.

He'd lost track of how many laps he'd done—somewhere up in the hundreds—and still he hadn't come up with any stupendous ideas by the time she returned, carrying two pink plastic basins filled with soap, lotion and washcloths. Over her shoulder rested at least a dozen towels.

"What's all that for?" he asked.

"I ran up to the O.R. to get you some scrub pants. I'm going to give you a bed bath and help you get changed."

* * *

"Like hell you are," Fig said, sounding all big and tough. "I am not a child. Nor am I incapacitated. I do not need to be given a bath."

Roxie had been a nurse long enough to know when someone was scared. And she wanted to help. "Maybe not, but in addition to getting you all cleaned up, it will relax you. I promise." Roxie would make sure of it. "People say I give one primo bed bath." She walked to the lone chair in the room and unloaded her towels.

"I bet they do." His words, coated with sarcasm and heavy with sexual innuendo, hit their mark.

While she knew he was only lashing out due to his own inner struggles, his words hurt. "What's that supposed to mean?" Roxie dropped the two basins, soap and lotion onto the counter by the sink. "I'm such a tramp you think I'd behave unprofessionally while bathing a patient? That I would take advantage of someone in my care by making inappropriate, unwanted sexual advances?"

"I didn't mean…"

"Well, what did you mean, then?" Roxie glared at him, her arms crossed over her chest, and she waited for him to answer.

"I'm an ass," Fig said, sitting heavily on the stretcher, looking down at the floor. "I'm sorry."

"I get it," Roxie said. "You're tense and uncomfortable and unhappy. I feel terrible even though I didn't ask you to get involved cleaning at my house, you insisted. And I told you not to go into that room, yet you went in anyway. I am trying to do what I can to make this easier for you. But I'll be damned if I'm going to stick around and be insulted just because you're in a bad mood."

Fig toed off his sneakers. "Okay." He lay down on the stretcher, resting his right wrist on his belly. "If you think it will help, you can give me a bed bath."

You can give me. "Oh, I *can,* can I? Maybe now I don't want to. There are lots of other things I could be doing right now." But none she'd *rather* be doing.

"Do you want my pants off or on?" he asked.

"Makes no difference to me."

He reached down with his left hand and fumbled with the button to his jeans. "You're going to stand there and watch me struggle?"

"Yes." It'd serve him right.

"No, you're not." He stared up at her. "Because you're too nice. And caring. And not at all mean. Come here," he said. Contrite. Not a command. A plea. "Please."

Her legs walked over to the stretcher.

"Don't leave me," he said quietly. "I need you."

That was all she had to hear. Roxie moved to the head of the bed, kissed his forehead and said, "You've got me." The idea excited her. Felt kind of girlfriendy. A new gig for her. She kinda liked the thought of taking care of him— her temporary man—looked forward to staying with him after surgery, to cooking and cleaning up after someone who'd actually appreciate it.

Roxie walked to the sink, adjusted the water temperature until she had it right where she wanted it and began filling one of the basins.

She returned to Fig. "I'm going to help you out of your pants," she explained, just like she would to any patient. She undid the button and lowered the zipper. "Bend your knees and lift up," she instructed.

He did. As she slid down his pants, his underwear came, too. Since he didn't seem to have a problem with it, she made sure to maintain his privacy by keeping him covered by the hospital gown. Then she slid both down his long legs, taking his socks with her as she did.

With one basin filled, she began filling the other and returned to the bed. "I'm going to remove your gown now."

Fig lay there with his eyes closed.

She slid the top half off his shoulders and down his arms, leaving it folded over his groin. Then she covered him from his neck to his ankles with towels, laying them crossways, pulling out the gown when she was all done.

When the second basin was filled she moved each to the over-the-bed table, set the height level with the mattress and got to work. "Let me have your left hand," she said. Fig lifted it. His eyes still closed.

Roxie washed his hand and between his fingers. She spent extra time on it because Fig seemed very conscious of the cleanliness of his hands, to the point he carried a hand sanitizer with him. Then she submerged his hand in the rinse basin. "Let it soak for a minute." In nursing school, while posing as a patient—in her bikini—for the demonstration on bed baths, the teacher had set each of Roxie's hands to soak in the bathwater. It'd felt so good Roxie made it a point to do the same for each of her patients.

"I'm going to start with your head." His beautiful head. "Lift." She slid a towel beneath it then dipped the first of her washcloths in the heated water of the other basin and squeezed out the excess. She cleansed him gently, carefully. After rinsing his face and behind his ears, Roxie dipped the cloth in the clean water, squeezed it until it stopped dripping and set it over his eyes and forehead.

Then she lowered the towel covering his colorful chest. As she bathed him, she admired the beautiful artwork covering his upper body, all outdoor landscapes, she realized, which stuck her as odd for a man who preferred the indoors. She read the words tattooed in script on scrolls swirling over the backdrop of lush flowering bushes and trees, snow-capped mountains and ocean sun-sets: "Nothing can bring you peace but yourself ~ Ralph Waldo Emerson," over his left pectoral. "Life is a sum of all your choices ~ Albert Camus," above his belly button. "To err is human, to forgive divine ~ Anon.," on his left shoulder. "Happiness depends on ourselves ~ Aristotle," on his right shoulder. "You only live once, but if you do it right, once is enough ~ Joe E. Lewis," curved around the outside of his right pectoral.

The proverbs resonated with her. "My favorite words of wisdom are 'Life may not be the party we hoped for, but while we're here we should dance.'"

"Who said it?" Fig asked.

"I have no idea." But that simple sentence had become the basis of her life, the impetus to have fun and find joy when and where she could.

After Roxie dried his torso, she took the lotion she'd left warming in the sink and massaged it into Fig's upper body, avoiding his right forearm. Usually she wore gloves when giving a bed bath. Today she didn't, relishing the smooth curve of each muscle, praying for healing at every raised scar from his painful past.

"Roll onto your left side." She assisted him, positioning his right arm on a pillow and sliding towels underneath him to catch any dripping water.

After bathing, drying and lotioning him, she worked her fingers into his tight muscles.

"That feels so good," Fig said.

Roxie smiled. "That's what I'm aiming for."

When she'd finished with his legs and feet, Roxie couldn't miss the bulge under the towel covering Fig's groin. She dipped a washcloth in the now sudsy water, wrung it out and placed it in his left hand. "You can do between your legs."

At that he opened his eyes. "I've been thinking about what you said earlier. Technically, I'm not your patient so you don't have to worry about adhering to any professional code of ethics."

She knew that, which was why she'd planned a little something special to help alleviate his distress. "I don't?" Roxie asked, knowing exactly where he was headed.

Fig shook his head. "And since we've already had sex, if you were to…let's say…make any sexual advances—which I wouldn't turn down, by the way—they wouldn't be at all inappropriate. In fact they'd be welcomed. Appreciated even." While giving a hand job during a bed bath certainly wasn't nurselike behavior, it could very well fall into the realm of girlfriendlike behavior. At least a dozen times over the years she'd worked at Madrin Memorial she'd walked into a patient's room to find the curtain drawn and the scent of sex heavy in the air.

Men liked it anywhere. Everywhere.

He still had an hour and a half before the earliest possible time the O.R. might call for him. There was plenty of time, but just to be sure… "Exactly what are you asking for, Fig?"

He took her hand and placed it on his erection so there'd be no doubt. "The bath helped. But I still feel wound tight. I want…"

"Something to release the built-up…tension?"

"Yeah." He closed his eyes and guided her hand over the top of the towel, along the length of him, while he lifted his hips into her touch.

"If you wanted to get rid of the towel," he added, "that'd be okay, too."

She smiled, starting to get into the game he played. "What if I don't want to use my hand?" Roxie asked seductively as she moved to the head of the stretcher and bent down close to his lips. "What if I wanted to use my tongue? Would that be okay?"

"Your mouth is perfection," he said, staring up into her eyes.

She dropped down for a kiss. He turned his head. She connected with his jaw. Again. Strike two. One more time and she'd call him on it. Or did she really want to know the truth? That her mouth was perfect to go down on him, but not good enough to kiss? He wasn't the first guy to avoid kissing her on the mouth. But his refusal hurt more than the others. Because what they had together—while still new—meant more. He meant more.

No. She would not go there. Today she was playing girlfriend.

But deciding not to use her mouth for anything more than talking and eating until he kissed her, she pulled away the towel, reached for the lotion, squeezed and watched ribbons of white cream twirl around his aroused flesh, all engorged and eager for attention.

She didn't make him wait.

When she squeezed her fingers around his thick, firm flesh and slid from the rounded tip down the smooth, impressive length to the bare skin at its base, Fig let out a pleasure-filled groan. A wonderful sound.

"You like?" she asked, knowing the answer.

"Oh, yeah." Having him in her palm felt so good, Roxie almost groaned, too. She moved her hand in long, slow strokes, lubricated by the lotion. The rise and fall of Fig's chest became more rapid, as did his thrusts to meet her.

Fig pulled at the towel covering his chest until it fell to the floor. His nipples beckoned her. Roxie bent to lick one, the roughened texture making her tongue tingle. She sucked it into her mouth. Okay, eating, talking and nipple sucking, but nothing else.

Fig clutched her head and leaned down to kiss the top of it. "I'll make it up to you." He strained against her palm. "Whatever you want, I'll do." He panted into her hair. "Anything. You feel so damn good. I'm going to…"

And with one final push that lifted his hips completely off the stretcher, Fig released all his tension into the towel Roxie had barely managed to toss on top of him.

While she cleaned him, Fig looked completely relaxed, maybe even asleep. His breathing returned to normal. His eyes closed. But when she covered him with fresh toweling and put up the side rails, he reached for her. "I'm going to take a nap." He sounded like he'd already started. "Come lie with me."

"There's not enough room."

He scooted over and patted the space he'd created to his left.

"I don't want to hurt you."

"Honey, I feel so good I am incapable of recognizing pain."

Good.

"Now come. Lie down with me." He yawned. "We hardly got any sleep last night."

She *was* kind of tired.

"Please," he said. "I need to have you close."

Roxie liked to be needed. So she slipped out of her sandals and carefully crawled up beside him. With the utmost care not to jostle his right forearm, she snuggled into his side, her head on his shoulder, her palm over his heart, her knee across his hips. "You comfortable?" she asked.

He nodded. "I like this," he said sleepily. "Just don't try to cook me breakfast," he mumbled.

What? She lifted her head to look at him. He was out.

Roxie closed her eyes, enjoying his strong arm heavy

across her back and the tiny twitches as his body fully relaxed in sleep.

While he was in surgery she'd run to visit *Mami* then
make a quick trip to the store for the ingredients to make
Mrs. Klein's fabulous chicken soup with matzo balls.
Jewish penicillin, she'd called it. Good for whatever ailed
you.

Fig was going to love it.

Roxie was in the process of stocking Fig's fridge with food
when his cell phone—which she'd held on to along with
all of his other valuables when he'd gone up to the O.R.—
rang for the third time. She rummaged around her purse
until she found it. The screen read: "Mom." Knowing how
much her mom worried when she couldn't reach her, Roxie
opened the phone. "Hello."

"Who's this?" an older female voice asked.

"Roxie. I'm a friend of Fig's."

"Where is he? What's wrong? Albert," she called out.
"Come quick. Something's happened to Ryan."

"He took a little fall. He's in surgery to repair…"

"He's in the hospital," Fig's mother yelled to someone.
"Get the car."

"I'm going back to the hospital now. The recovery room
called a few minutes ago and said he tolerated the procedure well and should be ready for discharge in a few
hours."

"They called you? Why did they call you? I'm his
mother. Alllbbbeeerrrttt," she yelled. "Oh, where is that
blasted man?" she muttered. "I want to speak to the nurses
myself. They need to know Ryan's medical history. He's
a very fragile young man."

He didn't seem fragile to Roxie.

"Come. Come. I'm waiting. What hospital is he in?"

"Madrin Memorial." Roxie almost said *ma'am*.

"I'll be there as soon as I can," Fig's mom said.

"You really don't have to…" The connection ended. "I have everything under control," she finished, although no one was there to hear her.

CHAPTER SEVEN

FIG felt absolutely horrible. Out of habit he scanned the recovery room for his mother, which was absolutely ridiculous since she was hours away and had no idea where he was. He retched again. The extra antinausea medication the nurse had shot into him wasn't working. Fig didn't care. "I want to go home," he told the nurse standing beside him, holding the small plastic bowl he was supposed to puke into.

"Not until you're taking oral fluids," she said.

The thought of swallowing anything made him retch again. "You said I could go after I peed." Which he'd done, into a plastic urinal container, with his nurse standing beside him—listening and watching as if he'd planned to substitute someone else's urine for his own. All while his ass hung out from the back opening of his hospital gown. The ultimate humiliation.

She held out a cup of water with a straw in it. "Once you're drinking I can discontinue your intravenous."

He would never drink that easily contaminated tapwater swill despite the lining of his throat feeling like it'd been impaled with thousands of tiny shards of glass. Fig only drank bottled water. From bottles he opened himself. "I *am* going home," Fig said. "Either discharge me or give me the papers to sign out against medical advice. I'm leaving either way. Where are my clothes?"

"Roxie took them. She said she'd bring you back clean ones to put on."

Damn it. He had to leave now. Before his lungs tightened to the point he could not choke in a breath. Before his eyes blurred and he started to shake. Before the doctor ordered a sedative to drug him into a complacency that would enable people to manipulate him as they pleased.

No. Fig wasn't a scared little boy anymore, and he'd walk out of here half-naked if he had to.

"I'm going to call your doctor," the nurse said in a huff and walked back to the nurses' station.

About a minute later Roxie strolled in with a brightly colored "Feel Better Soon" balloon floating from a red ribbon wrapped around her palm. "You've got Helen all in a tizzy. For a seemingly laid-back guy, you are one terrible patient." She plopped a grocery bag with his clothes on the foot of his bed.

"Take this out of me, will you?" Fig held up his left arm to show her his IV.

"I'm not on duty, and I'm not your nurse."

Fig tried to pick at the tape, only to find his right hand next to useless.

"Stop that."

Fig looked up at her, waited until her eyes met his so she'd know he was serious. "I am going home." He retched. Damn it.

Roxie grabbed the bowl and thrust it under his chin. He spit.

"He's having a bad reaction to anesthesia." His nurse returned. "Since it's so late, Dr. Rosen wants to admit him overnight."

"I am not staying. Take this out." He held up his left

arm. Or he'd find a way to rip it out himself. "You can't keep me here. I know my rights."

His nurse shook her head.

"Tell Dr. Rosen he can release Fig to my care. Ask him to prescribe a couple of Phenergan suppositories."

"I don't need to be released into anyone's care." Just dump him in his bed, let him sleep off this whole experience and he'd be back to normal come morning. Fig slid his legs over the side of the bed and fought against a swirl of dizziness to remain upright.

"Tell me what I need to know," Roxie said to the nurse, who handed her some papers.

"The surgery went well. The splint stays on for seven to ten days. He needs to call Dr. Rosen's office on Monday to schedule his first post-op visit. If all goes well, he'll likely be placed in a hard cast for six weeks." She sorted through the papers she'd handed Roxie and pulled one out. "He needs to begin active digit and shoulder range of motion exercises daily as of tomorrow. This is the instruction sheet. Oral pain medication every four to six hours as needed." The nurse looked at him. "If he can tolerate it."

"Stop talking like I'm not here." He dumped out the bag. Bless Roxie for bringing him sweatpants and a loose tee with big armholes so he could dress himself. He stood. Wobbled.

Roxie caught him up against her. "What's your rush? Got a hot date?"

He flashed her the best smile he could manage considering he felt so crappy. "Smokin' hot," he said, because Roxie was.

"Keep the arm elevated," the nurse went on. "Check nail beds and report any deepening or change in color. Sling with elbow at ninety-degrees flexion. You know all this stuff," she added.

"Yeah, but I want him to hear it." She pivoted Fig back to the bed and he sat. "Is it okay with you if I discontinue the IV?" Roxie asked the nurse.

"Go ahead." The plump woman turned away. "I'll call in for the new med orders."

Roxie removed the annoying tube from his arm and, after applying pressure, put on a gauze-and-tape dressing. "I'll help you get dressed," she offered.

"I don't need help," Fig said. He relied on no one. Trusted no one.

"All righty, then," she said, plopping into the chair facing his bed, leaning back and crossing her legs. "Get to it."

She wasn't going to force her assistance on him or lecture him about accepting help when he needed it? Well, what d'ya know? He decided to put on his pants first. Unfortunately for him, in the aftermath of his surgery and interminable retching, the simple act of untangling his clothing and shaking out his sweatpants tired him out. Pushing through it, he held the waistband in his left hand, leaned forward, planning to thread his feet into the leg holes—and kept on going.

Roxie caught him again. "You keep winding up in my arms and people are going to talk."

She sat him up.

"What do you think they'll say?" he asked, glad she kept the conversation light and casual instead of pointing out how weak and dizzy he was and how ludicrous it was for him to think he could go home on his own.

She knelt on the floor, slid the sweatpants up to his knees and lifted the hems until his feet popped out. Then she stood, hooked both hands under his armpits and helped him stand. "Probably something like, 'What is it about Roxie that even drugged-up post-op patients can't keep their hands—or in your case, hand—off of her?'"

He pulled up his pants with his left hand, dropped back onto the bed and waited for her to comment that he hadn't bothered with the underwear she'd brought for him. She didn't. "I bet they all wish they had your allure." He untied his gown at the neck and took it off. Then he eyed the shirt, trying to decide the best approach to put it on.

She laughed. "Is that what I have?" She stepped between his thighs, picked up the shirt and carefully worked it up his bandaged arm. "Allure?"

"In spades." He looked up at her. Roxie stretched the neck opening over his head. With her help, he pushed his left arm in then pulled the shirt over his belly.

She moved the chair close to the bed and pulled one of his feet into her lap. "You sweet-talker." And without another word, she slid on his sock and sneaker, tied his laces then did the same with the other foot.

The nurse returned. "You need to sign these papers." She pushed them across his over-the-bed table and handed him a pen.

How was he supposed to sign with his left hand? To get out of there, he'd find a way. He picked up the pen. Dropped it. Picked it up again, this time holding it tighter. Then, in a very careful—yet still illegible—attempt at a signature, and without reading a word, Fig signed every place the nurse pointed.

That done, he was free to leave. He went to stand.

"Hold up," Roxie said. "I'm going to run to the pharmacy to get your prescriptions filled, then I'll drive the car around. I'll call up to the nurses' station when I'm ready for you and your nurse will wheel you down."

"I'd rather go with you."

Roxie put her hand on his shoulder. "I know. But it's better if you rest for a few minutes." She plumped his pillow. "Lie back."

He did. Surprised at how good it felt.

"And you really need to try to drink."

His stomach clenched. "Would you pick me up a bottle of water or ginger ale?"

"Sure," she said, without question.

A short time later his nurse pushed him through the electronic doors leading to the outside, and the band of anxiety that'd tightened around his chest since he'd first arrived at the hospital loosened, enabling Fig to inhale a deep breath of fresh air. Freedom.

Roxie got out of her little red car—leaving his balloon floating in the backseat—and walked around the front of it to open the door for him.

A huge silver Mercedes crossover skidded to a stop, missing Roxie's rear fender by inches. It looked just like… It couldn't be.

His mother climbed out of the front passenger door. How the hell did she…?

"Oh, thank goodness, we're just in time," she yelled. "Wheel him over here. He'll be coming home with us."

"No," Fig said, rage using up what little energy he'd racked up from his rest.

"He doesn't know what he's saying. He's not well. Come. Come." His mother opened the rear door and waited, doing her best Impatient Lady of Power impersonation. His father stood and watched, like he always did, unwilling to make any attempt to control her.

Roxie came to stand beside him.

"What did you do?" he snapped. He didn't have the energy to deal with his mother's relentless efforts to get her way.

"Me?" Roxie asked. "I answered your phone—after the third time it rang in as many minutes, might I add—because I didn't want her to worry that you weren't picking up. I had no idea she'd charge into town and swoop down on us in full motherly dudgeon at the thought of someone else taking care of you."

"Swoop?" his mother said. "I most certainly do not swoop."

"I've got to get back to work," his nurse said. "Pick a car. Either car."

"The red one," Fig said.

"That vile creature must be the girl from the bar," his mother said to his father in a loud whisper audible to everyone within fifty feet of them. The way she said "girl" made her low opinion of the *girl* in question crystal clear.

"Mom," Fig warned.

"Yes," Roxie said, unfazed. "That would be me. The shiksa." She held out her hand to his mother, who now stood within reach. "I go by Roxie."

Fig tried to hide his smile. To his knowledge, his mom had never come across anyone like Roxie before. If he didn't feel so close to passing out he would have sat back and enjoyed the encounter.

His mother looked at Roxie like she had open sores. "What kind of…woman would stand between a mother and her son?" she yelled, clutching at her chest in a performance that garnered the attention of several passersby. "A shameless gold digger," she answered her own question then waited for Roxie's reaction.

"I've been called a lot of things in my day, and I'll cop to the 'shameless,' but 'gold digger' is a new one for me," Roxie said, stepping behind his wheelchair and pushing him toward her car. "You holding out on me, Fig?" She leaned forward to whisper in his ear. "Obviously I've been too free with my favors. From now on I'm going to hold out for some bling."

Only Roxie could make him smile at that precise moment in time.

"His name is Ryan," his mother snapped. "And he is coming home with *me*." She grabbed Roxie's arm.

Roxie stopped. "He's a grown man. Why don't we ask him what he wants to do?" She walked in front of the wheelchair. "Who are you going home with?"

Since neither would have accepted that he wanted to go home alone and all he needed was a ride, Fig said, "You," to Roxie. Then he picked up the plastic bowl in his lap and retched.

"Oh, dear," his mother cried out.

"Get me out of here," he said to Roxie.

"I am a registered nurse, Mrs. Figelstein, so you don't have to worry." Roxie pushed him the rest of the way to her car. "I'll take good care of him." She locked the wheels. "I've discussed the discharge orders with the recovery room nurse. I've picked up his medications, and I'll thank you to remove your hand from my arm so I can assist him into my car without hurting you."

"Where is she taking you, honey?" his mom asked. "I'll come by to get you settled in."

"Go home, Mom."

"I can't believe this," she said dramatically, dabbing at her eyes. "I dropped everything to travel for hours so I could be here to take care of you in your time of need, and you're turning me away?" she sobbed.

"I didn't ask you to come." He didn't want her here, didn't want her anywhere near him when he wasn't operating at full capacity.

"We'll follow you. Get in the car, Albert."

With a steadying hand from Roxie, Fig stood and stared down his mother. "If you come anywhere near where I'm staying, I will cut you out of my life for good. Same rules as my apartment. I mean it."

"It's okay," Roxie said in his ear. "I can handle her."

People only thought they could handle his mother. No one recognized her for the master manipulator she was until it was too late.

"I'll call you tomorrow," Fig said to his mother.

"You always say you'll call, but you never do," his mother countered.

"Because you don't give me a chance to."

"I'll call you tonight. To see if you need anything. We'll find a motel."

"Don't call me tonight because my phone will be off. And don't call me tomorrow because I'm getting a new number and I am not giving it to you."

His mother clutched at her heart again. "Oh, the pain of watching my son turn his back on me. After all I've done for him. My pills, Albert. Where are my pills?"

"Enough," Fig said. "You got me home last weekend with your unnecessary trip to the emergency room. The doctor said you'll outlive us all. Go home, Mom. If I need you, I'll call you."

With one last look at his mother's shocked face, Fig slid into the car, pulled the door closed and relaxed back in his seat.

When Roxie pulled out of the hospital parking lot, she glanced in her rearview mirror. "Woo wee. I thought for sure they'd follow us and I'd have to show off some of my tricky-bo-dicky driving skills to lose them." She actually sounded a bit disappointed at the missed opportunity. "I think on the scale of one to crazy, I'd rather have an inattentive, introverted, hoarding mother than a manipulative, histrionic, attention-seeking one," Roxie said matter-of-factly as she turned into Kyle's condo complex.

Just like that, at first meeting, Roxie had his mother's true nature pegged. "Neither one is a prize," Fig said, his stomach not feeling so good.

"You got that right," Roxie agreed. "So your mom's the reason you missed our date?"

"Yeah."

"Why didn't you say so?"

"Because I knew it was a ploy to get me home, but I let her suck me in with her tears and her desperate pleas. I was angry at her and myself. I didn't want you to think I was a pansy mama's boy running home every time she called." His stomach clenched. "I think I'm going to be sick." And he was.

Hours later—after he'd waited until his abdominal muscles ached like he'd been beaten and he felt so tired and drained he could barely lift his head—Fig allowed Roxie to give him the nausea medication. He appreciated that she did it quickly and efficiently and without making a big deal out of it. In fact she chattered on about random nothingness the entire time. "You smell like chicken soup," Fig pointed out after she'd finished; the smell not at all appealing.

"That's because while you were in here suffering and not allowing me to do anything for you, I made us a pot of my delicious chicken soup." She stripped off her exam glove and walked to the garbage. "Well, Mrs. Klein's delicious chicken soup. But she wasn't the one who spent the past three hours peeling, stirring and straining it, now, was she?"

Fig retched.

Roxie returned to the bed, sat down and rubbed his back. "The medicine should kick in in a few minutes. Don't worry, I won't force-feed you the soup tonight—even though you're not drinking near as much as you should be. Mrs. Klein always said it needs to sit overnight in the fridge so you can strain the fat in the morning."

At least that'd buy him some time.

"I wish you had asked me first. I don't like chicken soup," he lied. He used to love it until he'd figured out it was one of the many food sources his mother had probably used to poison him.

The next morning Roxie lay in bed listening to Fig's shallow breaths, watching his peaceful expression and relishing the warm, cozy feeling of waking up with him—even though she was the only one awake. She wished she could confide in him and tell him the truth about Johnny and the video. Seek his counsel on what she should do. But regardless of how close they'd become in such a short time, she barely knew him, had no idea how he'd react, and she wasn't ready to give him up. Not yet.

He stirred, gave a tiny stretch and turned onto his side. He'd be up soon. So she quietly slid out of bed and headed to the kitchen to get breakfast started.

So what if he didn't like chicken soup? She liked it. And once upon a time *Mami* had liked it. She could pack some up for Ali and Jared and Victoria and Kyle. It would not go to waste.

But she'd made it for Fig. Making chicken soup for someone was a labor of love, Mrs. Klein used to say. While Roxie didn't love Fig, he'd been a good friend to her when she'd really needed one. He'd taken down her video. He'd stood up for her to the fire marshal, and he'd given her a place to stay. He'd accompanied her to the hospital—twice—when he hated hospitals. So she wanted to demonstrate her appreciation by doing something special for him. That he didn't like, and didn't even appear interested in tasting, the soup she'd worked so hard on was disappointing.

But it wasn't the first disappointment she'd ever suffered, and most likely would not be the last. Roxie shook it off and opened the fridge. She took out the eggs and milk she'd bought yesterday—because Fig didn't have enough food in his refrigerator to feed a gerbil. She slid two pieces of split-top wheat bread into the toaster—in case all he could stomach was toast—and filled the kettle—in case he felt up to some coffee.

On the chance he was as hungry as she thought he'd be after last night's ordeal, she also got started on making him a nice "thanks for everything, I think you're special" breakfast.

Roxie cracked five eggs into a bowl and took down the cinnamon and vanilla and found she couldn't stop smiling. She loved playing pretend girlfriend, working in Kyle's bright kitchen cooking for her temporary man. If she'd been able to find a frilly apron in one of the drawers, she would have put it on and danced around—in a room devoid of clutter where she actually had space to prepare a decent meal and had access to pots and utensils without having to search for them.

"Whatever you're doing, stop," Fig commanded from the doorway to the bedroom. "Give me a minute and *I'll* make *you* breakfast."

"Don't be ridiculous," Roxie said. "You've only got one functioning arm and I've got two." She held them up and wiggled her fingers. "Besides, I've already started. Pick your poison. French toast made with delicious challah bread. Eggs. An omelet. Toast. Coffee. Oh, and there's O.J. in the fridge but I wasn't sure if you were a juice drinker in the morning."

He walked to the kitchen, looking tired and perturbed. "I can make my own breakfast," he grumbled.

"Then what's the sense of having *me* here?"

He pulled out a kitchen chair and sat down heavily. "Exactly."

What? "You don't want me here?"

He rubbed his hand over his face. "I can't do this. You insisted on staying last night. But I'm feeling much better this morning."

He didn't look much better. She wiped her hand on a towel. "I thought…" That he liked having her around. That he'd invited her to stay until they were done cleaning out the house. That last night he was just being a difficult patient. "I didn't realize…" That he'd intended for her to stay for only one night. That once they'd had sex he was done with her. Like all the rest of them. "I'll get my things."

"Roxie. Wait."

Absolutely not. She wouldn't stay where she wasn't wanted. But she'd taken responsibility for his care. "Let me see your right hand."

He held it out to her.

"Mild swelling. To be expected. Make sure you keep it elevated." She pinched his nail beds. "Good capillary refill. Move your fingers." He did. "Good range of motion." She turned to the bedroom. Would not get sappy. "Your home exercise plan is on the kitchen counter. Your prescription bottles are by the toaster. Don't forget to call Dr. Rosen's office to schedule your post-op visit."

"I'm sorry," he said.

And Roxie snapped. "Do you have any idea how many times you've apologized to me in the last forty-eight hours?"

He didn't answer.

"Way more than someone who wants to be my *friend*

should have to. But you're not interested in being friends, are you? No. You got what you wanted and now I'm being sent on my way."

"Sorry," a different male voice said.

Kyle stood at the front door, his key still in the lock, starring at Fig's shirtless torso. "You showed her your tattoos?"

"Don't you knock?" Fig asked.

"I came to check on you. I didn't think you'd let Roxie…" Kyle stopped.

"Don't worry about it," Roxie said to Kyle. "I have just been informed I've overstayed my welcome. I'll be gone in a few minutes."

"It's not like that," Fig said, his voice now an annoying buzzing in her ears.

"Where will you go?" Kyle asked.

At least one of them cared enough to ask. "I've got plenty of options," Roxie said. Although she didn't want to bother anyone, so probably a motel. Something cheap, since there was a good chance she would soon be unemployed.

"Since we expect your mom will be moving into the downstairs bedroom this afternoon, you can have Victoria's couch." He looked semihopeful.

Roxie smiled. "She didn't agree to let you share the master bedroom, after all."

Kyle shook his head. "Not unless Jake has a sleepover. But if you were to need the couch…"

"She'll probably send you here to sleep with Fig," Roxie said. "Victoria's mind is set. She doesn't want Jake to see his parents sleeping in the same bed until after you're married. There's no getting around it."

Roxie's mind was set, too. "I need to get my things." She turned and pounded down the hall to the bedroom. How could she have misread Fig? She picked up her bag from the floor and dropped it onto the bed. How could she have gotten so caught up in playing pretend girlfriend? Which, for a very short, very emotional twenty-four hours, had started to feel all too real. She put on a pair of denim capri pants, tied the T-shirt she'd worn to bed at her low back and slipped into her flip-flops.

She grabbed her watch from the table beside the bed and her lip gloss from the dresser beneath the mirror, and she was ready to go.

"You're being an idiot," Kyle yelled at Fig. "Roxie is my friend, and she deserves an explanation. Tell her. Or I will."

"Tell me what?" Roxie entered the open kitchen.

"Nothing," Fig said to Roxie. Then he stood and faced Kyle. "Don't do this."

"You care about her," Kyle said to Fig.

Seems he'd misread Fig, too.

"I can see this is ripping you apart," Kyle said.

That's when Roxie noticed how tormented and sad and downright distraught Fig looked. But he was the one who'd told her to go.

"Don't let her leave," Kyle went on. "Take a chance. Talk to her. Let her make her own choice."

Kyle walked to Roxie and eased the strap of her bag off of her shoulder. "Hear him out, Roxie. You will never find a better, more loyal and supportive man." He hugged her and whispered in her ear, "The good outweighs the inconvenient. I promise you."

His words made no sense.

Kyle walked to the door and set Roxie's bag beside it. "I'm leaving now. But I'll be waiting in the parking lot." He looked at Fig. "If Roxie leaves this apartment in less than fifteen minutes I am going to come back up here and beat you senseless."

"Oh, you think so?" Fig asked in honest challenge. "Even one-handed I can take you."

"So you'd rather fight than take a few minutes to tell me what's going on?" Roxie asked quietly.

Kyle escaped through the door and clicked it closed behind him.

"I'm a kook," Fig said. "A nut job."

"If you're trying to scare me into leaving, you'll have to do better than that." Roxie leaned a shoulder against the wall and crossed her arms at her waist, not knowing what else to do with them.

"You've got so much going on in your life right now. You deserve an easy man, not someone like me."

"I've never had easy a day in my life. I wouldn't know what to do with an easy man."

"In that case, can I make you some coffee?" Fig asked.

"I'm still trying to decide if I should stay or if I should let you get beat up," Roxie said, only half kidding. "So answer me this. Is Kyle right? Do you care about me? Is the thought of me walking out that door ripping you apart?"

Fig looked down at the floor and nodded.

Roxie's heart felt a tiny bit hopeful. "Then I'll make the coffee."

"No." Fig lifted the kettle in his left hand and walked to the sink.

"That's fresh water," Roxie said. "I filled it this morning."

Fig dumped it out, struggled to dry the inside with paper towels and refilled it using three containers of bottled water—that were not easy for him to open one-handed. But he didn't ask for help and Roxie didn't offer. He glanced at her on the way to the stove, his expression a mix of uncertainty and embarrassment.

"Does this all have to do with your frequent hand washing/sanitizing and why you won't kiss me?"

He rested his hip against the counter. "Noticed that, did you?"

"I'm a nurse. I have excellent assessment skills." Roxie walked to the cabinet where she'd seen the coffee mugs and took two down. Then she got two spoons from the silverware drawer.

Fig watched her every move.

"You going to answer me?" Roxie asked.

"It's indirectly related." He reached into a cabinet and took out individual-serving-size packets of instant coffee. He held them out to Roxie. "Would you…?"

She washed her hands in the sink then ripped the tops off the coffee packets.

"There's milk in the…"

Fig held out a handful of single-serving creamers.

Roxie peeled back the lids on four of them.

"Thank you," Fig said.

The coffee made, they both sat down at the table.

"The no kissing on the mouth, and the hand washing—which is not a compulsion, I'd like to point out… It's not like I scrub my hands raw, or anything. I just like them to be clean—started back when I was first diagnosed with leukemia. My mother lectured me on the risk of infection and how to protect against it. Constantly. For years. It is now hardwired into my circuitry."

"And you can put your tongue between my legs but not between my lips." She hesitated, thought about what she'd said and clarified, "These lips," while pointing to her mouth.

"It's a conundrum." He smiled and shrugged. "Can't explain it."

"So you're a selective germaphobe. That's the big secret?"

Fig stirred his coffee. "Have you ever heard of Munchausen syndrome by proxy?"

"Isn't it a form of child abuse?"

"It can affect adults, too. It occurs when an abuser, usually a mother, intentionally harms or fabricates an illness in her child that initiates a hospitalization."

There were some sick people in the world. "Are you trying to tell me your mother somehow convinced your doctors that you had leukemia when you didn't? Because I'm not buyin' it."

He shook his head. "No. I definitely had the leukemia. But during my remissions I suffered from debilitating headaches and forgetfulness and general malaise to the point I didn't feel well enough to leave the house. No one could identify a reason. Mom homeschooled me. Her life revolved around me, her every waking hour dedicated to me. She carted me to doctors and specialists. I underwent countless tests. All the while she soaked in the praise for what a wonderful, attentive mother she was, giving up her life to care for her sick son."

He stared into his coffee as he spoke. Roxie felt sorry for little Fig, sick, so alone and subjected to a controlling mother. But Munchausen by proxy was a hefty accusation.

"By the time I'd turned eighteen—" Fig took a sip of coffee and continued "—I was clinically depressed. Living at home. I had more bad days than good, and I couldn't visualize my future being anything but more of the same. One night I drank more of my dad's stash of expensive beer than usual and got totally wasted. Jacked up on liquid confidence, I stole the family Ford and, while speeding down the highway, decided to take control of my life…by ending it."

Roxie couldn't believe it. This strong, confident man had attempted suicide? As bad as things had gotten in her life, she'd never once considered it. "Your accident. The one you told me about." The one that'd left him scarred.

"Wasn't an accident at all."

"Oh, Fig. I'm so sorry."

"I'm not." He stared off into the living room. "I met Kyle in rehab and he saved my life, although it took him almost losing his to do it. I remember Mom coming into our room late one night. She'd befriended the staff, bribed them with cookies and treats and wasn't held to the same rules as other visitors. I heard her out in the hallway and pretended to be asleep—I did that a lot so she'd leave me alone. Anyway, she came in close to my bed and whispered, 'I'm so sorry, Ryan. I never expected it to go on this long, to make you so unhappy. It was selfish. I'll stop. I promise.'"

"What?"

"It didn't make sense to me at the time, either. But after Kyle's brush with death, when we sat down to try to make sense of what'd happened, I remembered Mom's words and the pieces of the puzzle started to come together."

"What happened to Kyle?" Roxie asked.

"Sorry," Fig said. "I got ahead of myself. In rehab, Kyle and I hit it off right from the start. I know it sounds pathetic, but he was my first real friend."

Roxie reached for his unbandaged hand and squeezed. For as difficult as her childhood had been, Fig's was worse.

"Long story short, after rehab and some convalescence at my house, my father got us both into the same college and we moved into an apartment close to campus. Mom was not happy about me moving out and refused to allow me to live in the dorms. Too many germs, she'd said. An apartment was the compromise."

"Sounds like an eighteen-year-old's dream, to be set up in an apartment with his buddy." Roxie would have loved an opportunity like that.

"It was. Until Mom started visiting. Daily. For hours at a time. She insisted on cleaning the apartment, doing our laundry and cooking for us. Kyle's mom had died a few years earlier and he didn't mind the attention as long as she was gone right after she did the dinner dishes."

"How long did she give you on your own before she started coming around?" Roxie asked.

"About a month. In that time I'd started to feel better." His face lit up at the memory. "Up until that point, it's the happiest I'd ever been. I had friends and went on dates. Then the headaches and nausea started up again. I began missing class. Mom suggested I move home but I refused. The symptoms got worse."

"You didn't relate the change in your health to your mom's visits?"

He looked up at her. "It was par for the course for me. I'd never gone more than a few weeks without relapsing. To be honest, I expected it."

"So what made you suspect your mom?"

"One weekend Kyle was up late studying. Mom had made us each a batch of brownies. She always packaged them separately, saying mine had herbs and supplements to help me get well, and while I was used to the slight change in taste—because she'd been giving them to me for years—Kyle might find the taste off-putting. But that particular night Kyle was so munched he didn't care. He devoured my pan of brownies. About three-quarters of the batch. In one sitting. An hour later he collapsed in my room and had a seizure."

CHAPTER EIGHT

"Ay Dios mio," Roxie said.

Fig remembered that horrible night, the fear and desperation, waiting for the ambulance and not knowing what to do. "The emergency room doc said Kyle demonstrated signs of acute poisoning. But they couldn't identify the source. They pumped his stomach and gave him all sorts of medication." Fig had broken down and cried with relief when, after hours of treatment, the doctor finally told him Kyle would be okay. "When he got well he was convinced there was something wrong with the brownies."

"Maybe he had a bad reaction to one of the supplements your mom added."

Fig had suggested the same thing. But, "He didn't exhibit signs of allergic reaction. The doctor was very clear. He suspected poisoning by an unidentified agent."

"But you ate the brownies. How come you weren't affected?"

"I'm not big on sweets. Mom knew that. I'd have one, maybe two small brownies a day. I usually wound up throwing half of them out because they got stale before I finished them."

"I can't believe it," Roxie said. "What kind of mother would poison her son's brownies?"

"One desperate for attention and validation. One desperate to be needed. My dad traveled a lot. Even when he was home he spent most of his time on the phone or relaxing in his den. And it wasn't just my brownies. Looking back, I remembered the drops I'd caught her putting in my soup one time, and my water glass another. 'Homeopathic remedies,' she'd said."

"And now you won't eat soup, and you'll only drink bottled water."

If only that were the extent of it. "It goes beyond that, Roxie. My mother, the woman who was supposed to love me more than anyone, the woman I trusted to care for me, who I'd thought wanted only the best for me, poisoned my food. For years. With the intent to make me sick."

"How do you know for sure? Did you confront her?"

Of course he had. "She denied it. To this day she insists she never gave me anything but what my doctors prescribed and recommended. I asked to see the bottles of the homeopathic preparations and herbs she'd added to my food. She came up with excuse after excuse. I searched for them, and never found one."

"Maybe…"

No. There were no maybes. "Within a week or two of removing every item of food she either made for me or bought for me from our apartment, and taking control of what I ate and where it came from, I began to feel healthy and strong. I know, in here—" he raised his fist to his heart "—that she did it. You saw how she is. Conniving. Manipulative. What's to stop her from trying again? What's to stop someone else from slipping something in my food for any number of reasons?"

"Do you honestly think I'm the type of person who would poison your food?"

"I know, I sound insane, and what I have going on is

not rational, but I refuse to lose one more day of my life because I feel too sick to go out and live it."

Roxie took a sip of coffee. "Have you talked to anyone about all this?"

"Kyle. And now you."

"I mean a professional."

He smiled. "I know. And no, I haven't."

"Maybe it's time you did. Because your issues with food obviously bother you to the point you're trying to hide them. In my opinion you've transferred control of your life from your mother to your irrational fear of being poisoned."

How the heck did she read people and situations so quickly and thoroughly and correctly?

"You know, I've got to tell you, we all have issues, Fig. You're really not all that special. Unless there's something else? Something that might crop up later tonight or tomorrow and have you wanting to get rid of me again?"

"No. And I didn't *want* to get rid of you. I thought..."

"Well, you may change your mind when you learn I don't like anyone to touch my belly button. I avoid foods with artificial red coloring and artificial sweeteners. I am fanatic about keeping my immediate living area spotless. And I have a thing about organization—especially in my closet."

"I can live with that." As long as she could put up with him. Please let her be willing to at least try.

"Now just so I'm sure I understand, I can stay here as long as I don't mess with your food or try to cook for you?"

"Yes."

"Do you have any problem cooking for me?"

"No."

She walked to the door, picked up her bag and turned

toward the bedroom. "Good. You feel up to making French toast?"

He smiled. "Sure."

"Thanks. I'm going to jump in the shower."

That was it. Done. Fig blew out a relieved breath. He'd shared his biggest secrets, and rather than bolting for the door, Roxie responded by asking him to make French toast while she went to take a shower. Granted, he'd known her for only less than two weeks, and they'd gotten off to a rather rocky start, but her actions affirmed what Fig was starting to feel in his heart. Roxie had definite long-term potential.

Did she have any idea how special she was? So different from all the other women he knew. Accepting. Honest. Roxie said what was on her mind and went after what she wanted. She played at tough but turned out to be sensitive and caring. She understood him and knew what he needed before he did. Fig could read her, too. He'd hurt her this morning. Roxie deserved better.

Before he could think better of it, determined to make amends, he had his right arm sealed in plastic wrap and was pushing open the bathroom door.

"You can't get that arm wet," Roxie cautioned as soon as he entered.

The fact that she didn't tell him to let her shower in peace was as good as an invitation. Fig dropped his boxers and pushed back the shower curtain.

"Oy," Roxie said in the process of rinsing shampoo from her hair, rivulets of suds streaming down her firm, tan, luscious body. Fig went from semierect to full-on let's-get-busy. "In order to stay here I have to put up with your freaky eating habits *and* have sex with you? It's too much. What's in it for me?"

That was the problem with not thinking a plan all the

way through. No protection. Fig climbed into the tub anyway, holding his right arm up and away from the spray of
the shower, and closed the curtain behind him. "I'll feed
you well and give you lots of orgasms." He hooked his left
arm behind her back and pulled her front flush with his.

Roxie wrapped her arms around his neck and rubbed
her warm, slippery, magnificent body from side to side,
her taut nipples scraping across his chest, her pelvis cra-
dling him, her bare mons igniting his fire.

She kissed his neck. "Works for me. What do you get
out of it?"

He hugged her close. "You." Day and night, to cuddle
up to in his bed and brighten his wide-awake hours.

"Smart man. I can be very useful to have around," she
said enticingly.

Of that he had no doubt.

"I can help you with your shower, for instance." She
stepped away, picked up the soap and nestled it between
her palms. She stroked it and twirled it sensually until a
foamy lather seeped between her fingers.

Fig's erection envied that soap, wanted to be that soap.
He swallowed. "You have an uncanny ability to know exactly what I need." When Roxie set her sudsy hands to his
chest, his man-parts sent out a flare of excitement that left
behind a residual intense yearning. His body throbbed with
a desire only Roxie could satisfy.

From his neck down her soft hands left no part of him
untouched, her movements more graceful and arousing
than purposeful. The experience: incredible. The end result: one clean, ready-for-sex man.

"I think you should get another tattoo," Roxie said.
"Around here." She drew a circle on his thigh. "An itty-
bitty raccoon."

Tease. He pulled her close, ran his hand down her back

and squeezed her right butt cheek. "How about you get one right here? To give me something to spank."

She actually trembled. Fig had never even considered spanking a woman prior to Roxie, had never been as scared and angry as she'd made him the night of the fire. But if she liked it he'd do it. Anything to please her.

"Rinse," she said.

He stepped beneath the warm water.

Roxie joined him, kissed his shoulder, his chest. "I am in love with your body." She accepted him. As is. Tattoos and quirks and all. It was time to show her how much that meant, how much he was starting to care for her.

"If I had two working hands, this is when I'd pick you up, slam your back to the wall and drive myself deep inside you."

"Ooohhh. Something to look forward to," she said as she took him into her hand and began a slow, sensual glide up and down his swollen shaft. It felt so good. She felt so good. Her long, thin fingers surrounding him, squeezing him, pushing him closer to the edge of ecstasy.

"But you need to take it easy," she said. "Let me do all the work." She went down on her knees.

"No," Fig said, reaching for her with his left hand and helping her up. "Today is all about you."

He closed the distance between them and pressed her back to the center wall, keeping his left side under the water. "Lift this leg." He tapped her right thigh. "Now wrap it around my waist. Open for me. Good girl."

He thrust along the seam of her sex, teasing and titillating, giving her a sample of what was to come. Roxie's breathing became deeper, her movements urgent. She rubbed his head, kissed his cheek, his chin and bottom lip.

Where normally he would have turned his head, Fig froze, waited to see what she'd do next.

"I want to kiss you in the worst way," she said, tracing his bottom lip with her finger.

Deep down he wanted her to kiss him. Wanted to kiss her. But when it came to actually doing it…he couldn't.

"Would it help if I told you I flossed, brushed my teeth and gargled before I got into the shower?" she asked.

In anticipation he'd join her? He leaned back and raised an eyebrow in question.

She nodded. "You, my friend, have a plethora of oral hygiene paraphernalia."

He liked a clean, healthy, as-germ-free-as-he-could-get-it mouth. He stared at her lips, wondered what they'd feel like pressed to his, what she'd taste like. His mom's words haunted him. *The human mouth is the dirtiest part of the body. It contains more germs than a toilet seat. Germs will kill you, Ryan. No kissing on the lips. Ever.*

Damn her. The last thing Fig wanted to think about when he looked at Roxie's beautiful lips was a toilet seat.

"Do you remember yesterday, on the stretcher in the E.R.?" She rocked along his length, ran her fingertips up and down his sides.

He nodded, although she made it difficult to think about anything other than her hands on his body and how much he wanted to get inside of her, to pleasure her over and over.

"When you said you'd make it up to me? Whatever I want, you'll do? Anything, you said."

Uh-oh. Fig swallowed, knew where this was headed.

"Well, I sure would like it if you'd kiss me."

Ka-pow! *Take that,* arousal. Dread replaced his elation of a moment ago. What woman would appreciate a man experiencing dread at the thought of kissing her? It wasn't normal. It made no sense. He knew that. But still… Now she'd get angry. She had every reason to. He was a mental case. He couldn't look at her. He stepped away and gave her room to leave.

"Hey," she said softly as she took his arm and brought him back to her. "If you're not ready, that's okay. I can wait, but not too long." She lifted his chin. His eyes met hers, soft and caring. "Promise me you'll work on it. To surprise me."

"I will." He buried his face in her neck. Thankful. Blessed to be with Roxie, who didn't make unrealistic demands and carry on when he couldn't meet them, who simply stated what she wanted, prepared to wait. He would reward her patience with the most amazing kiss ever. Hopefully. After he received some counseling. Which he would inquire about first thing Monday morning. For Roxie. For himself. For a future he'd never thought possible before today.

"I'm sorry I brought it up." She hugged him. "Can we get back to the celebration-of-me day?"

Of course they could. After he took care of a few small details. "You soak for a little while longer. Give me five minutes to get ready," Fig said. He whispered in her ear, "Then dry off and meet me in my bedroom, where we will commence with the Day of Roxie revelry." He kissed her temple. "Come as you are."

Okay. So when the idea of making their next few hours extraordinary and worthy of standing out above every other sexual encounter from Roxie's memory had popped into Fig's head, he'd failed to consider he had only one usable hand.

When Roxie exited the bathroom in full goddesslike nakedness—in way less than the five minutes he'd requested—he'd barely managed to get the bottom sheet on the bed.

"Mocha satin," she said, rubbing the still-folded top

sheet against her cheek. "These things are legit. Me likey."
She took over making the bed and winked. "Conserve your
first-day-post-op energy. You're going to need it." She had
the bed made in minutes.

He glanced at the candles he'd placed on each night-
stand. Without being asked, Roxie lit them while he closed
the blackout curtains.

"You're going all out," Roxie said.

"You're worth it," Fig responded. And she was. Even if
she didn't realize it. "Now lie down."

Roxie folded down the top sheet, crawled to the center of the queen-size bed—giving him a tantalizing view
of her nice, round posterior—and lay down on her back.
"This feels rather decadent." She eyed him askance. "But
a party of one is no party." She patted the bed beside her.

Even though the room wasn't completely dark, the light
from the candles danced on her beautiful skin. She looked
like a serving of rich caramel cream piped onto a bar of
mocha chocolate. Fig's mouth watered. Come to find out,
he had a sweet tooth, after all.

He grabbed a strip of condoms from the drawer by the
bed and held them out to Roxie. "You're in charge."

She scooted to the edge of the bed, eagerly ripped one
open and rolled it on. Fig called on every bit of control he
possessed to keep himself from tackling her and giving it
to her hard and fast. "On your back," he said. "Arms over
your head."

Roxie did as instructed because the command in his tone
excited her. She settled onto the silky sheets and reached
her arms—and what the heck, her legs, too—toward each
corner of the bed. Spread out, exposed and open, she was
his for the taking.

He watched her, a hint of domination in his gaze. Power.

And with no more than that look, Roxie's body heated and made itself ready to accept him.

"Tell me what you want," Fig said, still standing at the side of the bed.

She wanted him to tie her arms and legs in this exact position, to do wicked things that would make her scream out with pleasure. "You. I want you."

He joined her on the bed, careful of his right arm. At one point he winced.

"Are you sure you're up for this?" Roxie asked.

Fig settled on top of her, balancing his weight on his left elbow. He stared deeply into her eyes and slid the broad tip of his erection along her warm, wet path. All the way down then back up. Over and over. "I am definitely up for this."

Well, then, let's get started. Roxie tilted her pelvis, hoping with his next pass he'd slide inside.

He didn't.

"Have I told you how beautiful you are?" he asked instead.

She wasn't. Her face was too narrow, her eyes too prominent and her nose resembled a hawk's beak.

"You have the prettiest eyes. When I look into them I can tell exactly what you're thinking."

Oh, no, he couldn't.

And still staring down at her, he thrust deep. Filled her. Touched a part of her she didn't know existed until that very moment, making sex with Fig so much more than a mere physical encounter.

He pulled out and pushed in again. "Today is all about you." Out. In. "Tell me what you want, Roxie." Out. In. "What you *really* want."

She couldn't. Not yet. But there was one thing. "Make love to me." Not down-and-dirty-fill-me-drill-me sex. But slow, sweet, you're-worth-a-little-time-and-effort sex. The kind two people who cared about more than each other's bodies had. It'd be nice to experience that at least once.

Fig got an odd look on his face.

Roxie went hot with embarrassment. "Don't panic. I'm not saying I love you or anything." But if she let herself, she could. Oh, so easily. "I hardly know you."

"Yet you know more about me than friends I've had for years."

She liked knowing his secrets. If only she could share all of hers.

"You can," he said.

"Can what?" Roxie asked.

"Tell me whatever it is you're hiding."

How could he possibly…?

"When you're ready." He kissed her forehead. "Keeping secrets is going to give you wrinkles."

Roxie focused on relaxing her facial muscles. No stress or indecision or guilt here. "Are we going to spend our day talking? Because there are other things…"

"Wrap your legs around my hips."

Gladly.

He twirled the knuckles of his right hand around her nipple until it tightened into a hard, ticklish peak, and increased his thrusts. The nurse part of her wanted to tell him he shouldn't be using his right hand. The aroused woman part—who loved how he made her feel—took the nurse by the throat and squeezed so not even a peep of sound could escape.

"I wish I had two good hands so I could do everything I want to do to you."

"Improvise," Roxie suggested.

Fig lowered his mouth to her ear. "I'm going to make

you love me, Roxie," he whispered, his breath hot and heavy, his hips rocking into her.

He wouldn't have to work hard. It would take far more effort for her to make herself not fall in love with him. "Oh, you think so?" she asked, meeting each thrust.

He bent his knees, shifted up and drove into her, gliding along the exact spot that drove her wild.

"I know so." He lavished attention on the tiny cove at the base of her ear and Roxie reveled in the sensation of having each of her turn-on triggers engaged at the same time.

Soon they were both breathing too heavily to talk. They spoke with their bodies in a mix of tender touches and loving caresses. They communicated via escalating moans, desperate groans and deep, lingering sighs. Roxie had her legs clamped around him, urging him deeper—as if it were even possible.

Then he did something that sent a surge of wonderfulness loose inside of her and Roxie screamed out, "Just like that. Don't stop. Don't you dare stop."

Like he'd hit her power boost she thrust harder, moved faster, and squeezed him tighter than she'd thought herself capable. In return he thrust harder, moved faster and squeezed her tighter right back.

A few minutes later, lying replete on Fig's muscled chest while he twirled his fingers in her hair, unable to move more than her mouth, Roxie said, "We sure are well matched in the bedroom."

Fig kissed the top of her head. "It's a start."

On Sunday morning Roxie finished wiping the counters with a paper towel and said, "Sit. You made breakfast. I clean up. Then I've got to go."

Fig pulled out a chair, sat down and studied her like

he could tell she was hiding something. "What's on the schedule for today?"

"*Mami* made a list of things she wants me to bring over to Victoria's. After I stop by her room to pick it up I need to meet with Victoria to discuss my job and, if I still have one, to put in a request for some more time off." And pick up what she needed for Tuesday night. An ominous feeling of doom weighed heavily on her shoulders. She turned her back to Fig so he wouldn't see.

She hated not being totally honest with him. But he'd never approve, would no doubt want to be involved somehow and he wasn't up to it. As much as she didn't want him to know the truth, she worried about him, too. He looked absolutely drained from them spending the better part of the past twenty-four hours in bed. Not sleeping. Barely resting. They'd been insatiable for each other. He needed to relax and strengthen. Not worry about her. No. She'd handle it herself and put the ordeal behind her. Without Fig ever finding out.

"Then I'm going to the house to try to find everything," she said with forced vigor. "Then it's back to the hospital to wait for *Mami*'s discharge, and a trip to Victoria's to get her settled in."

"I'll come with you," Fig offered.

Any other time she would have taken him up on his offer. She liked having him around. But not today. "Don't be ridiculous." She washed the last of their silverware and set them in the dish rack to dry. "You need to elevate your arm and rest today. But thank you." She walked over to kiss the top of his head. "Really. I appreciate the offer. Now what do you need me to do for you before I go?"

"Leave me your brothers' names, addresses and phone numbers."

"Yeah. About that." She ran the ends of the scarf she'd

chosen as a belt through her fingers. "They're not going to come." They didn't care about her or *Mami* one bit. "And they probably won't appreciate you bothering them." And would be obnoxiously vocal about it, like they were back when she used to call them to ask them to come home.

He stood up and slid a pad and pen across the counter. "Names, addresses and phone numbers. You let me handle the rest."

"I don't…" How embarrassing to admit the only number she knew for certain was Ernesto's. While *Mami* wrote down the return addresses from the occasional Christmas cards she received, Roxie couldn't say for certain where any of her brothers lived.

As if he understood he tapped the pad and said, "Write down as much as you know."

"Your time would be better spent sleeping." She did as he asked. "Or preparing me a gourmet dinner."

Fig approached her with his arms open. She stepped between them and he hugged her close. "It's going to be fine, Roxie. They'll come. I'll make it happen."

Roxie pulled back to look at him. "What are you up to?" She studied his face, trying to find the answer. But he gave nothing away.

"It's better you don't know," he teased. "What time do you think you'll be home?"

Home. It would be so nice if this really were her home, and whenever she returned to it, Fig would be there waiting for her, making her feel safe and cared about. Happy.

But she was the pretend girlfriend, and he was her temporary man. Because *Mami* couldn't live alone, and as soon as her house was habitable, they'd both be moving back into it. And because Fig wasn't the only one with quirks he didn't want others to know about.

"I'll call you and let you know," Roxie answered.

"Call Kyle's house phone. My cell's turned off."

"Did you call your mom?" Roxie asked. She'd already spoken with hers, twice.

"I will," Fig said. "Later."

Roxie detached his cell phone from the charger and handed it to him. "Do it now. So she doesn't worry."

He put the phone down. "She'll worry no matter what."

"Did you ever think maybe if you called her on a regular basis and involved her in your life a bit more she wouldn't call you constantly or go to such extreme lengths to see you?"

Based on his expression, no, he hadn't.

"Either you forgive her for the past or you don't. Either she's in your life or she isn't. All or nothing. Anything less will be a stressor to you both. She'll always be seeking more of your time and attention. And you'll constantly be trying to put her off and make her go away."

"Short of moving back in with her, I'm not capable of giving her the amount of my time and attention she wants."

"Discuss it with her," Roxie suggested. "Set limits. But you'll have to give a little, too."

Fig stared down at the phone in his hands. "Do you think I'm crazy?" He looked up and smiled. "Maybe I should clarify. Crazy for forgiving her?"

"Honestly?"

Fig nodded.

"I don't think you have forgiven her. I think there's part of you that wants to, but a bigger part is still angry and hurt. And unsure. Because you never found out for certain if she purposely set out to hurt you."

"She was a good mom," Fig said. "She used to play with me for hours and read to me. Sing to me." His words drifted off as he remembered something. "She stayed with me and held my hand and refused to leave me alone through countless scary and painful procedures and tests. The leukemia was very real and we battled it for years. Without her, I think I would have given up. Yet she prolonged my suffering, to control my life. How am I supposed to deal with that?"

"You close the door on it and lock it away." Like she'd chosen to do with all the ways her mother had failed her. "Or you work things out with your mom." Roxie kissed his head. "If you want to move forward and heal, you need to choose."

On Tuesday night Roxie sat at the corner of the bar at O'Halloran's, praying the pain medication she'd convinced Fig to take after a particularly—purposely—energetic round of demanding sex kept him sound asleep for the time it would take her to accomplish her task and return to him.

"The usual to start?" Triple B asked.

Roxie nodded. He returned with an ice cold bottle of beer.

While she waited, she sipped the familiar brew to calm her nerves, she listened to the same old songs playing on the jukebox and watched the regulars drinking what they typically drank and doing what they typically did.

But for Roxie, tonight was no ordinary night at O'Halloran's.

"Well, well, well. If it isn't Roxie Loves Coxie."

His voice grated on her self-control, and she briefly considered breaking her beer bottle over his head. But then she wouldn't get what she needed, and he wouldn't pay for what he'd done, so she lifted it and took a sip of its bubbly goodness instead.

"Fancy meeting you here," he continued the charade.

As if their "date" hadn't been prearranged. "Hi, there,

Johnny." She wondered if that was his real name. "Nice to see you again." The remnants of that lie sat bitter on her tongue. But— Nothing to see here, folks. Just two old… friends meeting up for a drink.

As if on cue Triple B meandered over. "What'll you have?" He tossed a napkin on the bar in front of Johnny.

"A beer. Same as her."

Johnny leaned in to whisper in Roxie's ear. The stubble on his cheek grazing hers made Roxie cringe. She much preferred Fig's smooth skin. "Too bad we got all this bad business between us," he said. "We were good together. Had us some fun."

So she'd thought. Until the call she'd hoped was for a second date turned out to be for the purposes of blackmailing her. "You've got yourself some talent," she said.

"Maybe when this is all done we could…"

Not even if someone were holding a loaded gun to her head. "Maybe," she lied. Play the role. Draw him in. Get him talking. "Was it your buddy who filmed us?"

He nodded.

Come on. Talk. "I heard his breathing on the tape." His heavy, excited breathing.

"He likes to watch." Johnny smiled.

"If you'd let me know you were making a video of us, he could have come out of his hidey-hole and gotten closer to the action. I bet he would have liked that." The creeper.

"You mean you would have been okay with it?"

Perfect. "I might have been. If you'd asked real nice."

"I'll keep that in mind for next time."

You do that, scuz-bucket. "So where is he? Your friend."

"He's around."

Roxie scanned the bar, didn't see him.

Triple B delivered Johnny's drink, placing it on the bar with a bit more force than necessary. Johnny, however, was too busy staring at Roxie's cleavage in the low-cut blouse she'd purposely worn to notice Triple B's bulging biceps and step-out-of-line-and-I'll-beat-you-into-a-coma scowl. Roxie motioned her friend away.

"So you called this meeting, doll. What's up?" Johnny took a swig of beer.

Roxie leaned in close. "I pulled the switch," she said quietly. "The drugs for the tape. That was the deal."

Johnny looked around. "I heard you've been on vacation this week." He eyed her suspiciously.

"One of my best friends is the head nurse on 5E. I dropped in to visit her. She got called out on an emergency, asked me to give her keys to the charge nurse. I saw my opportunity and I took it. Since I wasn't on the schedule to work, if someone figures it out, there's no way they'll trace the switch to me."

Johnny smiled. "Smart girl. I knew from the moment we met you were perfect for the job." He ran a callused finger up and down her arm. "We could make a good team, you and me. In *and* out of the sack."

Roxie fought the revulsion of this man's touch and sat perfectly still. That he actually thought she was okay with being taken advantage of, videotaped and threatened with exposure. "Did you bring the tape?" Roxie asked.

Johnny nodded. "Just like you asked." He didn't offer any further information. He finished his beer and ordered another—for each of them.

Roxie didn't have time for this. She needed to get the tape and get the heck out of there. "Where is it?"

"My car."

Not the car. Triple B would totally freak if she got up to leave the bar with Johnny. "Ask your friend to bring it in." Then she'd have them both in the same place.

"What's your rush?" Johnny chugged from his second beer. "Drink up."

Roxie lifted her second "beer" to her lips. Triple B had replaced it with ginger ale, like she'd asked. She couldn't risk anything dulling her senses. "I've got a friend waiting on me," she lied.

"The pale, bald guy?"

So he *had* been watching her. "Yeah."

"He your boyfriend?"

"Patient," she answered, wanting to keep Johnny interested until they'd finished their transaction. "Friend of the family. So. We going to make the exchange or what? I've got to get back before he wakes up."

Johnny finished his beer. "Outside."

She grabbed her purse and stood. What else could she do? Halfway to the door Triple B bellowed, "Where you going, Roxie?"

She plastered a smile so he wouldn't know just how nervous she was. "Outside for a few minutes. I'll be back in to settle up."

"I left enough money for both of us," Johnny said.

Lord help her.

"Five minutes, Roxie." Triple B picked up his wooden drunk-slugger and slammed it down on the bar. "Or I'm coming out after you."

"That was quite a show," Johnny said when they reached the parking lot.

Fear crept up Roxie's spine. Had he figured her out?

Johnny laughed. "But you look like you can take care of yourself."

She almost collapsed with relief. "He worries. I went to school with his wife."

Johnny walked past car after car. She'd been so drunk the night they'd left together she had no recollection of what he'd driven her home in. Something moved on her right. Roxie halted.

"It's only Luke," Johnny said, taking her arm.

His friend. Two against one, not good. And now he was pulling her along, double not good. Roxie dug her heels into the gravel lot. "Look. I'd rather stay over here in the light so I can see what I'm doing," she tried.

"Come on." Johnny gave her a tug to get her moving. "I have a light inside my car."

Roxie wanted to run. But she needed him to take the pills. And she needed to get the tape. In a flash of morbid thought Roxie took solace in knowing if something happened to her, Victoria would see that *Mami* was taken care of.

"Hey, Luke," Johnny said into the darkness. "Roxie said next time you don't have to hide."

"I said maybe there'd be a next time." *Maybe as in never, you miscreant.*

Johnny stopped beside an old-style Cadillac parked in the shadows and opened the door. She could sense Luke close by. Johnny rummaged through a bag on the backseat and took out what looked like a DVD in a clear plastic case.

"How do I know that's of me?" she asked.

He held it up to show her "Roxie" written in black marker on the disk. But wait a minute. "Shouldn't there be a tape? From the video recorder?"

Johnny smiled. "I told you she was smart, Luke," he said and turned back to the bag. He emerged with three mini-camcorder tapes.

She held out her hand.

He held the disk and tapes out of reach. "What do you have for me?"

Roxie felt around in her purse and pulled out two sheets

of blister-packed Percocet pills and two of Vicodin pills. He reached for them.

"I give you the pills. You give me the tape. Like we agreed." Roxie's heart pounded. She could smell her own sweat. "At the same time."

Johnny stepped forward and held out the disk and tapes with his right hand. She took them with her left hand at the same time he snatched the pills from her right. There. It was done. But before relief could settle in, Johnny yanked her by the arm, turned her and forced her up against his car while he mashed his lips into hers.

"This is why you tried to screw me unconscious and insisted I take my pain medication afterward?" Fig's eerily calm voice penetrated the darkness. "If you want me to kiss you you're going to have to stop swapping spit with other men."

Oh, God. Not now. "It's not what you think," Roxie said, trying to push away from Johnny.

"Let her go," Fig demanded.

Johnny opened the front door of his car, reached inside and turned on his headlights, surrounding Fig in light. "Well, well, well. He sounds awful jealous for a patient," Johnny pointed out.

She should have inflicted a disorienting blow to his head when she'd had the chance.

"You told him I was your patient?" Fig asked. To anyone who didn't know him he'd come off completely calm and in control. But his right eye twitched, and his jaw looked made of stone.

"I don't want no trouble," Johnny said. "You can have her." He dropped his hands. "I'll just be on my way."

"No. Wait," Roxie said to him.

"You mean you want to come home with me and Luke, after all?"

"Roxie doesn't do tag team. Isn't that right, honey?" Fig asked. "Or was that a lie, too? Maybe we're not as well matched in the bedroom as you led me to believe."

This was a nightmare. Wake up. Wake up.

"Get lost, buddy," Johnny said. "She's made her choice. Get in the car, Luke." Johnny grabbed Roxie around the waist and started to push her through the open door. "Come on, baby. Me and Luke. We got what you need."

"No." Roxie tried to twist free.

Fig started toward her.

Car after car skidded in around them.

Johnny pushed her away. "You double-crossing bitch." He slammed his gigantic fist into her cheek.

Pain exploded on contact. Tiny pinpricks of light speckled the darkness. A black nothingness threatened. Wanting to be finished with this whole situation, wanting to be done with this night, Roxie didn't fight it.

CHAPTER NINE

BACK at the hospital. Again. Fig paced the E.R. hallway outside of Roxie's room. He couldn't tell which hand hurt worse, the one attached to his fractured wrist or the one that'd planted the knockout punch to the unchivalrous excuse for a man who'd struck Roxie.

"You are some piece of work." Kyle handed him a bag of ice. "You're going to need an X-ray, you know."

"Nothing's broken." Fig made a loose fist then, despite the pain, extended his fingers. "You haven't mentioned how you and Victoria happened to be in O'Halloran's parking lot at eleven-thirty on a Tuesday night. And why you didn't warn me what was going down."

"I don't know much more than you," Kyle said, his hands in his pockets. "I couldn't sleep on that couch Victoria banished me to, so I was awake when she tried to sneak out of the house."

"What is with the two of them?" Roxie, allowing herself to be used in some sting operation to capture a drug-dealing blackmailer—he found out after the fact—putting herself in danger. She and Victoria sneaking around, not confiding in the men responsible for protecting them.

Victoria stuck her head out into the hallway. "She's awake."

Finally. Some answers. Up to now all Victoria would say

is "it's not my story to tell." Fig followed Kyle into Roxie's room, which looked identical to the one he'd been in prior to his surgery. She lay on a stretcher, the top slightly elevated, with no pillow. Her left eye was almost swollen shut, the area surrounding it and her cheek an inflamed red that made Fig want to search out the goon from the parking lot and hit him again. He was in the E.R. somewhere. Fig had seen him come in.

"You hit him?" Roxie accused the second she saw him.

"He hit you," Fig explained.

"With your left hand?"

He held up his splinted arm. "Well, I couldn't use my right."

"How are you going to take care of yourself?"

She was worried about him?

"And if you're both here—" she pointed back and forth between Kyle and Victoria "—who's home with *Mami* and Jake?"

"Ali and Jared," Victoria answered.

"Then who's watching the baby?" Roxie asked.

"They brought him along," Victoria said. "Your mother is in love."

Roxie flung her arm over her forehead. "You should all be in your own homes in your own beds."

"I had to be there," Victoria said, standing next to the stretcher. "In case something went wrong. If Ali wasn't nursing, she would have come, too. She and Jared had a huge argument over it."

"We'd have had a huge argument, too, *honey*," Kyle said to Victoria, "if you'd taken the time to fill me in on your little plan."

"Which is why I didn't," Victoria countered.

"Would one of you please tell me what the heck is going on?" Fig asked. Loudly.

Roxie clamped her eyes closed and brought her hands up to her temples. "Keep it down, will ya? Lady with a closed head injury here."

"Sorry," he whispered.

"That's it. I'm going to start charging," she said to him. "Fifty dollars every time you do something that warrants an apology to me. Effective immediately." She held out her hand.

"Start me a tab," he said. "You know you're awful chipper for someone who was mauled and beaten in a dark parking lot."

"That little hit?" She waved him off. "My brothers used to hit me harder than that. He caught me by surprise is all."

One more reason to hate her brothers. "Can we focus on the reason you were in O'Halloran's parking lot to begin with? Why you snuck out of my bed to meet a blackmailer? Why half the town's police force and men in official-looking black cars knew about it and I didn't?" That last part hurt. Did she not think she could trust him? After everything they'd shared?

Roxie turned to face the wall. "I'd rather not talk about it."

"We'll wait outside," Victoria said, taking Kyle by the hand.

"But I want to know, too," Kyle complained.

Victoria pushed him out of the room.

After the door closed behind them, Roxie didn't move. "You didn't take your pain medicine."

He was a pro at faking it and pretending sleep. "You weren't yourself at dinner. You seemed antsy and distracted." The sex had been different, too. Dispassionate. Desperate. Almost impersonal.

"So you followed me?"

"If you'll remember, I asked you what was wrong." At

least half a dozen times. "I was worried about you. Talk to me," Fig said quietly.

"I didn't want you to find out." She sounded so miserable his heart ached for her. "To know the truth."

"Whatever it is, it's okay." He approached the stretcher. "We'll get through it."

"We? We'll get through it?" She gave an emotionless chuckle. "You'd be wise to run or you'll get brought down right along with me. *Ay Dios mio.* Your parents will be in town to see it happen."

"I won't run. I can't. I'm falling in love with you, Roxie. And when you love someone…"

"You have known me barely two weeks. The worst damn two weeks of my miserable life, as it turns out. You're nuts to think you love me," she said. "Hell, I'm so screwed up right now *I* don't even love me."

"Roxie…"

"Don't 'Roxie' me, all calm as can be. I'm giving you an out. Take it. Trust me, you'll be glad you did."

"Let me help you."

She laughed. "You can't even help yourself. How are you going to help me? Come tomorrow everyone will know. I'll be even more of a pariah than I am now. And you, adding fuel to the fire. 'If you want me to kiss you you'll have to stop swapping spit with other men.'"

"I walked up to see you kissing another man. I'm sorry if the sight of it upset me."

"I was wearing a wire, Fig. Lord knows how many people heard you admit you couldn't bring yourself to kiss me because of where my mouth has been."

That's not what he'd said.

"I wonder how the newspaper will spin that in the not-so-flattering article they are sure to be working on as we speak. Hmmmm." She tapped her chin. "I can picture the headline. 'Not Only Is the Whack-Job Hoarder's House Too Filthy to Live In, But She's Been with So Many Men Her Mouth is Too Dirty to Kiss.'"

"I'm sorry. I didn't mean…"

She turned away from him and held out her palm for another fifty dollars. "You can go now."

"Don't do this, Roxie. Don't push me away. Whatever has you so upset, it can't be as bad as you think."

"You have no idea."

"Maybe…"

"Maybe nothing. The police confiscated all the tapes from the video. In their entirety. And nothing stays secret in Madrin Falls."

"The video's old news. People have already seen it."

Roxie seemed to deflate. "Not all of it."

"What?"

She let out a deep breath. "There was more. Johnny only uploaded the first half."

Now it made sense. "He threatened to upload the second part."

She nodded. "This time I got in touch with Victoria, who worked with the hospital investigators, the DEA and the police to set up tonight's fun."

"But why? It's more of the same. No one's going to care."

"It is not more of the same," she snapped. "I let him do things to me. Perverted, embarrassing things. And I liked them," she said defiantly. "Before you, sex had become boring. Routine."

Before him. If she weren't so upset he would have puffed up with pride and smiled.

"I needed more," she continued. "Johnny offered me an opportunity to explore new avenues to find satisfaction and I accepted. Willingly. I enjoyed myself more than I had in months. Maybe years. Tomorrow everyone will know the full extent of just how freakishly screwed up I really am."

"Roxie. There's nothing wrong with experimenting." In fact the thought excited him. "With two consenting adults finding pleasure in a way that's agreeable to them both. You're not a freak. You're not screwed up."

"Says the man who refuses to kiss me because my mouth is too dirty, who won't let me cook for him because he thinks I'm out to poison him and who won't leave the house without hand sanitizer in his pocket. I'm sorry if your opinion of freakish behavior doesn't mean all that much."

Someone knocked at the door. Without waiting for a response Victoria stuck her head in. "The police are here, Roxie. They need to speak with you."

"Goodbye, Fig."

He did not like the finality in her tone. "I'll be right outside."

"No. I want you to leave. I'm tired. Exhausted, actually. I can barely handle my own problems without yours adding to the enormous mound. I've enjoyed playing temporary pretend girlfriend. But reality check. We're from two different worlds with enough baggage between us to sink an ocean liner. Focus on yourself. Fix yourself. Find a nice Jewish girl and have a nice perfect life."

Two police officers entered the room.

Victoria took him by the arm. "There'll be no changing her mind tonight." She guided him to the door. "When she's ready for discharge, I'll bring her home with me."

"But…"

"You need to come now," she whispered as they exited the room. "There's a reporter from the newspaper nosing around. Kyle's got him cornered in the lounge."

* * *

After driving for hours, not wanting to return to the condo to see reminders of Roxie and feel the loss and frustration of not being able to hold her, comfort her and reassure her, Fig pulled into the parking lot of the only decent motel in town. He sat for a few minutes, wondering if this was the right thing to do, and decided, yes. It was time. Past time. He wanted to be the man Roxie confided in, trusted with all her secrets and turned to with confidence when she needed help. He wanted to enrich her life, not add to her burdens. To do that he had to start somewhere. So he got out of his car, climbed the stairs to the second floor, walked halfway down the row of rooms and knocked on his parents' door.

Roxie awoke to a large hand gently shaking her shoulder. "Time to wake up," a male voice said, startling her.

"Hey," the voice said. "It's okay. It's me. Kyle."

Kyle? In her bedroom? She lifted her head, and pain sliced through it. "Ow." She tried to open her eyes. The left one achieved only a squint. Memories of last night came pouring back. Johnny. The punch. The complete video in the hands of the police. Victoria's old, like-sleeping-on-burlap-covered-straw couch.

And Fig. Gone. Because she'd pushed him away. Because he'd let her.

The pain traveled to her heart.

"I was told to wake you up by nine," Kyle said, standing over her.

"Nine?" Roxie sat up. "Where's *Mami?*"

"Shoot," Kyle said. "Would you lie back down?"

Roxie looked up at him to see if he was serious.

He held up notepaper with Victoria's neat handwriting on it. "Number two," Kyle said. "I was supposed to help you sit up in case you got dizzy."

Roxie smiled. That was Victoria, Miss Organization/ Delegation. "I'm not dizzy," Roxie said. "What's number three?"

"Bring you fresh water." He pointed to a glass on the coffee table. "Four. Offer you acetaminophen or ibuprofen in case your head hurts." He pointed to two pill bottles beside the water. "Five. Make you breakfast. Six. Tell you to read the newspaper. Seven. Get you to your house by ten."

"Well, check, check, check and check." She picked up the newspaper from the coffee table and flung it, Frisbee style, into the open stairwell leading to the front door. "You can cross me reading that rag off your list. Not gonna happen."

"You hungry?" Kyle asked.

"No."

"Okay. I'll make you some toast." He pointed to his list. "You see this small writing here? Victoria said not to take no for an answer." He turned toward the kitchen.

"Can you say whipped?" Roxie called after him.

"Whipped. And enjoying every minute of it. Well, except for sleeping on the couch. There are fresh towels in the bathroom if you want to shower."

"Why's it so quiet here?" Roxie asked. "Where is everyone?"

"Victoria has your mom and Jake over at your house."

"What?" Roxie jumped up. The room spun. "Whoa." She plopped back down.

Kyle stuck his head out of the kitchen. "If you fall down and hurt yourself I'm going to be royally pissed."

"*Mami*'s not strong enough. Her heart. What was Victoria thinking?" She popped the cap on the acetaminophen and swallowed back a few with a water chaser.

"Relax. Have you ever known Victoria to overlook a

detail? Jared changed shifts with another doc. He'll be on-site for the duration of your mom's visit. And he pilfered some stuff from the E.R. just in case."

Roxie fingered the swollen tissue on her face. "What did you tell *Mami* about my eye?"

"That you got hit trying to stop a father from beating his son outside the convenience mart."

Genius. Roxie smiled. "Who thought of that?"

"You're welcome," Kyle said with a smile of his own.

"Now all we have to do is keep her away from the newspaper."

"Victoria hid her glasses."

Ten minutes later Roxie had freshened up and was ready to go. "I need a ride," she said on her way out the door.

"You're going to get me into trouble for not feeding you." Kyle followed after her, holding a piece of toast.

Roxie stopped short, surprised to see her red car parked in Victoria's driveway.

"Fig drove it over from the bar," Kyle said. "And he borrowed my pickup, so I'll drive you in your car."

Roxie fished her keys out of her oversize bag. "I'm perfectly capable of…"

Kyle plucked them from her hand. "Number eight. I'm to drive because your vision is impaired."

"Does that woman miss anything?"

"Actually, Fig added that one."

She turned to Kyle. "Fig?" He didn't hate her? Hadn't left town?

"The calls started coming in around five this morning."

Welcome to small-town U.S.A. "Threats to run me out of town? Reports of cross burnings on my lawn?"

"If you want to know, read the article in the paper."

Not a chance.

"He was here by six-thirty and he and Victoria set to

work making lists. Newsflash, Fig can be almost as anal as Victoria is."

"God help us," Roxie joked.

"Have a care with his heart," Kyle said seriously. "I've never seen him as upset as he was last night when you went down. And we've been through a lot together."

"You would honestly let your friend get involved with someone like me?" Roxie asked. The town's good-time girl?

"Fig is a very good judge of character," Kyle answered. "And for the record, I was the one who encouraged him to come for a visit to meet you. Now get in the car. We're on a tight schedule."

Kyle turned onto her street and Roxie couldn't believe the congestion, cars and trucks lining the sidewalks. A news van sat parked on her neighbor's lawn. "This is a nightmare," she said, envisioning pandemonium when she stepped out of the car. Cameras flashing. People yelling taunts and insults. "Nothing better to do on a Wednesday morning? Worthless busybodies. Doesn't anyone work a day job anymore?"

Kyle squeezed the car into a space between her neighbor's chain-link fence and the portable carport Roxie had erected to hide the grotesque pile of discarded children's toys and equipment *Mami* had accumulated.

"Come to think of it," Roxie continued. "Why aren't you at work? And Victoria? Is that Ali on the front lawn? She's on maternity leave. She shouldn't be here. And if Jared's here and that's Ali's gramps standing next to her, who's watching little James? Have you all gone insane?"

"We're your friends, Roxie. We're all here today because you need us to be." Kyle reached down between his seat and the door and handed her the newspaper he'd tried to foist on her earlier. "Now stop being a pain in the ass and read the damn article. You made the front page." He unfolded it and held it open in front of her face. "Number six on my list. Read it."

"'Local Nurse a Local Hero Who Needs Our Help.'" Roxie read the headline. A blown up, black-and-white copy of her hospital ID badge photo was centered beneath it. "What?" She looked at Kyle.

He smiled.

Roxie looked through the car window to see that while some people were standing around watching the spectacle, the majority were working. *Mami* sat in a chair on the porch with Jake at her side. A blonde woman Roxie recognized from the hospital came out of the house carrying a large white garbage bag. She stopped in front of *Mami,* who examined the bag, which Roxie knew would be labeled with the name of the person it was intended for. *Mami* nodded and pointed. The blonde walked to Victoria, who stood in the middle of the fray with a clipboard. Victoria pointed to the left. The woman walked to a sign with Ernesto's name on it and set the bag on the pile.

"Victoria's carrying a clipboard," Roxie noted.

"She loves to be in charge, that woman of mine." Kyle looked out the window at his fiancée. "Look over there."

Roxie looked in the direction of his finger. "Jeez Louise. Fig has one, too."

"Read the rest. I'm stuck hostage until you do because I can't open my door. So get to it." He looked at his watch. "Number seven. Get you to the house by ten. I have eight minutes."

Roxie scanned the article. "Local nurse the victim of a sexual predator/narcotics dealer...volunteered to help catch him without regard for her reputation or personal safety... As a result, law enforcement obtained records and videotapes implicating the suspect and an accomplice in fraudulent activities at dozens of hospitals across New York State… The hero and her mother need our help."

"I was a victim?"

"Yes. You were." Kyle crossed something off his list. "And if Fig chose to play around with the facts a bit, so be it. He can be a master manipulator when it suits him."

"It's in his genes."

"But he uses it for the greater good. Speak of the devil."

Roxie's door opened and there stood Fig, dressed in work clothes and a baseball cap. He held out his left palm to help her out of the car. Roxie flipped it over and kissed his still-slightly-swollen, bruised knuckles before exiting.

Kyle climbed out behind her.

Fig kissed her left cheek gently. "Does it hurt?" he asked quietly and kissed her temple.

Not anymore. He kissed her forehead. Her nose. He set his right cheek to hers, the corners of their mouths almost touching. "Don't give up on me, Roxie," he whispered. "I'm going to beat it. I'm going to be a man you're proud to be with."

He already was.

"I love you," he said. "It came out of nowhere. I didn't plan for it to happen. But here we are. I spent a miserable night without you, not knowing what today would bring."

From the minute he'd exited her hospital room, Roxie had been miserable, too. But, "You can't. It's too soon."

"Yes, I can." He shifted to look at her face. "We've been through so much in such a short time. I know what I feel. It's okay if you don't…"

"If worrying about you and wanting to take care of you and missing you every minute we're not together means I love you, then I do. But…"

"No buts." Fig touched a finger to her lips. "For now

let's just leave it at we love each other. We'll work the rest
out later."

A horn honking "La Cucaracha" had everyone stopping
what they were doing to look out at the street in front of
the house. A refurbished 1960s-style car with gleaming
chrome fenders pulled to a stop, and a huge Latino man
climbed out of the front passenger door.

"Which one's that?" Fig asked.

"What do you mean which one? I don't recognize him.
It's not like I know every man in town." She tried to step
away.

"Stop," Fig said. "You have to stop twisting what I say.
Which brother is that?"

"That's one of my brothers?" *Ay Dios mio.* He did not
look happy. "This was a bad idea."

Fig waved him over.

"Stop that. What the heck are you doing?"

"We need to finish this, Roxie. Today's the day."

Two equally huge men climbed out of the backseat and
the driver drove off. Roxie glanced at the condition of the
house and yard, mortified it looked nothing like it had fifteen years earlier.

Fig stepped forward to greet her brothers.

Roxie headed for the porch, grabbing Jared on the way.
"You got a defibrillator somewhere? My brothers showed
up, after all." Even if *Mami* didn't need it, Roxie might.

"It's going to be fine." Jared wrapped an arm around her
shoulders. "Ali." His wife looked up from stacking hundreds of plastic take-out containers. "You got my bags?"
Ali nodded.

Roxie climbed the steps. *"Hola, Mami,"* she said.

Her mother stood and took Roxie's face between her
hands. *"Mi querida hija.* Look at your beautiful face. That
man should be arrested."

"Sit. I need to tell you something."

"Mami," a loud booming voice called out.

Roxie recognized that voice, Roberto, her oldest, meanest brother, and froze, scared to look at him.

Her mother clutched her chest and grabbed for the broken porch railing. Jared reached out to steady her. "Keep breathing, Mrs. Morano." Ali walked up beside Roxie and rubbed her back. "You, too, Rox."

"Funny how you could be a grown, independent woman one second and feel like a scared five-year-old girl the next," she whispered to Ali as her brother's large stride ate up the distance to the porch.

"It's going to be okay," Ali said.

Roxie knew better.

"Hey, bug eyes," Roberto said when he reached her. "Great job taking care of the home front."

Bug eyes. No one dared call her that to her face in years. How he used to make her cry.

"Roberto, mi hijo," Mami said with reverence, reaching up a hand to touch him as if to confirm he was real and not an apparition.

"Si, Mami. And I brought Miguel, Cruz and Ernesto with me. We'll have this place cleaned out and fixed up in no time."

"You can't…" *Just come in here and take over,* Roxie wanted to say.

But *Mami* said, "See, Roxie. I told you they'd come."

Roberto flashed an evil smile from over *Mami's* shoulder as he bent to hug her.

Why exactly did they come? Roxie wondered. Why now, when she'd called each one of them so many times over the years without so much as a call back from all but Ernesto? What had Fig done?

"Will you two keep an eye on *Mami?*" Roxie asked

Jared and Ali, who both nodded. Confident her mother
was in good hands, she went to find Fig, taking the long
way around the yard to avoid her other brothers—having
no desire to see Ernesto in particular after the nasty messages he'd left on her cell phone after "accidentally coming across" her video online.

She slipped in between two small box trucks…and ran
into Fig's parents on the sidewalk.

A bullet between the eyes seemed like the only way
to improve upon this day. She forced a smile. "Hello, Mr.
and Mrs. Figelstein. What brings you here?" *Come to see
Roxie's beautiful home? To meet her warm, welcoming
family? To see what a wonderful choice your son has made
in picking a woman to fall in love with?*

To Roxie's complete and utter shock, Fig's mother flung
herself at Roxie's chest and clamped her arms around her
midback, pinning Roxie's arms at her sides. Roxie briefly
contemplated the best defensive wrestling maneuvers to
ward off the unprovoked attack and escape the pythonlike
squeeze without hurting the smaller woman, until Mrs.
Figelstein said, "Thank you. For convincing Ryan to come
talk to me. For giving me back my son."

That's when Roxie realized Fig's mother was actually
hugging her…and how good it felt to be hugged right then.
And she burst into tears. Not the ladylike kind, either. "I'm
sorry." She'd been holding in so much for so long it was
getting harder and harder to contain all the emotion. She
tried to pull away so she could go someplace private to
get herself together. "It's been a difficult few days."

Fig's mom didn't let go. "There, there." She patted between Roxie's shoulder blades like she was burping a baby.
"Ryan's told us what you've been going through. You get
it all out, honey. Albert. My purse. Get the dear girl some
tissues."

Honey? Dear girl? Self-pity outburst over. Somewhere between the front of the box trucks and the rear, she'd slipped into an alternate reality.

"What's going on here?" Fig yelled. "What did you do?" He peeled his mother off and pulled Roxie into his arms.

"She didn't do anything." Roxie sniffled. "I kind of lost it for a minute."

"Jared told me what happened." He ran his fingers through her hair and eased her head to his shoulder. "I'm sorry."

She held out her hand for a fifty.

"Will you take it in trade?" he asked quietly.

She nodded. And felt her spirits lift instantly.

"Look at that, Albert. Our Ryan is in love."

Fig let out a breath. "A few more days and they'll all be gone," he whispered.

"What if we don't survive it?" Roxie whispered back.

"I hear you make a chicken soup with matzo balls that will make me weep," Mrs. Figelstein said. "That's a very important skill for a woman running a Jewish household. Have you considered converting?"

Roxie lifted her head and looked at Fig. "Did she just…?"

Fig raised his eyebrows and nodded. "Yup."

"We don't have to make any decisions now," his mother added.

"We?" Roxie asked Fig quietly.

"As long as she's willing to raise the children Jewish. You are, aren't you, Roxie?"

"Am I pregnant and don't know it?" Roxie whispered.

"Enough, Mom," Fig warned. "Did you do what I asked?"

"Sandwiches, drinks and chips for one hundred will be delivered promptly at noon."

"I said for fifty," Fig clarified.

"Well, dear. I made Daddy drive me past on our way to the deli and it's a good thing I did. No self-respecting Jewish mother would ever host a party that did not provide enough food for everyone in attendance. You remember that, Roxie. Now come." She took Roxie by the arm. "Introduce me to your mother."

That was a terrible idea. "I don't think…"

Someone yelled out, "Roxie." Ali.

And Roxie ran.

Mami, who'd been doing so well since the fire, sat in her chair, rocking and looking down at the ground. "What happened?" Roxie asked, dropping to her knees at *Mami*'s feet.

"I wanted to show them," *Mami* mumbled. "I decide. It's not all garbage."

"Si, Mami," Roxie agreed. "They're your things. You decide. Just like on the TV show."

"But look." *Mami* pointed to her brothers, who stood amidst the now organized mess of her front yard, pitching bag after bag haphazardly into the back of a box truck like they were tossing trash into a Dumpster.

"Stop," Roxie yelled, walking to her brothers. "These are *Mami*'s things that she's collected for you for years." She lowered her voice. "While I couldn't care less what you do with them after you drive them away, you will respect them, and respect her wishes while you're here."

"You going to make us, Roxie?" Ernesto asked, his words oozing contempt. "Or are you going by a porn name these days?"

"Sticks and stones," Mrs. Figelstein said from beside her, then Fig's mother opened fire. "You ought to be ashamed of yourself." She took on Ernesto. "Talking to your little sister like that. The poor girl was drugged and abused and it was an absolutely horrific experience for her."

The woman had Jewish guilt down.

Ernesto looked stricken.

"The four of you, coming here and upsetting your mother. Get down from that truck," she demanded. When Roberto didn't move she yelled, "Right. Now," in a voice worthy of a military drill sergeant. And well, what do you know? Her big, tough bully of a brother listened. "You all go and apologize." She pointed to the porch. "This. Instant."

Roxie leaned in to Fig. "Your family is awful big on apologies."

He gave her a small half smile.

"Move it," Fig's mother said with authority, as if anyone who didn't would suffer severe consequences.

Her brothers didn't know what to make of her—a vicious ankle biter yapping at four Rottweilers, holding them entranced. Then they looked at Fig's dad, who may not talk much but stood tall and protective behind his wife. They glanced from Jared and Ali, who stood on the porch with *Mami,* to Roxie and Fig, Victoria and Kyle and dozens of other friends and coworkers and even some townspeople she'd never met, who'd all come to stand beside her.

For the first time in her life, Roxie didn't have to go it alone. She felt weak with relief.

Fig stepped forward to confront her brothers in semiprivate. "The terms you all agreed to were you come home, make nice and clean out the house without upsetting your mother. You want me to stick to my end of our deal you'd better stick to yours."

"You're right, ma'am," one of her brothers, either Miguel or Cruz, said to Fig's mom. And he led the other three up to the porch to *Mami.*

"She's amazing," Roxie said to Fig.

He actually looked a little proud as he watched his mom follow Roxie's brothers. "She has her moments."

"So you had a nice talk with her?"

"Most of the night. I'm sorry she brought up…"

Roxie held out her hand. "I think that makes two hundred dollars you owe me. How *will* you work it off?" she teased.

"The only way to find out is if you come home with me at the end of the day." He looked hopeful. But was prolonging their relationship really the way to go? So they loved each other. He didn't live in Madrin Falls, and Roxie couldn't leave *Mami* and couldn't afford, nor did she want to hire on, a live-in caregiver. It was her responsibility to care for her mother.

"I know how to make you say yes," Fig said. He leaned close. "Sorry. Sorry. Sorry. Sorry. Sorry. There," he said. "That will keep me busy all night long."

He was right, that did get her to say yes. And after a brief nap when they got back to his place, he did keep busy. All. Night. Long.

CHAPTER TEN

ON THURSDAY morning, after answering a knock on the condo door, Fig said goodbye to the mysterious visitor he did not invite in and turned to her, holding out a police evidence bag containing a DVD with her name on it and three small camcorder cassettes. The same ones Johnny had given her and the police had later retrieved from her purse and taken into evidence while she'd been unconscious.

Was it possible? Could the nightmare of Johnny be over without Madrin Falls—and the internet porn-loving community at large—being privy to a second installment?

As if he could read her mind, Fig smiled and nodded.

Roxie ran to him and threw her arms around his neck. "How did you…?"

He hugged her close. "All I'm at liberty to share is I acquired them through legal means, they are no longer evidence and can be dealt with as you see fit."

Bonfire! "Thank you." She kissed his neck. "I can't tell you how much this means to me."

"Then why don't you show me?" Fig suggested, stepping back.

They'd been at it most of the night. Even she was exhausted, and she hadn't undergone major surgery a few days prior. "You can't possibly…"

Instead of walking to the bedroom like she'd first

thought, Fig stopped at the hall closet, took out a second bag, this one a nondescript red plastic shopping bag with handles, and walked it over to her.

Roxie peeked inside. Couldn't believe it. She looked up at Fig.

"I don't know what went on after the first few minutes of the video," he said, taking her back into his arms— her new favorite place to be. "And I don't care. But if you want to play and experiment I'm all in. If this bag doesn't contain what you're looking for, then we'll keep shopping until we find it."

How was she ever going to leave him when it came time to return home with *Mami?* For the next ten days they lived like honeymooners, working at her house during the day and indulging each other's sexual fantasies at night.

On day one, Fig started counseling four times a week.

On day two, *Mami* agreed to attend counseling.

On day three, *Mami* canceled the counseling appointment Roxie had made on day two.

On day four, her brothers returned to their homes, *Papi*'s and their secondhand "booty" transported out of town in the three small box trucks that'd been parked in front of her house, one driven away by Roberto, one by Ernesto and one by Cruz.

No tearful goodbyes there. But Ernesto did apologize for his porn comment and promised to stay in touch.

On day five, Fig's parents returned home, after garnering Roxie and Fig's assurances that they'd visit within the next two weeks. With *Mami*.

On days six, seven, eight and nine, Roxie's house was repaired and outfitted with new flooring and carpeting, a fresh coat of paint and a brand-new kitchen. All covered by insurance.

But like every brief bit of good in Roxie's life, on day ten reality intervened to put an end to her happiness.

"I don't want to go," she said to Fig over a delicious farewell breakfast of mushroom-and-Swiss-cheese omelets.

"It's not the end of us," Fig emphasized.

But it was the end of spending their nights, mornings and evenings together. Just the two of them. It was the end of impromptu private discussions and cuddle sessions on the couch. Roxie picked at the half of her omelet her stomach refused to accept. "We'll see each other every day." Fig reached out to take her cold hand into his warm one.

But it wouldn't be the same.

"We'll find a way to make it work, Roxie." He squeezed.

"But your job and your apartment. I can't ask you to stick around Madrin Falls knowing it may be years before I can give you more than a few stolen hours here and there." She felt her face heat. "I mean, assuming that's what you want."

Fig released her hand, slid back his chair and patted his lap. "Come."

She loved that even at almost six feet tall she wasn't too big to curl up on Fig's lap.

He wrapped his arms around her and kissed her head through her hair. "You didn't ask me to stay, I offered. Yes, I'd like more than a few stolen hours here and there, but I understand your situation. I applaud your dedication to caring for your mother. And I'm willing to take whatever time you have available to keep you in my life. I love you." He kissed her head again.

"I love you, too," Roxie said. So much. Partly because he accepted her decision to move back in with *Mami* without trying to change her mind. Because if he'd asked her not to, if he'd suggested she hire a caretaker and invited her to live with him full-time, she may not have been able to refuse.

That night they exchanged "I love yous" again—via cell phone—each alone in their own bed. As Roxie had suspected, it wasn't the same. Her heart—heck, her entire body and soul—ached for him.

Two days later, after rising early to clean up *Mami*'s breakfast mess in the kitchen then working her first twelve-hour shift in weeks, Roxie returned home to find four garbage bags of clothes, an old plastic dollhouse and a slightly rusted scooter on the brand-new beige carpeting of her living room.

"What is this?" she yelled at the top of her lungs.

Mami walked in from the direction of her bedroom, where she'd spent most of her time since they'd returned home, despite the family room being completely accessible and fully functional with new slipcovers on the sofas and a brand-new TV—a housewarming gift from Fig.

"They're from the church," *Mami* answered as if Roxie hadn't seen hundreds of similar bags before. Served her right for asking a stupid question.

"No." Roxie put her hands on her hips. "They are not staying. We talked about this. It took dozens of people four days to clean out this house. We both agreed we never wanted to go through that again."

"It's only a few things. For the next time the boys come."

Not again. Please, not again. Roxie's insides felt hollow except for a blistering hot ball of despair deep in her gut.

Mami scanned the room. "We have plenty of space now. If it upsets you I can put them in the boys' room." She started to drag one of the bags down to the raccoon room, as she and Fig now referred to it.

"Stop," Roxie said.

She did.

Right then and there Roxie made a decision. "I won't stay here if you continue to take in donations from the church. Either I load this stuff into my car this minute and I'll drop it back at the church tomorrow on my way home from work, or I'm moving out."

"You won't even know it's here." *Mami* dragged the first bag down the hall.

Yes, she would. "You need help to deal with this problem, *Mami*." Roxie's eyes filled with tears. "I will drive you to counseling. I will shop for you and take you to the doctor and church. I will continue to pay the bills. I will hire on a person to stay here with you so you're not alone. But I refuse to live here day after day and watch this house go to ruin. Not again."

Mami returned to the family room and dragged a second bag and then a third down the hall without further comment.

Roxie went into her bedroom to pack.

Fig glanced at his watch. Again.

"What's up with you?" Kyle asked from across the kitchen table.

"Today was Roxie's first day back at work. She was supposed to call when she got home." Two hours ago.

"Did her dirtbag brothers cash their checks?"

"Yeah."

Kyle shook his head. "Man, I don't believe it. Forty thousand dollars gone like that." He snapped.

Not that Fig minded spending it, and its loss in no way impacted his life, but he'd honestly—and mistakenly, as it turned out—thought to entice her brothers with the money, but once they arrived and witnessed the devastation firsthand, they'd do the right thing out of a sense of family, not monetary gain.

Wrong.

"How'd she react to you having to pay her brothers to come home?" Kyle asked, taking another cookie and dunking it in his coffee.

"She doesn't know."

"I think she suspects," Kyle said.

Because she's so smart and observant. "Maybe. But I fed her a story that I called each brother and told them I was the producer of a nationally syndicated hoarding show, and I was scheduled to begin filming on location at Roxie's house. That I did a pretend interview with questions intended to enrage them and provoke them to return home to clean out the house before taping for the show began."

In fact he'd tried that scenario with Roberto. Who'd called him some—what he suspected were—choice names in Spanish, then told him to go to hell so there'd be no misunderstanding. But Fig refused to let Roxie down. So he'd spoken in the universal language of U.S. currency.

Someone knocked on the door. Fig opened it to find Roxie, her eyes wet and rimmed in red, holding two overstuffed duffel bags, looking seconds from breaking down.

At the sight of him she dropped her bags and lunged toward him.

Fig opened his arm to catch her.

She held him tight. "Do you think it'd be okay for me to stay with you for a few days?"

Forever. "For as long as you want."

She said, "Thank you," then started to cry.

He eased her into the condo so Kyle could scoot out the door to drag in the duffels then leave.

"I can't do it," she said in between hiccuping breaths. "Not again." Fig calmed her down enough to explain what had her so upset.

"Who's with your mom now?" he asked.

"I arranged for her friend from church to stay with her for a few days. But I'll need to make more permanent arrangements."

"Tomorrow," Fig said. "We'll take care of it tomorrow."

He walked her to the couch and pulled her down onto his lap.

"I like it when you say 'we.'" She cuddled into his chest.

"Well, I like saying 'we,'" Fig said. And he liked being part of a "we."

Roxie looked up at him, her eyes sad. "Thank you," she said. "For taking me in. For understanding me and knowing me—the real me—and still loving me."

"And thank *you*," Fig said in return. "For taking *me* into your heart. For understanding me and accepting me—the real me—and still loving me right back."

Then, staring deeply into the loving brown eyes of the woman he planned to spend the rest of his life with, Fig knew no time would be more perfect. So without a care for germs or bacteria or sickness, with his full focus on showing the woman in his arms how much he truly loved her and wanted her in his life, Fig dipped his head and set his lips to hers.

EPILOGUE

Three months later

"Sí. Sí. Adiós, Mami," Roxie said, ending the call.

Fig put down his book and watched her pad barefoot across the white tile floor of their two-week beachfront vacation rental to drop her phone in her purse on the kitchen counter. Then she joined him out on the lanai, bending beneath the huge umbrella to remove his baseball cap and kiss the top of his head. "Fight it all you want, my love. But in the three days we've been here, you have actually started to get some color."

Yeah. An unappealing, unattractive, uncool pink.

She walked to the edge of their small wooden patio and stared out to the ocean less than one hundred feet away. "This is so much more beautiful than I'd ever imagined."

"It's exactly as I'd imagined it." Heat. Sand. Salty air. The beautiful blue-green water and palm trees he'd seen only in pictures. A completely relaxed Roxie wearing a teeny, tiny, hot-pink string bikini, showing lots of deliciously smooth, deeply tanned skin, adorned with a dangling gold belly button ring, sipping an iced strawberry margarita. Beautiful curves, enchanting smiles and contagious laughter. Perfection.

"How's your mom doing?" Fig asked.

Roxie slid the wicker chair beside him into full sun and sat down. "The change is unbelievable. Marvela—" who now lived with Roxie's mother and, in lieu of rent, supervised and assisted her "—has them both volunteering at a local day care twice a week. *Mami* is the on-site grandma for the three-year-olds." Roxie sipped her icy beverage. "At an invite from Ali's gramps, she's attending activities at the senior center, and she's knitting afghans and baby blankets for the women's crisis center. I've never heard her so happy." Roxie set her drink in a shady spot and reclined, tilting her face up to the sun. "It's like my moving out improved her quality of life."

"Finally agreeing to attend therapy improved her quality of life," Fig said. "You taking a stand shocked her into compliance."

"If only I'd done it sooner. All those years…"

"Nuh, uh, uh," Fig said. "The past is in the past. Nothing we can do about it today."

She held up a hand to shade her eyes and looked at him. "Stop throwing my words back at me."

He smiled. "They're good words." That Fig had needed to hear a few times himself—well, in addition to a couple of dozen counseling sessions—before he'd effectively tucked his past into a pocket of his memory, never to be lamented over or angered by again.

"Victoria's pregnant," Roxie said. "Jake blurted it out when they had *Mami* over to dinner on Friday."

Fig was happy for his friends. "That's what she and Kyle wanted." He eyed Roxie. "What about you? Do you want children?"

She laughed. "Could you imagine me a mother?"

Actually, yes, he could. "I think you'd make a terrific mother." Loving. Attentive. Dependable.

"I think I'd be annoyingly strict," she said with a scowl.

"Good," Fig said. "I'll be the fun parent." She balled up her napkin and threw it at him.

"I have a surprise for you." He handed Roxie the rectangular box with the now flattened red bow he'd stashed in his shorts pocket that morning. "I thought maybe we could try out something new tonight."

Roxie smiled—bless her adventurous soul—sat up and plucked the box from his hand. She shook it and held it up to her ear. "Fur-lined nipple clamps?"

Next time. "You'll have to open it to find out."

She pulled one end of the ribbon to unravel the bow then undid the knot and dropped it on the table. She lifted the lid. At the sight of all the pink tissue paper stuffed inside she looked up at him like he was playing some type of prank. "Is there even anything in here?"

"Keep looking."

She took out each small piece of crumpled paper until she came upon the one that contained her surprise and began to unwrap it.

Fig went down on one knee at her feet.

"Ay Dios mio," she said in awe, at the two-carat teardrop diamond engagement ring he'd bought for her.

Fig took it from her hand. "Roxie Morano, knowing you has changed my life." He held the ring out to her. "I look forward to each new day, knowing you'll be a part of it. I love you more than anything. And if you'll do me the honor of becoming my wife, I will devote the rest of my life to taking care of you and making you happy."

Rather than the thrilled expression he'd hoped for, Roxie looked confused. "I thought you said this was for tonight?"

"It is." He kissed her knuckles. "I was hoping we could try out making love as an engaged couple. That's something we haven't done before. What do you think?"

"Are you sure?" she asked, hesitantly extending her fingers.

Fig looked up at her. "I'm sure." He slid the ring into place. "I love you, Roxie. Will you marry me?"

"Lord help you, Fig. I hope you don't live to regret this." She jumped up and pulled him up with her. "Yes." She flung her arms around his neck. "Yes, I'll marry you. And I promise to take care of you and try my hardest to make you happy right back."

Thank you. Fig let out a relieved breath and hugged her close. "I made reservations at the nicest restaurant in town so we could celebrate island style."

Roxie pulled back a bit to look at him. "I kind of miss our cozy dinners when you used to cook for me every night." She caressed his head. "Do you think we could eat in tonight?"

She rubbed against him.

"Anything you want."

"I'd like that chocolate pudding pie you make for dessert."

He smiled, grabbing her butt with one hand and holding her still so he could do a little rubbing of his own. "The one with the whipped cream?" That she liked to "eat" in bed?

"Yeah," she said a little breathlessly as she rocked into his touch. "That's the one. Ya know—" she set her fingertips to his shoulders "—you're starting to feel a little hot. I think you need some more suntan lotion."

Their favorite tropical form of foreplay. Fig feared he'd go hard at the scent of coconut from now on. "But that always leads to..." he said innocently as he guided her to the sturdier of the two chaise longues, pulling at the strings of her top on the way.

"Exactly," Roxie said as she untied the strings of her

bikini bottom, exposing the fist-size raccoon tattoo on her right butt check.

Fig pushed down his shorts and stepped out of them, thankful for the good sense that prompted him to pay extra for the most secluded cabin available.

And under the late-afternoon sun, to the sound of the ocean waves crashing into the shore, covered head to toe in protective SPF 50, Fig made love to his fiancée, in a way he was sure she'd never been made love to before.

* * * * *

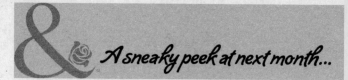

A sneaky peek at next month...

Medical Romance™

CAPTIVATING MEDICAL DRAMA—WITH HEART

My wish list for next month's titles...

In stores from 4th May 2012:

☐ Sydney Harbour Hospital: Lexi's Secret – Melanie Milburne

& West Wing to Maternity Wing! – Scarlet Wilson

☐ Diamond Ring for the Ice Queen – Lucy Clark

& No.1 Dad in Texas – Dianne Drake

☐ The Dangers of Dating Your Boss – Sue MacKay

& The Doctor, His Daughter and Me – Leonie Knight

Available at WHSmith, Tesco, Asda, Eason, Amazon and Apple

Just can't wait?

Visit us Online

You can buy our books online a month before they hit the shops! **www.millsandboon.co.uk**

0412/03

Book of the Month

MILLS & BOON

BOOK OF THE MONTH &

MARGUERITE KAYE

Rake
WITH A FROZEN HEART

We love this book because...

Rafe St Alban is the most dark-hearted, sinfully attractive rake in London. So get ready for fireworks when he sweeps prim Miss Henrietta Markham off her feet in Marguerite Kaye's compellingly sensual story of redemption!

On sale 4th May

Visit us Online

Find out more at
www.millsandboon.co.uk/BOTM

0412/BOTM

MILLS & BOON ® Book Club

2 Free Books!

Join the Mills & Boon Book Club

Want to read more **Medical** books?
We're offering you **2 more**
absolutely **FREE!**

We'll also treat you to these fabulous extras:

- Books up to 2 months ahead of shops
- FREE home delivery
- Bonus books with our special rewards scheme
- Exclusive offers and much more!

Get your free books now!

 Visit us Online

Find out more at
www.millsandboon.co.uk/freebookoffer

SUBS/ONLINE/M

Special Offers

Every month we put together collections and longer reads written by your favourite authors.

Here are some of next month's highlights— and don't miss our fabulous discount online!

On sale 20th April   On sale 20th April   On sale 20th April

Find out more at
www.millsandboon.co.uk/specialreleases

*Visit us
Online*

0412/ST/MB369

Mills & Boon® Online

Discover more romance at
www.millsandboon.co.uk

 FREE online reads

 Books up to one
month before shops

 Browse our books
before you buy

...and much more!

For exclusive competitions and instant updates:

 Like us on **facebook.com/romancehq**

 Follow us on **twitter.com/millsandboonuk**

 Join us on **community.millsandboon.co.uk**

 Visit us Online   Sign up for our FREE eNewsletter at
www.millsandboon.co.uk

WEB/M&B/RTL4